VALLEY OF THE SHADOW

A Sister Fidelma Mystery

Also by Peter Tremayne
and featuring Sister Fidelma

Absolution by Murder
Shroud for the Archbishop
Suffer Little Children
The Subtle Serpent
The Spider's Web

VALLEY OF THE SHADOW

A Sister Fidelma Mystery

Peter Tremayne

HEADLINE

First published in 1998 by
HEADLINE BOOK PUBLISHING

10 9 8 7 6 5 4 3 2 1

British Library Cataloguing in Publication Data

Tremayne, Peter, 1943–
Valley of the shadow
1. Fidelma, Sister (Fictitious character) – Fiction 2. Nuns – Ireland – Fiction 3. Detective and mystery stories
I. Title
823.9′14 [F]

ISBN 0 7472 2016 6

Typeset by Palimpsest Book Production Limited,
Polmont, Stirlingshire
Printed and bound in Great Britain by
Mackays of Chatham PLC, Chatham, Kent

HEADLINE BOOK PUBLISHING
A division of Hodder Headline PLC
338 Euston Road
London NW1 3BH

For Father Joe McVeigh of Fermanagh – in memory of our public debate on the values of the Celtic Church and the Brehon Law system at the Irish Book Fair, March, 1994. Thanks for being a supporter of Sister Fidelma!

Even though I walk through the valley of the
shadow, I will fear no evil, for You are with me,
Your staff and crook are my comfort.

Psalm 23

HISTORICAL NOTE

The Sister Fidelma mysteries are set during the mid-seventh century A.D.

Sister Fidelma is not simply a religieuse, formerly a member of the community of St Brigid of Kildare. She is also a qualified *dálaigh*, or advocate of the ancient law courts of Ireland. As this background will not be familiar to many readers, this foreword provides a few essential points of reference designed to make the stories more readily appreciated.

Ireland, in the seventh century A.D., consisted of five main provincial kingdoms: indeed, the modern Irish word for a province is still *cúige*, literally 'a fifth'. Four provincial kings – of Ulaidh (Ulster), of Connacht, of Muman (Munster) and of Laigin (Leinster) – gave their qualified allegiance to the *Ard Rí* or High King, who ruled from Tara, in the 'royal' fifth province of Midhe (Meath), which means the 'middle province'. Even among these provincial kingdoms, there was a decentralisation of power to petty-kingdoms and clan territories.

The law of primogeniture, the inheritance by the eldest son or daughter, was an alien concept in Ireland. Kingship, from the lowliest clan chieftain to the High King, was only partially hereditary and mainly electoral. Each ruler had to prove himself or herself worthy of office and was elected by the *derbfhine* of their family – a minimum of three generations gathered in conclave. If a ruler did not pursue the commonwealth of the people, they were impeached and removed from office. Therefore the monarchial system of ancient Ireland had more in common with a modern-day republic than with the feudal monarchies of medieval Europe.

Ireland, in the seventh century A.D., was governed by a system of sophisticated laws called the Laws of the *Fénechas*, or land-tillers, which became more popularly known as the Brehon Laws, deriving from the word *breitheamh* – a judge. Tradition has it that these laws were first gathered in 714 B.C. by the order of the High King, Ollamh Fódhla. But it was in A.D. 438 that the High King, Laoghaire, appointed a commission of nine learned people to study, revise, and commit the laws to the new writing in Latin characters. One of those serving on the commission was Patrick, eventually to become patron saint of Ireland. After three years, the commission produced a written text of the laws, the first known codification.

The first complete surviving texts of the ancient laws of Ireland are preserved in an eleventh-century manuscript book. It was not until the seventeenth century that the English colonial administration in Ireland finally suppressed the use of the Brehon Law system. To even possess a copy of the law books was punishable, often by death or transportation.

The law system was not static and every three years at the Féis Temhrach (Festival of Tara) the lawyers and administrators gathered to consider and revise the laws in the light of changing society and its needs.

Under these laws, women occupied a unique place. The Irish laws gave more rights and protection to women than any other western law code at that time or since. Women could, and did, aspire to all offices and professions as the coequal with men. They could be political leaders, command their people in battle as warriors, be physicians, local magistrates, poets, artisans, lawyers, and judges. We know the name of many female judges of Fidelma's period – Bríg Briugaid, Áine Ingine Iugaire and Darí among many others. Darí, for example, was not only a judge but the author of a noted law text written in the sixth century A.D. Women were protected by the laws against sexual harassment; against discrimination; from rape; they had the right of divorce on equal terms from their husbands with equitable separation laws and could demand part of their husband's property as a divorce settlement; they had the right of inheritance of personal property and the right of sickness benefits. Seen from today's perspective, the Brehon Laws provided for an almost feminist paradise.

This background, and its strong contrast with Ireland's neighbours, should be understood to appreciate Fidelma's role in these stories.

Fidelma was born at Cashel, capital of the kingdom of Muman (Munster) in south-west Ireland, in A.D. 636. She was the youngest daughter of Faílbe Fland, the king, who died the year after her birth, and was raised under the guidance of a distant cousin, Abbot Laisran of Durrow. When she reached the 'Age of Choice' (fourteen years), she went to study at the bardic school of the Brehon Morann of Tara, as many other young Irish girls did. Eight years of study resulted in Fidelma obtaining the degree of *anruth*, only one degree below the highest offered at either bardic or ecclesiastical universities in ancient Ireland. The highest degree was *ollamh*, still the modern Irish word for a professor. Fidelma's studies were in law, both in the criminal code of the *Senchus Mór* and the civil code of the *Leabhar Acaill*. She therefore became a *dálaigh* or advocate of the courts.

Her role could be likened to a modern Scottish sheriff-substitute, whose job is to gather and assess the evidence, independent of the police, to see if there is a case to be answered. The modern French *juge d'instruction* holds a similar role.

In those days, most of the professional or intellectual classes were members of the new Christian religious houses, just as, in previous centuries, all members of professions and intellectuals were Druids. Fidelma became a member of the religious community of Kildare founded in the late fifth century A.D. by St Brigid.

While the seventh century A.D. was considered part of the European 'Dark Ages', for Ireland it was a period of 'Golden Enlightenment'. Students from every corner of Europe flocked to Irish universities to receive their education, including the sons of the Anglo-Saxon kings. At the great ecclesiastical university of Durrow, at this time, it is recorded that no less than eighteen different nations were represented among the students. At the same time, Irish male and female missionaries were setting out to reconvert a pagan Europe to Christianity, establishing churches, monasteries, and centres of learning throughout Europe as far east as Kiev, in the Ukraine; as far north as the Faroes, and as far south as Taranto in southern Italy. Ireland was a by-word for literacy and learning.

However, the Celtic Church of Ireland was in constant dispute with Rome on matters of liturgy and ritual. Rome had begun to reform itself in the fourth century, changing its dating of Easter and aspects of its liturgy. The Celtic Church and the Eastern Orthodox Church refused to follow Rome, but the Celtic Church was gradually absorbed by Rome between the ninth and eleventh centuries while the Eastern Orthodox Churches have continued to remain independent of Rome. The Celtic Church of Ireland, during Fidelma's time, was much concerned with this conflict.

One thing that marked both the Celtic Church and Rome in the seventh century was that the concept of celibacy was not universal. While there were always ascetics in both Churches who sublimated physical love in a dedication to the deity, it was not until the Council of Nicea in A.D. 325 that clerical marriages were condemned but not banned. The concept of celibacy in the Roman Church arose from the customs practised by the pagan priestesses of Vesta and the priests of Diana. By the fifth century Rome had forbidden clerics from the rank of abbot and bishop to sleep with their wives and, shortly after, even to marry at all. The general clergy were discouraged from marrying by Rome but not forbidden to do so. Indeed, it was not until the reforming papacy of Leo IX (A.D. 1049–1054) that a serious attempt was made to force the western clergy to accept universal celibacy. In the Eastern Orthodox Church, priests below the rank of abbot and bishop have retained their right to marry until this day.

The condemnation of the 'sin of the flesh' remained alien to the Celtic Church for a long time after Rome's attitude became a dogma. In Fidelma's world, both sexes inhabited abbeys and monastic foundations which were known as *conhospitae*, or double houses, where men and women lived raising their children in Christ's service.

Fidelma's own house of St Brigid of Kildare was one such community of both sexes in Fidelma's time. When Brigid established her community at Kildare (Cill-Dara = the church of oaks) she invited a bishop named Conlaed to join her. Her first biography, written in A.D. 650, in Fidelma's time, was written by a monk of Kildare named Cogitosus, who makes it clear that it was a mixed community.

It should also be pointed out that, showing women's co-equal role with men, women were priests of the Celtic Church at this time. Brigid herself was ordained a bishop by Patrick's nephew, Mel, and her case was not unique. Rome actually wrote a protest in the sixth century at the Celtic practice of allowing women to celebrate the divine sacrifice of Mass.

To help readers locate themselves in Fidelma's Ireland of the seventh century, where its geo-political divisions will be mainly unfamiliar, I have provided a sketch map and, to help them more readily identify personal names, a list of principal characters is also given.

I have generally refused to use anachronistic place names for obvious reasons although I have bowed to a few modern usages, eg: Tara, rather than *Teamhair*; and Cashel, rather than *Caiseal Muman*; and Armagh in place of *Ard Macha*. However, I have cleaved to the name of Muman rather than the prolepsis form 'Munster', formed when the Norse *stadr* (place) was added to the Irish name Muman in the ninth century A.D. and eventually anglicised. Similarly, I have maintained the original Laigin, rather than the anglicised form of Laigin-*stadr* which is now Leinster.

Armed with this background knowledge, we may now enter

Fidelma's world. The events of this story occur in the month known to the Irish of the seventh century as *Boidhmhís*, the month of knowledge, which later calendars would rename *Iúil*, or July, after the Latin fashion from Julius Caesar who reformed the Roman calendar. The year is A.D. 666.

Finally, in chapter two there is an oblique reference to Fidelma's lack of respect for Abbess Ita of Kildare. The reason why can be found in the short story 'Hemlock at Vespers', first published in *Midwinter Mysteries 3*, edited by Hilary Hale, Little, Brown & Co, London, 1993, reprinted in *Murder Most Irish*, edited by Ed Gorman, Larry Segriff and Martin H. Greenberg, Barnes & Noble, New York, 1996.

Principal Characters

Sister Fidelma of Cashel, a *dálaigh* or advocate of the law courts of seventh-century Ireland
Brother Eadulf of Seaxmund's Ham, a Saxon monk from the land of the South Folk

At Cashel

Colgú of Cashel, king of Muman and Fidelma's brother
Ségdae, bishop of Imleach, Comarb of Ailbe

At Gleann Geis

Laisre, chieftain of Gleann Geis
Colla, tanist or heir-apparent to Laisre
Murgal, Laisre's Druid and Brehon
Mel, Murgal's scribe
Orla, sister to Laisre and wife to Colla
Esnad, daughter of Orla and Colla
Artgal, a warrior/blacksmith of Gleann Geis
Rudgal, a warrior/wagon-maker of Gleann Geis
Marga, an apothecary
Cruinn, the hostel keeper at Gleann Geis
Ronan, a warrior/farmer of Gleann Geis
Bairsech, his wife
Nemon, a prostitute

Brother Solin, a cleric from Armagh
Brother Dianach, his young scribe

Ibor of Muirthemne
Mer, a messenger

Elsewhere

Mael Dúin of the northern Uí Néill, king of Ailech
Ultan, bishop of Armagh, Comarb of Patrick
Sechnassuch of the southern Uí Néill, High King at Tara

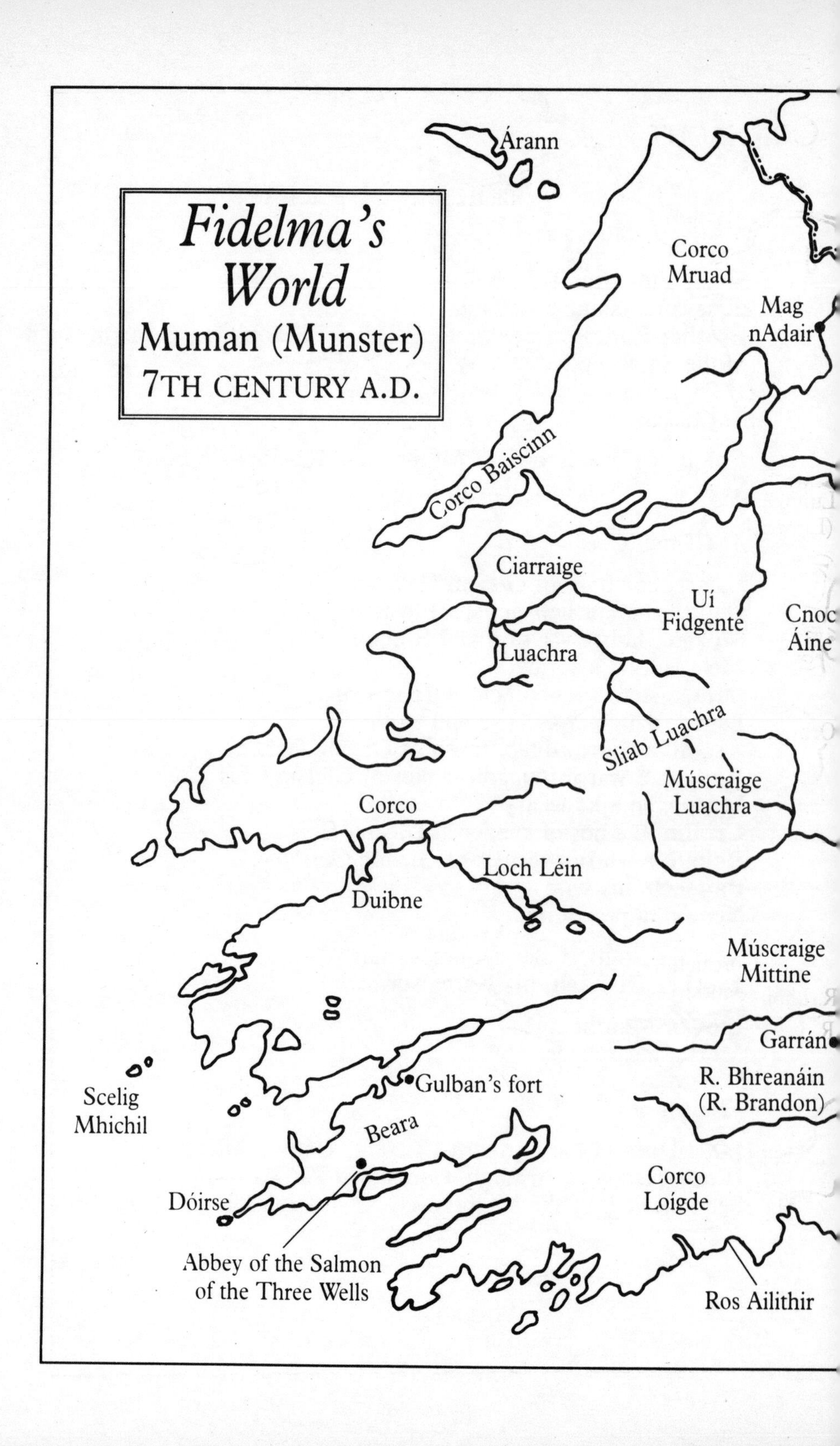
Fidelma's World
Muman (Munster)
7TH CENTURY A.D.
Árann
Corco Mruad
Mag nAdair
Corco Baiscinn
Ciarraige
Uí Fidgente
Luachra
Sliab Luachra
Múscraige Luachra
Corco
Loch Léin
Duibne
Múscraige Mittine
Garrán
Gulban's fort
R. Bhreanáin (R. Brandon)
Scelig Mhichil
Beara
Corco Loígde
Dóirse
Abbey of the Salmon of the Three Wells
Ros Ailithir

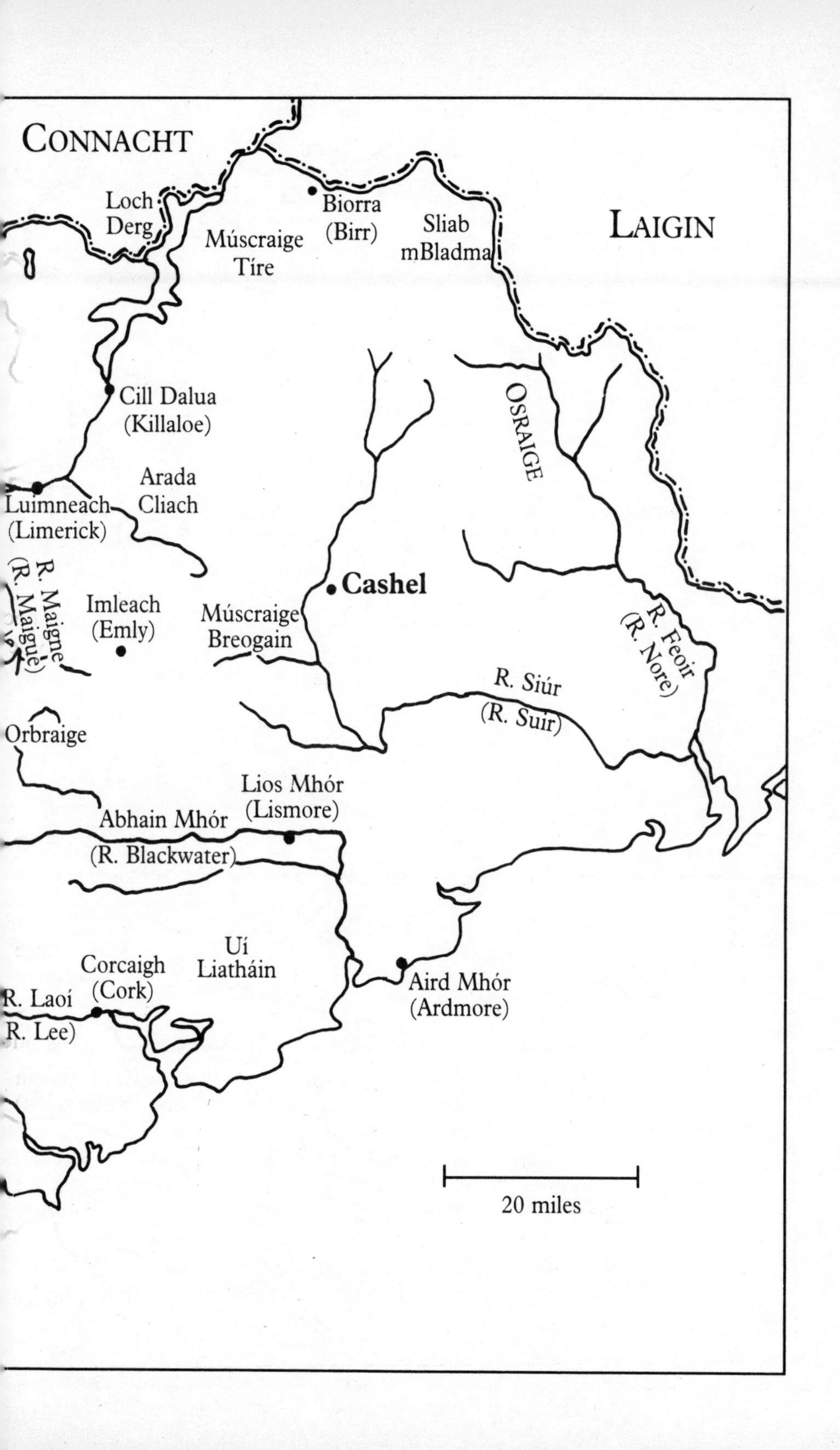
CONNACHT
Loch Derg
Biorra (Birr)
Múscraige Tíre
Sliab mBladma
LAIGIN
Cill Dalua (Killaloe)
OSRAIGE
Arada Cliach
Luimneach (Limerick)
R. Maigne (R. Maigue)
Imleach (Emly)
Cashel
Múscraige Breogain
R. Feoir (R. Nore)
R. Siúr (R. Suir)
Orbraige
Lios Mhór (Lismore)
Abhain Mhór (R. Blackwater)
Uí Liatháin
Corcaigh (Cork)
R. Laoí
R. Lee)
Aird Mhór (Ardmore)
20 miles

Chapter One

Hunters were coming. Humans. The baying of their hounds echoed eerily through the narrow glen. Rising swiftly from the waters of a small central lake, a speckled, white-rumped, curlew flapped upwards, announcing its annoyance at having to leave a potential meal of choice crab behind; its long down-curved beak giving forth a haunting, plaintive cry – 'coo-li!', 'coo-li!'. It rose upwards into the air until it became a mere black speck, moving in ever widening circles, against the cloudless azure sky. The only other object in that blue canopy was the large, bright, gold-white orb of the sun now settling towards the western half of the sky and whose rays caused the indigo waters of the lake to sparkle like a myriad of bright, glittering jewels as the beams caught it.

It was a hot, lazy day. But now, the sluggish atmosphere was being disturbed as a general alarm began to spread. An otter, with its long body and powerful tail curving behind, ran swiftly for cover with a hunched and rolling gait. On a mountain track, a fallow deer buck, with broad blade antlers, still covered by velvet growth, which would shortly be discarded when the rutting season arrived, halted with its nostrils quivering. Had the baying of the hounds not warned it, the peculiar scent of man, its only feared predator, would have caused the beast to turn and scramble upwards, over the shoulder of the hill away from the approaching menace. Only a single animal remained nibbling on the gorse and heather, apparently unconcerned by the frenzy which seized its fellow beasts. On a rocky protrusion stood a small, shaggy-haired, sure-footed feral goat, with its spreading horns. With its jaws rhythmically munching, it continued in its indifferent, lethargic stance.

Below, part of the valley was covered with a thicket of shrubs and trees which came down almost to the lakeside. This wood spilled through the northern end of the valley, tumbling to within fifty yards of the lake where low gorse and heather took over and spread through the rest of the basin. Most of the woodland growth consisted of the thorny brushwood of the blackthorn, with its tooth-edged toughened branches, looking little different from the cherry plums which grew amidst it, thickening the spread of the broad trunk oaks with their massive crooked branches and spreading crowns. Along a narrow, dark passage through this forest came the sound of a physical presence pushing rapidly through the restraining branches and the clinging shrubbery.

Out of the woodland thicket there burst the figure of a young man. He skidded to a halt, his chest heaving as he vainly sought to control his erratic, gasping breath. His eyes widened in dismay as he saw the vast, coverless expanse of valley before him, the sides moving gently upwards to the rock-strewn hills. A soft groan of despair came to his lips as he sought for a means of concealment in the bare landscape before him. He turned back towards the thicket but the sounds of his pursuers were close. Behind him, still concealed by the dense wood, he could hear them. The baying of the hounds had turned into frenetic yelps of excitement as they sensed the nearness of their prey.

Grim desperation etched the young man's features. He began to stumble forward again. He wore a long costume of rough brown homespun, the habit of a religious. It was torn and some thorny branches had attached themselves to it where the wool had proven too strong for the smaller twigs to rip entirely away. Mud and even blood, where the thorns had encountered flesh, stained the young man's clothing. Two things confirmed that the garment was, indeed, that of a religious. Firstly, he wore his head shaven at the front to a line from ear to ear, his hair flowing long at the back, in the fashion of the tonsure of St John which was affected by the religieux of Ireland. Secondly, around his neck he wore a silver chain on which was hung a silver crucifix.

The young man, who was in his early twenties, would have been handsome but now his features were twisted in anxiety, his face bore the numerous scratch marks of passing undergrowth. Traces of blood and bruising were to be observed on his ruddy cheeks. Above all, it was the fear in his wide dark eyes that distorted his features. The young man had given himself up to fear, his entire body oozed fear like the sweat which poured from it.

With a smothered cry, he turned and began to run towards the lake, his hands grabbing at his long habit, to stop it encumbering his feet and make his progress easier. He had long ago lost his sandals. His feet were bare, lacerated and caked with mud and blood. He was oblivious to the pain, for pain was the last thing that seemed to permeate his thoughts. Around his left ankle he wore an iron circlet of the sort hostages or slaves wore, for there was a circular link through which a chain or rope might be passed.

The young man had only proceeded a few yards towards the lake when he realised the futility of seeking any sanctuary there. There were only a few shrubs around it and nothing else. It had, for too long, been used as a watering spot by the wild life for there was not even long grass or gorse growing around it. Countless creatures had masticated the verdure into a short stubble over the years. There was no place for concealment.

With a curious whine of desperation, the young man paused and threw up his arms in a helpless gesture. Then he spun round towards the sloping hills where the feral goat still stood in aloof indifference. He began to scramble desperately upwards. His foot caught on the rag of the torn hem of his habit and he tripped and fell heavily; the little breath he had left was knocked from him.

It was at that moment that the first of his pursuers emerged from the forest behind.

Three men on foot came running out of the woods, each holding a leash at the end of which was a large mastiff, each beast straining and pulling, jaws slavering, yelping eagerly as they saw their prey. The three huntsmen spread out slightly but the young man was too exhausted to endeavour to escape. He had raised himself on an elbow and half lay, half sat, gasping as the men approached. There was a fearful resignation on his features.

'Don't unleash the hounds,' he cried breathlessly, anxiety edging his voice, as the huntsmen came within earshot. 'I will not run any more.'

None of the three made any reply but came to a halt before the young man, their hands firm upon the leashes so that the great hounds were almost within touching distance of him. They strained forward, whining in their eagerness to be at him, the spittle on their muzzles, their great rough tongues almost able to touch his skin. He could feel their hot breath and he cringed away.

'Keep them back, for the love of God!' cried the young man as his backward evasive movement caused them to strain forward further with snapping jaws.

'Do not move!' ordered one of the huntsmen roughly to the young man. He gave a swift tug on the leash to bring his animal under control. The other men quieted their dogs.

Now, out of the woods, came a fourth figure on horseback. At the sight of this figure, the young man's eyes flickered nervously. The corners of his mouth pinched as though he feared this figure more than the straining mastiffs before him. The figure was slender, seated at ease in the saddle, and rode with loose rein, allowing the horse to amble forward as if out for a morning ride without an urgency to be anywhere. The rider paused for a moment, gazing upon the scene.

The rider was a young woman. A helmet of burnished bronze encased her head, under which no hair escaped so tight did it fit. A thin band of twisted silver was set around the helmet meeting at the centre with a gleaming semi-precious stone. Apart from that single circlet of silver, she wore no other jewellery. No cloak adorned her shoulders and her clothing was a simple saffron-coloured linen dress pulled in at the waist with a man's heavy leather belt with a purse attached. From this belt, an ornate knife in a leather scabbard hung on her right side while on her left a longer scabbard was balanced with the intricately worked handle of a sword protruding from it.

The face was slightly rounded, almost heart-shaped and not unattractive. The skin was pale although there was a slight blush on the cheeks. The lips were well shaped but a trifle pale. The eyes cold and sparkling like ice. A cursory glance would have made one think the woman was young and innocently attractive but a second glance might cause one to dwell on the hardness of the mouth and the curious menacing glint in the fathomless eyes. The corner of her mouth twisted slightly as she saw the huntsmen and their dogs threatening the figure of the young man on the ground.

The leader of the huntsmen glanced over his shoulder and smiled with satisfaction as the woman walked her horse across to them.

'We have him, lady,' he called, stating the obvious with satisfaction.

'That you do,' agreed the woman in an almost pleasant tone which made her voice sound the more menacing.

The young man had recovered some of his breath now. His right hand was twisting nervously at the silver crucifix which he wore around his neck.

'For pity's sake . . .' he began but the woman held up a hand in a gesture calling for silence.

'Pity? Why do you expect pity, priest?' she demanded in a hectoring tone. 'I have enough pain of my own to cry for another's pity.'

'I am not responsible for your pain,' returned the young man defensively.

The woman gave a sharp bark of staccato laughter which caused even the straining hounds to turn their heads momentarily at the unexpected discordant noise.

'Are you not a priest of the Faith of Christ?' she sneered.

'I am a servant of the True Faith,' the young man agreed, almost defiantly.

'Then there is no mercy for you in my heart,' the woman replied sourly. 'On your feet, priest of Christ. Or do you wish to begin your journey to the Otherworld laying down? It makes little difference to me.'

'Mercy, lady. Let me depart in peace from these lands and, I swear, you will never see my face again!'

The young man scrambled to his feet and would have rushed to her stirrup to plead at her foot had he not been held back by the threatening hounds.

'By the sun and the moon,' the woman smiled cynically, 'you almost persuade me that I should not pour water on a drowning mouse! Enough! Nothing emboldens wrong doing more than mercy. Bind him!'

The last order was directed to her huntsmen. One of them handed the leash of his dog to another, drew a large dagger-like knife and moved to the nearest clump of blackthorn, cutting a stout pole some five feet in length. He returned, taking a rope, which he had carried wound around his shoulder, and motioned the young man to come forward. Reluctantly he did so. The pole was placed behind his back, between it and his elbows, and then the arms were tied so that the wood acted almost in the manner of a painful halter.

The woman looked on approvingly. When the binding was completed, by the expedient of another piece of rope tied loosely around the neck of the young man with the other end held in the hand of a huntsman, the woman nodded in satisfaction. She glanced up at the sky and then back to the group before her. The hounds had quieted, the excitement of the hunt having receded.

'Come, we have a long journey before us,' she said, turning her horse and moving off at a walking pace back towards the forest path.

The huntsman leading the prisoner advanced after her with the other two and the hounds bringing up the rear.

Stumbling, the young priest cried out once more.

'For the love of God, have you no mercy?'

The huntsman jerked quickly on the rope, tightening it around the hapless young man's neck. He turned to his charge with a black-toothed grin.

'You'll survive longer, Christian, if you save your breath.'

Ahead of them, the mounted figure of the woman continued on without concern. She stared straight ahead with a fixed expression. She rode as if she were alone, ignoring those who came behind her.

High up on the hillside, the feral goat stood, watching their disappearance back into the wood, with the same indifference that it had displayed throughout the encounter.

And eventually the circling curlew returned downwards to the lakeside in search of its interrupted meal.

Chapter Two

The religieux sat on a small boulder by the side of the gushing mountain stream, soaking his feet in the crisp cold water with an expression of bliss on his upturned face. He had his homespun brown wool habit hitched to his knees and his sleeves were rolled up as he sat in the hot summer sunshine, allowing the water to gurgle and froth around his ankles. He was young, and thick-set and wore the *corona spina*, the circular tonsure of St Peter of Rome, on his otherwise abundant head of brown, curly hair.

He suddenly opened his eyes and gazed reprovingly at a second figure standing on the bank of the stream.

'I believe that you disapprove, Fidelma,' he said chidingly to the tall, red-haired religieuse who was watching him. The young, attractive woman regarded him with eyes of indiscernible colour, perhaps blue, perhaps green, it was difficult to say. The downward droop of her mouth indicated her displeasure.

'We are so near our journey's end that I merely feel we should be moving on instead of indulging ourselves in pampering our bodies as if we had all the time in the world.'

The young man smiled wryly.

'*Voluptates commendat rarior usus*,' he intoned by way of justification.

Sister Fidelma sniffed in annoyance.

'Perhaps the indulgence is rare and thereby the pleasure is increased,' she admitted, 'nevertheless, Eadulf, we should not delay our journey longer than is necessary.'

Brother Eadulf rose from his perch with a sigh of reluctance and waded to the bank. His face, however, wore an expression of satisfaction.

'*O si sic omnia*,' he announced.

'And if everything were thus,' rejoined Fidelma waspishly, 'we would have no progress in life because it would be one long indulgence in bodily pleasure. Thank God that winter was created as well as summer to balance our sensitivities.'

Eadulf dried his feet roughly on the hem of his habit and slipped on his leather sandals.

They had paused in this spot to take a midday meal and fodder their horses on the green grass along the bank of the stream. Fidelma had tidied away the remains of their meal and repacked the saddle bags. It had been the strong midday summer sun that had persuaded Eadulf to cool his feet in the cold stream. He knew, however, that it was not his indulgence that really perturbed Fidelma. He had observed her growing anxiety these last twenty-four hours even though she did her best to keep her apprehension hidden from him.

'Are we really so near?' he asked.

Fidelma replied by pointing to the tall peaks of the mountains whose foothills they had entered that morning.

'Those are the Cruacha Dubha, the black ricks. This is the border of the lands of the clan of Duibhne. By mid-afternoon we should be in the country of Laisre. It is an almost hidden valley up there by that high peak which is reputed to be the highest mountain in this land.'

Brother Eadulf stared upwards at the bald peak which towered among the surrounding heights.

'Are you regretting that you rejected your brother's offer to send warriors to accompany us?' he asked gently.

Fidelma's eyes flashed a moment and then she shook her head as she realised that Eadulf meant well.

'What point is there in this entire journey if warriors have to protect us? If we have to spread our teachings and Faith at the point of a sword then those teachings and our Faith must surely not be worth the hearing.'

'Sometimes men, like children, will not sit and listen until they are made to,' observed the Saxon philosophically. 'A stick for the child – a sword for the adult. It helps concentrate the mind.'

'Something to be said in that,' agreed Fidelma. She paused and added: 'I have known you too long to attempt to keep the truth from you, Eadulf. Certainly, I am apprehensive. Laisre is a law unto himself. While honour and duty make him answerable to my brother in Cashel, Cashel might be a million miles away.'

'It is hard to believe that there is still an area of this land where the Faith is unknown.'

Fidelma shook her head.

'Not exactly unknown; rather it is known but rejected. The Faith reached these shores scarce two hundred years ago, Eadulf. There are still many isolated parts where the old beliefs die hard. We are a conservative people who like to hang on to old ways and ideas. You have been educated at our ecclesiastical schools yourself. You know how many cleave to the old path and the old gods and goddesses . . .'

Eadulf nodded reflectively. Only a month ago he had returned with Fidelma to Cashel after spending a short time in the valley of Araglin where they had encountered Gadra, a hermit, who held staunchly to the old religion. But the Faith was still young in many other lands. Eadulf, himself, had been converted only after he had reached young manhood. He had once been hereditary *gerefa* or magistrate to the thane of Seaxmund's Ham in the land of the South Folk before he had fallen in with an Irishman named Fursa who had brought the Word of Christ and a new religion to the pagan Saxons. Soon Eadulf had forsworn the dark gods of his fathers and became so apt a pupil that Fursa had sent him to Ireland, to the great ecclesiastical schools of Durrow and Tuam Brecain.

Eadulf had finally chosen the path to Rome rather than Iona. It had been attending the debate between the advocates of the Roman liturgy and the observances of Columba in Whitby that Eadulf had first worked with Fidelma, who was not only a religieuse but an advocate of the Irish courts of law. They had been through several adventures together. And here he was, back in Ireland, as special envoy to Fidelma's brother, Colgú, king of Muman, on behalf of the new archbishop of Canterbury, Theodore of Tarsus.

Eadulf knew well the extent to which people preferred to cling to old ways and old ideas rather than leap into the untried and unknown.

'Is this chieftain, Laisre, whom we seek, so fearful of the Faith?' he inquired.

Fidelma shrugged.

'Perhaps it is not Laisre who is to be feared but those who counsel him,' she suggested. 'Laisre is the leader of his people and will respect caste and status. He is willing to meet with me and discuss the matter of establishing a permanent representation of the Faith in his lands. That is a sign of a liberal attitude.'

She paused and found her mind turning over the events of the previous week; thinking of the day on which her brother Colgú of Cashel, king of Muman, asked her to meet him in his private chamber . . .

There was no doubting that Colgú of Cashel was related to Fidelma. They shared the same tall build, the same red hair and changeable green eyes; the same facial structure and indefinable quality of movement.

The young king smiled at his sister as she entered the room.

'Is it true what I hear, Fidelma?'

Fidelma looked solemn, the corner of her mouth quirked downwards.

'Until I know what it is that you have heard, brother, I can neither verify nor deny it.'

'Bishop Ségdae has told me that you have surrendered your allegiance to the House of Brigid.'

Fidelma's face did not change expression. She moved to the fire and sat down. It was her right to be seated in the presence of a provincial king, even if he had not been her brother, without seeking permission. It was not only her rank as an Eóghanacht princess that gave her this right, though that enforced it, but that she was a *dálaigh*, an advocate of the law courts, qualified to the level of *anruth* and thus could even sit in the presence of the High King himself if he invited her to do so.

'You have heard correctly from the lips of your "Hawk of the Borderland",' she replied quietly.

Colgú chuckled. Bishop Ségdae's name meant 'hawk-like' and he presided at the abbey of Imleach, which name meant 'borderland'. Imleach was the great ecclesiastical centre of Muman and it vied with Armagh as the chief Christian centre of Ireland. From a child, Fidelma had loved words and their meanings and often delighted in playing word games.

'Then Bishop Ségdae is right?' Colgú pressed with some surprise as he realised what this meant. 'I thought that you were committed to serve the House of Brigid?'

'I have withdrawn from Brigid's House at Kildare, brother,' Fidelma confirmed with a degree of regret in her voice. 'I could no longer give fidelity to the Abbess Ita. It is a question of . . . of integrity . . . I shall say no more.'

Colgú sat opposite her, leaning back in his chair, legs outstretched, and gazed thoughtfully at his sister. Once she had set her mind to something it was little use pressing her further.

'You are always welcome here, Fidelma. You have rendered several services to me and this kingdom since you quit Kildare.'

'Services to the law,' corrected Fidelma gently. 'I took an oath to uphold the law above all things. By service to the law, I have fulfilled my service to the lawful king and therefore this kingdom.'

Colgú grinned; the same quick urchin grin that Fidelma often acknowledged an amusing point with.

'I am lucky, then, to be the lawful king,' he replied dryly.

Fidelma met her brother's glance with grave humour on her features.

'I am glad that we are in such agreement.'

Colgú, however, was serious again.

'Is it your wish to stay in Muman now, Fidelma? There are plenty of religious houses here which would welcome you. Imleach for one. Lios Mhór for another. And should you wish to remain here in the palace of Cashel, you would be more than welcome. This is where you were born and this is your home. I would value your daily counsel.'

'Wherever I may serve best, brother. That is my wish.'

Her brother glanced at her searchingly for a moment and then said: 'When Bishop Ségdae mentioned that you had quit Kildare, I confess that I had thought that your reason might be a wish to travel to the kingdom of Ecgberht of Kent.'

Fidelma raised her eyebrow in an involuntary gesture of surprise.

'Kent? The kingdom of the Jutes? Why so, brother? Whatever made you think that?'

'Because Canterbury is in Kent and isn't that the place to which Brother Eadulf must return?'

'Eadulf?' Fidelma blushed but raised her chin aggressively. 'What do you imply?'

'I hope that I imply nothing,' returned Colgú with a knowing smile. 'I simply observe that you have spent much time in the company of the Saxon. I see the way that you and he respond to each other. Am I not your brother and have no reason to be blind to such things?'

Fidelma compressed her lips with an embarrassed expression which she contrived to turn into quiet irritation.

'That is foolish talk.' The vehemence in her voice was just a little too artificial.

Colgú regarded her long and thoughtfully.

'Even the religious have to marry,' he observed quietly.

'Not all religious,' pointed out Fidelma, still flustered.

'True,' agreed her brother, 'but celibacy in the Faith is reserved only for those who follow the lives of aesthetics and hermits. You are too much of this world to follow that path.'

Fidelma had now contained her embarrassment and restored her composure.

'Well, I have no plans to go to the kingdom of the Jutes, or any other land outside my own.'

'Then, perhaps, Brother Eadulf will renounce his allegiance to Canterbury and settle among us?'

'It is not my position to forecast the actions of Eadulf, brother.' Fidelma replied with such irritability that Colgú smiled disarmingly.

'You are angry that I am so forward, sister. But I do not raise this matter from idle curiosity. I want to know just how you feel and whether you are contemplating leaving the Muman.'

'I have answered that I am not.'

'I would not blame you. I like your Saxon friend. He is good company in spite of being a son of his people.'

Fidelma made no reply. There was silence for a while and then Colgú stretched himself languidly in his chair and his expression became troubled as his mind seemed to turn to another subject.

'In truth, Fidelma,' he said at last, 'I need your services.'

Fidelma's expression was grave.

'I was expecting something of the sort. What is it?'

'You are skilled in problem solving, Fidelma, and I wish to take advantage of that gift once more.'

Fidelma bowed her head.

'What talent I have is yours to command, Colgú. You know that.'

'Then I will confess that I did ask you here with a specific purpose in mind.'

'I had no doubt of it,' she replied solemnly. 'But I knew that you would have to approach it in your own way.'

'Do you know the mountains to the west known as the Cruacha Dubha?'

'I have never been amongst those mountains but I have seen them from a distance and have heard stories about them.'

Colgú leant forward in his chair.

'And have you heard stories of Laisre?'

Fidelma frowned.

'Laisre, chieftain of Gleann Geis? There has been some talk about the man recently among the religious here at Cashel.'

'What have you heard? You may speak freely.'

'That his people still follow the old gods and goddesses. That strangers have not been welcome in his lands and that the brothers and sisters of the Faith go into his lands at their own risk.'

Colgú gave a sigh and lowered his head.

'There is some truth to this. But the times change quickly and Laisre is apparently a man of intelligence. He now realises that he cannot remain a barrier to progress for ever.'

Fidelma was surprised.

'Do you mean that he has converted to the Faith?'

'Not quite,' admitted Colgú. 'He is still a fierce adherent of the old ways. However, he is willing to consider the arguments with an open mind. There is much opposition among his people, however. So the first step is a negotiation . . .'

'A negotiation?'

'Laisre has sent word to us that he is willing to negotiate with me a means whereby he will give permission for members of the Faith to build a church and a school in his territory which will eventually replace the old pagan sanctuaries.'

'The term "negotiate" implies that he wants something in return. What is his price for allowing the building of a church and school in his land?'

Colgú shrugged slightly.

'That price is one that we have to find out. But I need someone who can negotiate on behalf of both this kingdom and the Church.'

Fidelma stared thoughtfully at her brother for a moment or two.

'Are you suggesting that you want me to go to the Cruacha Dubha and negotiate with Laisre?'

Inwardly, she was surprised. She had thought that Colgú was merely seeking her advice on the matter.

'Who is more assiduous in negotiating and who is more knowledgeable about this kingdom and the needs it has?'

'But . . .'

'You can speak as my voice, Fidelma, as well as that of Bishop Ségdae. Find out what Laisre wants; what he expects. If the terms be reasonable, then agree with him. If they be unconscionable then you may tell him that the king and his council must take them into consideration.'

Fidelma was thoughtful.

'Does Laisre know that I am coming?'

'I did not presume on your agreement, Fidelma,' smiled Colgú. 'He merely asked for an envoy of the Faith to be in his lands by the start of next week and that it should be an emissary worthy of my charge. Will you accept?'

'If it is your wish that I represent you and Bishop Ségdae. Why isn't the good bishop here, by the way, to express his views on this matter?'

Colgú grimaced wryly.

'He is. I have the old "hawk of the borderland" waiting outside until I had talked the matter over with you. He will advise you of his views on the matter later.'

Fidelma examined her brother suspiciously.

'You were sure that I would go then?'

'Never,' Colgú assured her with a smile which did not give weight to his reply. 'But now that you are going, I want you to take a company of my champions with you. My knights of the Golden Collar.'

'And what would Laisre say if I came riding into his territory with a band of Niadh Nasc at my command? If I am sent as an emissary, then an emissary I must be. He would only see the company of warriors as an insult and an intimidation to a negotiation. Warriors have no place in the negotiation of the establishment of a church or a school. I will ride alone.'

Colgú shook his head vehemently.

'Alone into the Cruacha Dubha? No, that you will not. Take one warrior at least.'

'One warrior or ten, they are all warriors and will cause affront. No, I will take only another member of the Faith to express our peaceful intent.'

Colgú studied her face for a moment and then gave a grimace of resignation, realising that she had made up her mind and when his sister had made up her mind Colgú knew that it was useless to attempt to change it.

'Then take your Saxon along,' he insisted. 'He is a good man to have at your side.'

Fidelma glanced swiftly at her brother but this time did not blush.

'Brother Eadulf may have other things to do – it is surely time that he returned to the archbishop of Canterbury who sent him to you as an envoy?'

Colgú smiled gently.

'I think that you will find that Brother Eadulf is willing to bide a while longer in our kingdom, sister. Nevertheless, I do wish you would allow yourself to be accompanied by my warriors.'

Fidelma was adamant.

'How can we demonstrate that the Faith is the path of peace and truth if we go with force to make converts? No; I say again, brother, if I am sent to negotiate with Laisre and his people, I must go demonstrating that I place my trust in my Faith and my reliance on a truthful tongue not a sword. *Vincit omnia veritas!*'

Colgú was amused.

'Truth may well conquer all things but knowing when and to

whom that truth should be spoken is the secret. Since you are fond of Latin tags, Fidelma, I give you this advice – *cave quid, dicis, quando et cui.*'

Fidelma bowed her head gravely.

'It is advice that I shall bear in mind.'

Colgú arose and went to a cupboard, taking from it a small wand of white rowan wood on which was fixed a figurine in gold. It was the image of an antlered stag, the symbol of the Eóghanacht princes of Cashel. Solemnly, Colgú handed it to his sister.

'Here is the emblem of your embassy, Fidelma. By this wand you derive authority from me and speak with my voice.'

Fidelma rose, knowing well the symbolism of the wand.

'I will not fail you, brother.'

Colgú gazed fondly on his sister, then held out both hands and placed them on her shoulders.

'And since I cannot persuade you to take a troop of warriors with you, I can offer you the next best thing.'

Fidelma frowned as Colgú turned and clapped his hands. The door opened and his Brehon and chamberlain entered. They were followed by Bishop Ségdae, an elderly hawk-faced man whose features seemed to fit his name. They had obviously been waiting outside for this moment. They bowed briefly to Fidelma in respectful greeting. Then, with no word being spoken, the chamberlain moved forward to Colgú's left side. He carried a small wooden box. He held out the casket towards the king.

'I have been meaning to do this for some time,' Colgú confessed in a confidential tone, as he turned to open the box. 'Especially after you thwarted the Uí Fidgente in their plot to destroy my kingdom.'

He took out a length of golden chain. It was a simple and unadorned piece some two feet in length.

Fidelma had seen other kings of Cashel perform the ceremony and she suddenly realised what was about to take place. Even so, she was surprised.

'Do you mean to raise me to the Niadh Nasc?' she whispered.

'I do,' confirmed her brother. 'Will you kneel and take the oath?'

The Niadh Nasc, the order of the Golden Chain or Collar, was a venerable Muman nobiliary fraternity which had sprung from membership of the ancient élite warrior guards of the kings of Cashel. The honour was in the personal presentation of the Eóghanacht king of Cashel and each recipient observed personal allegiance to him, being given, in turn, a cross to wear which had originated from an ancient solar symbol for it was said the origins of the honour were shrouded in the mists of time. Some scribes claimed that it had been founded almost a thousand years before the birth of Christ.

Slowly, Fidelma sank to her knees.

'Do you, Fidelma of Cashel, swear on all that you honour to defend and guard the legitimate king of Muman, the head of your house, and receive in brotherhood and sisterhood your companions who bear the order of the Golden Chain?'

'I swear it,' whispered Fidelma and placed her right hand in that of her brother, Colgú the king.

He took the length of golden chain and wrapped it around their joined hands in a symbolic act of binding them.

'Conscious of your loyalty towards our person, house and order, and of the solemn vow you have sworn to obey, defend, protect and guard the same, so now do we bind you with this chain to our service and invest you as a Niadh Nasc. Let death and not dishonour sever these links.'

There was silence for a moment and then, with an awkward laugh, Colgú unwound the chain and raised his sister to her feet, bestowing a kiss on both her cheeks. Then he turned back to the box and took out another length of golden chain. This time there was a singularly shaped cross attached to the end of it, a white cross with rounded ends in which a plain cross was inserted. It was the insignia of the order, a cross that was old before Christian symbolism. Gravely, Colgú placed it around his sister's neck.

'Any person within the five kingdoms of Éireann will know this insignia,' he said solemnly. 'You have refused the protection of my warriors in the flesh but this will afford you their protection in spirit because anyone who offers offence to a member of this order also offers offence to the kings of Cashel and the brethren of the Niadh Nasc.'

Fidelma knew that her brother was making no idle boast. Few were admitted to the order, even fewer women achieved the honour.

'I will wear this insignia with honour, brother,' she said quietly.

'May it protect you in your journey to the Forbidden Valley and your negotiation with Laisre. Also, Fidelma, remember my exhortation – *cave quid, dicis, quando et cui.*'

Beware what you say, when and to whom.

Her brother's advice was echoing in Fidelma's mind as she brought her attention back to the grim forbidding peaks of the mountain range above her.

Chapter Three

The climb upwards through the foothills into the mountains took much longer than Eadulf had expected. The track twisted and turned like a restless serpent through precipitous embankments of rock and earth, crossing gushing streams that poured from the towering mountain peaks, through dark wooded glades and across open rocky stretches. Eadulf wondered how anyone could live in such an isolated habitation for Fidelma assured him this was the only route into the region from the south.

As he peered upwards towards the impossible heights, his eye caught something flashing momentarily. He blinked. He had seen the flash at least two or three times before on their upward climb and, at first, he thought that he had merely imagined it. He must have betrayed his concern, perhaps by a tightening of his neck muscles or straining his head too long in the direction of the point of the glinting light, because Fidelma said quietly: 'I see it. Someone has been watching our approach for the last half hour.'

Eadulf was aggrieved.

'Why didn't you tell me?'

'Tell you what? It should be no surprise that someone watches strangers riding through these mountains. Mountain folk are a suspicious people.'

Eadulf relapsed into silence. Nevertheless, he continued to keep a wary eye on the surrounding hills. To his perception, the flash was the sun striking on metal. Metal meant weapons or armour. That always meant a potential danger. The journey continued in silence for a while and still they climbed higher. At one point they were forced to dismount, so steep and rocky did the path become, and lead their horses upwards.

Eventually, Eadulf was about to ask Fidelma if she thought that there would be much further to climb when the pathway suddenly curved around the shoulder of the mountain and, unexpectedly, a broad glen stretched away before them. It was heather filled with a mass of red, orange and green gorse presenting a strange ethereal spectacle. And still the higher mountain peaks seemed as distant as before.

'This journey is neverending,' Eadulf grumbled.

Fidelma paused and turned in her saddle to regard the Saxon sternly.

'Not so. We have but to cross this great glen and pass through those peaks beyond. Then we shall be in the territory of Laisre; in Gleann Geis itself.'

Eadulf frowned momentarily.

'I thought that you had never been in this territory before?'

Fidelma suppressed a sigh.

'Nor have I, though I have passed it by.'

'Then how . . . ?'

'Ah, Eadulf! Do you think our people have no knowledge of the making of maps? If we don't know how to cross our own country, how could we send missionaries across the great lands to the east?'

Eadulf felt a little foolish. He was about to speak again but he suddenly observed that Fidelma's body had tensed and she was staring across the glen before them, looking upwards into the sky. He followed her gaze.

'Birds,' he remarked.

'The ravens of death.' Her voice was low.

The dark specks were circling against the azure sky, seemingly moving lower and lower in a spiral.

'A dead animal, no doubt,' Eadulf suggested, adding: 'A big one to attract so many scavengers.'

'Big, indeed,' agreed Fidelma. Then she nudged her horse forward with a determined movement. 'Come on, it is on our way, and I have a mind to see what attracts so many scavengers.'

Reluctantly Eadulf followed her. Sometimes he wished that his companion was not always filled with curiosity about things. He would rather press on out of the heat of the day and reach their destination quickly. Several days in the saddle was enough for Eadulf. He would prefer a comfortable chair and a mug of mead which had been left to chill in some icy mountain stream.

Fidelma had to guide her horse carefully, for the superficially level valley floor was deceptive. The clumps of heather and brambles grew at depths over an uneven terrain. An entire army could have hidden out of sight among the gorse and heather. Their coming had set off an alarmed croaking chorus among the wheeling birds who stopped their whirling descent and rose reluctantly higher.

Abruptly, Fidelma halted her horse and stared at the ground before her.

'What is it?' demanded Eadulf, coming up behind her. She said nothing but sat like a statue in her saddle, staring with her features drained of blood.

Frowning, Eadulf edged forward and looked towards the object of her horror-filled eyes.

His face also went ashen.

'*Deus miseratur . . .*' He began the first line of Psalm 67 and then halted. It seemed inappropriate. There had been no mercy shown to those who comprised the curious altar of death before them. Around the rough ground there lay over a score of bodies; naked bodies of young men, arranged in a grotesque circle. That they had met their deaths violently was obvious.

Fidelma and Eadulf sat still on their horses, looking down at a ring of naked bodies, unable to comprehend what their eyes accepted.

Still without speaking, Fidelma finally slid from her saddle and moved forward a pace or two. Eadulf swallowed hard, dismounted and, taking the reins of both horses, loosely tethered them to a nearby bush. Then he moved forward to join Fidelma.

She stood, hands folded in front of her, her lips compressed in a thin line. There was a slight twitching of a nerve in her jaw which betrayed the emotion her features did their best to conceal.

She took another step forward and let her eyes travel intently around the circle of death. That the naked, male bodies had been carefully laid out after they had met their deaths, there was no question.

Fidelma's shoulders braced and her jaw thrust out a little as if she were preparing herself for a difficult task.

'Should we not remove ourselves lest those responsible return?' Eadulf urged nervously, glancing about him. But the valley seemed devoid of life save the flock of night-black ravens still gathering in the sky above, flying in a chaotic croaking cloud. Some were moving hesitantly down again as if unsure of what their senses told them – that here was rich pickings, carrion for the eating. But some sense told them there was movement among the corpses, living humans who could do them harm. A few, braver than the rest, actually landed a short distance from the circle. Eadulf, in disgust, as they hopped cautiously to the nearest corpses to inspect them more closely, reached down and picked up a stone. He did not hit the ugly black bird at which he aimed but the action itself was enough to cause it to take flight again with an angry squawk which warned its fellows that there was danger below. Some of them still alighted on the ground nearby but out of range and watched with glinting hungry eyes.

'Come away, Fidelma,' urged Eadulf. 'This is not a sight for your eyes.'

Fidelma's green eyes flashed dangerously.

'Then whose eyes is it a sight for?' Her voice was sharp. 'Whose sight, if not that of an advocate sworn to uphold the laws of the five kingdoms?'

Eadulf hesitated awkwardly.

'I meant . . .' he began to protest but Fidelma cut him short with a sharp gesture of her hand.

She had turned and dropped to one knee by the nearest body and began to inspect it. Then, slowly, one by one, she began to move around the circle of bodies repeating her examination, pausing by one body for a longer period than the others. Eadulf gave an inward shrug and, although his eyes kept flickering across the surrounding countryside, he passed the time trying to make some sense from the grim pile of cadavers.

That they were all young males, perhaps the youngest was no more than sixteen or seventeen, the eldest no more than twenty-five, was the first and immediate thing that struck him. They were all naked; their pale skins, parchment white, showed that they were unused to any stage of nudity in life. He also noted the bodies were arranged in a circle with each body placed with the feet towards the centre of the circle. Each body also lay on its left side. He also noted that there were no signs of blood or disturbance of the ground around the circle. To Eadulf this meant that the young men had not been slaughtered at this spot. He was pleased by his deduction.

Fidelma had finished her examination and rose to her feet. There was a small stream about ten yards away and, without a word, she turned and walked with a studied determination towards it. Bending before it, she washed her hands and arms and then splashed the cold water on her face.

Eadulf waited patiently. He had been long enough in the five kingdoms of Éireann to know how fastidious the Irish were about cleanliness. He waited patiently until she had finished. When she returned, her face was still sombre and she halted again before the circle of bodies.

'Well, Eadulf, what have you observed?' she asked, after a pause of a moment or so.

Eadulf started in surprise. He had not realised that she had noticed his inspection. He thought rapidly.

'They are all young men,' he offered.

'That is true.'

'They have been lain out in some sort of order, in a circle, and they were not killed here.'

Fidelma raised an eyebrow in query.

'Why do you think that?'

'Because if they had been killed here then there would have been a struggle. The ground around is not disturbed nor is it bloody. They were killed elsewhere and placed here.'

She nodded appreciatively at his observation.

'What about their feet?'

Eadulf looked at her curiously.

'Their feet?' he faltered.

She pointed downwards.

'If you examine their feet, you will see that each young man has callouses, sores and blisters, as if they have been forced to walk over rough ground or for many miles. The abrasions are recent. Doesn't that contradict your argument that they were carried here?'

Eadulf thought furiously.

'Not necessarily,' he said after a moment. 'They may well have been marched a distance to the place where they were killed and then brought here after death to be laid out in this curious fashion.'

Fidelma was approving. 'Well done, Eadulf. We'll make a *dálaigh* of you yet. Anything else? You have not mentioned the marks of a leg-iron around their left ankles.'

In truth, Eadulf had not spotted these abrasions which, since Fidelma pointed them out, were now clear. However, Fidelma went on: 'Did you count the number of bodies?'

'About thirty, I think.'

There was a momentary expression of annoyance on her features.

'One should be more accurate. There are precisely thirty-three bodies.'

'Well, I was near enough,' he replied defensively.

'No, you were not,' she countered sharply. 'But we will return to that in a moment. You mentioned that they were laid out in some sort of order. Do you have any other observations?'

Eadulf regarded the circle and grimaced.

'No.'

'You have no comment to make on the fact that they were laid on their left side, every one of them with their feet placed towards the centre of the circle? Does that not mean anything to you?'

'Only that it must be some form of a ritual.'

'Ah, a ritual. Look again. The bodies are placed on their left side. Start at the top of the circle and follow round . . . they are placed facing right-hand-wise. In other words – sunwise, what we call *deisiol*.'

'I am not sure that I follow your meaning.'

'In pagan times we performed certain rites by turning *deisiol* or sunwise. Even now, at a burial, there are many among us who insist on walking round the graveyard three times sunwise with the coffin.'

'You mean this might be a pagan symbol?' Eadulf shuddered and raised a hand to cross himself, a gesture he thought better of.

'Not necessarily,' Fidelma reassured him. 'When the Blessed Patrick was given land at Armagh, on which he eventually raised his church, it was said that he had to walk *deisiol* around it holding a crozier and, in that fashion, solemnly consecrated the land to the service of the Christ by using our ancient customs and rites.'

'Then what are you saying?' frowned Eadulf.

'That these bodies are laid out as part of a ritual but what form of ritual – pagan or Christian – we must endeavour to find out by other observations.'

'Such as?'

'Have you observed the manner in which these unfortunates were precipitated from this world?'

Eadulf confessed that he had not.

'Have you ever heard of The Threefold Death?'

'I have not.'

'There is an ancient tale that once, long ago, our people forsook the ancient moral code of our Druids and fell to the worship of a great golden idol called Cromm Cruach, the god of the Bloody Crescent, to whom human sacrifices were offered. He was worshipped on the Plain of Adoration, Magh Slécht, in the time of the High King Tigernmas, son of Follach. His very name meant "lord of death".'

'I have not heard this tale before,' Eadulf said.

'It is a period in our history which adds no pride to our people in the telling of it. The people finally tired of Tigernmas and he was mysteriously slain during the frenzied worship of the idol and our people returned their allegiance to the gods of their forefathers.'

Eadulf sniffed disapprovingly.

'I see little difference between worship of an idol and worship of the pagan gods. Neither was the true god.'

'You have a point, Eadulf, but at least the old gods did not demand the blood sacrifice that Cromm Cruach did.'

Eadulf ran a hand through his hair.

'But what has this to do with . . . what was it? . . . The Threefold Death?'

'It was the death which Cromm Cruach demanded, according to Tigernmas.'

'I still do not follow.'

Fidelma waved a hand towards the bodies.

'Each of these young men has been stabbed. Each has been garroted and each has had their skull crushed by a blow to the head. Does that imply anything to you?'

Eadulf's eyes widened.

'This is your Threefold Death?'

'Exactly so. Each of these forms was a means of death. Every young man bears the marks of the same manner of dying. And furthermore, did you note the marks on their wrists?'

'Marks?'

'The burn marks of ropes. Their wrists were secured, presumably at the time of their deaths, and then the ropes were untied.'

Eadulf shivered and genuflected.

'Do you suggest that they are the victims of some sacrificial rite?'

'I enumerate the facts. Any conclusion would be no more than speculation.'

'But if what you say is so, then you are suggesting that this is a pagan sacrifice and imply that the worship of the idol you mentioned, Cromm, still survives.'

Fidelma shook her head.

'Tigernmas was said to have been the twenty-sixth king after the coming of the sons of Míle who brought the children of the Gael to Éireann. He ruled here a thousand years before Christ came to this world. Even his Druids turned on him because of this evil practice. To suggest the worship of Cromm still exists would be illogical.'

Eadulf pursed his lips a moment.

'There is some deviltry here, though.'

'In that, you are correct. I mentioned the number of bodies – thirty-three in all . . .'

'And you implied that this number has some significance,' interposed Eadulf hurriedly.

'When the evil gods of the Fomorii were overthrown, it is said that they were commanded by thirty-two chieftains plus their High King. The great Ulaidh hero Cúchulainn slew thirty-three warriors in an evil fairy castle. When the Dési were expelled from Ireland by Cormac Mac Art they had to spend thirty-three years wandering before they could settle down. Thirty-three champions including the king died in Bricriu's hall . . . need I go on?'

Eadulf's eyes slowly widened.

'You are saying that the number thirty-three holds special significance in the pagan traditions of your people?'

'I am. What we see here is some ancient ritual. The Threefold Death and the placing of the bodies in a sunwise circle and the number of the bodies all add to the ritual. But what the meaning of this ritual is, that we must discover. There is one other important observation which you have neglected to mention.'

Eadulf's eye scanned the circle.

'What is it?' he asked uncertainly.

'Examine that body and tell me what you see,' she said, indicating a particular corpse with a wave of her hand.

Distastefully, Eadulf picked his way across the bodies and looked down. He gasped and crossed himself.

'A brother,' he whispered. 'A brother of the Faith. He wears the tonsure of St John.'

'Unlike the others, this one has cuts and lacerations to his legs and arms and face.'

'Does this mean that he was tortured?'

'Perhaps not. It looks more likely that he was running through some brambles from which he sustained such cuts and scratches.'

'Yet this brother in Christ was ritually slaughtered.' Eadulf was aghast. 'His cloth did not save him from this mean death. You have already said yourself what this means.'

Fidelma stared at him uncertainly for a moment.

'I have?'

'It is obvious.'

'If it is so, then tell me.'

'We are heading to this Forbidden Valley where a pagan chieftain rules and who, by your very words, is opposed to the Truth of Christ's Teaching. You are fond of quoting Latin proverbs Fidelma. I give you one. *Cuius regio eius religio*.'

For the first time since they had witnessed the horrendous sight Fidelma let a smile play around her lips at Eadulf's observation.

'The ruler of a territory chooses its religion,' she echoed in translation.

'This chieftain, Laisre, is a pagan,' went on Eadulf hurriedly. 'And is this not some pagan symbolism which is meant to frighten or intimidate us?'

'Intimidate us to prevent us from doing what?' demanded Fidelma.

'Why, from going on into Gleann Geis to negotiate the establishment of a Christian church and school there. I think that it is meant as an insult to your brother as king and Ségdae as bishop of Imleach. We should leave this place immediately. Turn around and head back to a Christian land.'

'Ignore our mission?' Fidelma asked. 'Is that what you mean? To flee from here?'

'To return here later with an army and put the fear of God into these pagans who have thrown such a deliberate insult before us. Yes, that is what we should do. I'd come back here in force and wipe this nest of pagan vipers from the face of the earth.'

Standing there by the corpses it was easy to get worked up. Eadulf did so, becoming red in the face in his fury.

Fidelma was pacifying.

'The first thought that crossed my mind, Eadulf, was as you have eloquently expressed it. But it is an obvious thought. An obvious reaction. If this sight was meant for our eyes, perhaps it is too obvious. Do not ignore the shadows cast by bright lanterns.'

Eadulf felt calmer in spite of his fear and anger as he tried to fathom her meaning.

'What does that mean?'

'It was an aphorism of my master, the Brehon Morann of Tara. The things that are obvious are sometimes an illusion and the reality lies hidden behind them.'

She paused and screwed up her eyes, focussing them on something on the ground not so far away.

'What is it?' asked Eadulf, wheeling round in the direction in which her gaze became fastened in case some new danger threatened.

The sun's rays had struck something laying on the gorse several yards away and were reflecting off it.

Fidelma said nothing but made her way towards it, pushing through the stubby gorse before bending down and coming up with the object in her hand.

Eadulf could hear her inward gasp of breath.

He moved quickly to her side to stare down at what she held.

'A warrior's torc,' she observed unnecessarily. Eadulf knew enough to recognise the golden collar which was once widely worn by the élite champions of the Irish and the Britons as well, even among the Gauls of more ancient times. The collar was nearly eight inches in diameter consisting of eight twisted wires soldered into cast terminals. There were intricate lines of beading, cast dots and tiny punch marks in concentric circles. It was a work of burnished gold, the polish of the metal work showing that the torc had not been discarded long.

Fidelma examined the markings thoroughly and then handed the torc over to Eadulf.

He was surprised by the lightness of the object, thinking at first that it was made of solid gold. However, the terminals were hollow and the twisted strands weighed very little.

'Is there a connection?' he asked, inclining his head towards the bodies beyond.

'Perhaps. Perhaps not.'

Fidelma took the torc back from his hands and placed it carefully in her *marsupium*, the satchel which hung at her waist.

'Whether there is or not, one thing is certain; it had not lain here long for it is too bright and newly polished. A second thing is certain: it belonged to a warrior of some quality.'

'A warrior of Muman?'

She shook her head negatively.

'There is a subtle difference in the designs used by the artists of Muman and those of other kingdoms,' she explained. 'I would say this torc was crafted among the men of Ulaidh, somewhere in the north.'

She was about to turn away from the spot when she appeared to notice something else. A grim look of satisfaction crossed her features.

'Here is proof of your assertion, Eadulf,' she announced, pointing.

He moved across to examine the ground. There was a muddy patch in an otherwise stony landscape from which the gorse grew irregularly. He could see that this area was criss-crossed with ruts.

'This shows that the bodies were brought here on wagons. See the deeper ruts? Also the ones that are not so deep? The deeper ruts indicate the heavily loaded wagons and those that are not deep show them after the bodies were offloaded.'

She stared at the markings and walked along them for a short distance. Then she halted reluctantly.

'We cannot follow them now. Our first priority is to complete our journey to Gleann Geis.' She stared in the direction the tracks led. 'The tracks seem to come from the north, they are difficult to follow over the stony ground. I would say that they came from beyond those hills.'

She extended her arm to indicate where she meant. For a moment she stood undecided before turning to survey the ever-growing horde of impatiently chattering crows and ravens with distaste.

'Well, there is little enough we can do for these poor devils. We do not have the time, nor strength, nor tools to afford them a proper burial. But perhaps God created scavengers for just such a purpose.'

'At least we should say prayers for the dead, Fidelma,' Eadulf protested.

'Say your prayer, Eadulf, and I will add my amen to it. But we should leave as soon as we may.'

Sometimes Eadulf felt that Fidelma took the religious part of her life less seriously than she took her duties as an advocate of the law. He gave her a disapproving glance before he turned and blessed the circle of bodies before him and began to intone in Saxon:

> 'Dust, earth and ashes is our strength,
> Our glory frail and vain;
> From earth we come, to earth at length
> We must return again.
> When in life we feed on flesh of beasts,
> of fowls and divers fish;
> But in death for crawling worms
> Ourselves become a dish.'

Suddenly, two large crows, more courageous than their fellows, rose in the air and then fell on one of the bodies, sinking their claws into the pale flesh. Eadulf swallowed, left aside his verseful prayer and muttered a quick blessing for the repose of the souls of the young men before backing hurriedly away.

Fidelma had untied their mounts from the bush where Eadulf had left them and was now holding the fretful horses. The animals were unnerved not only by the stench of corruption but by the ravenous chorusing of the birds as they set to. He mounted as she did and they began to ride away.

'As soon as we are able, I want to return to this spot and follow those tracks to see if we may learn something further,' she announced, glancing over her shoulder to the distant hills.

Eadulf shuddered.

'Is that wise?'

Fidelma pouted.

'Wisdom has little to do with it.' Then she smiled. 'By my reckoning, we are only a short ride away from Gleann Geis. It lies beyond these next hills, westward there across this valley. We will see what Laisre has to say. If he maintains that he knows nothing then we can swiftly conclude our business there, return and follow these tracks.'

'It might rain soon and wash them away,' Eadulf said automatically and perhaps with a little hope in his voice.

Fidelma glanced at the sky.

'It will not rain between now and the day after tomorrow,' she said confidently. 'With luck it may remain dry for some days.'

Eadulf had long since given up asking how she could foretell the weather. She had explained many times about observing patterns in plants and clouds but it was beyond his understanding. He now simply accepted that she was invariably correct. He glanced back to the gorging ravens and shuddered visibly.

Fidelma, noticing his look of repulsion, said: 'Be philosophical, my brother in Christ. Are not ravens and crows part of the great Creation and do not those scavengers have a part ordained by the Creator?'

Eadulf was unconvinced.

'They are the creations of Satan. None other.'

'How so?' demanded Fidelma lightly. 'Do you question the teachings of your own Faith?'

Eadulf frowned, not understanding.

'Genesis,' quoted Fidelma. '"God then created the great sea-monsters and all living creatures that move and swim in the waters, according to their kind, and every kind of bird; and God saw that it was good. He blessed them and said, 'Be fruitful and increase, fill the waters of the seas; and let the birds increase on land.'"' Fidelma paused and pulled a face. '"*And every kind of bird,*"' she repeated with emphasis. 'Genesis does not say, every kind of bird except the carrion.'

Eadulf shook his head, unwilling to accept her quotation.

'Who am I to question the Creation? But God gave us free will and in that he allowed me to express my repugnance for such creatures.'

Fidelma could not help a mocking grimace. If she were truthful, she would have to admit that she enjoyed her exchanges on the Faith with Eadulf.

They had left the vast black mass of croaking scavengers, which now carpeted the ground, well behind them, increasing the pace of their horses.

'What do you propose to do when we meet with this Laisre?' demanded Eadulf. 'I mean about these corpses? Do you intend to demand his explanation of them?'

'You sound as though you presume him guilty.'
'It seems a logical assumption.'
'Assumptions are not facts.'
'Then what do you intend to do?'
'Do?' She frowned for a moment. 'Why, follow my brother's advice. Beware what I say, when and to whom!'

Chapter Four

They had barely ridden a mile across the valley when they heard the sound of approaching horses. Immediately before them was an entrance to what appeared to be a ravine, opening between two granite heights and through which the track they were taking disappeared. It was from this direction that the sound of the horses could clearly be heard.

Eadulf, nervous and still sickened by the sight he had witnessed, began to look around immediately for some cover. There was none.

Fidelma halted her horse and sat at ease, merely awaiting the appearance of the riders, and curtly ordered him to do likewise.

A moment or so later, a column of about a score of warriors burst out of the gorge on to the plain just in front of them. Their leader, a slender figure, saw them at once and, without faltering, led the column at a breathless pace to within a yard or so of them. Then, as if at some given signal not obvious even to the discerning eye, the band of horses halted in a cloud of dust with a sound of snorting breath and an occasional whinny of protest.

Fidelma's eyes narrowed as she examined the leader of the band of horsemen. The rider was a slightly built woman of about thirty years. Dark hair, almost the colour of jet, tumbled in a mass of curls from her shoulders. A thin band of twisted silver around her forehead kept it in some semblance of order. She wore a cloak and carried a long scabbard with a workman-like sword and an ornate knife on her right side. The woman's face was slightly rounded, almost heart-shaped and not unattractive. The lips full and red. The skin pale. The eyes were dark, flashing with challenge.

'Strangers!' Her voice was harsh and seemed at odds with her appearance. 'And Christians at that. I know you from your attire. Know that you are not welcome in this place!'

Fidelma's mouth was a thin line at the discourtesy of this greeting.

'The king of this land would be displeased to know that I am not welcome here,' she replied softly.

Only Eadulf could recognise the quiet tone which bespoke her suppressed anger.

The dark-haired woman frowned slightly.

'I think not, woman of the god Christ. You are speaking to his sister.'

Fidelma simply raised an eyebrow in cynical query.

'You claim to be the sister of the king of this land?' she asked in disbelief.

'I am Orla, sister to Laisre, who rules this land.'

'Ah.' Fidelma realised that the woman had placed a different interpretation on what was meant by king. 'I do not speak of Laisre, *chieftain* of Gleann Geis; I speak of the king of Cashel to whom Laisre must bend his knee.'

'Cashel is a long way from here,' shot back the woman in annoyance.

'But Cashel's reach is sure and firm and it extends justice into all the far corners of the kingdom.'

Fidelma spoke with such assured firmness that Orla's eyes narrowed suspiciously. She appeared to be unused to being answered with confidence and as an equal.

'Who are you, woman, who rides so unconcerned into the land of Laisre?' Her dark eyes flashed in dislike at Eadulf, who sat quietly behind her. 'And who are you who dares to bring a foreign cleric into this land?'

A burly warrior from the column of horsemen edged his mount forward. He was an ugly looking man, with a bushy black beard and a scar above one eye, the mark of an old wound.

'Lady, no need to ask more of these people who wear the emasculate robes of their alien religion. Let them be gone or let me drive them forth.'

The woman, Orla, gave the warrior a glance of irritation.

'When I need advice, Artgal, I shall consult you.' And with this dismissal, she turned back to Fidelma. There was no change of expression on her hostile features. 'Speak, woman, and tell me who dares lecture the sister of the chieftain of Gleann Geis on the duties of her brother.'

'I am Fidelma . . . Fidelma of Cashel.'

Whether by design or accident, Fidelma made a slight movement in her saddle at which the cross of the Golden Chain, hidden in the folds of her clothing, slipped out and the sunlight struck it momentarily causing the dark eyes of Orla to glimpse it. They widened perceptibly as she recognised it for what it was.

'Fidelma of Cashel?' Orla repeated in a hesitant tone. 'Fidelma, sister of Colgú, king of Muman?'

Fidelma did not bother to answer the question but assumed that Orla knew the answer already.

'Your brother, Laisre, is expecting my embassy from Cashel,' she went on, as if disinterested in the reaction she had provoked. She reached behind her into her saddle bags and drew out the white wand with the golden stag atop it, the symbol of her embassy from the king of Cashel.

There was a silent pause as Orla stared as if mesmerised by it.

'Do you accept the white wand or do you choose the sword?' Fidelma demanded with a hint of a smile on her features. Envoys going into a hostile land presented either the wand or the sword as a symbolic challenge to peace or war.

'My brother is expecting a representative of Cashel,' Orla admitted slowly, raising her eyes from the wand to Fidelma's face, her expression unsure. There was an unwilling note of respect in her voice now. 'But that representative is one who should be qualified to negotiate with Laisre on ecclesiastical matters. Someone qualified to . . .'

Fidelma suppressed an impatient sigh.

'I am an advocate of the Brehon Courts, qualified to the degree of *anruth*. I am the negotiator whom he is expecting and I speak in the stead of my brother, Colgú, his king.'

Orla failed to disguise her surprise. The qualification of *anruth* was only one degree below the highest that the ecclesiastical and secular colleges of Ireland could bestow. Fidelma could walk and talk with kings, even the High King, let alone petty chieftains.

The dark-haired woman swallowed hard and, while she was undoubtedly impressed, her features remained harsh and unfriendly.

'As representative of Laisre of Gleann Geis, I bid you welcome, *techtaire*.' It took Eadulf some moments to recognise the ancient word for an envoy. Orla continued: 'But as representative of the new religion of Christ, I say that you are not welcome in this place. Nor is the foreigner whom you bring with you.'

Fidelma leant forward, her voice sharp and clear.

'Does that imply a threat? Are the sacred laws of hospitality abrogated in the land of Laisre? Is it the sword you accept instead of this?'

She held up the white wand again, thrusting it forward almost aggressively towards Orla. The sun sparkled brightly on the gold figure of the stag.

Orla's cheeks coloured and she raised her chin defiantly.

'I imply no threat to your life. Nor even his life.' She jerked her head towards Eadulf. 'No harm will come to you nor to the foreigner while you extend your protection to him. We are not barbarians in Gleann Geis. Envoys, under law, are regarded as sacred and inviolable and are treated with utmost respect even though they be our bitterest enemies.'

Eadulf moved uneasily for there was still a deadly serious threat behind what she was saying.

'That is good to know, Orla,' Fidelma replied easily, relaxing and replacing the wand in her saddle bag. 'For I have seen what happens to people to whom such immunity from death is not given.'

Eadulf's jaw slackened and he felt a sudden panic. If Orla and her warriors were responsible for the deaths of the young men across the valley then Fidelma, in admitting knowledge of the corpses, was putting their lives in considerable danger. He had thought she was going to be circumspect about the gruesome find. Then he suddenly became aware of the distant squawking of the birds of prey and he glanced anxiously over his shoulder. It was obvious that something was amiss across the glen in the direction where the corpses lay and the warriors of Orla's bodyguard must surely have spotted the ravening carrion birds anyway.

Yet Orla was regarding Fidelma with some bewilderment. She had apparently not taken in the swirling cloud of distant ravens.

'I have no understanding of your meaning.'

Fidelma indicated across the valley with one arm in a careless gesture.

'Can you see the black of the battle ravens there? They feed on corpses.'

'Corpses?' Orla jerked her gaze up, apparently seeing the birds for the first time.

'Thirty-three young men who have suffered The Threefold Death.'

Orla's jaw suddenly clenched; her face was white as she brought her gaze back to Fidelma. It took her a moment or two to frame an answer.

'Is this some jest?' she demanded coldly.

'I do not jest.'

Orla turned to the black-bearded warrior whom she had previously rebuked for his interruption.

'Artgal, take half of our men and see what this evil gathering means.'

Artgal was glowering with suspicion.

'It may be some Christian trap, lady.'

The woman's eyes flashed angrily.

'Do as I say!' The voice was like a whiplash.

Without another word, the warrior, Artgal, signalled a section of the mounted warriors to follow him and he rode off in the direction where the distant birds were circling and diving.

'The Threefold Death, you claim?' the woman almost whispered after he had gone. 'Are you sure this was the manner of death, Fidelma of Cashel?'

'I am sure. But your man, Artgal, will confirm what I say on his return.'

'The blame for this is not to be laid on the people of Laisre,' the woman protested. There was a curious expression on her features as if she was trying to overcome her fear. 'We know nothing of this matter.'

'How can you be so sure that you speak for all the people of Laisre?' asked Fidelma ingenuously.

'I am sure. I speak not only for my brother but as wife of his tanist, the heir-elect, Colla. You have my word.'

'A great evil has been committed in this valley, Orla. I am charged by my oath to discover the cause of it and who is responsible. That I mean to do.'

'But you will not find the answer in Gleann Geis,' replied Orla sullenly.

'Yet it is to Gleann Geis that we are now proceeding,' Fidelma said with confidence. 'The sooner we get there the better. So my companion and I will leave you to await the return of your warriors and continue on.' She looked towards Eadulf and gave a brief motion of her head, as if indicating him to follow, and, without another word, she nudged her horse forward, passing Orla and the remaining mounted warriors. After but a moment or so's delay, Eadulf followed. The warriors were staring in some bewilderment at Orla who sat still, doing nothing to impede their progress.

Confidently, Fidelma walked her horse into the mouth of the gorge where the pathway became stony, indicating it had once been the bed of a flowing stream. How long it had been dried up was difficult to tell; perhaps for centuries. It twisted and turned with precipitous granite walls rising over a hundred feet on either side almost cutting out the light. They were in a semi-gloom from the moment they entered the passage. From an entrance of perhaps ten yards' width, the gorge narrowed until there was only room for two horses to move comfortably abreast.

It was only after they had ridden some way that Eadulf decided to break the silence.

'Do you . . . ?' he began but stopped suddenly as his voice boomed back in resounding echo against the walls of the narrow defile. He paused a moment and then lowered his voice to a whisper but even the whisper sounded like sepulchral echo. 'Do you think that the woman, Orla, and her warriors killed those young men?'

Fidelma contrived to shrug without articulating a reply. Her face was set and stern.

'The surprise on Orla's face seemed genuine enough,' Eadulf went on doggedly.

'Nevertheless, had I not been who I am, I doubt that we would be proceeding with our journey. Orla and her warriors seem to have little liking for those of our Faith.'

Eadulf shivered and raised a hand to cross himself then caught himself and dropped it to his side. Habit caused action to lose meaning.

'I did not know such heathen areas existed in this land. There is much to fear here.'

'Fear is self-destructive, Eadulf. And you should not fear someone because they do not share your belief,' chided Fidelma.

'If they are prepared to use the sword against those whose belief is not their own – yes, there is much to fear,' Eadulf replied, almost hotly. 'We have doubtless seen some grotesque ritual sacrifice back there in the valley, perpetrated by these pagans. I fear for our safety.'

'Fear is not required. But caution is the watchword. Remember what Aeschylus said – excessive fear always makes men powerless to act? So rid yourself of any fear and apply watchfulness and caution and by this means we will discover what is the truth.'

Eadulf sniffed disdainfully.

'Perhaps fear is a means of protection,' he protested, 'because fear makes us cautious.'

'Fear never makes anything virtuous. I give you an aphorism of Pubilius Syrus – what we fear comes to pass more speedily than what we hope. If you fear in this place, your fear will create that unnameable thing you fear. You have nothing to fear but fear itself. There is nothing to fear here but the evil deeds of men and women and we have stood up to evil men and women before and been victorious. So let it be now.'

She broke off, holding her head to one side.

They became aware of the sound of a horse behind them moving rapidly through the gorge.

'They are coming after us,' hissed Eadulf, turning in his saddle, but the ravine twisted and turned so much there would be nothing to see until the rider was almost upon them.

Fidelma shook her head.

'They? See what fear does to judgment? It is only one horse coming along behind us and that undoubtedly belongs to Orla.'

Eadulf had barely opened his mouth to reply when the dark-haired woman came abruptly round a corner of the granite rock, saw them and halted her horse.

'I could not let you enter Gleann Geis without the courtesy of an escort. I have left my men to deal with . . .' She hesitated and made a gesture with her hand as if it would describe the horrendous scene of the dead bodies on the plain behind. 'Artgal will report anything he may find which can help to solve the riddle of this slaughter. I shall accompany you to my brother's ráth.'

Fidelma inclined her head in acknowledgment.

'We appreciate your courtesy, Orla.'

The dark-haired woman edged her horse forward into the lead and they proceeded at a walking pace.

Fidelma opened the conversation again.

'I am led to understand that you disagree with your brother, Laisre, that the Faith should be recognised in this land?'

Orla smiled sourly.

'My brother has accepted that the word of your Faith is strong in the five kingdoms. There is scarcely a petty kingdom or chief who disputes the message of this foreign god. Laisre is chieftain but we may not all agree with his action.'

Eadulf went to say something but ended up in a fit of coughing as he caught Fidelma's warning eye.

'So? You feel that the Christ is an alien god and not the one god of all the world?' mused Fidelma.

'We have our own gods who have served us since the beginning of time. Why abandon them now, especially in favour of one who is borne to this country on the tongues of Romans and Roman slaves who could never conquer us in warfare but now conquer us with their god?'

'A unique way of looking at things,' remarked Fidelma. 'But you forget that our people have accepted a god of the east as the universal god but we worship him in our own way, not in the ways dictated by Rome.'

Orla pursed her lips cynically.

'That is not what I hear. There are those of your Faith who, as you rightly say, refuse to accept the dictates of Rome but many others who do. Ultan of Armagh, for example, who says he has authority throughout the five kingdoms and sends his representatives to all the corners of this land, demanding allegiance.'

A frown passed Fidelma's brow so quickly that it might not have been noticed.

'Have you received such envoys from Ultan?'

'We have,' Orla admitted unabashed. 'This same Ultan who calls himself the Comarb, the successor of Patrick, who brought the Faith of Christ to this land. This same Ultan who claims that all dues of the new Faith should be his.'

Fidelma felt obliged to point out that the scribes of the abbey at Imleach disputed Patrick's claims to be the first to have brought the Faith to Éireann and especially Muman. Had not Muman been converted by the Blessed Ailbe, son of Olcnais, who served in the house of a king? Had not Ailbe befriended and encouraged Patrick? Had it not been Patrick and Ailbe, working together, who had converted Oengus Mac Nad Froich, king of Cashel, to the Faith? And it was Patrick who agreed that the royal city of Cashel should be the seat of Ailbe's church in Muman. All this came tripping to her tongue, but she remained silent. Much could also be learnt through silence.

'I have no liking for your Faith or those who propound it,' confessed Orla honestly. 'Your Patrick converted the people by fear.'

'How so?' asked Fidelma keeping her voice calm.

Orla thrust out her chin, the better to make her point.

'We may live in a remote part of the world, but we have bards and scribes who have recounted the stories of how your Faith was spread. We know that Patrick went to Tara where he caused the Druid Luchet Mael to be burnt in a pyre and when the High King, Laoghaire, protested, Patrick brought about the death of others who refused to accept the new Faith. Even the High King Laoghaire was told that he would die on the spot unless he accepted the new Faith. Didn't Laoghaire summon his council and tell them: "It is better for me to believe than to die" – is this a logical way to win people to a Faith?'

'If what you say is the truth then it is not a logical way,' Fidelma agreed quietly, though with a slight emphasis on the word 'if'.

'Do members of your Faith lie, Fidelma of Cashel?' the woman sneered. 'Ultan of Armagh sent my brother a gift of a book, *Life of Patrick*, written by one who knew him, one called Muirchú, and in which these truths are recorded. Not only that but we are told that Patrick journeyed to the fortress of Míliucc of Slemish, where he had lived before running away to Gaul and converting to the new Faith. Hearing Patrick was nearing his fortress, so fearful of this Patrick was the chieftain, that he gathered all his valuables and his household, his wife and children, and he shut himself in his ráth and set fire to it. What fear could a man stir in another to make him end his life so horribly? Do you deny that this is so recorded?'

Fidelma sighed softly.

'I know it is so recorded,' she admitted.

'And as it was written, so was it done?'

'We are told to believe the word of Muirchú, but it was the chieftain's decision to end his life rather than believe and serve the eternal God.'

'Under the ancient laws, we are told that what we believe is a matter for our conscience only. Belief is our choice so long as what we believe does not harm others. Your Patrick's conversion of the five kingdoms was through a presentation of a single choice – believe or die by his hand.'

'By the hand of God!' snapped Eadulf, finally no longer containing his silence.

Orla raised her eyebrows and turned in her saddle.

'So? The foreigner speaks our language. I had begun to think that you did not or else that you were dumb. What land do you come from?'

'I am Eadulf of Seaxmund's Ham in the land of the South Folk.'

'And where is that?'

'It is one of the Saxon kingdoms,' explained Fidelma.

'Ah, I have heard of the Saxons. Yet you speak our language well.'

'I have studied in this land some years.'

'Brother Eadulf is under the protection of the hospitality of my brother Colgú of Cashel,' interposed Fidelma. 'He is an envoy from the archbishop of Canterbury in the land of the Saxons.'

'I see. And the good Saxon brother disputes my understanding of Muirchú's account of Patrick's life?'

'Some things may not be taken so literally.' Eadulf felt moved to make a defence.

'The book is not true then?'

Fidelma groaned softly as Eadulf reddened in annoyance.

'It is true, but . . .'

'How can it be true and yet not to be taken literally?' smiled Orla icily. 'There is some necromancy here, surely?'

'Some things are symbolic, meaning to impress the concept by means of stating a myth.'

'So none of the people Patrick is said to have killed were actually killed?'

'That is not what . . .'

Fidelma interrupted.

'We are coming to the end of the gorge,' she announced thankfully as she saw that the ravine was widening into a broad valley. 'Is this Gleann Geis?'

'It is the Forbidden Valley,' confirmed Orla, turning away from Eadulf and gazing up at the cliff above them. She suddenly issued a shrill whistling sound like a bird cry. At once, a deeper answering cry sounded. The figure of a sentinel appeared high above them, gazing down. It was then that Fidelma realised this passage into Gleann Geis was well protected for no one could move in or out without the consent of those who controlled this narrow pass.

Chapter Five

Gleann Geis was spectacular. The floor of the valley was a level plain through which a fair-sized river pushed its sedate way, apparently rising at the far end from a turbulent mountain stream, cascading over precipitous waterfalls that dropped for incredible distances. Then it raced its way into another fissure, much like the dried-up gorge through which they had made their entrance. It passed through the gap in the granite barrier on its journey out of the glen. The valley floor was covered mainly in cereal and grain fields, cultivated yellowing squares of corn and wheat, set among swathes of grazing land on which cattle herds stood out as bright groups of brown, white and black against the green carpet. A few small white flocks of sheep and goats were dotted among them.

It occurred to Eadulf immediately that here was a fruitful valley; rich with pastoral land as well as cultivated areas. It was surrounded by a natural fortification. The walls of the encircling mountains stretched away with their lofty, unscalable heights which sheltered the valley from the winds. He was able to pick out buildings which seemed to cling to the sides of the mountains. Most of them appeared to be erected on little terraces. The same blue-grey granite blocks that were used in the walls of the buildings were also used in the barriers which created the terraces.

There was no need to ask which of the several buildings in the glen was the ráth of Laisre. Towards the head of the valley, in splendid isolation and set upon a single large mound of a hill, were the walls of a large ráth, or fortress, its bulwarks following the contours of the hill. Eadulf was unsure whether the hill, perhaps hillock was a better description for it rose less than a hundred feet from the valley floor, or so he estimated, was a natural phenomenon or not. Eadulf knew that some of the heights on which such fortresses were built were man-made and he wondered at the incredible time and labour of ancient times involved in producing such an elevation. They were too far away to see the detail but he knew that the great walls must stand twenty feet high.

It was an impressive valley – yes; but even with its width and its length, Eadulf felt an overwhelming claustrophobia as he gazed upwards at the surrounding mountains. He had a feeling of being shut in, of being imprisoned. He glanced at Fidelma and found that she, too, had been intently examining the breath-taking landscape and there was the same degree of awe on her features.

Orla had been watching their expressions as they surveyed their surroundings with a faintly scornful smile of satisfaction on her lips.

'You may now understand why this is called the Forbidden Valley,' she observed.

Fidelma regarded her gravely.

'Inaccessible – yes,' she agreed, 'but why forbidden?'

'The bards of our people sing of the time beyond time. It was in the days when Oillil Olum was said to have sat in judgment at Cashel and when we dwelt outside the boundaries of this place. We dwelt in the shadow of a mighty Fomorii lord who devastated our lands and our peoples by his greed and lust. Eventually our chieftain decided to move our people away from the reach of the Fomorii tyrant, seeking a new land to settle in. So it was we eventually came to this place. It was, as you see, a natural fortification against the enemies of our people. There is only one path into it and the same path out . . .'

'Except the river,' Eadulf pointed out.

The woman laughed.

'Only if you are a salmon can you hope to enter the valley that way. The river cuts through the rock and over many rapids and waterfalls. No boat can get up or down. No, this is a natural fortress and only those we invite in may enter. To those we do not wish to greet in friendship, it remains the Forbidden Valley. A few sturdy warriors may hold the gorge, as you have seen.'

'I also see that you have an abundance of warriors, unusual in a small clan,' observed Fidelma.

Orla was deprecating.

'None are professional such as those that you have at Cashel. Our clan is too small. Each of our warriors has other tasks to fulfil. Artgal, for example, is a blacksmith and has a small farm. Each man, in turn, serves when needed to ensure our safety against potential enemies. Though, for the most part, we are secured by nature's decree.'

'An enclosed form of life,' Eadulf sighed. 'How many dwell under the rule of Laisre?'

'Five hundred,' Orla admitted.

'It occurs to me that if you have lived here for generations, surely it restricts your growth as a people?'

Orla frowned trying to understand Eadulf's oblique point.

'What my brother in Christ is saying,' intervened Fidelma, conscious of his line of thought, 'concerns the matter of incestuous marriage.'

Orla looked surprised.

'But incest is forbidden by law.'

'Surely in a small community, locked within this valley for years . . .' Eadulf began to explain.

Orla understood and stared at him in disapproval.

'The *Cáin Lánamna* states that there can only be nine types of marriage and this we adhere to. We are not as primitive as you would paint us, Saxon. Our bards keep strict genealogies and we have the services of a matchmaker who travels on our behalf.'

'Who administers the law among you?' interrupted Fidelma intrigued.

'My brother's Druid, Murgal. He is our Brehon as well as spiritual guide. His reputation is without equal in this part of the country. You will soon encounter him for he will negotiate for Laisre. But we delay, let us proceed to my brother's ráth.'

Fidelma glanced surreptitiously at the woman. She began to respect Orla's firmness of mind and easy authority, although she disagreed with her philosophy.

The road they were taking led from the gorge slightly downhill to a large sprawl of granite boulders. From their midst, standing by the roadside, there arose a large carved statue of a male figure, almost three times as big as a man. It was sitting cross-legged, one leg slightly tucked under the body. From its head great antler horns rose up. Around the neck, was a hero's gold torc. The arms were held up so that the hands were on a level with each shoulder. In the left hand, a second hero's torc was grasped while in the right hand a long snake was held, the hand gripping the serpent just behind the head.

Eadulf's eyes almost started from their sockets as he viewed the great pagan idol.

'*Soli Deo gloria!*' he gasped. 'What is that?'

Fidelma was unperturbed.

'It is Lugh Lamhfada – Lugh of the Long Hand – who was worshipped in ancient times . . .'

'And still is, here,' Orla reminded her grimly.

'An evil apparition!' breathed Eadulf.

'Not so,' Orla said sharply. 'He is a god of light and learning, renowned for the splendour of his countenance; the god of all arts and crafts; the father of the hero Cúchulainn by the mortal woman Dechtíre. The god whose festival we celebrate at the feast of Lughnasadh which is next month when we harvest our crops.'

Eadulf crossed himself swiftly as they passed the impassive seated figure whose grey stone eyes stared at them indifferently.

They rode silently along the valley road towards the distant ráth. Eadulf found himself confirmed in his first thoughts that this was a wealthy enclave. The mountains which gave protection from the winds also encouraged crops to grow while, at the same time, by catching the rain clouds, causing the valley to be fertile. Here and there, the heavy rainfalls over the millennia had formed little patches of bogland but, all in all, it was fecund country with trees bearing fruits as well as an abundance of grain crops. Sheep, goats and cattle held to the high ground pastures.

As they passed, now and then, people stopped to stare at them; some greeted Orla with familiarity which she acknowledged. Fidelma had the impression from their appearance that here, in spite of a difference of religion, dwelt a content and self-sufficient people. It puzzled her for it did not seem to balance with the terrible sight which had met their eyes in the glen outside this valley.

As they approached the grey granite walls of the ráth, Fidelma saw that it was no mere ornamental fortress. In spite of the natural defences of the valley which surrounded it, its great walls and battlements, as well as its situation at the head of the valley, were so constructed that, should a hostile force break through the gorge, a few warriors could still defend it from an entire army. It had been constructed by experts in the martial arts. Again the question crossed Fidelma's mind why such a small clan would need to have such defensive structures in a valley already naturally defended?

Of course, in the old days, when tribe fought against tribe for the best territories and to increase their wealth, such fortresses were widely spread throughout the five kingdoms. Cashel itself had been raised to protect the Eóghanacht from their more jealous neighbours, just as the other great fortress capitals of Tara, Navan, Ailech, Cruachan and Ailenn had also been built. But, while this ráth was nowhere near the size of the others, it was a strong and well-built fortress with several buildings of two and even three storeys in height. She could even observe a large squat watch tower.

She was aware of several sentinels staring down at their approach from the walls of the ráth and women as well as men were crowding to see their arrival. Two warriors stood before the open gates of the fortress. Fidelma noticed that these were heavy timber doors of oak, reinforced with iron and iron hinges. She noticed that the hinges were well greased and the doors, though standing wide open, had the appearance of being other than mere ornaments. Above this gateway, a banner of blue silk on which was embroidered a hand holding a sword aloft, was fluttering in the breeze – the emblem of the chieftain of Gleann Geis.

A tall, fair-haired warrior, standing by the gate, held up his hand in respectful greeting.

'You have returned without your escort but with two strangers, Orla. Is anything amiss?'

'I am escorting the emissary from Cashel to my brother, Rudgal. Artgal and the others will follow soon. There was . . . was a matter they had to investigate.'

The fair warrior's eyes narrowed suspiciously as his glance fell first on Fidelma and then on Eadulf. But he stood aside respectfully while Orla led the way through the gates into a large flagged courtyard surrounded by a large complex of buildings. The square was traditional with a large oak tree growing in its centre. Eadulf was now observant enough about custom to know that the tree was the *crann betha*, the tree of life, or totem of the clan. Eadulf knew that the tree symbolised the moral and material well-being of the people. If disputes arose between opposing clans that one of the worst things that could happen was that the rival clan raided the other clan's territory to cut down or burn their rival's sacred tree. Such an act demoralised the clan and caused their rivals to claim victory over them.

Two young boys came running forward as Orla slid from her horse.

'The stable lads will take your horses,' Orla announced as Fidelma and Eadulf followed her example and dismounted. The boys took the reins from them while they unstrapped their saddle bags.

'I presume you will want to refresh yourselves from the arduous journey before you meet my brother and the others?' the wife of the tanist continued. 'I will show you to our guests' hostel. After you have bathed and eaten, my brother Laisre will doubtless want to greet you in the council chamber.'

Fidelma indicated that arrangement suited them well. One or two people crossing the courtyard of the ráth greeted Orla and then turned their gaze on Fidelma and Eadulf with undisguised interest. Orla made no attempt to explain who they were. A young girl came running forward.

'What brings you back so early, Mother?' she demanded. 'Who are these strangers?'

Fidelma could see the likeness between Orla and the girl immediately. The girl was about fourteen, not much more. Her manner of dress and jewellery showed that she was past the age of choice in that she was regarded as an adult. She had her mother's dark, abundantly curly hair and flashing eyes. In spite of her youth she was attractive and aware of her allure for she carried herself with a coquettish self-aware attitude.

Orla greeted her daughter with absent-minded distance.

'Who are these Christians, Mother?' insisted the girl, obviously recognising their manner of dress. 'Are they prisoners?'

Orla frowned slightly and shook her head.

'They are emissaries from Cashel, Esnad. Guests of your uncle. Now be off with you. Plenty of time to greet them later.'

The young girl, Esnad, turned an openly speculative gaze on Eadulf.

'That one is foreign but quite handsome for a foreigner,' she ventured with a flirtatious expression.

Fidelma tried to hide her amusement while Eadulf blushed furiously.

'Esnad!' snapped her mother in irritation. 'Be off!'

The girl turned with a backward smile at Eadulf and walked slowly across the courtyard, her hips swaying slightly suggestively. Orla heaved a sigh of exasperation.

'Your daughter is at the age of choice?' observed Fidelma.

Orla nodded.

'It is hard to find a husband for her. I fear that she has her own ideas. She is a trial, that one.'

She continued on, leading them to a large two-storey building set against one of the outer walls of the ráth. Orla opened the door and stood aside.

'I will send the hostel keeper to you and, when you are refreshed, she will bring you to Laisre's chamber.'

She inclined her head briefly to Fidelma and then left them to their own devices.

In the security of the main room of the guests' hostel, a room where the guests obviously ate and where meals were prepared, Fidelma threw her saddle bags on to the table and sank into the nearest chair, giving a deep sigh of exhaustion.

'I have spent too long on horseback, Eadulf,' she remarked. 'I have forgotten what it is to relax in a chair.'

Eadulf glanced around at the accommodation. It was a comfortably decorated room with a fire already lit above which a cooking pot was steaming and emitting pleasant aromas.

'At least Laisre's guests seem well provided for,' he muttered. The room stretched the entire length of the building and there was a long table with benches on either side and a couple of more elaborate wooden chairs. This was obviously the dining area. At the far end, by the fire, were all the accoutrements for cooking. There were four doors leading to other rooms on the lower level. Eadulf put down his saddle bags and crossed to them, taking a quick look inside.

'Two bathing rooms,' he announced. He opened the other doors, grunted in disgust and crossed himself. 'The others are the *fialtech.*' The Irish term came easily to him for the 'veil house' was a colloquialism for a privy and had been picked up from the Roman concept. Many religious believed that the Devil dwelt within the privy and it had become the custom to make the sign of the cross before entering it.

A wooden staircase led to the upper level. Here Eadulf found there were four small rooms, cell-like affairs. He peered into each one in turn, noticing the wooden cots already laid out with their straw mattresses, woollen blankets and linen sheets. After a moment or so he retraced his steps downstairs to where Fidelma was still stretched in her chair.

'There seems to be two other guests,' he observed. 'Rich guests by the look of their baggage in the cubicles. And one is obviously a cleric.'

Fidelma looked up in surprise.

'I was not told to expect anyone else at this meeting. Who could it be?'

'Perhaps Bishop Ségdae has sent some other cleric to represent him and the abbey?' hazarded Eadulf.

'Hardly likely since he concurred with Colgú's delegation of me. No, no cleric from Imleach would come here.'

Eadulf gave a shrug.

'Didn't the woman, Orla, say that Ultan of Armagh had sent an emissary to them? Well, we shall know soon enough who the cleric is and who his companion is. We . . .'

He was cut short when the door of the hostel burst open and a portly, elderly woman bustled in. She wore a beaming smile and walked with a rapid gait, hands folded in front of her. She bobbed swiftly towards Fidelma and then made a similar obeisance to Eadulf. Her eyes twinkled from beneath deep folds of flesh. She seemed almost spherical in girth.

'Are you the hostel keeper?' asked Eadulf, regarding her with slight awe, for she seemed to fill the room with her presence.

'That I am, stranger. I bid you welcome. Tell me how may I serve you?'

'A bath,' Fidelma requested immediately. 'And then . . .'

'Food,' interposed Eadulf, in case she neglected his order of preference.

The wreaths of flesh quivered.

'A bath you shall have and that immediately, lady. Since we already have guests, the water is even now heated. And there is food ready to be served.'

Fidelma rose and indicated her satisfaction.

'Then proceed to draw a bath for me . . . what is your name?'

The hostel keeper bobbed again towards her.

'I am called Cruinn, lady.'

Fidelma tried hard to keep a straight face for the name implied one who was round and the name certainly fitted the circular shape of the hostel keeper. The woman stood smiling, apparently unaware of the struggle taking place to mask her features.

'Tell me, Cruinn,' Eadulf intervened, catching Fidelma's eye and distracting the woman in case Fidelma lost her struggle, 'who is staying in the hostel with us?'

The fat woman turned to him.

'Why, someone who believes in your God. A noble from the north, I think he is.'

'A noble from the north?' Fidelma intervened, abruptly serious.

'Well, he is richly dressed and with much fine jewellery on him.'

'Do you know his name?'

'No. That I don't. But the other, his companion, is called Brother Dianach and is his servant, so I believe.'

'They are from the north, you say?' repeated Fidelma as if to make sure there was no mistake.

'From the distant kingdom of Ulaidh, I am told.'

Fidelma stood thoughtfully.

'If this is Ultan's emissary, I wonder what Armagh seeks in this . . .' She nearly said 'godforsaken place' but it seemed, as the populace did not believe in God, it was not the best of descriptions. Orla had said that Ultan of Armagh had sent gifts to Laisre the chieftain. Gifts from Armagh. But that didn't make any sense. Why would Armagh send gifts to a pagan chieftain in a kingdom where it had no jurisdiction and where the people did not even follow the Faith? The rotund hostel keeper interrupted her thoughts.

'I have little idea who they are or what they want. I only know that people come and stay and then I must work. Better people stay where they belonged than travelled from one place to another.' Cruinn sighed deeply, a curious wheezy sound and an action which caused her figure to wobble dangerously. 'Well, it is not my place to complain but that is my view. Come, lady, I will draw your bath first.'

'I will wait here,' Eadulf offered, 'and perhaps there is mead that I might refresh myself with while I am waiting?'

'You will find it in the cask there,' indicated Cruinn, speaking over her shoulder as she propelled Fidelma to one of the bathing chambers. 'But the second bathing tub is ready should you wish to take your bath now.'

Eadulf caught Fidelma's eye and bit his lip.

'In that case, it will save time if I bathed now.' He gave in reluctantly.

As a Saxon he always found the bathing customs of the people of Éireann somewhat extreme. They washed twice daily, with the second wash being a full body bath. Every guests' hostel had its bath house or houses, each with a large tub or vat for which there were several names but most usually *dabach*. After the bath, guests would anoint themselves with sweet scented herbal potions.

Not content with a complete bath in the evening, which was called *fothrucud*, they would, immediately on rising in the morning, wash their face and hands. In both bathing and washing they used a tablet of a scented fatty substance called *sléic* or soap, which they applied with a linen cloth and worked into a lather. They would even have, at certain times, ritual steam baths in what they called *Tigh 'n alluis* or 'sweating houses' where, in a small stone cabin, great fires were kindled so that the place became heated like an oven and the bather would enter and stay until they were perspiring after which they came out and plunged straight into a cold stream. Eadulf disapproved of this practice vehemently. Surely this was a way to an early grave? His own people were not so enamoured of bathing.

The upper classes of the Saxons bathed weekly, usually a swim being deemed sufficient for the cleansing process. Eadulf was not a dirty person in body, manners or habit but he still felt that the bathing rituals of Éireann were excessive.

An hour later they were finishing their meal when the door of the hostel opened and in came a heavy-jowled man. That he was a cleric was not in question. He wore the tonsure of St Peter but he was clad not in the simple robes that most religieux wore but in elegant silks and embroidered linens and with a bejewelled crucifix the like of which neither Fidelma nor Eadulf had seen since they were in Rome together. Fidelma eyed the man in disapproval. Here was someone whose riches seemed to betray the very teachings of Christ.

The eyes of the man were dark and watchful. They had a curious quality of staring, unblinkingly, like the eyes of an animal watching its prey. The eyes were made small by the largeness of the surrounding features. He was a short man, stocky rather than fat, although the fleshy face made one think he was obese until one noticed the powerful muscular shoulders and thick arms.

'I am Brother Solin,' he announced officiously, 'secretary to Ultan, archbishop of Armagh.' He intoned his introduction in accents which corroborated that he was from the kingdom of the Uí Néill of Ulaidh. There was something about him which caused Fidelma to take an immediate dislike to him. Perhaps it was the way he stared at her with an almost speculative gaze which left no doubt that he was a man judging her as a woman and not as a person. 'Orla has informed me of your arrival. You are Sister Fidelma and you must be the foreign cleric.'

'You are a long way from Armagh, Solin.' Fidelma rose, unwillingly, but courtesy prompted her to be civil in respect to the position of the northern religieux.

'As you are from Cashel,' the stocky man replied, unperturbed, coming forward and seating himself.

'Cashel is the royal seat of this kingdom, Solin,' responded Fidelma coldly.

'Armagh is the royal seat of the Faith in all five kingdoms,' the man replied with an airy dismissal.

'That is a question to be debated,' snapped back Fidelma. 'The bishop of Imleach makes no such recognition of Armagh.'

'Well, it is a debate of such delicacy that we should leave it for a future time.' Solin dismissed the matter with an air of boredom.

Fidelma stood her ground. She decided to be direct.

'Why is the secretary of Ultan of Armagh in this small corner of my brother's kingdom?'

Solin poured a mug of mead from the jug on the table.

'Does Cashel forbid wandering clerics?'

'That is no answer,' Fidelma responded. 'I think you are hardly in the category of a *peregrinator pro Christo*.'

An angry look came into Solin's eyes.

'Sister, I think you forget yourself. As secretary to Ultan . . .' he protested.

'You secure no privileges of rank before me. I am envoy to my brother, the king of Cashel. Why are you here?'

The blood drained momentarily from Solin's face as he fought his rage at being so bluntly addressed. Then he regained his composure with a tight smile.

'Ultan of Armagh has sent me to the farthest corners of the five kingdoms to see how the Faith prospers. He has sent me with gifts to distribute . . .'

The door opened again with abruptness.

It was Orla. She entered with an annoyed expression furrowing her features.

'What does this mean?' she snapped. 'My brother is being kept waiting. Is this the courtesy Cashel extends to its chieftains?'

Solin smirked, rising from his seat.

'I was just trying to persuade the good sister to accompany me to the chieftain's council chamber,' he said obsequiously. 'She seemed more concerned with the reasons for my presence in Gleann Geis.'

Fidelma opened her mouth to challenge his lie but then snapped it shut. She turned to Orla and met her anger with a stony look.

'I am ready. Precede us.'

Orla raised an eyebrow, disconcerted for the moment by the haughty expression on Fidelma's face for she was quite unused to having her authority challenged. Without a further word, she led the way from the hostel. Eadulf and Solin brought up the rear.

The chambers of Laisre were housed in the largest of the buildings in the ráth. A centrally situated three-storey building which, when entered by the great door, revealed a large reception chamber with passageways leading left and right and with a stone stairway to the rooms above. A tall inner door then gave entrance into a large chamber. There were several people gathered there in the high-ceilinged, smoky room. Large tapestries draped the walls and hanging lamps illuminated the room, although the central fire, on which logs were blazing, gave out a strong glowing light and was the cause of the smoky atmosphere.

A couple of deer hounds lay at full length before the roaring fire. To one side of them was a large ornate carved oak chair. Clustered around it were several men and women of the chieftain's immediate circle. Two warriors guarded the interior door and a third stood just behind the oak chair of office. Fidelma recognised this third warrior as the black-bearded man, named Artgal, who had accompanied Orla when they had first encountered her.

It needed no introduction to identify Laisre, the chieftain of Gleann Geis, even if he had not been sprawling in the great oak chair. Knowing that Orla was his sister Fidelma could distinguish him at once for the resemblance was truly remarkable. He had the same structure of face, the same dark eyes and hair and the same manner of expression. Had he not worn a long wispy dark moustache she would have said they were two peas from the same pod. In fact, as she examined him more closely, she realised that he and Orla must be twins. He was a man of slender looks and handsome with, perhaps, the fault of knowing it. He was not remotely like the image that Fidelma had conjured of a pagan chieftain at Cashel. She had imagined a wild, unruly man. But, pagan as he was, Laisre was poised, impeccable in his manners and with all the appearance of civility.

As Orla conducted them into the chamber Laisre rose from his chair of office and came forward to greet Fidelma in token of her rank, of which Orla must have informed him. His hand was outstretched.

'You are well come to this place, Fidelma of Cashel. I trust your brother, the king, is well?'

'He is, by the grace of God,' replied Fidelma automatically.

There was a smothered exclamation from one of the men in the room. Fidelma turned an inquiring look in the direction of the group.

Laisre grimaced apologetically. There was a humour in his eyes.

'Some here may ask the question, by the grace of which god?'

Fidelma's eyes found the man from whom the sound had come. He was a tall, thin man, with iron-grey hair and distinctive parti-coloured robes, embroidered with gold thread, and a gold chain of office around his neck. He met her gaze with unconcealed hostility. His face had an almost bird-like quality, scrawny with a prominent Adam's apple which bobbed furiously as he swallowed, which seemed to be a constant habit. His deep black eyes, unblinking like a serpent, smouldered with a deep emotion.

'Murgal is entitled to express his opinions,' she observed coldly, turning back to Laisre.

Fidelma was aware that the thin man had started in surprise. Even Laisre was astonished that she could identify Murgal.

'Do you know Murgal?' the chieftain asked hesitantly, unable to see the simple logic by which she had arrived at her identification.

Fidelma suppressed a smile of self-satisfaction at the effect she had caused.

'Surely everyone knows the reputation of Murgal and that he is a man of principle and learning . . . and of propriety,' she replied solemnly, determined to take the best advantage she could before entering into the negotiations with Laisre. It was always best to start out by wrong-footing one's adversaries. She had merely made a deduction. Orla had boasted about Murgal, her brother's Druid and Brehon. She had, in fact, never heard of Murgal before. But who else would be standing so close to his chieftain and wearing such a chain of office? It was pure bluff and she had succeeded with it. The knowledge of the envoy of Cashel would now be whispered around the council chamber of Gleann Geis.

Murgal's mouth had compressed. His eyes became hooded as he regarded her, assessing her qualities as his opponent.

The significance of the interaction of the initial clash was lost upon all but Fidelma and Murgal.

'Come forward, Murgal, and greet the envoy and sister of Colgú of Cashel,' Laisre ordered.

The tall man came forward and bowed slightly in deference to her rank.

'I, too, have heard of Fidelma, daughter of Faílbe Fland of Cashel,' he greeted in a curious whispering pitch, a slightly wheezing tone as if he were a sufferer from asthma. 'Your reputation has preceded you. The Uí Fidgente have long memories and their defeat last winter has been attributed to you.'

Was there some subtle threat implied in his words?

'The defeat of the Uí Fidgente, after they tried to overthrow the rightful king of Cashel, was brought about only by their own vanity and avarice,' replied Fidelma calmly. 'For that they have been justly punished. However, as a loyal servant of Cashel, I am pleased when any who nurture treachery to Cashel are uncovered, just as I am sure that Laisre, as a loyal servant of Cashel, is also pleased.'

Murgal blinked slowly, the lids of his eyes drooping as if he were tired and needed to close them. He was beginning to realise that he had met an opponent of wit and perception who would need to be treated with skill and discretion.

'Your principles are a thing to be admired – the surety of knowledge that one serves a rightful cause against wrong must surely be a comfort?' he replied.

Fidelma was about to respond when Laisre, smilingly, took her arm and turned her from Murgal saying, 'Well, there is nothing wrong in principle though it is often easier to fight for a principle than to adhere to its precepts. Come, Fidelma, let me introduce you to my tanist, Colla, the husband of my sister Orla.'

The man standing next to Orla took a pace forward and inclined his head in salutation. The tanist was the heir-elect in any tribe or kingdom. Colla was the same age as Laisre but standing a good head taller than his chieftain. That he was a man of action there was little doubt. He had the build of a warrior. His skin was bronzed by the sun which contrasted with the fiery copper redness of his hair and bright blue eyes. He was not handsome but had a subtle masculine attractiveness which Fidelma could not fail to notice. Perhaps it was his manner, some inner quality of strength or the lazy smile on his features, which made him seem easy going and affable but did not conceal the steel of his character to the discerning eye. He was dressed in accoutrements for war and his sword was slung in workman-like fashion.

'I rejoice at your safe arrival here, Fidelma,' he greeted in a deep, booming voice that caused Fidelma to start for a moment. 'My wife, Orla, has told me of the horror which you encountered in the glen beyond and I can only assure you that I will do everything in my power to find the culprits and bring them to justice. The reason for that senseless slaughter must be uncovered for it does not reflect well upon our people.'

Fidelma regarded him gravely for a moment and then asked in an innocent tone: 'Why do you say it was senseless slaughter?'

The tanist started in surprise.

'I do not know what you mean.'

'If you do not know the reason for it, why do you say it was senseless slaughter?' she explained carefully.

There was an awkward silence for a moment or two and then Colla shrugged.

'It is just a matter of expression . . .'

Laughter interrupted him. Laisre was consumed with mirth.

'You have a sharp wit, Fidelma. Our negotiation will prove interesting. But, in seriousness, when Orla and Artgal reported this matter, we were all perplexed. The Uí Fidgente have been quiet since your brother's army crushed them at the Hill of Áine last year. Until that time they had been the only hostile raiders in this land. Some of the tribes beyond this valley had their herds depleted by raids. But why kill these strangers and in such a fashion? Who are these strangers that have been killed? Where did they come from? No one seems to offer any answers to these perplexing questions as yet.'

Fidelma was suddenly interested.

'Are we certain that they are strangers?'

Laisre was self-assured.

'Artgal examined the features of each corpse in turn. We are not such a large community here that thirty of our young men can go missing without our knowing of it. He recognised no one.'

'Thirty-three, in fact,' replied Fidelma, turning purposefully to Murgal. 'Thirty-three corpses. A strange number is thirty-three. Thirty-three spread in a sunwise circle. Each corpse slain by three different methods – The Threefold Death.'

There was a chill silence in the council chamber; so quiet that one could hear the soft snoring of one of the deerhounds against the crackle of the fire. No one made any reply. All understood the significance of what she was saying. The symbolism meant much to those who followed the old paths of worship. Finally Murgal took an angry step forward.

'Speak on, envoy of Cashel. I believe there is an accusation behind your speech.'

Laisre looked uncomfortably towards his Brehon.

'I hear no accusation, Murgal,' he admonished. Then turning to Fidelma he continued pleasantly, 'The idea that we of the old religion hold human sacrifices, which is what I have heard some of the clerics of your Faith preach, is a nonsense. Even in the ancient stories about the worship of the idol Cromm, it was the Druids who are said to have stood against the king, Tigernmas, who introduced the worship of Cromm, and it was they who brought about his destruction and an end to that vile cult.'

'Nevertheless,' Fidelma pressed, 'I merely point out the symbolism of these deaths. Such symbolism draws one to the inevitable questions and ones that need to be answered.'

Orla, who had taken a stand near her husband, sniffed deprecatingly.

'I have already explained to Fidelma of Cashel that she cannot look to Gleann Geis for responsibility for these deaths.'

'I did not suggest that the responsibility lay in Gleann Geis. But responsibility rests somewhere. I would ask permission to withdraw from your council for a few days and proceed with an investigation immediately, before the signs are destroyed by wind and rain.'

It was clear that Laisre was not happy at the proposal. Yet it was Colla who spoke for him.

'Obviously, there is much to be discussed between Gleann Geis and Cashel,' he ventured, speaking directly to Laisre. 'The negotiations are important. Time cannot be wasted. Because of that factor, let me then make a suggestion, my chieftain. Give me permission to ride out with half-a-dozen warriors and investigate in the place of Fidelma of Cashel. While she concludes the business that brought her to Gleann Geis, I will see what can be learnt about these deaths and then return to make a report to her.'

Laisre appeared relieved at the suggestion.

'An excellent idea. We are agreed to it.'

Fidelma was about to express her dissatisfaction and point out that as a trained *dálaigh* of the courts she had more experience in assessing such matters than Laisre's tanist but the chieftain went on: 'Yes; make ready, Colla. Take Artgal and as many men as you feel that you need. You do not have to leave until dawn tomorrow. So tonight we will hold our feast to welcome the envoy of Cashel as we have planned.' He turned to Fidelma with a smile. 'A commendable plan of action, do you not think so, Fidelma of Cashel?'

Fidelma was still going to disagree when Murgal interrupted with a tone of satisfaction.

'I am sure that Colla will find that there is no blame that will attach itself to Gleann Geis.'

Fidelma glanced at him with irritation.

'I am sure your tanist will discover that.'

Murgal returned her look and knew what she was implying. He clearly debated momentarily whether he should take open offence at her words but she turned away to conceal her annoyance at how she had been deflected from her purpose.

Eadulf was a little concerned and wondered whether Fidelma would press the matter further. It did not need someone with prudence to realise that there was no way that Fidelma would be given permission by the chieftain of Gleann Geis to leave the negotiations and follow an investigation concerning the slain men. Thankfully, so far as Eadulf was concerned, Fidelma seemed to realise as much for she finally inclined her head in acceptance of the situation.

'Very well, Laisre,' she said, 'I shall accept this proposal. I will need to make a full report on this matter to my brother when I return to Cashel, so all that Colla can discover, however much he deems it of insignificance, will be of interest to me.'

'Then I shall leave with my men at break of day, Fidelma of Cashel,' the tanist assured her.

Laisre beamed with satisfaction.

'Excellent. Now let us turn our minds to other matters. I have neglected my duties as host. Have you met Solin, secretary to Ultan of Armagh and a leading cleric of your Faith?'

Fidelma did not bother to turn in Brother Solin's direction. Out of the corner of her eye she had been aware that Solin had been standing with Eadulf and had been whispering in his ear. Eadulf looked uncomfortable and had removed himself a pace or two.

'I have already met Brother Solin,' she said in a voice which evinced no pleasure at the meeting.

'And Brother Dianach, my scribe?' queried Solin coming forward. 'I do not think that you have met him?'

There was something pompous about the way he said it, as if making the point that he was a man important enough to have a scribe with him. Fidelma turned to examine the thin, slightly effeminate young man whom Solin now pushed forward. He was hardly out of his teens with a pale, spotted face and a badly shaved tonsure in the manner of those of the Roman creed. The boy was nervous and his dark eyes would not meet her gaze, giving him the appearance of shiftiness. She felt sorry for the gauche youngster.

'*Salve*, Brother Dianach,' she greeted in Roman fashion, trying to put the boy at his ease.

'*Pax tecum*,' he stammered in reply.

Fidelma turned back to Laisre.

'I would also take this opportunity to introduce Brother Eadulf, an envoy from the Archbishop Theodore of Canterbury in the land of Kent.'

Eadulf took a pace forward and bowed slightly from the neck, first to the chieftain and then generally to the assembly.

'You are welcome to this place, Eadulf of Canterbury,' greeted Laisre, having a little difficulty in pronouncing the foreign names. 'For what purpose do you honour our little valley with a visit? The Archbishop Theodore, of the distant land you come from, has surely no interest in what transpires in this part of the world?'

Eadulf was diplomatic.

'I am sent as an envoy to the king of Cashel only. But while enjoying his hospitality, I have taken the opportunity to visit the far corners of his kingdom to discover how his people prosper and in what manner.'

'Then you are thrice welcome to observe how we do so,' replied Laisre solemnly. He glanced again at Fidelma. 'And now . . .'

'Now,' Fidelma said, reaching into her robe and bringing forth the white wand of office and, at the same time, drawing out her dagger. 'We must observe custom.' She held out the dagger hilt towards Laisre in one hand and the wand with the stag's head in the other.

Laisre knew the protocol. He reached out a hand and lightly tapped the wand with his forefinger.

'We receive you as envoy of Colgú,' he intoned solemnly before stepping back and waving his hand to the hovering servants who brought chairs and placed them in a semi-circle before his chair of office. Several of the people stood back while Laisre indicated Fidelma and Eadulf to be seated. Murgal, Colla, Orla and Solin were the only others who seated themselves while the chieftain returned to his chair.

'Now to the purpose of the negotiation . . .' Laisre began.

'As I understand it,' intervened Fidelma, 'the purpose is to agree a means whereby the abbot-bishop of Imleach is empowered to build a church of the Faith here in Gleann Geis as well as a school. Am I correct?'

Laisre seemed disconcerted for the moment at her swift summary.

'You are correct,' he agreed.

'And, in return, what is it that you expect from Imleach?' asked Fidelma.

'What makes you think that we expect anything of Imleach?' Murgal intervened in a suspicious tone.

Fidelma smiled at him with an expression which showed little humour.

'The very word we are using to describe what we are about to do – negotiation – makes me think so. Negotiation implies a bargain. A bargain means to make some form of agreement involving a compromise. Or am I mistaken?'

'You are not mistaken, Fidelma,' Laisre replied. 'The bargain is simple – in return for permission to build a church and to teach children here in Gleann Geis we would want assurances that there will be no interference in the religious life of Gleann Geis, in our pursuing the faith of our forefathers, in following the path of our ancient beliefs.'

'I see.' Fidelma frowned slightly as she considered the matter. 'But why should we build a church and a school if we are not allowed to proselytise the people? Why have a church or a school at all if no one is allowed to go to them?'

Laisre exchanged a glance with Murgal and then seemed to weigh his words carefully.

'The fact is, Fidelma of Cashel, we do have a Christian community here in Gleann Geis.'

Fidelma was surprised but tried not to show it.

'I do not understand. I have always been told that Gleann Geis was a bastion of the old faith, the old ways. Is this not so?'

'So it is,' interrupted Murgal, his voice brittle. 'And so it should remain.'

'This is a wrong attitude,' Laisre rebuked him. 'The times have changed and we must move with them or perish.'

Fidelma turned to examine him with interest. She wondered if she had underestimated the chieftain. It was clear that some among his people disapproved of his contact with the bishop of Imleach but now he was displaying the quality of a firm leader of his people.

Murgal gave a loud hiss of annoyance.

There was an uncomfortable silence before Laisre proceeded.

'Over the years our men and women have intermarried with surrounding clans and through this means we have maintained our strength as a people. We have obeyed the ancient laws against incest and so we have survived strong and healthy. But the wives and husbands who have been brought into our midst have often been of the new religion. They have come to Gleann Geis bringing the new Faith and many have raised their children in it. This community is so sizable now that they demand a church and a priest of the Faith to see to their spiritual needs; they demand a school where they may learn about their Faith.'

Colla muttered something indiscernible.

Laisre ignored him. He turned directly to Fidelma.

'There are some among us who recognise the inevitability of the triumph of your Faith. In these last two centuries the five kingdoms have been transformed whether some of us like it or not.'

'A fundamental tenet of our law is that no one dictates what gods or goddesses we follow,' Murgal intervened. 'Since the time when those of the new Faith subverted our kings, we have been told which gods we can pray to. We are told that we can only pray to three . . .'

'There is only one God!' exploded Eadulf, unable to keep aloof from the argument.

'One?' Murgal sneered. 'Do you not know your own Faith? There are three, those you call the Holy Trinity. And do you not also pray to a goddess, the mother of your Christ?'

Fidelma shook her head.

'That is not how we, of the Faith, view these matters, Murgal,' she remonstrated softly. Then to Laisre she said, 'But surely this is no place to discuss theology, nor was it for that purpose that I came to Gleann Geis.'

The chieftain lowered his head for a moment in thought and then he indicated his agreement.

'We may discuss the freedom of the individual and the freedom of religion at some other time,' Fidelma added.

'Then remember,' Murgal said, 'when you speak of freedom, our religion is wedded to the soil of this place; it is the religion of our ancestors for countless generations going back into the mists of time itself. Know then, that it is a hard thing to eradicate entirely from the soil in which it has grown, in which it has been nurtured and borne fruit. Remember that freedom from the bondage of soil is no freedom for the tree.'

Fidelma began to realise that Murgal was no mere unquestioning spokesman of a dying faith. He was a spiritual man of deep thought. In him, Fidelma realised that she had found an adversary not to be underrated.

'I shall remember what you say, Murgal,' she acknowledged. 'But our immediate task is to make an agreement, that is, if you wish to have a church and school in this valley. I had been given the impression that the council had already agreed to this for I did not come here merely to debate theology.'

Laisre coloured a little.

'I called you here, Fidelma, because it is my wish that my people have these things so that all their beliefs are satisfied. While some of my council inevitably disagree to changes, the greater good of the greater number of my people must remain my guide.'

'Then I am ready to discuss these practical matters.'

Laisre stood up abruptly.

'I have decreed that the opening session of our negotiations will begin tomorrow morning at the sounding of the horn. We shall meet here in the council chamber and discuss such matters as may be pertinent. But as for this evening, I have provided a feasting and an entertainment to welcome you into our valley. The horn will summon you to the chamber for the feast.'

Chapter Six

Fidelma had been surprised that she had not been permitted a private meeting with Laisre to discuss the chieftain's own attitudes. There were a few hours before the evening feast was due to start which Fidelma felt could have been profitably spent in some preliminary discussions on attitude. It appeared that there was some schism among the leaders of the clan over the matter. She had been politely told that neither Laisre nor Colla could make themselves available. Therefore, she and Eadulf found themselves left to their own devices; ignored, though politely so, for everyone in the ráth, including Brother Solin and his young scribe, seemed to have disappeared.

It was Fidelma who suggested that they might usefully examine the fortress and its grounds. It was inevitable that they decided to take a turn around the battlements of the ráth, the wooden walkway which circled the interior of the granite walls. Should the fortress ever be attacked, warriors could take their place in defensive positions, covering the approaches with their bows.

'It is the only place that I have noticed, at the moment, where we might not be overheard,' Fidelma commented as she looked around her. 'It is a place to be remembered when we need to be discreet.'

They paused at an open stretch of the wall, well away from a sentinel who stood above the gateway.

'Is there something disturbing you then that you should seek privacy?' Eadulf queried.

'A few matters still disturb me,' Fidelma acknowledged. 'Do not forget there is the riddle of the thirty-three bodies to be resolved.'

'So you do not trust Colla to come up with any real evidence for the slaughter?'

'That should be obvious,' she replied waspishly. 'Perhaps Laisre does have a valid reason to keep us here but I have the feeling that he does not want us investigating that matter further. I have a feeling we are being manipulated. Why are we dismissed to our own resources when we could have conducted much of the business that brings us hither within these precious hours, which we are now wasting?'

'Well, there is little we can do since Laisre has already set the time for the negotiations. Colla will be on his way at that time.'

Fidelma raised a shoulder and let it fall in an eloquent shrug.

'I fear whatever report he brings back will not add to our knowledge. There is something more immediate that concerns me. The presence of this cleric from Armagh. It is curious that he has suddenly appeared in this place at this particular moment. And where is he and his young scribe at this moment? Is he in discussion with Laisre on some matter to which I am not privy and, if so, why?'

'Surely his presence cannot mean anything sinister?' Eadulf was surprised at her suggestion.

'Surely it can,' replied Fidelma seriously. 'This is an isolated community which usually shuns the representatives of the Faith. Yet now they not only send for a representative from Imleach, which is the main centre of the Faith in Muman, but we find a cleric from Armagh here as well. Not just a cleric but Ultan of Armagh's own secretary. You already know that Armagh is the main centre of the Faith in Ulaidh. Thirty years ago Cummian, who was the bishop there, sought Rome's blessing to call himself archbishop and principal bishop of all the five kingdoms. Imleach does not recognise that office. True that Ultan is recognised as Comarb, or successor, of Patrick but Armagh has no right here. And I have no liking for this man Brother Solin. We must be on our guard for I fear there is something amiss.'

Eadulf was surprised at her attitude but did agree that Brother Solin was not a person to be liked.

'He is not a pleasant man. He is a sly person.'

'Sly? In what manner?' Fidelma demanded quickly. 'Do you have some reason for saying so?'

'He spoke to me in the council chamber while you were engaged with Laisre.'

'So I noticed. I saw that you stepped away from him as if you had been insulted.'

Eadulf knew Fidelma too well to comment on the sharpness of her vision.

'He tried to persuade me that my loyalty should lie with Armagh as the supreme authority of the Faith in the five kingdoms. He claimed kinship with me by virtue of the fact that we both wear the tonsure of St Peter of Rome.'

Fidelma chuckled softly.

'And what did you say to that?'

'Little enough. I thought I would let him have his say in order to find out what he was about. He was very concerned to try to make me accept that Ultan of Armagh was the chief bishop of all Ireland.'

'As I have said before, Armagh is not supreme, though its bishop affects the title "archbishop". The title our people accord to the bishop of Armagh is Comarb of Patrick; that is, the successor of Patrick, just as the bishop of Imleach is accorded the title of Comarb of Ailbe. Both Armagh and Imleach are coequal among the centres of the Faith here.'

'Brother Solin seems to think that is not so. He told me that anyone who bears the tonsure of Rome should shun the company of those who do not accept the authority of Armagh.'

Fidelma was annoyed.

'I know that Ultan has ambition for his *paruchia* but that is nonsense in itself. What did you reply?'

Eadulf thrust out his chin.

'I restrained myself from telling him what I felt. I merely pointed out that Theodore, the archbishop of Canterbury, has sent me as emissary to the court of Colgú of Cashel and to no other king or bishop in the five kingdoms.'

Fidelma smiled briefly.

'And how did Brother Solin react to that?'

'He inflated his cheeks like a fish and his face grew red with mortification. It was then I stepped away from him and ended the discourse.'

'Strange, though, that he should have thought he could speak to you in such a fashion,' she mused.

Eadulf coloured a little.

'I think he wanted to separate us,' he confided.

'In what way do you mean?'

'I believe that he did not realise that we were old friends and thought that I was merely travelling with you. I think that he hoped to isolate you in your mission here.'

'For what purpose?'

'I am not sure. I believe that he was actually trying to warn me that it would be better if I travelled on alone rather than be with you.'

Fidelma was intrigued.

'He made a threat?'

'I do not think it was a threat . . . not exactly.'

'Exactly what, then?'

'He spoke in hypothetical abstractions so that I was unsure of his true meaning. All I know is that he means you no good.'

'We will keep a close watch on Brother Solin, then. We must discover what he is up to.'

'That he is up to something there is no doubt, Fidelma,' affirmed Eadulf.

There was a short silence before Fidelma spoke again: 'This feast this evening will be a formal affair so I am told. You know that there is a priority of places at such gatherings?'

'I have been in Éireann long enough to know this,' he acknowledged.

'Very well. I shall be seated with Laisre and his immediate family simply because I am sister to the king of Cashel. I would imagine Brother Solin will be seated with the *ollamhs* and the learned men like Murgal. You will probably find yourself seated on the same table with Brother Solin's young scribe – Brother Dianach. He is not only young but artless. Try to see what information might be garnered from him about the motivations of his master. I would be happier knowing exactly what Solin is up to in Gleann Geis.'

'I will do what I can, Fidelma. Leave that to me.'

Fidelma paused for a moment, pursing her lips in thought.

'I thought this negotiation was going to be a simple matter, Eadulf. Now I am not so sure. There is something odd going on here, something beneath the surface that we must uncover. I can feel it.'

A hollow cough interrupted them. They had been so intent in their discussion they had failed to notice that a fair-haired warrior had approached them. The man stood a few yards away regarding them quizzically. It was the same warrior who had greeted Orla at the gates of the fortress.

'I noticed you and the Brother standing here, Sister, and wondered if there was anything that you needed?' he ventured.

'No, we were merely taking the evening air before the feast,' Eadulf explained.

Fidelma was looking at the warrior with interest, taking in his features for the first time. He was a strong-looking man, the fair hair was the colour of harvest corn and his eyes were light blue. He was in his early thirties. He wore an old-fashioned lengthy moustache on his upper lip which came past the sides of his mouth to his jaw bone, adding years to his age. He carried himself well.

'Why do you address me as "Sister"?' Fidelma suddenly asked sharply. 'Those who do not follow the Faith do not usually do so.'

The warrior let his eyes meet hers for a long moment, cast a quick look at Eadulf and dropped them again. Then he glanced along the walkway as if fearing to be overheard, before placing his hand inside his shirt and pulling out something on the end of a leather thong. It was a small bronze crucifix.

Fidelma regarded it thoughtfully.

'So, you are a Christian?'

The man nodded quickly and put the crucifix back into his shirt.

'There are more of us here than Murgal the Druid likes to admit, Sister,' he answered. 'My mother came here to marry a man from Gleann Geis and when I was born she raised me secretly in the Faith.'

'So when Laisre said that he wanted a church and school for the Christian community here, for those already raised in the Faith,' mused Eadulf, 'he was not telling a lie?'

The fair-haired man shook his head.

'No, Brother. For many years our community has pressed our chieftain and his council to allow us a priest to tend to our needs. They have refused until recently. Then we heard the joyful news that Laisre had sent to Imleach and Cashel for just such a purpose.'

'And what is your name?' asked Fidelma.

'My name is Rudgal, Sister.'

'And you are a warrior, I see.'

Rudgal chuckled slightly.

'There are no professional warriors here in Gleann Geis. I am a wagon maker by trade but answer Laisre's call every time he needs the services of warriors. Each man here pursues his own calling. Even Artgal, who Laisre considers his chief bodyguard, is also a blacksmith.'

Fidelma remembered what Orla had told her.

'And why do you make yourself known to us, Rudgal?' asked Eadulf.

Rudgal looked swiftly from one to the other.

'In case there is any service I can render. Call upon me should you need anything that is in my power to provide.'

There came the sound of a horn close by. Rudgal gave a grimace.

'Ah, the trumpet! We are summoned to the feast.'

Eadulf found, even as Fidelma had predicted, that Laisre was a strict traditionalist. Everyone had gathered in the large anteroom before the council chamber of the ráth. This was now converted into the feasting hall. Three officers of Laisre's household went into the hall first. Murgal, as official advisor to Laisre, a *bollscare*, or marshal, to regulate the order of precedence of those about to be seated, and the trumpeter or *fearstuic*. At the sound of the next single blast on his horn, Laisre's shield bearer and others carrying the shields or standards of Laisre's warriors entered. The shields were then hung on hooks above the chairs according to ranks.

At the third blast, the bearers of the emblems of those of other ranks went in and fixed these devices to indicate where each guest would sit. Finally, at the fourth blast of the trumpet, the guests all walked in leisurely, each taking their seat under their own shields or emblems. In this manner, all unseemly disputes or jostling for places were avoided. No man or woman sat opposite another, as only one side of each table was occupied. This rigid adherence to an order of priority was, Eadulf noticed, the strictest rule.

Large wooden tables had been set up in the chamber. Laisre's marshal continued to fuss about to assure himself that every person was seated in their proper place according to their rank. Sometimes, or so Eadulf had been told, it was known that serious arguments could break out over the seating arrangements at a feast.

At the top table, Fidelma was seated next to Laisre by right of being an Eóghanacht princess. On her other side was Colla, the tanist, then his wife Orla and their daughter, Esnad. Other members of the chieftain's family were ranged on both sides. The warriors were seated at another table; the intellectuals, men like Solin and Murgal with others Eadulf could not identify, were seated at another table. Eadulf's table apparently contained those of lesser professional rank. Sub-chieftains and minor functionaries sat at yet another table.

Eadulf noticed that Brother Solin's scribe, Brother Dianach, had taken the next seat to his left, just as Fidelma had anticipated. Eadulf decided to begin the conversation by remarking on this emphasis on placing people thus as if it were a strange custom to him. The young cleric overcame his apparent shyness to shake his head in serious reproval at Eadulf's implied criticism.

'In my father's time, it was the placing of Congal Cloén below his proper place at the banquet of Dún na nGéid, which was the main cause of the Battle of Magh Ráth,' he said in quiet seriousness.

Eadulf decided to develop the conversation.

'What battle was that?'

'It was the battle at which the High King, Domnall mac Aedo, annihilated Congal and his Dál Riada allies from across the water,' answered the young scribe.

An elderly man, seated on the opposite side of Dianach, who had introduced himself as Mel, scribe to Murgal, intervened.

'The truth of the matter was that the battle marked the overthrow of the old religion among the great kings of the north.' There was disapproval in his voice. 'True there was an argument about the insult offered Congal as to where he was seated at the feasting table. But so far as the great chieftains of Ulaidh were concerned, they had long resisted the new Faith and the Christian king Domnall mac Aedo was determined to impose it on them. Their resistance finally came to an end with their defeat by Domnall mac Aedo at Magh Ráth. The old faith was thereafter confined to the small, isolated clans.'

The young scribe, Brother Dianach, tried to repress a shiver and crossed himself.

'It is true the Faith triumphed after the battle at Magh Ráth,' he conceded, 'and thanks be to God for that. It was told that just before the feast two horrible black spectres, one male and one female, had appeared to the assembly and, having devoured enormous quantities of food, vanished. They left a baleful influence. So it was that King Domnall had to lead the forces of Christ against the forces of the Devil. He overcame them, *Deo favente*!'

The elderly scribe, Mel, uttered a laugh of derision.

'When did you say this happened?' Eadulf ignored him and addressed the boy as if he were in sympathy with him.

'It was in my father's time; scarcely three decades ago when he was a young warrior. He left his right arm behind at Magh Ráth.'

It was only then that Eadulf realised that he had heard of the battle before. He had studied at Tuam Brecain and in that ecclesiastical college there had been an elderly teacher called Cenn Faelad. He had been a professor of Irish law but had also written a grammar of the language of the people of Éireann which had helped Eadulf increase his knowledge of the language. Cenn Faelad walked with a limp and, when Eadulf had pressed him, he had revealed that as a young man he had been wounded in a battle which Eadulf, mishearing the pronunciation, had thought was called 'Moira'. As Tuam Brecain was already a leading medical college as well as having a faculty of law and of ecclesiastical learning, Cenn Faelad had been taken there and the abbot, himself a skilled surgeon, had brought him back to health. There Cenn Faelad had stayed learning law instead of war and becoming one of the greatest Brehons of the five kingdoms. Eadulf was about to turn to his companion with this contribution to the conversation when he was interrupted.

Laisre had stood up and the trumpeter gave a further blast on his horn to bring the assembly to silence. Eadulf wondered for a moment if Laisre was actually going to say a *Deo gratias* to bless the meal, before he realised his mistake. Laisre merely gave a traditional formal welcome to his guests.

The servants then came in bearing great trays of food and pitchers of wine and mead. Eadulf noticed that the hot plates of meat which were carried in were formally presented in order of rank as well. Particular joints were reserved for certain chiefs, officials and professionals according to their status. The *dáilemain*, the carvers or distributors of food, went down the tables offering joints to each person in turn. Using the left-hand fingers to catch hold of the joint, the recipient would cut off the required piece of meat with a knife held in the right hand. Each person was careful to respect the area of the joint from which they could cut their meat. It was a great insult if a forbidden joint was inadvertently taken. There was even a law, Brother Dianach, growing quite loquacious, advised Eadulf, which penalised the person who took the *curath-mir*, or hero's morsel, a special choice joint reserved for the person who was acknowledged, by general consent, to have performed the bravest and greatest exploit among the guests.

Dishes of breads, fish and cold meats followed the hot meat, and there were bowls of fruit aplenty, all served with pitchers of imported wine or jugs of local mead and ale. The fact that Gleann Geis was able to import wine, although Eadulf assessed it was not a particularly good wine or that it had not travelled well from Gaul, indicated that its chieftain prided himself on his table. Eadulf had taken two clay goblets of the wine before he realised that it was leaving a bitter taste in his mouth and decided to change to drinking the local rich honey-mead.

Each person was given a *lambrat*, a hand cloth, to wipe their hands after the meal.

During the course of the meal, Eadulf did his best to pump the young cleric about the reasons for his journey with Brother Solin. The young man, with an innocence which made Eadulf wonder if it was artfulness, seemed more interested in asking him questions about life in the Anglo-Saxon kingdoms and, having learnt that Eadulf had actually been to Rome, would answer no question until Eadulf had talked about the city and the great churches there. Eadulf, in fact, learnt little and, the wine souring his mouth, he drank more mead than was good for him. Wisely, the young cleric had started with a beaker of ale which he made last throughout the meal and which he only sipped at.

'My father was a warrior of the Dál Fiatach in the kingdom of

Ulaidh until he lost his arm at Magh Ráth,' Brother Dianach finally replied in answer to Eadulf's insistence. In fact, Eadulf's indulgence had caused him to lose any subtlety in his questioning. 'But that was long before I was born. I was sent to Armagh to study with the religious and that was when I learnt to be a scribe.'

'But how did you come here?'

'With Brother Solin,' replied the young man innocently to Eadulf's exasperation.

'This I know, but why were you chosen to accompany Brother Solin?'

'Because I was a good scribe, I suppose,' Brother Dianach replied. 'Also because I was fit. It is a long journey from Armagh to this kingdom.'

'Why send Brother Solin here at all?' Eadulf encouraged.

The young man heaved a sigh at Eadulf's continued repetition of this particular question.

'That is something known only to Brother Solin. I was taken aside by my superior and told to report to Brother Solin with my stylus and writing boards and told to do as he bid me do.'

'Surely you were told more?' Eadulf demanded, the alcohol making him sound aggressive.

'Only that we would be on a long journey and to prepare myself for such. I was told that I would be doing the work of God and Armagh.'

'And Brother Solin explained nothing of the purpose for this journey? Not even some stray comment as you passed along the way?'

Brother Dianach shook his head emphatically.

'But assuredly you were curious?' Eadulf was like a dog worrying a bone.

'Why are you so interested in the business of Brother Solin?' the young man finally was pressed into asking. 'Brother Solin says that curiosity, with ambition, are two scourges of the unquiet soul.'

Eadulf was exasperated but he realised that he had pressed the point too far.

'Surely he who is not curious is an enemy of knowledge? How can you learn anything when you are not curious?' he responded defensively.

Brother Dianach regarded Eadulf's flushed face with distaste. He would say no more about the matter and turned to Mel, the elderly scribe, on his other side, ignoring Eadulf who suddenly felt a little foolish. He was not that imbued with alcohol that he had lost all sensitivity. He cursed himself for having mixed the bad wine with the potent mead.

At the top table Fidelma knew that it was bad manners to inquire further of Laisre or his tanist about matters concerning the forthcoming negotiations. The feasting hall was the place where weapons and matters of politics and business were traditionally left outside. So Fidelma had turned the conversation to the history of the people of Gleann Geis for she liked to learn as much as she could about various parts of the country. But the conversation was somewhat guarded and stilted.

She was, therefore, somewhat thankful when some musicians were admitted to the hall. Laisre had explained that, unlike most chieftains, he refused the presence of musicians during the feast. Only after the meal had been eaten did he allow them to enter and provide entertainment.

'To play music during a meal insults both cook and musician and kills conversation,' he explained.

Now, as more wine and mead were circulating among the guests, a harper entered and came forward, carrying a small hand-held *cruit*, or harp, and sat himself cross-legged on the floor in front of his chieftain on the other side of the table. He struck up an energetic tune, nimble fingers moving with an astonishing and complex motion, striking the difficult modulations in perfect harmony, completing the cadences in a rich yet delicate manner. The tinkling of the higher notes, supporting the deeper tones of the bass strings, was soothing to the ears.

At the end of the piece, Orla leant towards Fidelma: 'You see that even we poor pagans can find enjoyment in our music.'

Fidelma ignored Orla's furtive gibe.

'My mentor, the Brehon Morann of Tara, once said that where there is music there can be no evil.'

'A wise observation,' Laisre agreed. 'Now choose a song, Fidelma, and my musicians shall demonstrate their talent for you.'

The *cruit* player had been joined by another harpist who played a *ceis*, a smaller harp which was square shaped and, as Fidelma knew, was used to accompany the *cruit*. A *timpan* player, with his eight-stringed instrument, played with a bow and a plectrum, also joined the group together with a piper and his *cruisech*.

There were usually three kinds of music which were popular at feasting. The *gen-traige*, which incited the listeners to merriment and laughter and produced lively dance tunes; the *gol-traige* which expressed sorrow and laments, sad songs of the death of heroes;

and the *súan-traige* which was a softer form of music, like songs of unrequited love and lullabies.

Music had always been an essential part of Fidelma's childhood. The palace at Cashel was never wanting in musicians, songsters and ballad makers.

She was thinking about a choice of song when Murgal, who was seated alongside Brother Solin at the adjacent table, lurched to his feet. His face was flushed and Fidelma saw at once that he had indulged freely in the wine.

'I know a song that will be to the taste of an Eóghanacht princess,' he sneered. 'I will sing it:

> 'The fort on the great Rock of Muman,
> Once it was Eoghan's, once it was Conall's,
> It was Nad Froích's, it was Feidelmid's.
> It was Fíngen's, it was Faílbe Fland's.
> Now it is Colgú's;
>
> 'The fort remains after each in his turn –
> And the kings sleep in the ground.'

There was a roar of laughter from the warriors at their table and many banged their knife handles on the wooden boards in appreciation.

There was no doubting what Murgal was saying. The message was that the authority of the kings of Cashel was transitory.

Laisre's face became an angry mask.

'Murgal, the wine is in and your wit is out! Would you insult your chieftain by demeaning him in the eyes of his guests?'

Murgal turned to his chieftain, still smiling a slightly vacuous grin, the wine giving him courage.

'Your Eóghanacht guest desired a song. I merely supplied one which paid tribute to her brother at Cashel.'

He sat down heavily in his seat, still smiling. Fidelma saw Brother Solin smirking at what he imagined was her discomfort. She became aware of a young woman on the other side of Murgal, a slender blonde-haired woman, rather attractive. Her face was without emotion and she was looking at the table before her, clearly discomfited by her drunken companion.

Laisre was turning to apologise to Fidelma but Fidelma rose to her feet. She allowed a soft smile to spread as if she was sharing Murgal's joke.

'Murgal has made a good song,' she announced to the company, 'although I have heard better and certainly in better tune. Perhaps I might bring him the latest composition of the bards of Cashel?'

Then without more ado, she tossed back her hair from her face and began to sing, softly at first but then with growing resonance. Fidelma had the gift of music and the lilting soprano of her voice caused a stillness to fall within the feasting hall.

> 'He is no branch of a withered tree,
> Colgú, prince of the Eóghanacht,
> Son of Faílbe Fland of noble deeds,
> Lofty descendant of Eoghan Mór,
> Sprung from the race of Eber the Fair
> Who ruled Éireann from the banks of the Boyne –
> south to the Wave of Cliodhna.
>
> 'He is of the stock of a true prince,
> A tree sprung from the roots of the forest
> sanctuary of Éireann,
> The just heir of Milesius,
> The sum of a great harvest with fruit of many
> trees,
> Each as ancient as the oldest oak,
> The crown above a multitude of branches.'

She sat down amidst an uncomfortable silence. Then Eadulf, not really understanding the nuances of the exchange, and carried away by his indulgence in alcohol, hearing only that Fidelma had sung as sweet a song as ever he had heard, began to clap loudly. His applause eventually caused Laisre to follow his example and soon a polite tribute rippled around the chamber. When it died away Laisre turned to his musicians and bid them play softly.

In her song, Fidelma had answered Murgal's cynical sneer that the Cashel kings were mortal and their authority was only brief. She had pointed out how the Eóghanacht claimed to be descended from the Eber, son of Milesius, leader of the Milesians, the first Gaels to land in Ireland. From Eber had descended Eoghan Mór, the founder of the royal dynasty of the Eóghanacht. The subtlety of the song reminded her listeners of the status she held.

Laisre glanced at her contritely.

'I apologise for Murgal's lack of etiquette.'

He referred to the fact that it was a rigid rule that a guest was not to be insulted within a feasting hall.

Fidelma spoke without rancour.

'As you rightly observed, Laisre, it was the wine that made him forget though, as Theoginis once said, wine is wont to show the mind of man.'

The sound of someone being smacked across the face was so abrupt that the soft music of the *cruit* player faltered and died away for there was a series of sounds which followed in quick succession. First a chair went over backwards, crockery plates crashed and splintered on the floor and there came an angry but almost suppressed exclamation. All eyes in the feasting hall were drawn to the table where Murgal was standing swaying on his feet once again; this time, however, one hand was nursing a reddening cheek, his eyes were glowering at the fair-haired woman who had been sitting next to him and who now was on her feet as well, standing facing the Druid.

It was the slim woman whom Fidelma had noticed. Her face was now contorted with anger.

'Pig and son of a pig!' she hissed and then turned abruptly and exited from the feasting hall without a backward glance. A plump woman rose from another table and went trotting out with an angry look in Murgal's direction. Fidelma realised it was the hostel keeper, Cruinn.

Murgal seemed to quiver with anger and then he, too, left the feasting hall. A moment later one of the warriors, the fair-haired Rudgal, rose and hurriedly followed Murgal from the room.

Fidelma, watching, turned with a glance of inquiry towards Laisre.

'Some domestic matter, I suppose?' she asked innocently.

'No, Marga is not wife to Murgal,' Orla replied cattily before her brother could speak. 'But Murgal has a wandering eye.'

Esnad, the young daughter of Orla, began to chuckle and then, catching sight of an angry glance from her father, Colla, pouted and made no further sound.

Laisre flushed slightly.

'It is not a matter to be commented on before strangers at a feasting,' he snapped at his sister. Orla grimaced at her brother to express her annoyance before sitting back. Laisre resumed a more considered expression towards Fidelma.

'Suffice to say, wine can make a lout of the best of us,' he observed, trying to make a joke out of the matter.

'Wine is like rain. If it falls on a bog, it makes it the more foul. But on good soil, it wakens it to bloom and radiance,' observed Colla, who had not spoken at the table for some time. It was clear that he had little respect for Murgal.

'This Marga is an attractive woman,' Fidelma observed. 'Who is she?'

'She is our apothecary,' replied Laisre distantly. Fidelma observed a colour on his cheeks. Then, as if he felt he should reply to her comment, added: 'Yes, an attractive woman.'

Fidelma was surprised.

'So young and an apothecary!'

'She is qualified under the law.' It was said defensively by Laisre.

'I would have expected no less.' Fidelma's soft reply had a note of rebuke in it. 'Does she reside in the ráth?'

'Yes. Why do you ask?' Colla asked sharply.

'Oh,' Fidelma decided to turn the subject at the suspicion voiced in Colla's reply, 'it is always wise to know where an apothecary resides.'

One of the musicians had resumed his interrupted long, interminable song, singing in a form without instrumental accompaniment, his voice rising and falling. It was an old, old song, about a young girl who was being lured by unseen forces towards a mountain top where she would eventually meet the fate which the gods had set for her. Fidelma suddenly felt an empathy with the heroine of the song. Something had drawn her to this valley and it seemed there were unseen forces dictating her fate.

Chapter Seven

It was still early when Fidelma decided to leave the feasting hall. There was music being played and the wine and mead continued to circulate. She made her excuses to Laisre, telling him that she was tired after travelling the long journey from Cashel. He made no protest. As she passed through the hall, Fidelma quietly signalled to Eadulf to follow her. He rose unsteadily, and somewhat reluctantly, and did so. He was aware that he had imbibed a little more than was good for him and tried hard to compensate for it by moving slowly and deliberately.

Outside it was surprisingly light. The moon was full, hanging like a bright white orb in the cloudless sky. The sky itself was a glitter of light with numerous stars winking across the canopy. Fidelma was waiting for him by the door. She had not noticed his slow, uncertain gait.

'Let us walk around the walls of the ráth,' she instructed rather than suggested. She led the way up the steps to the battlements where a soft night breeze ruffled her hair. She could see some shadowy figures farther along the wall, young men and women who had absented themselves from the feast to pursue their own amorous interests, and so she stopped, gazing up at the night sky. In the distance they could hear the occasional sound of laughter and the faint sounds of music. From the courtyard below a woman laughed lasciviously and there was a deep chuckle from her male companion. Fidelma shut her mind to the extraneous sounds and inhaled softly as she gazed at the breath-taking magnificence of the spectacle of the night-sky.

'*Caeli enarrant gloriam Dei*,' she whispered.

Eadulf caught the words as he leant against the parapet of the wall by her side. He rubbed his forehead and tried to concentrate. He knew that they were from one of the Psalms.

'The heavens bespeak the glory of God,' he translated approvingly, trying not to slur his words.

'Psalm nineteen,' Fidelma confirmed, continuing to study the sky. Then, after a second or two, she turned abruptly. 'Are you all right, Eadulf? Your speech sounds unusual.'

'I am afraid I have taken a little too much wine, Fidelma.'

She made a clicking sound of disapproval.

'Well, I shall not let you go until you tell me what you have learnt from Brother Solin's scribe, the young Dianach.'

Eadulf pursed his lips in disgust. Then he groaned as his world momentarily swam.

'What is it?' demanded Fidelma anxiously as he raised a hand to his forehead.

'Bad wine and even worse mead.'

'Do not expect sympathy for that,' she admonished. 'Let me hear about Brother Dianach.'

'Only that he is either a most naive young man or a consummate actor. He ventured no explanation of what is behind Solin's visit here. He claimed that Brother Solin does not confide in him.'

Fidelma pushed out her lower lip in an expression of annoyance.

'Do you believe him?'

'As I say, it is hard to tell whether he is guileless or well versed in the craft of deceit.'

'According to Brother Solin, he is merely on a mission from Armagh to ascertain the strength of the Faith in the extremities of the five kingdoms,' mused Fidelma.

'Why can't there be truth in that?'

'Why not send to the ecclesiastic centres of the five kingdoms and ask the abbots and the bishops, who could tell Ultan what he wants to know, whereby the information could be relayed within a week compared to what Brother Solin would find out within a year? There is something illogical in that.'

Eadulf still felt too befuddled from the wine to work out any alternative possibilities and so did not comment further on the matter.

'I hadn't realised that you sung so well.' He suddenly shifted the subject of the conversation.

'It was not the quality of my song but its meaning that was important,' Fidelma replied with grim satisfaction. 'Did you notice the scene with Murgal? I mean the incident with the girl, not the one about the song?'

'I doubt whether anyone in the feasting hall failed to notice it. She was rather attractive.'

'Did you notice the reason for the exchange?'

'As a matter of fact, I think Murgal was attempting to be too friendly with the girl and she became tired of his lewdness.'

This seemed to coincide with Orla's spiteful remark about Murgal.

She stared out across the shadowy moonlit valley. It was an eerie yet beautiful sight.

'So what do you make of this pagan world, Eadulf?' Fidelma asked after a while.

Eadulf reflected for a moment before replying. He tried to make some sense from his befuddled thoughts.

'No more or less than any other world. Here there be people, pagan or no, with the same ill-behaviour, jealousies and pretensions as any spot in Christendom. But the sooner you conclude your business, the sooner we can be removed from it. I prefer the easy gaiety of your brother's palace at Cashel.'

'Have you forgotten something?' Fidelma was slightly amused.

'Forgotten?' Eadulf groaned, thinking more of finding his bed than anything else. 'Forgotten what?'

'Thirty-three young men slaughtered at the gate to this valley.'

'Oh, *that*!' Eadulf shook his head. 'No, I have not forgotten that.'

'*That!*' mimicked Fidelma and then added, with seriousness: 'There may be people here with the same emotions as any place in Christendom but there is also an evil that has struck this place and I shall not rest until I have discovered its meaning.'

'I thought you were going to wait to see what Colla, the tanist, discovers,' Eadulf returned, trying hard to suppress a yawn and not succeeding.

'I do not trust Colla to bring me an accurate observation. Anyway,' she brought her gaze back to the night canopy, 'perhaps we should retire and prepare ourselves for tomorrow. It is no good leaping to conclusions before we have information.'

She turned and led the way back down the wooden stairway. As Eadulf moved forward after her, he found himself stifling another groan as his world began to sway again. He held on to the rail for dear life. Fidelma pretended that she had not heard his moan as he stumbled behind her. All the same, she kept a solicitous eye on her companion to ensure that he reached his bed in the guests' hostel in safety. Once they had arrived back and Eadulf had stumbled into his bed chamber, Fidelma waited a while and then looked cautiously into his room.

Eadulf was sprawled face downward on the bed, still fully clothed, a soft snoring emanating from his prostrate figure. Normally, Fidelma was not a person to approve of anyone who could not hold their liquor but she had never known Eadulf to be indulgent in spirits. She gave him the benefit of the doubt and stayed to take off his sandals and spread a blanket over his recumbent body.

Fidelma rose early as was her custom. She found that she was the first to bathe out of the four guests at the hostel. She completed her toiletry and dressed before going back down to the main room of the hostel where Cruinn, the rotund hostel-keeper, was preparing the first meal of the day. By that time she found, to her utter surprise, Eadulf was up. He was sitting, unshaven and dishevelled, with his head in his hands obviously feeling the affects of the evening's feasting. As she sat down opposite him, he raised his head with a groan and blinked sleepily.

'God's curse on all cocks!' he muttered. 'I had barely fallen asleep when that damned cock began to crow and dragged me from my rest. It sounded like the choir of devils from the infernal regions.'

Fidelma neglected to tell him that he had been dead to the world for most of the night in an alcohol-induced slumber. She frowned in mock admonition.

'I am surprised that you ask God to curse the cock of all birds when it is sacred to the Faith.'

'How so?' demanded Eadulf, still drowsy and rubbing his forehead.

'Don't you recall the story of how, after the Roman soldiers crucified Jesus, they were cooking a cock? One of them reported to his fellows that there was a rumour among the followers of Christ that he would return to life on the third day. A second soldier mocked the idea and made a jest saying that it would no more come to pass than the dead cock would crow. Whereupon the dead bird arose from the cauldron and flapped its wings and cried out "the son of the virgin is safe"!'

Eadulf, in spite of his headache, had to admit that the Irish words '*mac na hóighe slán*' fitted well into the pattern of the sound of a cock crow. Then a dim memory stirred.

'I read a similar story in a Greek Gospel. The *Gospel of Nicodemus*. Except that it was Judas Iscariot's wife who was cooking the cock and tried to reassure the betrayer of Christ. The bird flapped its wings and crowed three times but there was no meaning to the sound.'

Fidelma laughed good naturedly.

'You must allow our bardic traditions to interpret tales so that they have substance for our people.'

Eadulf remembered his headache and groaned again.

'I do not need a cock crowing to affirm me in my Faith. But I do need the cock to be silent when I am trying to seek rest or how can I have a clear mind to follow my Faith?'

'Cock or not, I think the answer to your lack of rest may be found elsewhere. Truly, did you not hear the saying that wine is gold in the evening but lead in the morning?'

Eadulf was about to open his mouth to reply when Brother Dianach, the young scribe, joined them. Silently Eadulf cursed his fresh scrubbed and bright countenance and the ebullient greeting to Fidelma and his look of disapproval at the haggard Eadulf. His shyness seemed to have entirely vanished.

Having exchanged morning greetings, Fidelma asked where his master, Brother Solin of Armagh, was that morning.

'He was not in his chamber,' replied Brother Dianach, 'so I expect that he has already risen and gone out.'

Fidelma glanced to Eadulf but the Saxon monk was too intent on dealing with his own crapulousness.

'Then, indeed, he was abroad very early. Is that his custom?'

The young monk nodded an unconcerned affirmative as he sniffed the aromatic air.

The rotund Cruinn bustled over to them, bringing a tray with fresh baked bread, still fragrant from the oven, with clotted cream, fruit and cold meats, and a jug of mead. Having set down the tray, the corpulent hostel-keeper requested their leave to return to her own house for, she said, she had promised to go picking healing herbs with her daughter. Fidelma took it on herself to dismiss her with thanks, saying that they would be able to manage. As Cruinn left, Eadulf reached out a shaky hand immediately for the jug of mead. He grinned weakly at Fidelma's disapproving stare.

'*Similia similibus curantur*,' he muttered, pouring the mead from the pitcher into the beaker.

'Oh no, Brother.' The young Brother Dianach turned on him in reproof. 'Like things are not cured by like things. You are quite, quite wrong.'

The young man looked so totally serious that Eadulf paused with the beaker midway to his lips. Fidelma grinned mischievously.

'And what would your advice be, Brother Dianach?' she prompted.

The young man turned his gaze to Fidelma and reflected on the matter earnestly.

'*Contraria contrariis curantur* . . . opposites are cured by opposites. That is the principle that is taught at Armagh. Just consider the affect of giving things that produce the same illness to one who already has it. It merely increases the illness. Surely the root of all medicine is to counter the illness by using that which gives the opposite affect not that which enhances the condition?'

'What do you say, Eadulf?' chuckled Fidelma in amusement. 'You have studied medicine in Tuam Brecain.'

In silent answer, Eadulf gulped at the contents of the beaker, shutting his eyes and shivering with a look halfway between agony and ecstasy. He gave a long, drawn out gasp of pleasure.

Brother Dianach gazed at him in astonishment.

'I did not know that the Saxon brother had studied at one of our great schools of medicine,' he remarked sharply. 'You did not say this last night. However, you should know that you should not be taking alcohol to counter your intemperance. It is a shameful thing, Brother.'

Eadulf closed his eyes, groaned and poured a second beaker of the mead and made no reply at all. While Fidelma and Brother Dianach concluded eating their first meal of the day, Eadulf barely touched anything substantial. When the young monk had excused himself to return to his room, Fidelma leant across and touched Eadulf's arm.

'Do not lecture me,' groaned Eadulf before she could say anything. 'Let me die in peace.'

'All the same, the young boy is right, Eadulf,' she said seriously. 'You need your wits about you today. Too much mead will dull them.'

Eadulf forced his eyes open.

'I swear that this is all I shall take. Just enough to get me started through the day. At least the mead has cured my pounding head . . . for the moment.'

'Then let us go for a walk and prepare ourselves for the negotiations. Did you hear, by the way, what Brother Dianach said about Brother Solin?'

Eadulf began to rise. He frowned.

'Only that he had gone out early. Why? Is there something else to be learnt from that?'

'Rather than having gone out early, he did not even come in at any time during the night.'

Eadulf looked at her with interest.

'How do you know?'

'I was up before your infamous cock crowed. Brother Solin's door was open just as it had been when I retired to my room last night. The coverlet of the bed was undisturbed just as it had been last night. The logic is that he never came back to the hostel.'

Eadulf ran a hand reflectively through his hair.

'He was still in the feasting hall when we left, wasn't he? No, wait a moment. Young Brother Dianach had retired early. A pious, sober body is that one. Now, I seem to recall that Brother Solin left not long afterwards. Before we did. In fact, shortly after Murgal made his dramatic exit.'

'So where has he been all night?'

'Are you saying that it may have some bearing on what he is doing here?'

'I do not know. But we must watch out for Brother Solin. I do not like him.'

They were about to leave the hostel when the door opened and the object of their conversation entered. He looked startled at seeing them standing as if waiting for him and then hurriedly composed his features into a bland smile, wishing them a good morning.

'We have not been outside to see if it is good or not,' Fidelma returned innocently. 'Is it so?'

'You should rise early, as I do,' Brother Solin said unperturbed, moving to the table and seating himself. He began to help himself liberally to the food which remained on the tray. There was no doubting that he was in good appetite.

'Have you always been an early riser?' continued Fidelma, her tone guileless. 'I have difficulties, don't you, Eadulf?'

'Oh, indeed, I do,' agreed Eadulf, entering into the spirit of the banter. 'Especially this morning, I was disturbed by that confounded cock crowing. Is that what plucked you from your slumber, Brother Solin?'

'No, I was awake earlier. I have always been an early riser.'

Eadulf exchanged a glance with Fidelma but she shook her head, not wishing Eadulf to accuse Brother Solin openly of telling an untruth.

'I suppose it is good to begin the day with a strenuous walk before breakfast?' she prompted, returning to the table and sliding back into her seat.

'Nothing like it,' agreed Brother Solin complacently, tearing a piece of bread and helping himself to another slice of cheese.

Eadulf started to cough to smother his indignation. One thing he had noticed, and he was sure Fidelma had noticed the same, was that Brother Solin was wearing the same clothes that he had worn on the previous evening during the feast. A man of Brother Solin's standing would always have extra clothing to change into for special occasions.

Fidelma had also noticed that Solin had not changed his clothes since the previous evening and spoke hurriedly in case Eadulf was going to comment on the fact.

'Perhaps you would go to my cell and collect the material I have brought for the meeting with Laisre and his council?' she asked him pointedly.

Eadulf took the hint and went up to the bed chambers, pausing at the top of the stair to listen to the rest of the conversation.

'Are there good places to walk around here, Brother Solin?' he heard Fidelma asking.

'Indifferently good,' replied the cleric.

'Where did you go?'

'Beyond the cluster of houses at the fork of the river, just a quarter of a mile from the gates of the ráth,' came back the reply readily enough.

The answers were given with such assurance that Eadulf knew that Fidelma would not be able to shake Solin from his story that he had simply been walking early. What could the cleric from Armagh be up to? Indeed, were they being unjust in suspecting that he was involved in anything subversive at all?

As if she had read his very thoughts, Eadulf heard Fidelma lower her voice confidentially.

'Since we are alone, Brother Solin, let me ask you, between ourselves, why are you really here?'

There was a pause and then Brother Solin chuckled deeply.

'I have told you before, Sister Fidelma, and yet you do not believe me.'

'I would like to hear the truth.'

'Whose truth? You do not like my truth, so what must I say?'

'Do you take an oath, by the body of Christ, that you are on a mission from Ultan of Armagh merely to assess the strength of the Faith in the five kingdoms? Why? Armagh has no jurisdiction here. This is where the bishop of Imleach rules.'

Brother Solin chuckled wheezily.

'You have studied in Tara, Fidelma of Cashel. I have even heard of you from Ultan. The Brehon Morann of Tara was your mentor. Your advisor in the Faith was Abbot Laisran of Durrow and you were a novice at Kildare. You joined Abbess Étain of Kildare as advisor at the council in Whitby. From there you were asked by Ultan of Armagh to go on a mission to Rome. Only since you have returned have you decided to stay under your brother's protection at Cashel.'

Fidelma was astounded at how much the man knew about her.

'You seem to know much, Brother Solin,' she admitted.

'I am Ultan's secretary, as I have already said. I need to know much.'

'It does not answer my question. Armagh is not accepted as the mother-church of this kingdom.'

'The point that I was making, Sister, is that you have travelled enough to know something of the rights of the Uí Néill kings. And just as the Uí Néill kings assert their rights to the High Kingship and dominion over the five kingdoms, so does Armagh assert its rights to the ecclesiastical kingdom of all Ireland.'

Fidelma was unruffled.

'I know the dissensions between the Uí Néill and the Eóghanacht over the symbolism of the High Kingship,' she affirmed cautiously. 'There are few living in the five kingdoms who do not know that. The Uí Néill have been claiming for many years that the kingship of Tara should have power over all five kingdoms. When the kings of Ireland first met and decreed that they should elect a High King from among them, it was never meant as an autocratic office but one of a "precedence of honour". Each High King was to be elected by and from the ranks of each royal dynasty in turn. It was an honour, a token of respect, not a giving of power. Look in the laws of the five kingdoms and turn to the laws of kingship. Show me a law that even admits there is an office in the five kingdoms greater than that of the provincial king?'

Brother Solin sat back with a derisory grin.

'I expected that an Eóghanacht princess would be able to quote me the law when it favours Cashel.'

'I speak as a *dálaigh*,' returned Fidelma firmly. 'If I spoke as an Eóghanacht princess I would quote the law of the *Uraiccecht Bec* – "greatest over kings is the king of Muman".'

'The Uí Néill do not agree.'

'Naturally.' Fidelma could not keep the sneer out of her voice.

'Yet you have in the past acknowledged Sechnassuch as High King. You have been to Tara and served at his court? You have even acknowledged Ultan as archbishop.'

'I was summoned to Tara to help solve the mystery of the theft of the High King's sword. I recognise the High Kingship out of courtesy for the sacredotal honour as envisaged by the kings. But no Eóghanacht would admit that the king who sits in Tara has supreme authority over these southern dominions. Nor did I, in calling Ultan by the Greek title of *archiepiskopos*, do anything more than attempt to translate our Irish title of Comarb of Patrick. For an archbishop superintends the bishops of his province, just as the Comarb of Ailbe of Imleach does here in Muman.'

Brother Solin shook his head slowly.

'There is a time coming, Fidelma, when the High Kingship will not be just an empty title. The only way to make this land great, not just a land with quibbling provincial kingdoms, is through a strong High King who unites all the kingdoms within his grasp.'

Fidelma's eyes flashed dangerously.

'And that High King would be one of the Uí Néill, of course?'

'Who better to lead than the descendants of Niall of the Nine Hostages? Last night you claimed Eóghanacht descended from Eber, son of Milesius. But do not the Uí Néill have a similar claim from Eremon, who was the elder son of Milesius, who ruled the north? Did not Eremon slay Eber when he tried to usurp that power?'

Fidelma's voice had not raised during this exchange in spite of the agitation of Brother Solin. She still kept it low and even.

'I have met with Sechnassuch, son of Blathmaic, who sits on the throne at Tara. He is a man of principle and would not hunger for power in the way you described. He claims Tara in accordance with the custom of precedence. He obeys the laws of the five kingdoms.'

'Sechnassuch? The whelp of Blathmaic mac Aedo Sláine!' It was a derisory, automatic ejaculation. Then a strange look came across Brother Solin's face. It was as if he had regretted the outburst. His attitude changed abruptly.

'You are right, Fidelma.' His voice was suddenly ingratiating. 'Sometimes I let my dreams for a better system of kingship of this land stand in the way of reality. You are right, of course. Absolutely right. Sechnassuch would not subvert his office.'

Fidelma knew Brother Solin had realised that he had said too much. Yet it was not enough to allow her to glimpse a reason why the cleric was in Gleann Geis.

'You have still not explained why Ultan should send a representative to this lonely outpost of Christendom?' she pressed. 'He could find out the standing of the Faith by a far more simple means.'

Brother Solin shrugged eloquently.

'Perhaps, he had heard of the difficulties that Imleach had in converting this area to the True Faith and asked me to bring a mission here to see what might be accomplished? Perhaps it is a coincidence that I have arrived just when you are negotiating a means whereby Imleach might bring lightness to this black valley.'

'Three false statements,' snapped Fidelma, quoting the triads of Éireann. '"Perhaps", "may be" and "I dare say"!'

Brother Solin chuckled in appreciation at her erudition.

'Well, Sister, if there is anything further that I may advise you on . . . ?'

Eadulf was bending forward to witness the exchange when he heard a hollow cough behind him.

'Are you unwell, Brother?'

Eadulf straightened up with a red face and found the young Brother Dianach regarding him curiously. He had entirely forgotten that Dianach had gone to his bedchamber.

'I felt a little dizzy,' he muttered, trying to think of some excuse for his position. 'Putting your head between your knees is good for the condition.'

'So that is what you were attempting?' Eadulf could not tell whether Brother Dianach was being sarcastic or not. 'A dangerous thing to do on the stairs. Still, I trust you will be better but I fear you have the wrong philosophy towards maintaining a healthy body. Excuse me, Brother Eadulf.'

The young man passed down the stair before Eadulf could think of a suitable reply. He felt annoyed with himself. Brother Dianach was surely suspicious now as to why Eadulf was crouching at the head of the stairs. It must have been obvious that Eadulf was listening to the conversation below.

Brother Solin looked up as his scribe came down into the room and smiled briefly.

'Good morning, Brother Dianach. Do you have your stylus and clay tablets ready?'

'I do,' the young man replied.

Brother Solin returned his gaze to Fidelma.

'I do not think we need say more on this subject now that we are clear about it?' he asked, a slight emphasis in his voice.

Fidelma returned his gaze evenly.

'I agree,' she said. 'For the time being.'

Brother Solin stood up and wiped the residue of food from the corners of his mouth.

'Come with me, Brother Dianach,' he instructed, moving to the door. 'We must prepare ourselves for this morning's council.' He cast a glance at Fidelma which she could not interpret.

As soon as the door had closed behind them Eadulf came stumbling down the stairs.

'Dianach caught me listening at the top of the stairs . . .' he began.

'Did you hear what passed between us then?' interrupted Fidelma sharply.

'I did. I thought . . .'

'Brother Solin is obviously concealing something,' Fidelma interrupted. 'Ultan of Armagh would have no concern about this backwater. There is something else going on here. But what? I am most frustrated. What is Solin really up to?'

'There is a philosophy that if you have to lie then you should incorporate as much of the truth in the lie as permissible,' Eadulf volunteered.

Fidelma stared at Eadulf for a moment and then smiled broadly.

'Sometimes you remind me of the obvious, Eadulf,' she said. She paused reflectively. 'He was certainly lying about where he has been during the night. Yet when I asked him where he had walked this morning, he was able to describe exactly where without hesitation. Perhaps that was where he actually was? I think, after this morning's negotiation is over, we might restore ourselves by going for a walk in that direction and seeing what we can discover.'

She glanced through the window. The hour was growing late.

'We do not have long before the council is in session. I think we should have a brief walk now, if only to clear our heads.'

Brother Eadulf looked pained.

'I fear it will take more than a walk to clear my head, Fidelma. That bad wine even now permeates my body from head to toe. I feel I need more than fresh air to sustain myself for the morning.'

As ailing as he felt, Eadulf, nevertheless, allowed Fidelma to cajole him into accompanying her. He would have rather flopped back on his bed and gone to sleep again. He felt nauseous and faint. His skin was sweaty and irritating and his mouth was dry.

Outside in the ráth, several people were abroad and hurrying about their day's tasks in spite of the fact that the feast had not ended until dawn for many of them. Eadulf and Fidelma were greeted without any sign of animosity and, indeed, a few were most friendly. All, however, seemed curious as they examined Fidelma. Her reply to Murgal's song seemed to be a topic of gossip.

As they were crossing the courtyard of the ráth towards the gates, Fidelma halted and indicated a cart being dragged through the gates by a small, sturdy ass. It appeared loaded with plants of many sorts. Urging on the ass to greater exertion as it struggled to pull its load was a tall, slender woman.

Fidelma nudged Eadulf.

'Isn't that Murgal's erstwhile companion at last night's feast?' she whispered. Eadulf raised his bleary eyes and recognised the woman immediately, in spite of the cloak and hood wrapped around her. She wore a dress which was more drab than the one she had worn on the previous evening.

Fidelma moved immediately towards her and Eadulf followed.

'Marga, is it not?'

The woman swung round to face her. Fidelma found herself looking into pale blue eyes, so pale that they reminded her of ice. There seemed no expression in the pallid features on which she looked. The long tresses were the colour of harvest corn. Fidelma had been right in her assessment on the previous evening. The woman was attractive. She did not alter that appraisal. Marga was tall and in spite of the long flowing black cloak, which seemed to enhance her pallidness and fair hair, Fidelma knew that her body was supple and well shaped, from the previous evening, and she appeared to move with a lithe, cat-like agility.

Her voice, when she spoke, was no more than a sibilant whisper.

'I do not know you, Fidelma of Cashel. How come you make so free with my name?'

'Your name was told me just as someone has told you my name and so I greet you. Am I incorrect that you are Marga the apothecary?'

'I am Marga and I heal in the name of Airmid, the goddess who guards Dian Cécht's secret Well of Healing.'

Her statement was issued as a challenge but Fidelma did not rise to it.

Airmid was one of the old goddesses. Fidelma knew the story well. She was daughter of the god of medicine, Dian Cécht, and sister of Miach, who was also a physician-god. When Miach proved to be a better physician than his father, the angry god slew his son. Out of his grave there grew three hundred and sixty-five herbs of healing. Airmid was said to have gathered the herbs from her brother's grave and laid them out on her cloak in order of their various healing properties. Dian Cécht, still jealous of Miach, overturned the cloak in a rage and hopelessly confused the herbs so that no human would ever learn the secret of immortality by their use.

'May health be your portion, Marga the Healer,' replied Fidelma gravely. 'I hope that you have learnt some of the secrets that your god, Dian Cécht, would have kept from us.'

Marga's eyes narrowed fractionally.

'Do you challenge my knowledge, Fidelma of Cashel?' she whispered threateningly.

'Why would I do that?' Fidelma asked innocently, realising that the girl was of a tempestuous nature. 'My knowledge of the ancient tales is a poor one. But everyone knows what Dian Cécht did in anger in order to prevent the knowledge of healing being fully learnt by mortals. I thought . . .'

'I know what you thought,' snapped Marga, bending to the ass's harness. 'By your leave, I have much to attend to.'

'As do we all, each in his or her own way. But there are some questions I would like to put to you.'

Marga bridled immediately.

'But I do not wish to answer them. Now . . .'

She made to move but Fidelma, smilingly, put out a hand to stay her. Fidelma had a powerful grip and Marga actually winced.

'I have no other time to put them.' Fidelma examined the cart closely. 'You appear to have been gathering herbs and plants for remedies?'

Marga was unbending.

'As you can plainly see,' she replied stiffly.

'And you practise your apothecary within the ráth?'

'I do.'

Her eyes flickered momentarily to a corner of some buildings across the courtyard, focussing on a tall building of three storeys with a curious squat tower at one end. Fidelma followed the involuntary movement and saw a mart at one corner. Outside the door, bundles of dried herbs were hanging.

'So that is your apothecary shop?'

Marga shrugged almost insolently but Fidelma did not appear to mind.

'I cannot see the purpose of these questions,' the pale-faced herbalist said impatiently.

'Forgive me,' replied Fidelma contritely. 'It is my friend here . . .'

Eadulf was momentarily startled and then tried to compose his features.

The pale blue eyes flickered over him without changing expression.

'You see,' Fidelma went on confidentially, 'my friend imbibed too much of the juice of the vine last night.'

'Gaulish wine!' sniffed Marga. 'It rots in the transport unless it is good. But Laisre is unable to afford better except for himself and his family. Well, there were plenty of others who took more of it than was good for them.'

'You mean Murgal?' Fidelma asked quickly.

There was a pause.

'You have sharp eyes, Christian. Yes, I mean Murgal. But that is none of your business . . .'

'Of course not,' smiled Fidelma. 'But my friend here is in need of a herbal remedy for his distemper. He thought that he might be able to purchase something from you.'

Eadulf was surprised at the lie for he knew as much about herbal remedies as most, having studied the subject. Marga eyed him sourly. Eadulf flushed before her withering gaze.

'I suppose you have a headache and feel uncomfortable in the stomach?'

Eadulf nodded, not trusting himself to speak.

The apothecary turned and rummaged in her cart. She drew forth some root leaves eight inches in length, tapering below into a winged stalk, with veins on it. Eadulf recognised them at once. The thimble shape of the foxglove was a common enough plant in the hedges, ditches and wooded slopes.

'Use the leaves only, boiled in water. You drink the infusion. It will taste bitter but you will eventually feel its advantageous effects. Do you understand, Saxon?'

'I do,' responded Eadulf quietly.

He took the leaves from her and reached into his purse.

'A *screpall* is the smallest coin I have,' he muttered, handing it to her, but Marga shook her head.

'We have no use for coins in our valley, Saxon. We rely mainly on barter even if we deal with the outside world. Keep your coin and take the leaves as the charity of a pagan to a Christian.'

Eadulf began to thank her gravely but Fidelma interrupted with a smile.

'I suppose a number of people have been struck with the effect of bad wine?'

'Not many. Those who drink wine in preference to mead have developed the capacity to accept its potency.'

'Were there any affected last night, though?'

Marga shrugged.

'A few. Most of the pigs prefer to lay about and sleep it off.'

'Does Murgal usually consume so much?'

Marga's eyes narrowed in temper and then she seemed to change her mind and relax.

'Well, he has not sought my aid nor would I have given it to him. I'll applaud you for this, Fidelma of Cashel: last night you answered the pig well.'

'You do not like him?'

'Hadn't you noticed?' Marga jeered.

'I had.'

'Murgal thinks that he can take what he wants in life. He dared lay his sweaty paws on me. Now he has reason to know that he should not take such liberties.'

'I see,' Fidelma said gravely.

Marga glared at her in suspicion.

'Is that what you wanted to know?' she demanded with some petulance.

'Not all,' Fidelma smiled. 'Eadulf here truly did want something to purge him of his feelings of discomfiture.'

Marga examined them suspiciously for a moment before going to the ass's head and beginning to lead it away across the courtyard. Then she halted abruptly and turned back to Eadulf.

'Have a care with that infusion of those leaves, Saxon,' she called. 'Unless taken correctly the plant has a poisonous property. The correct dosage varies in each person. For you, I would say no more than a sip or two.'

Then she turned again, dragging the ass after her in the direction of her apothecary.

Eadulf let out a sigh of relief and wiped his brow.

'I am glad she finally said as much,' he observed quietly, staring in disgust at the leaves.

'Why so?' Fidelma queried with interest.

'Because, knowing herbs as I do, I thought she was doing her best to poison me. Had she not warned me, and had I known nothing about these leaves, I might be dead soon after drinking the brew. A sip is one thing but drinking the entire concoction is something else.'

Fidelma turned her head and glanced after the disappearing figure of the apothecary with interest.

'Maybe she didn't like you at first, Eadulf,' she smiled thinly.

'As a stranger, as a Christian or as a man?' mused the Saxon.

Fidelma chuckled.

'Well, at least she now likes you well enough to advise against your premature death.'

Chapter Eight

A horn blast shattered the air.

'That is the signal for the start of the council,' Fidelma advised Eadulf. 'Put those leaves away and let us make our attendance.'

Eadulf groaned loudly.

'I do not think I can last out such a meeting,' he protested. 'I swear I feel like death.'

'You may die after the council,' she replied cheerfully. Unwillingly, Eadulf followed her towards the chieftain's building in the ráth.

Several people were moving towards it but they stood aside to allow Fidelma and Eadulf to enter first. In the antechamber, the tall, fair-haired warrior, Rudgal, was waiting for them. As they entered, he moved towards them and saluted Fidelma solemnly.

'Please accompany me, Sister.' Then, after a moment, he added: 'You, also, Brother.'

He led them through the door into the council chamber where Laisre was already seated on his chair of office. The signs of the feasting of the previous night had been cleared away and a semi-circle of chairs had been arranged before Laisre. To the chieftain's right was an empty seat where the tanist should have sat. Clearly Colla had already departed on his errand of investigation. Behind Colla's empty chair was seated Orla but there was no sign of her daughter, Esnad.

To the left was a seat with Murgal sprawled on it. He looked as bad as Eadulf felt with red-rimmed eyes and pale face. There was still an angry red mark on his cheek. Behind him was a small table at which the elderly scribe, Mel, with whom Eadulf had spoken the previous evening, sat ready with his stylus and clay writing tablets.

Fidelma was shown to a chair in the centre of the semi-circle. A chair had also been placed for Eadulf, just to one side of Fidelma's seat. Behind, Brother Solin and Brother Dianach were seated. The other chairs were filled with the lesser dignitaries of Gleann Geis while behind them, pressing around, some of the people of the valley were crowded to hear what their chieftain would negotiate with the representative of the distant king of Cashel. The hubbub was loud and it was not until the horn blasted again that the noise eventually died away.

Murgal rose slowly to his feet.

'The council is now in session and, as Druid and Brehon to my chieftain, it is my right to speak first.'

Eadulf started in surprise at the man's discourtesy when he declared that he should speak before his chieftain. Fidelma, seeing Eadulf's concern, leant towards him and whispered: 'It is his right under the law, Eadulf. A Druid may speak before a king.'

Murgal apparently did not notice this exchange for he moved to the side of Laisre's chair of office.

'You will know that I am opposed to this negotiation. Let my objection be recorded.'

He glanced to Laisre who nodded and added for the benefit of Mel, the scribe: 'So it is said, so let it be written.' He turned back to Murgal and indicated that he should continue.

'Laisre's ancestors ruled us well. They kept us from outside harm over the years, refusing to have anything to do with those who looked enviously at our pleasant valley. It is a rich fertile valley. Uncorrupted. Why? Because we have forbidden this valley to those who would bring changes from outside. Three years have passed since we accepted Laisre as our chieftain, for his *derbfhine* elected him in due manner to be the head of his household and made him lord over us.

'But now my chieftain has seen fit to send to Cashel and ask for an embassy for the purpose of discussing the establishment of an alien religion in our land.'

In spite of his feeling of indisposition, Eadulf felt he could not let the matter pass without protest.

'A religion that all the kings of Éireann have accepted and which has been freely practised for over two centuries in the five kingdoms.' He was sarcastic, unable to keep his annoyance under control. 'Foreign religion, indeed!'

There was a gasp of horror from the assembly and even Fidelma looked uncomfortable. Murgal had turned in annoyance to Laisre. He was about to open his mouth but the chieftain stayed him with an upraised hand. Laisre leaned forward in his chair and addressed himself to Eadulf directly.

'I shall overlook your outburst this time, Saxon, because you are a stranger in this land and do not know its ways sufficiently to curb your tongue. You do not have the right to speak at this council. It is only that you travel as a companion with Fidelma of Cashel that you are even allowed to sit in this chamber. Even if you had the right to speak you may not interrupt the opening addresses. Only when the opening arguments have been placed will the accredited delegates debate their worthiness.'

Eadulf flushed with mortification and sank down into his chair. Fidelma was glaring at him in disapproval.

Murgal smiled triumphantly and continued.

'We have seen what this alien religion brings. Strangers from over the water who do not know our ways or customs and who would dictate to us. Strangers who insult our procedures so that they have to be rebuked.'

Eadulf ground his teeth at the way Murgal had seized on his lack of knowledge about protocol to strengthen his argument.

'Our brethren outside of the protection of these mountains may well have succumbed to the foreign teachings. It does not make it right nor is it an argument that we must also accept this religion. I say it must be rejected and our mountain barriers used to exclude its pernicious teachings. That is my position as Druid, Brehon and advisor to the chieftain of Gleann Geis.'

Murgal sat down amidst the many mutterings of approval from the people in the chamber.

Laisre nodded to the horn player who let out another blast to silence the chamber.

'Murgal has a right to speak before all others. It is my right to speak next. I am, like Murgal, an adherent of the true deities of our people, the gods and goddesses whom our forefathers worshipped and who have protected us since time began. But my duty as chieftain is to extend the hand of protection to all the people of this clan. Before I sent to the bishop of Imleach to suggest that we could negotiate a settlement for those of this clan who have adopted the ways of the new Faith, I pondered the matter carefully. I decided that he could send someone to discuss how best we could reach such an agreement. Imleach has long wanted to build a Christian church and a school in our valley.

'But I am a pragmatist. Because many of our people have married outside of this valley, we have to accept some of us now believe in this new Faith. Some have tried to hide that fact because they think it will displease me. In truth, it does make me unhappy. I will not deny it. Suppress the new Faith was one argument that I was counselled. But the people of Gleann Geis are my children.'

Murgal looked defiantly at him but he kept silent. Laisre paused a moment to reflect and then continued.

'That would have been a short-sighted policy, for what one prohibits becomes something that is eagerly sought after. So rather than give sustenance to those who would worship the new Faith, I now say give it freedom and let it wither naturally.'

Another outburst of low muttering followed Laisre's speech.

Fidelma, looking slightly puzzled, stood up.

'I am here not to argue for the new Faith or against the old Faith. I am here as an envoy of Cashel to negotiate with you on matters which I had been informed your mind was already agreed upon.'

To Eadulf's surprise, she sat down. The brevity of her statement even surprised Laisre who looked disconcerted.

'Surely you would want to make some argument for your Faith?' he faltered.

Even Murgal was looking nonplussed.

'Perhaps she has no arguments?' he sneered.

Eadulf leaned forward.

'You can't let these pagans denigrate the Faith,' he whispered. He used the Irish term *pagánach*.

Murgal had good hearing.

'Did I hear the Christian Saxon call us pagans?' he cried out in a loud voice.

Eadulf was about to reply when he remembered the proscription against speaking. He said nothing.

'Let him confirm that he called us pagan, lord,' urged Murgal.

'Your hearing is as good as anyone's,' Laisre replied. 'It is the term that those of the new Faith often call us.'

'I know it,' affirmed Murgal. 'And the very word *pagánach* is not even a word in the language of the children of Éireann. What better proof of their alien philosophy is this use of that word?'

'We do not seek to argue that *pagánach* is a word now adopted into our language,' intervened Brother Solin wheezily. 'It is from the Latin *paganus*.'

Murgal was smiling broadly.

'Exactly! Even in Latin it describes correctly what I am – a person of the country, *pagus* – as opposed to the *milites* or the soldiers who march through the country devastating it. You Christians are proud to call yourselves *milites*, enrolled soldiers of Christ, and look down on the civilians or *paganus* who you would trample on. I am proud to be called *pagan*! It is an honourable estate.'

Fidelma had known that Murgal was a clever man but she was

surprised that he had such a knowledge of Latin. She rose to her feet once more.

'I repeat, I am not here to discuss theology. I am here only to discuss how best we might agree a practical matter.'

Orla rose abruptly from behind Colla's empty chair. She was clearly enjoying the argument.

'If my husband were here, he would challenge this representative of Cashel. But I have a right to speak at this council not only in my husband's stead but as the sister of the chieftain.'

'Let Orla speak!' came a cry which gathered momentum from the seated dignitaries and those standing behind them.

Laisre motioned his sister, Orla, forward.

'There is no secret that I and Colla, my husband, have disagreed with Laisre, my brother. He has refused Imleach's attempt to bring Christianity to this valley for years and now he has invited members of the Faith to bring their alien teachings here. My brother, Laisre, is foolish if he thinks that allowing this new Faith to be practised here would see a swift destruction of it. Look at the position of this Faith throughout the five kingdoms. Two centuries ago Laoghaire of Tara took such a view that there was always room for another religion in the land and that suppressing it would merely make it breed faster. He allowed the followers of the Briton, Patrick, to have freedom to worship their God. Two centuries later there are only a few tiny outposts in the five kingdoms where we still follow the gods of our ancestors. The new religion dominates everywhere. Give it breathing space and it will choke the rest of us.'

There was a banging of feet and applause as Orla resumed her seat.

To Fidelma's irritation, Brother Solin had risen to his feet.

'Since Fidelma of Cashel will not debate with you, I, as representative of the Comarb of Patrick, who sits in Armagh, feel that I should take up the challenge she discards so lightly. I ask your indulgence to address this council.'

Fidelma's face had taken on a stony look and she was staring straight ahead. Her mind was working rapidly. This was not the negotiation that she had been expecting. No one had given her any indication that this was to be a debate on theology in which her task was to seek proselytes. She felt that she was being manoeuvred into a debate as a distraction. But why?

Laisre asked Brother Solin to stand forward and invited him to speak.

Brother Solin shot a glance of triumph at Fidelma.

'What is it that you fear about the religion of Christ?' he demanded looking at Murgal.

'Simply, that it destroys the old.'

'And is that a bad thing?'

Murgal smiled threateningly.

'We worship the ancient gods and goddesses who are the Ever Lasting Ones. Your Christ was executed and died. Was he therefore a powerful warrior? Did he have thousands defending him? No, he was a lowly carpenter who, irony of ironies, died on a tree!'

Murgal looked around him with a self-satisfied grin and added: 'You see, I have studied some of this religion of Christ.'

Brother Solin had reddened at the gibe.

'It was so ordained that the Christ, who was the Son of God, should die to bring peace to the world. God so loves this world, we are told, that he gave his only son to die for it.'

'Such a god,' sneered Murgal. 'He had to kill his own son to show love! Was he jealous of his son? Your God's son is as poor as his father!'

Brother Solin began to choke angrily.

'How dare you . . . ?'

'Loss of temper is no argument.' Clearly, Murgal was enjoying himself. 'Tell us what your God taught? We would like to hear. Was he a strong god? Did he teach resistance to those who would enslave people? Did he teach self-reliance or the practice of what is good and just? Did he teach resistance to those who do wrong? No, for I have heard it with my own ears. He taught poverty of spirit. It is written in your sacred texts – "Blessed are the poor in spirit for theirs is the kingdom of heaven". Your God's heaven is not the Otherworld where justice, morality and manly self-reliance are rewarded in the hall of the heroes who sit with the Ever Living Ones.

'Indeed, your God taught that if someone struck a man on one cheek, that person should offer the other cheek to be struck, thus courting further injury and oppression and inviting wrong doing. Surely the Brehons teach that those who court oppression share the crime? When men are poor in spirit then the proud and haughty in spirit oppress them. When men are true in spirit and determined to prevent wrong then the people benefit. Do you not agree with that, Brother Solin?'

Brother Solin was furious. His anger made him look pitiful and inarticulate in front of the assembly. Fidelma had already assessed that it needed a finer intellect than Brother Solin to do battle with glib-tongued Murgal. She shook her head slightly and whispered across to Eadulf: 'The triads of Éireann say three laughing stocks of the world – a jealous man, a parsimonious man and an angry man. Brother Solin has walked directly into the trap that Murgal has prepared.'

Brother Solin was continuing on, unaware of the impression he was giving.

'The Christ said – "Blessed are you that weep now, for you shall laugh. Blessed are you that mourn, for you shall be comforted and Blessed be you poor for yours is the kingdom of heaven."'

'Nice promises but only to be fulfilled in the Otherworld,' sneered Murgal. 'But it is poor teaching for this world. Poverty of person leads on from poverty of spirit. This religion was obviously conceived by a tyrant who wanted to see the poor continue in their poverty while he grew rich and fat on their misery.'

'Not so, not so . . .' cried Brother Solin losing all attempt at composure.

Fidelma stood up abruptly.

She said not a word but the very fact of her rising and her silence caused every voice to fade so that silence gradually permeated the room. She waited until it was so encompassing that even the smallest whisper could be heard.

'I was misinformed,' she began softly. 'I was told that this was to be a negotiation on practical matters. Not a theological debate. Should you have required representatives to discuss theology then you should have told the bishop of Imleach who would have sent you scholars who would match your scholars. I am but a simple servant of the law of this land. I shall commence my journey home to Cashel this afternoon and I shall take back the message that the chieftain of Gleann Geis has been unable to make a decision on this matter. Cashel will not send anyone to Gleann Geis again until it is assured that a decision has been made.'

As she turned, Eadulf rose unsteadily, groaning inwardly at the very idea of commencing such a journey in his condition.

'An admission of defeat?' cried Murgal. 'Do you admit that Christians cannot argue logic with a Druid?'

Fidelma halted and looked in his direction.

'You are acquainted, I suppose, with the triads of Éireann?'

'A poor Brehon I would be if I was not,' replied Murgal complacently.

'Three candles that illuminate every darkness: truth, nature and knowledge,' she quoted and then turned away towards the door.

This time she did not even stop when she heard Laisre's voice call out to her to do so.

The warrior, Rudgal, looking uncomfortable, barred the doorway as she reached it, resting his hand lightly on his sword hilt. He looked apologetic.

'My chieftain calls on you to stay, Sister,' he muttered. 'He has to be obeyed.'

He was taken aback by the green fire that danced in Fidelma's eyes.

'I am Fidelma of Cashel, princess of the Eóghanacht. I stay for no one!'

How she did it not even Eadulf knew but her sheer presence caused Rudgal to fall back a pace and she had swept through the door and out into the courtyard. She did not pause to see if Eadulf was following but walked quickly across the courtyard of the ráth to the guests' hostel. Inside she made straight for a pitcher of water and poured herself a drink.

Eadulf hastened in after her and closed the door. He looked at her nervously but found that her face was creased with laughter. He shook his head in bewilderment.

'I do not understand.'

Fidelma was good humoured.

'Whether this was Laisre's design or not, this council was a charade. It was set up either to waste time or to distract us from the business we were sent here to conduct. What I have to decide is why and who is responsible. And, further, was that idiot Brother Solin part of this deception?'

'I still do not understand.'

'Instead of getting down to the business we were meant to arrange, Murgal deliberately tried to lead us into the time-wasting morass of arguing our differing philosophies. If I had accepted that as the starting point, we would have been arguing here for weeks. Why? What purpose would that serve? The only thing to do was to take the stand I did and to call their bluff.'

'Will their bluff be called?' demanded Eadulf.

There came the sound of voices growing nearer.

Eadulf glanced out of the window.

'It is Brother Solin and his scribe. He does not look in a good mood.'

A moment later Brother Solin burst into the room; his face was still red with mortification.

'Little you did to support me in spreading the Faith,' he snapped at Fidelma without preamble. 'All you have done is insult our hosts and deny any means whereby we might arrange to bring the Faith to this valley.'

'It is not my task to support you in theological debate,' Fidelma returned, causing Solin to blink at her sharpness. If he had expected her to acquiesce to his dominance, he had quickly learnt. She turned to Eadulf. 'Go and saddle our horses and I shall be along directly. I'll pack and bring our bags.'

Reluctantly, Eadulf departed on his mission.

Brother Solin looked aghast.

'You mean to go through with it? You cannot leave here now!'

She regarded him coldly.

'Who will stop me? And what business is it to you?'

'You mean to leave here, having insulted the chieftain and his council in such a manner?'

'The chieftain and his council have insulted me by not discussing the business that had been arranged.'

Brother Solin spread his hands in helpless agitation.

'But surely there must be give and take to everything? These people want assurances about the Faith and it is our moral duty to give them those assurances. To each, something of the Faith and . . .'

'Poor Brother Solin,' Fidelma said with a harshness in her voice that belied her solicitude. 'You do not see, or do not wish to, that you were being manipulated into an unending debate, wasting time in arguing small points of theology. I am unsure if you be knave or fool. Why do you wish to waste time which might elsewhere be spent profitably? Did you really think that this was the opportune moment to attempt to convert Murgal and his followers to the Faith? You should have remembered the wise saying *fere libenter homines quod volunt credunt* – men usually believe what they want to believe.'

'I do not know what you mean,' Brother Solin said defensively.

She examined his features carefully.

'Perhaps, perhaps not. I would not like to think that you knowingly played a part in this distraction.'

She turned and ran up the stairs and picked up her saddle bags and then gathered Eadulf's from his room. Then she returned to the main room.

'Perhaps our paths may cross again, Brother Solin, but I shall not wish that day will come speedily,' she said icily and, before he could reply, she had left the hostel and crossed towards the stables.

Eadulf was waiting with their mounts. He looked pale and was clearly not in the best of health. Fidelma felt sorry for him but all depended on what she did now.

'What do we do?' he muttered. 'We are being watched by a group at the council chamber door.'

'Then we shall depart exactly as we said.'

Fidelma swung up on her horse. Eadulf followed her example and Fidelma led the way to the gates of the ráth. The warriors standing there watched them, nervously glancing towards the door of the council chamber, unsure of what they should do. They finally moved aside and let Fidelma and Eadulf through.

Outside Eadulf groaned.

'I will not be able to ride far without a rest, Fidelma. I am still ill with the bad wine.'

'You will not have to,' she assured him.

'I wish you would tell me what exactly you have in mind,' he grumbled.

'Exactly? That I cannot. For I might have to change my plan as minute passes minute.'

Eadulf stifled another groan. He would do anything for an hour on a bed. Even half an hour.

'Then you do have a plan?' he asked hopefully.

'Of course. Shall I wager a *screpall* to a *sicuil* with you? You see the cluster of houses by the river fork?'

Eadulf glanced ahead and answered in the affirmative.

'That is the very place where Brother Solin said he walked early this morning,' Fidelma went on. 'Well, my wager is that by the time we get there we shall be overtaken by a rider from the ráth who will beg us, in the name of Laisre, to return and crave our forgiveness for the events of this forenoon.'

'Knowing you, Fidelma,' sniffed Eadulf, with resignation, 'I am not likely to take your wager. But at times I wish we could follow some easier path.'

It was Laisre himself who caught up with them just before they reached the wooden bridge which crossed the river to the group of buildings forming the closest settlement to the ráth. The chieftain of Gleann Geis looked suitably chastened.

'Fidelma of Cashel, I apologise. It was my fault for letting the council get out of hand.'

They had stopped their horses before the bridge and sat astride them facing one another.

Fidelma did not reply.

'You were right, Fidelma,' pressed Laisre. 'You did not come hither to engage in a discourse about philosophy but to discuss some practical arrangements. It was Murgal who allowed his hostility to sweep him away into such . . .'

Fidelma held up a hand.

'Are you saying that you wish the council to reconvene to discuss the practical matter?'

'Of course,' Laisre agreed at once.

'Your Druid and council do not seem to be in accord with you on this matter of allowing a Christian church to be built in this valley.'

'Come back and you shall see.' Laisre was almost pleading.

'If I return . . .' Fidelma paused significantly. 'If I return, there would have to be conditions governing this matter.'

Laisre's expression changed to one of suspicion.

'What conditions?' he demanded.

'Your council will have to meet and make a decision before I enter into any discourse with you; decide, that is, whether you want this church and school or not. If the answer is negative, as it seems to be at this time, then I shall return to Cashel without further waste of my time. If the answer is affirmative, then we can deal with the practical matters. But that negotiation will now be between you and I and no other member of your council. I do not want to provide a theatre for Murgal to display his abilities as play-actor.'

Laisre raised his eyebrows.

'Is that how you see Murgal?' he demanded in surprise.

'Can it be that you do not?' she retorted.

Laisre looked pained for a moment and then, abruptly, he started to laugh heartily. Finally he shook his head.

'There is something in what you say, Fidelma. I admit it. But do not underestimate his serious intent.'

'No,' replied Fidelma quietly. 'That I do not.'

'Then you will agree to return? I cannot guarantee that Murgal will apologise to you.'

'I do not ask that he does. All I ask is that whatever discussion your council wants to hold on this matter, it does so before I start to discuss practical arrangements with you.'

'You have my word.' Laisre thrust out a hand. 'My hand on it, Fidelma of Cashel.'

Fidelma glanced closely at him but did not take it.

'Before we conclude, and as we speak in honesty, Laisre, what is Brother Solin of Armagh doing here?'

Laisre looked startled.

'I thought he was here at your behest? He came bearing gifts from Armagh.'

'My behest?' Fidelma controlled herself. 'Is that what he has told you?'

'No, but he is of your Faith. I suppose that I presumed . . .' He shrugged. 'Then all I know is that he is a traveller who sought our hospitality. We do not deny him that on grounds that he is of a different faith.'

It was only then that she accepted Laisre's hand.

'I accept your word, Laisre. Eadulf and I will return, shortly.'

Laisre appeared puzzled.

'You will not ride back with me now?'

'We want to look around your pleasant valley a while. We shall return soon.'

Laisre hesitated and then shrugged.

'Very well. Thank you for agreeing.' He nudged his horse and went back in the direction of the ráth at a canter.

Eadulf looked wistfully after him.

'I could have gone back to sleep for a while,' he moaned. 'I do not see the purpose in these games, Fidelma.'

'It is called diplomacy, Eadulf,' grinned his companion. 'The problem is that I do not know who is representing whom. Now let us see if this group of houses will reveal the information I want to know.'

They rode across the bridge into a tiny square surrounded by half-a-dozen homesteads. The largest was a sizable farmhouse. The others appeared to be no more than cabins which could belong either to people with small fields to work or the workers on the larger farm.

A large, red-faced woman was standing leaning against the door of the big farmstead watching their approach with unconcealed curiosity. Fidelma had noticed her immediately they had paused by the bridge to talk with Laisre. The woman looked a typical farmer's wife, she was thick-set with muscular arms, ready to do a day's work in the fields. She had been studying them carefully and with a degree of hostility on her features.

'Health on you, good woman,' greeted Fidelma.

'My man is at the council,' snapped the woman in an unfriendly tone. 'He is Ronan and he is lord of this place.'

'I am come from the council myself.'

'I know who you are.'

'Good.' Fidelma swung herself down from her horse. 'Then I do not have to explain.'

The woman scowled discouragingly.

'I told you that my man was away.'

'It was not your man that I came to see. You say you know who I am. Good. What is your name?'

The woman looked suspicious.

'Bairsech. Why do you want to know? What is it you want?'

'To talk, that is all, Bairsech. Do you have many people living in this settlement?'

'Twice twenty,' the woman replied indifferently.

'Did you have a visitor last night?'

'A visitor? We had several. My man was at the feasting, as was his right, and three cousins stayed with us, having come down the valley to attend. It is a long journey back at night, especially when one has drink taken.'

Fidelma smiled, trying to put the still hostile woman at ease.

'You are wise, Bairsech. But were there any other visitors, other than your cousins, that stayed here? I mean,' she decided to be explicit, 'a thick-set man who is currently a guest at the ráth.'

The woman's eyes narrowed.

'Thick-set? A man with his head cut in that ridiculous manner which your companion wears?'

Eadulf flushed in irritation at the reference to his tonsure but kept silent.

'The same.'

'A man in fine clothes? Oh yes, he was here. I saw him leaving this morning when I was up to milk the cows, leaving my man still snoring abed. Yes. He was here.'

'Does he know your man, then – know Ronan?'

'I said he was here in the settlement. He was not staying with our household.'

She jerked her head towards a small building set apart from the others with its own stable and an adjacent field in which half-a-dozen cattle were grazing peacefully.

'That is where he stayed.'

Fidelma turned to gaze upon the small building with interest.

'And who dwells there?'

'A woman of the flesh,' replied the other disapprovingly. It was a euphemism for a prostitute.

Fidelma's eyes widened in astonishment. She had not expected a prostitute to be dwelling in this isolated valley, let alone in such a small hamlet.

'And does she have a name, this woman of the flesh?'

'She is called Nemon.'

'Nemon? An inappropriate name for one of her calling it would seem.'

Nemon was the name of one of the ancient war goddesses. It meant 'battle-fury'.

'I spit on the name,' the burly woman suited the word to the action, 'I have told my man that she should be driven away from here. Yet the farmstead is her property and she is under the protection of Murgal.'

'She is? And you say that the man I described stayed with her last night?'

'I did.'

'Then we will go and see what Nemon has to say about this. Thank you, Bairsech, for your time and courtesy.'

They left the woman still scowling in suspicion after them.

Eadulf had slid off his horse by now and together they walked across the settlement, leading their horses.

'Who would have thought our pious brother from the north was a frequenter of women of the flesh,' he chuckled.

'We do not know that for sure,' Fidelma reproved him. 'All we know is that he did not return to the guests' hostel and appears to have stayed the night at the house of a prostitute. It does not imply that he is a frequenter of such places. The fact that this Nemon is under the protection of Murgal is a more interesting aspect of this affair.'

They walked up to the door of the cabin and tapped upon its oak wood panels.

A moment later it opened and a woman stood regarding them with the same hostility on her features as that of the farmer's wife.

She was a fleshy woman, in her fourth decade of life, with straw-coloured hair and ruddy features. Her face was heavy with make-up, the eyebrows dyed with berry juice and her lips crimsoned. She had been attractive once; but that must have been some years ago and now she had a voluptuousness that was gross rather than alluring. She examined them for a moment with her dark eyes and then focussed over their shoulder to where Bairsech, the wife of Ronan, still stood watching their every move with unconcealed curiosity.

'Her nose grows longer each day,' the woman muttered. 'Bairsech is a name which suits her well.' Fidelma suddenly realised that the name could be applied to a brawling woman. Then the woman stood aside and motioned them in. 'Come inside and do not give her the pleasure of examining us further.'

They hitched their horses to a small post outside the building and entered.

It was a comfortable room but not inviting.

'Are you Nemon?'

The woman nodded.

'You are strangers to the valley.' It was a statement not a question.

'You do not know why we are here?'

'I know nothing and care less. I care only for my comfort and my time is gauged in what I may profit from it.'

Fidelma turned to Eadulf.

'Give Nemon a *screpall*,' she instructed.

Unwillingly Eadulf took the coin out of his purse and handed it to the woman. She almost snatched it out of his hand and examined it suspiciously.

'Money is rare in this valley. We usually barter. But money is therefore thrice welcome.'

She assured herself that the coin was genuine before regarding them with a question on her features.

'What is it you want? Not my services,' she added, laughing lewdly, 'that's for sure.'

Fidelma shook her head, hiding her distaste at even the suggestion.

'We want a few moments of your time, that's all. And the answers to some questions.'

'Very well. Ask your questions.'

'I am told that you had a guest here last night.'

'Yes.'

'A man from the ráth? Thick-set. Wearing fine clothes with his head in a tonsure . . . cut in the fashion of my friend here?'

'What of it?' Nemon made no attempt to disguise the fact.

'When did he come?'

'Late. After midnight, I believe. I had to dispense with two customers to accommodate him.'

'Why?'

'He paid me.'

'Yet a stranger . . . would you not have been better served to continue with your local clients than serve a stranger who might visit you only once?'

Nemon sniffed.

'True enough. But Murgal was with him and told me that I would not lose by it.'

'Murgal?'

'Yes. He brought the man to me. Solin was the man's name. I remember now.'

'And Murgal the Druid to Laisre brought the man from the ráth to you and asked you to . . . to bestow your favours on him?'

'Yes.'

'Did Murgal give you a reason why you should do this?'

'Do you think that people give me reasons for what they do? I ask no questions so long as I receive money for my services.'

'Have you known Murgal long?'

'He is my foster-father. He looks after me.'

'Your foster-father? And he looks after you?' Fidelma's voice took on an air of cynicism. 'Have you known any other life but the one you now pursue?'

Nemon laughed disdainfully.

'You are disapproving? Do you think I should be like Ronan's woman across the yard there? Look at her, a woman who is younger than I am but who looks old enough to be my mother. Old before her time because she is condemned to go out into the fields at the crack of dawn and milk the cows while her husband lies in a drunken slumber. She has to plough fields and dig and sow and harvest while he rides about pretending to be a great warrior, not a lord, as he claims, but merely a sub-chieftain of this pitiful collection of hovels. No, I want no other life than the one I have. At least I sleep in fine linen sheets and for as long as I like.'

The derision on the woman's face was plain.

'Yet I notice that you have a small farm to run,' Eadulf pointed out. 'There are cows outside to be milked. Who does your work if you do not?'

Nemon screwed up her face in an ugly gesture.

'I only keep them because they are money. I would sell them tomorrow if the price was right. They are too much hard work. But, as I said, this valley is mainly a place of barter, so I must expect cows, goats, chickens, eggs and the like in place of coins.'

'Thank you for speaking with us,' Fidelma abruptly said, rising to leave.

'No thanks are necessary. You paid me for my time. Come again, if you need more conversation.'

Outside the cabin of Nemon, Eadulf exchanged a wry look with Fidelma.

'Do you think that Murgal was appeasing Brother Solin in some way?'

Fidelma looked speculative as she considered the question.

'You mean, he bribed him? He used Nemon to put Solin in a good mood in order to take part in this morning's play-acting at the council meeting?'

Eadulf nodded.

'Perhaps,' agreed Fidelma. 'Perhaps Brother Solin simply cannot resist the comfort that a woman like Nemon can provide. Maybe he asked Murgal where he might find such comfort. Murgal seems to have ideas in that direction himself.'

'You refer to the incident with Marga, the apothecary?'

Fidelma did not reply but mounted her horse.

Bairsech, the wife of Ronan, was still standing outside her door, her broad arms folded, and watching them with intense dislike as, together, they began to ride slowly away from the group of farm buildings over the bridge in the direction of the ráth.

'I wonder if Ultan of Armagh knows that his secretary is the sort of person to visit a woman of the flesh?' mused Eadulf.

Fidelma was serious.

'I doubt it. Ultan is in favour of the new ideas emanating from Rome on the celibacy of clergy.'

'It will never catch on,' Eadulf averred. 'It is true that there are always going to be some aesthetics but for all the clergy of the Faith to take such vows is demanding too much of human beings.'

Fidelma gave him a sideways glance.

'I thought you approved of the idea?'

Eadulf coloured but did not answer.

'Well, at least we have solved the mystery of where Brother Solin was last night,' he said hurriedly.

'Yes, but not why. We will have to keep a watch on both Murgal and our Brother Solin.'

Eadulf sighed.

'All I want, at the moment, is to be able to stretch out and sleep until my head stops pounding.'

Chapter Nine

They rode slowly back to the ráth. There were only a few people about. It being midday, most had retired for the midday meal. Eadulf was still moaning about his headache and Fidelma, finally taking pity on him, suggested that he go straight to the hostel while she stabled the horses. He received the suggestion without demur and he left her outside the stables and made his way across the stone-flagged courtyard. Fidelma led the two horses inside and took them to the far stalls which were the only empty ones. There was no sign of the two boys who usually looked after the stables but it did not take her long to unsaddle the horses and provide them with fodder and water.

She was bending in the stalls to retrieve the discarded saddle bags when she heard someone enter the stable. She was about to stand up when she heard Brother Solin's voice speaking in a defensive tone. She hesitated for a moment and then some instinct made her sink back to her knees behind the cover of the stall's panels.

There were two voices. It was easy to recognise the sibilant wheezy tones of Brother Solin but she could not recognise the second voice. It was young and masculine. What made her hesitate in identifying herself was the fact that this second voice also spoke in a northern accent. She edged carefully to the entrance of the stall and managed a quick glance around its shelter. Brother Solin and a young man were standing just inside the doors of the stable. She darted back behind the cover of the wooden stall.

'There,' came Brother Solin's tones, 'at least we can be unobserved.'

'It matters not whether we are observed or not,' replied the younger voice. There was anger in his tone.

'On the contrary,' Brother Solin replied suavely, 'if anyone here knew that you were here to spy among these people they would not take kindly to it. They might decide to do something . . . shall we say, drastic?'

'A harsh word is "spy" especially from such as you,' sneered the young man. 'And what of your own mission here?'

'Do you question my right to be in this place?'

'Right? What right? I certainly question your intentions.'

'Listen, my young friend,' Brother Solin seemed unperturbed, 'and listen to me well. I advise you to stay out of the business of Armagh. You think that you are immune because of those whom you serve? Well, there are greater powers than your master and they will not tolerate interference.'

There was an angry intake of breath from the younger man.

'Make no idle threats with me, pompous cleric, for your cloth will be no protection from the wrath of him I serve.'

There was a sudden silence.

Cautiously, Fidelma raised her head over the edge of the wooden stall again and this time saw the stocky figure of Brother Solin standing alone by the door, staring out of it. It seemed his adversary must have left. Brother Solin stood for a moment or two, as if deep in thought, and then he shrugged his shoulders and also left.

Fidelma came out of the stall and stood undecided for a while, trying to put an interpretation on what she had heard. Suppressing a sigh at the impossibility of the task, she turned back and picked up the saddle bags. She went to the door, hesitating to make sure no one observed her. She caught sight of Brother Solin entering the apothecary shop across the courtyard.

She hurried across the courtyard to the guests' hostel.

Cruinn, the portly hostel-keeper, was preparing the midday meal. She looked up with a fleshy smile as Fidelma entered.

'Your companion, the foreigner, has gone to bed,' she announced with some amusement. 'But there be many men in the ráth doing likewise this day. Will you sit down to a meal?'

Fidelma indicated that she would and that she would first have a word with Eadulf to see how he fared. She was about to go up when the portly woman cleared her throat as if embarrassed.

'Might I have a word, lady, while we are alone?'

Intrigued, Fidelma turned back to her in curiosity.

'Feel free to speak,' she invited.

'I have been told that you are a *dálaigh*, familiar with our laws. Is that so?'

Fidelma nodded affirmatively.

'Do you know all about the laws on marriage?'

Fidelma was not expecting such a question and raised her eyebrows in surprise.

'I know the text of the *Cáin Lánamna*, yes.' She smiled encouragement at the nervous woman. 'Are you thinking of marriage,

Cruinn? Best you should consult with Murgal. He would know your pagan ceremonies.'

The hostel keeper shook her head, wiping her hands on a large saffron-coloured apron.

'No; not him. I want some advice. I will pay, though I have not much.'

So anxious was her face that Fidelma took her by the arm and made her sit down on a bench at the table while she took a seat opposite.

'You may ask my advice for nothing, Cruinn. If it is so important to you. How may I help?'

'I want to know . . .' The elderly woman hesitated and then proceeded carefully. 'I want to know whether a woman of lowly position can marry a person of chiefly blood. Is there danger that the marriage might not be legal?'

Fidelma was quietly amused. She was about to ask what chief Cruinn planned to marry but felt that it was a silly mockery on her part.

'It depends on the position of the chieftain. Is he of royal lineage?'

'No. He is an *aire coisring*, a chieftain of a small clan,' the woman replied immediately.

'I see. Well, usually, the more formal types of union should be of partners from the same social class. Even a *bó-aire* is expected to marry the daughter of a man of equal rank. But such marriages between the lower class and higher class are known.'

Cruinn looked up swiftly, almost eagerly.

'And is the marriage valid?'

'Oh, of course. But I warn you that the financial burden of a socially mixed marriage falls more heavily on the family of the partner of the lower class. I will tell you this: if it is the woman who is of the lower class, as you seem to indicate, then her family has to supply two thirds of the cattle of joint wealth. It is a great step to take and think well on it, Cruinn, before you agree to any such liaison.'

Cruinn shook her head and smiled thinly.

'Oh no, it is not my marriage, for I have been most happily married and have a child. Though my man is dead, I am content. No, I ask on behalf of someone I know who would never bother to ask.'

Fidelma hid her smile. The woman would surely not ask such questions for a friend. Fidelma was sure that it was a personal matter but could not imagine Cruinn winning the heart of even the lowest lord of a clan. She realised that she was prejudiced, of course, but that realisation could not prevent the feeling of amused cynicism arising.

'Tell your friend to think well on it, then, for there is an ancient triad which says it is a misfortune for the offspring of a commoner to aspire to marriage with the offspring of even the lowest grade of lord.'

Cruinn stood up and bobbed in gratitude.

'I will remember and am grateful for your advice, lady. Now I will prepare your meal.'

Thinking it was a curious world, Fidelma hurried up the stairs to deposit her saddle bags in her room before turning into Eadulf's chamber with his bags.

Eadulf lay stretched on his bed with his eyes shut.

'How are you?' she asked sympathetically, putting his bags on a nearby table.

Eadulf winced at the sound of her voice and did not open his eyes.

'I think it is time to sing a *cepóc* for me but do not sing it too loudly.'

Fidelma grinned. A *cepóc* was a funeral dirge, a lament for the passing of someone into the Otherworld.

'Have you tried the infusion that Marga gave you?' she inquired, feeling solicitous.

'I will, as soon as that portly virago vanishes from the kitchen.'

'The woman Cruinn?'

'The same,' sighed Eadulf. 'She tried to make me eat some squishy mess when I came in. Another herbal remedy. I swear she is trying to kill me. She told me that it would help me recover and that she ought to know good medicines for she was often gathering herbs for the apothecary.'

'Well, you are no use to me until you recover your senses, Eadulf,' Fidelma said. 'I am going down to eat now. Get better as soon as you can.'

Downstairs she found that Brother Dianach had arrived and was already seated at his meal. Cruinn had already laid out the food and departed. Fidelma greeted the young monk and sat down. There was no sign of Brother Solin nor of the newcomer to the ráth.

'Is Brother Solin ailing?' she asked, suddenly remembering that she had last seen him entering the apothecary shop.

Brother Dianach looked up in surprise.

'Ailing? No. What makes you think so?'

Fidelma decided to keep her own council.

'So many people seem caught with the affliction of the bad wine of last night.'

Brother Dianach sniffed in disapproval.

'I did warn Brother Eadulf this morning that like does not cure like.'

'So you did,' Fidelma replied absently picking at her food. 'I thought I heard that there was another guest arriving here in the ráth?'

Again Brother Dianach was unresponsive.

'I have not heard so.'

'It was another traveller from Ulaidh.'

'No. You are surely mistaken.'

There was a sound on the stair and Eadulf, pale and wan, came down and, without a word to them, began to prepare some infusion from a small bag of medicines that he usually carried. Fidelma noticed that he did not use the foxglove leaves that Marga had given him. However, she knew that Eadulf was well enough trained in the art of herbal mixtures to trust he knew what he was doing.

After a while he came to the table with a beaker of some aromatic brew and began to sip it with closed eyes.

'*Similia similibus curantur?*' Brother Dianach gibed derisively.

'*Contraria contrariis curantur,*' replied Eadulf with a shudder. 'I will see you later.' He rose looking pale and unsteady, still bearing his beaker of liquid and retired to his room.

The door opened and Brother Solin entered. He seemed flushed and agitated.

'Is the hostel keeper here?' he demanded. 'I am hungry.'

Fidelma was about to say that he could help himself to food when Brother Dianach leapt to his feet.

'I will bring you the food, Brother Solin.'

Fidelma stared at the thick-set secretary in disapproval.

'Your nose is bleeding, Solin,' she remarked dispassionately. She also noticed that the front of the man's linen shirt was badly stained with wine and there were some dried flecks over his forehead. Someone had recently thrown wine in the cleric's face, of that she was certain.

Solin grimaced and drew out a cloth to hold to his nose. He offered no explanation but regarded her with censure in his eyes.

'I hope this afternoon will see better progress on the matter of bringing the Faith to this place.'

'You caused this morning to be wasted,' she replied coldly.

Brother Dianach hurried back with the plate of food for his master and resumed his seat with an unhappy expression.

Solin scowled at Fidelma.

'Wasted? There is no waste when one preaches the Word. If you would not defend your Faith before these pagans, then it was up to me to do so.'

In spite of their earlier argument, Solin could not apparently understand that he had incurred Fidelma's censure.

'Did you not see that Murgal was trying to lead me into the trap of arguing theology to waste time and avoid the main purpose of my visit here?' she demanded.

'I simply saw that, sooner than stand up for your Faith, you removed yourself from the hall and left the pagans victorious!' snapped Solin. 'And I will pass that information on to Ultan of Armagh to whom you may have to answer.'

'Then you are blind as well as a fool, Solin. You may pass my opinion on to Ultan as well.'

Having finished her meal, Fidelma rose and left the hostel. She was intrigued as to who the mysterious young man from Ulaidh was but needed to discover the fact without arousing attention.

At the gate she recognised one of the two warriors who stood talking there. The fair-haired Rudgal, the secret Christian. She walked across the courtyard and greeted him by name, nodding in affable fashion to the second man.

'I hear that there is another visitor to this ráth from the north?' she began.

Rudgal gave her an appreciative glance.

'There is little that escapes you, Fidelma of Cashel,' he replied. 'Yes, while you and the Saxon were down in Ronan's hamlet below, a merchant arrived.'

'A merchant? What is his merchandise?'

Rudgal did not seem particularly interested.

'He is a dealer in horses, I believe,' he said dismissively.

Rudgal's companion grimaced cynically, an expression which was not lost on Fidelma. She turned to him inquisitively.

'You disagree?'

'A horse dealer?' the man replied skeptically. 'That one has the mark of a professional warrior on him.'

Fidelma examined Rudgal's companion with interest.

'You seem to have observed him closely. Why do you say he has the mark of a warrior?'

Rudgal coughed harshly. It was an obvious signal and the other man shrugged, leaving with a muttered apology about being needed elsewhere.

Rudgal was on the point of leaving also when Fidelma stayed him.

'What did your companion mean?'

'Only that a man can be many things,' he replied indifferently. 'As you know, Sister, I am a wagon maker by trade and yet I am called to serve Gleann Geis as a warrior when needed. Just as Ronan is a farmer as well as a warrior.'

'Has this horse trader moved on? Or is he staying in the ráth?'

'We have no room at the guests' hostel, so Laisre has suggested that the merchant stay at Ronan's farmstead.'

'Is he there now?'

'He has returned to the ráth and is in conversation with Laisre in the council chamber.'

'I see. And where is his merchandise? Is that at Ronan's farmstead?'

Rudgal frowned.

'Merchandise?'

Fidelma was patient.

'If he is a trader in horses, he must have horses to trade. I am interested in horses. I would like to see what he has to offer. We can see Ronan's pastures below us from here. I see no herd of horses grazing there among the cows.'

For a moment Rudgal looked baffled.

'I don't know. Perhaps you should speak with him.'

Fidelma gazed after the disappearing warrior for some moments as Rudgal swung down the hill away from the ráth.

She suddenly became aware of someone hurrying by and she turned, finding herself contemplating the angry face of Orla, wife of the tanist, as the woman headed towards a building near the gates.

'You look distressed, Orla,' she called, forcing the wife of the tanist to stop in her tracks. 'Can I be of service?'

The handsome woman stared at her a moment; she swallowed hard but the anger did not go from her features.

'May the goddess of death and battles curse all you Christians,' she said with venom. 'You claim piety, chastity and humility but you are nought but animals!'

Fidelma was astonished.

'I do not know what you mean. Perhaps you should explain.'

Orla thrust out her chin.

'I will kill that fat pig, Solin, if he comes near me again!'

'I hope you did not waste good wine on him,' smiled Fidelma, suddenly remembering Brother Solin's appearance.

Orla stared at her.

'Wine?'

'I presume it was you who doused Brother Solin with wine?'

Orla shook her head.

'Not I. I would not waste even bad wine on the pig.' Without another word, Orla passed on leaving Fidelma with a thoughtful expression on her features. Fidelma turned back into the ráth and began making her way across the courtyard.

A voice hailed her.

It was Marga, the apothecary, who approached.

'Do you take me for a fool?'

Fidelma kept her features composed. Two angry women in as many minutes?

'Why would you think that I might do so?' she countered with interest.

'This morning you came to me and sought a cure for your foreign friend's hangover. Were you testing me?'

'Why would I be testing you?'

'Who knows your motives? Your Saxon friend had enough knowledge to provide his own medication. I learnt that he has studied at Tuam Brecain and is learned enough without the necessity of consulting me.'

Fidelma remained quiet for a moment.

'How did you learn that he studied at Tuam Brecain?' she asked after a moment's consideration.

Marga was exasperated.

'You answer my questions with questions! Don't think that you can keep secrets in such a small place as the ráth of Laisre.'

'Forgive me,' smiled Fidelma gently. 'It is a habit. I have been a *dálaigh* for too long to change it. Ah, but I think I know. Brother Solin paid you a visit this morning.'

Obviously, young Brother Dianach had told Solin and Solin had passed on the information when he went into Marga's apothecary that morning.

Marga shot her a look of dislike and spun on her heel and strode off.

Fidelma stood looking after her a moment or two before resuming her path towards the main building of the ráth where the council chamber was.

The saturnine figure of Murgal greeted her at the door.

'So you have decided to come back?'

He evinced no pleasure in the fact.

'That much is obvious, Murgal. Why do you seek to make your chieftain's task difficult?'

Murgal smiled thinly.

'You must already know that I disagree with what my chieftain is doing. Why, then, should I make his path easier?'

'I was led to believe that a decision was already made. If so, you should abide by that decision.'

'A decision made arbitrarily is not binding on all the people.'

'Are you telling me that Laisre made the decision to send to Imleach and Cashel without discussing the matter with his council?'

Murgal hesitated, made to open his mouth and then thought better of it.

Fidelma waited a moment and when Murgal continued his silence she added: 'We may not agree on a common faith but one thing we both believe, Murgal, and that is the rule of the law. Your chieftain's word is inviolable once given. You are a Brehon, Murgal. You have sworn an oath; an oath that is sacred, and that oath is to uphold the law.'

Murgal shook his head disdainfully.

'But my oath is not valid according to your Faith because it is not an oath to your God.'

'You are not speaking to any foreign cleric, Murgal. Christian or not, I am of the same bloodline as Eber the Fair. You have sworn your oath even though the sea rise and engulf you or the sky fall upon you. You are sworn to hold fast to the law. You will do so.'

'You are a strange woman, Fidelma of Cashel.'

'I am a product of my people, just as you are.'

'I am an enemy to your Faith.'

'But you are not an enemy to our people. If Laisre's word was given in accordance with the law, then you know you are sworn to uphold it.'

The doors of the council chamber opened and Laisre came out. He was followed by the young man Fidelma had seen at the door of the stable. She examined the newcomer carefully.

He was about thirty. Not tall but muscular in spite of the loose clothing he wore. His dress was not that of a warrior and certainly not the finery of a noble. But her quick eyes saw what the warrior at the gate of the ráth had observed. The young man carried himself in a particular way. He wore a sword slung on his hip and a dagger in his belt. They gave the impression that they were not for show. The deep brown eyes of the man were restive, examining and assessing things as quickly as did Fidelma. His brown hair was well cut, his moustache was trimmed. The clothes did not seem to suit his figure at all, as if he had put them on by mistake.

Laisre had evidently not been expecting to see Fidelma and Murgal together.

He halted, his eyes darting from one to the other in question and then seeing that they were not overtly in enmity he stepped forward again with a forced smile.

'We have another stranger travelling through our land. Fidelma of Cashel, Murgal, may I present Ibor of Muirthemne?'

The young man took a step forward and jerked his head forward in a perfunctory bow.

'Lady, your reputation precedes you. Your name is spoken of with affection even at Tara.'

'You are gracious, Ibor,' Fidelma replied. 'And you are also many miles from your home in Muirthemne.'

'It is the lot of a merchant to seldom stretch his limbs beside his own hearth, lady.'

'I am told that you are a horse trader.'

The young man nodded affirmation. He had a warm, open face, Fidelma thought, almost boyish.

'You have been told correctly, lady.'

'Then I would like to see your horses for I am much interested. Where is your herd grazing?'

'I have no herd,' the young man returned without embarrassment.

It was Murgal who spoke now, framing the question that Fidelma was about to ask.

'A trader in horses without horses? That requires some explanation.'

Undeterred, the young man chuckled.

'Oh, but I do have *a* horse. I have brought a horse to sell.'

'Just one?' Murgal asked somewhat surprised. 'It is a long journey from Muirthemne just to sell a single horse.'

'True,' Ibor assented. 'But it is such a horse and it is such a price that I am expecting to raise! I expected to sell it for thirty *séds*.'

'Thirty *séds*?' exclaimed Murgal. 'A large sum for one animal.'

'You said – expected?' Fidelma said quickly.

'I had heard that Eoganán, the chieftain of the Uí Fidgente, was looking for a thoroughbred horse and for an animal of great worth he would be prepared to pay a price that would make my journey worthwhile. I had found such an animal, a horse raised among the Britons which I brought to Éireann. I thought I would make the sum from Eoganán and it alone would recompense me for the long journey.'

Fidelma regarded him with suspicion.

'But Eoganán was killed at the Hill of Áine six months ago.'

Ibor of Muirthemne raised his hands in a gesture of hopelessness.

'That I only found out when I arrived in the country of the Uí Fidgente. There I found the new chieftain, Donnenach, trying to restore the shattered fortunes of his defeated people . . .'

'Defeated by Fidelma's brother, Colgú of Cashel,' interposed Murgal maliciously.

'After the Uí Fidgente under Eoganán had plotted Cashel's overthrow,' Fidelma replied in annoyance. It was not the first time that Murgal had tried to present Cashel's defeat of the Uí Fidgente as if it were Cashel's responsibility.

'Yes, but I knew none of this,' Ibor of Muirthemne pointed out disarmingly.

'News does not take that long to travel to Muirthemne, surely?' queried Fidelma.

'I was in the kingdom of Gwynedd, among the Britons, when all this happened,' protested Ibor. 'I was there arranging the buying of horses. I returned to Ulaidh about a month ago and the news was so old that no one bothered to relate it. I took the horse that I had especially chosen and set out for the country of the Uí Fidgente . . .'

'Wasn't it difficult to bring a thoroughbred horse out of Ulaidh when the law of the *Allmuir Sét* would have stipulated its sale only within the boundaries of Ulaidh?' asked Fidelma ingenuously.

The young man hesitated and then shrugged.

'I had special dispensation from the king of Ulaidh,' he explained hurriedly. 'I did not learn the news about the defeat of the Uí Fidgente until I reached their lands where I had been expecting to find Eoganán.'

'Then what brought you here? The Uí Fidgente live beyond the northern mountains,' Fidelma asked.

'I told you,' the young man was a little aggrieved, 'there was devastation and destruction there. No one wanted to barter for a thoroughbred horse when their cattle herds had been taken for fines. I did not want to take the horse north again and so I came here. One of the Uí Fidgente told me that Laisre of Gleann Geis was a shrewd judge of horse flesh.'

Fidelma turned to Laisre with curiosity.

'And have you made a judgment on the beast?'

'I have not seen the horse as yet. Ibor has just arrived and the horse is stabled below at Ronan's farmstead. I shall see it within the next day or so once our guest has rested from his journey.'

'Yes,' agreed Ibor. 'I promised Ronan's woman, Bairsech, that I would return to bathe and refresh myself from my journey and I am already late. So forgive me, I must go now.'

'I will escort you as far as Ronan's farmstead,' Murgal announced. 'I need to go in that direction. My . . . my foster-daughter lives within Ronan's hamlet.'

'That is good of you, Murgal.' The words were not reinforced by his tone of voice. The young man did not seem pleased to have Murgal's company. He turned courteously to Fidelma. 'I am honoured to have met you, Fidelma of Cashel.'

'I am always interested in meeting a trader in horses, especially one who travels great distances to come to this small corner of the kingdom of Cashel.'

Together, he and Murgal left the ráth.

'A personable young man,' remarked Laisre as he and Fidelma stood watching them leave.

Fidelma was cynical.

'A foolish young man.' When she saw Laisre look at her questioningly, she continued: 'It is a fool who rides alone through the country of the Uí Fidgente with a valuable horse in these turbulent times.'

'Perhaps it is not so dangerous in the country of the Uí Fidgente as you may think,' Laisre commented. 'Brother Solin and his young acolyte were there a few days ago.'

Fidelma did not hide her reaction of surprise.

'Brother Solin actually came here by way of the lands of the Uí Fidgente? Surely that was a curious choice of route?'

'It is a logical route from the northern kingdoms,' returned Laisre.

'I suppose it is,' Fidelma conceded reluctantly. 'But not one that I would venture.'

'My council and I will be gathering later this afternoon to iron out our differences and we may plan to resume our negotiation tomorrow before noon. I apologise once again for this morning. Murgal is an honest man but he is not yet convinced that tolerating the new Faith will bring us anything but a disappearance of our people. He fears the changes it will bring.'

'It is an understandable attitude,' accepted Fidelma. 'However, Heraclitus once said that nothing is permanent in this life but change.'

Laisre smiled wanly.

'A good saying but it will take much to change Murgal's mind.' He paused and then added: 'We will have another feasting tonight.'

Fidelma winced slightly.

'Perhaps you will excuse Brother Eadulf and myself?'

The chieftain frowned slightly. To refuse to attend a feast was approaching an insult. Fidelma knew the laws of hospitality. She went on hastily: 'I am under a *geis*, a prohibition that on each day after the full moon, I must spend the evening with simple fare and in meditation of my Faith.'

Laisre's eyes widened a little.

'A *geis*, you say?'

Fidelma nodded seriously. A *geis* was an ancient prohibition, a taboo or a bond which, when placed on someone, compelled them to obey the injunction. The concept of the *geis* still survived in the Brehon Laws. The legendary warrior-hero of Ulaidh, Cúchulainn, had been given a *geis* never to eat the flesh of a dog. Trapped by his enemies, he eventually had to eat dog flesh and this infringement brought about his inevitable death. The ignoring or transgression of the prohibition exposed the one on whom the *geis* had been placed to rejection by society and would place them outside the social order.

Fidelma told the lie after the briefest struggle with her religious conscience. Did not the Brehon Morann say: 'Never to lie is to have no lock to the door of your house. Mendacity is permissible as a means of protection from a greater evil.' She knew that Laisre could understand and would not question such a prohibition.

'Very well, Fidelma. I will press you no further.'

'There is one thing, however . . .' Fidelma stayed him.

'You have but to ask.'

'Is there a library at the ráth?'

'Of course.' Laisre seemed momentarily indignant. 'It is not only Christians who keep libraries.'

'I did not mean to imply otherwise,' Fidelma pacified. 'Where do I find this library?'

'I will show you. It is, in fact, under Murgal's control as my Druid and Brehon.'

'Will he mind if I examine it?'

'I am his chieftain,' Laisre replied curtly in explanation.

He led the way across the courtyard to the same building where the apothecary's shop was placed. There was a main entrance, a little further beyond the shop, and through this door was a flight of wooden steps leading to other storeys. Laisre climbed the stairs to the third and final storey and proceeded along a passage which led into a square tower room. The squat tower dominated the ráth.

'That is Murgal's apartment.' Laisre indicated an adjacent room. 'And here is the library.'

Fidelma entered a single, small chamber with the walls lined with wooden pegs from which hung book satchels, each satchel filled with a particular leather-bound volume.

'Were you looking for something particular?' Laisre asked as Fidelma moved down the lines of pegs and satchels, searching each book's title in turn.

'I am looking for the law books.'

Laisre pointed to several works in one corner. He stood hesitating as she began to peer through them. Fidelma took no further notice of him and he finally cleared his throat.

'Then if you have no further need of me . . . ?' he queried.

Fidelma looked up, as if she had forgotten his existence, and smiled apologetically.

'I am sorry. I will not be long in looking up the reference I require. But you need not wait for me. I can find my own way back.'

Laisre hesitated, then nodded in acknowledgment.

'Then, unless our paths cross later, I will see you in the council tomorrow before noon.'

Fidelma turned back to the book satchels as he left. She was looking for a copy of a specific law text and wondered if the Brehon had it in his collection of the score or so of legal texts.

She finally found what she was looking for. It was a tract called the *Allmuir Sét* or sale of foreign goods. She spent half an hour reading the text before replacing it in its satchel and rehanging it on its peg.

She left the room with a contemplative expression on her face and retraced her steps down the stairs to the courtyard, making her way confidently to the hostel.

Chapter Ten

Fidelma was crossing the courtyard when the sound of clattering hooves at the gate of the ráth made her turn. The sound announced the arrival of a body of horsemen. She immediately recognised Colla and Artgal at their head. They came to a halt and began to dismount. Fidelma walked across to where Colla was loosening his saddle girth.

'So, Colla, what news?' she demanded without preamble.

The tanist of Gleann Geis looked up sourly. Colla was not apparently overjoyed to see her.

'A wild goose chase,' he announced. 'I expected little else.'

'What did you find?' she pressed.

'Little enough,' he said dismissively. 'The ravens had feasted well. Little to be seen. My men and I followed some tracks but they soon vanished in the stony ground. All I could tell was that the tracks led towards the north.'

'And?' encouraged Fidelma. 'Did you follow them?'

'The ground was stony, as I said. The tracks soon vanished. We looked around for as long as we could but there was little else to do but return.'

Fidelma's eyes narrowed in dissatisfaction.

'So that is what I must report to Cashel? That thirty-three young men died here in some ritual slaughter and there was nothing to be done?'

Colla stood up and faced her defiantly.

'I cannot conjure a reason from nothing, Fidelma of Cashel. Not even you could have followed a non-existent track.'

'Yet you say that the tracks led north? How far did you follow them?'

'As far as the spot where they could no longer be seen.'

'But what country lies to the north?' Fidelma pressed.

'The Corco Dhuibhne are immediately to the north of these valley lands.'

Fidelma pressed her lips together for a moment.

'They are a pleasant enough clan, whose chieftain, Fathan, I know. This evil does not bear their mark. What other lands are there beyond here?'

'Well, to the north-east is the country of your own cousin, Congal of the Eóghanacht of Loch Léin, king of Iarmuman. Do you see his hand in this?'

Fidelma had to admit that she did not.

'But beyond him is the land of the Uí Fidgente,' she said reflectively.

Colla's eyes narrowed.

'Is it a scapegoat you seek?' he asked. 'The Uí Fidgente are a devastated people. Your brother defeated them at Cnoc Áine. They are weak and not capable of any hostile action. Do you wish to pursue them into oblivion?'

'Only if they are responsible for this outrage,' Fidelma affirmed.

'Well, one thing – they are a Christian people so surely that eliminates them from your suspicions?' Colla was scornful.

Artgal came forward to take the tanist's horse and lead it away into the stables. He also dismissed the other warriors back to their dwellings.

Fidelma gazed in silence at Colla for a moment before speaking and, when she did so, she was deliberate in her tone.

'For the time being, Colla, without evidence, we cannot say who slaughtered the young men, except that the manner in which their bodies were laid out indicates that the culprit wanted to indicate a pagan symbolism to any who found them . . . unintentionally or intentionally.'

She thanked him coldly for his efforts and strode back to the guests' hostel.

There was only one person about and that was Eadulf. He was now sitting helping himself liberally to a pitcher full of cold water.

'Feeling any better?' she asked encouragingly.

He raised bloodshot eyes and forced a smile. His face was still pale.

'A little but not much.'

'Are you in a mood to accept an invitation from Laisre to another feasting?' she asked keeping her expression serious.

Eadulf groaned aloud and put his head in his hands.

Fidelma smiled maliciously.

'I thought not. Have no fear. I have already declined in both our names.'

'*Deo gloria!*' he intoned piously.

'A quiet evening is called for, I think. Our business should be concluded tomorrow and then we can leave to search the plain and see what we may find out about the slaughtered young men.'

Eadulf was not enthusiastic.

'I thought we were waiting for Colla?' he objected.

'He has already arrived back,' Fidelma explained shortly. 'He has discovered no more than we already knew.'

Eadulf raised his head and contrived to look interested in spite of his condition.

'Did he follow the tracks?'

'He said that he lost them in the hills to the north.'

'But you don't believe him?'

Fidelma sat down and poured herself a beaker of cold water from Eadulf's pitcher.

'I do not know. He might be telling the truth. It is stony ground in that valley. Why come back with such news so soon? If it were some conspiracy to keep us occupied for a while, he could certainly have spent a few days pretending to search before returning.'

'I suppose so,' Eadulf conceded.

Brother Dianach entered. He bade them a polite good evening.

'Are you going to the feasting tonight?' he inquired with an air of innocence, looking directly at the suffering Eadulf.

'No,' Fidelma replied shortly.

'If you forgive me, then, I am going to bathe before the feasting.'

They ignored him and he delayed only a moment before going into the bath house.

'There is another guest come to the ráth,' Fidelma told Eadulf after they heard the splashing of water from the next room.

'Yes? Who?' Eadulf wondered at her confidential tone.

'A young man from Ulaidh?'

'Another visitor from Ulaidh?' Eadulf was surprised.

'Exactly my reaction. He calls himself Ibor of Muirthemne and says he is a *cennaige* or trader in horses.'

'You sound as if you do not believe it?'

Fidelma nodded.

'He does not know his law of dealing in horses from overseas.'

'Should he do so?'

'Any competent trader would know the basic laws.'

'So he is not a trader in horses. So who is he and why is he here?'

'I wish I knew. He does have the bearing of a man used to arms. And remember that we found a warrior's torc near the bodies of the young men and that torc was of northern workmanship? I feel . . .'

The door opened boisterously and the corpulent figure of Cruinn entered.

'I hear there is another feasting tonight,' she greeted them. 'However, I thought I would see if you required anything from me beforehand.'

'Brother Eadulf and I will not be going to the feasting,' Fidelma informed her.

The eyes of Cruinn showed surprise in her fleshy face.

'Not going?' she repeated as if it were an unheard-of thing. 'But it is Laisre who is hosting the feast.'

'We will not tax your services too much,' Fidelma informed her, ignoring her disapproval. 'If you could prepare a dish of cold meats and some bread that will be food enough.'

Cruinn glanced at Eadulf's haggard features.

'I could also prepare a hot broth. A broth of leeks and oats with herbs added.'

Eadulf's tongue flickered over his lips with anticipation.

'It sounds the very thing that is needed to settle a rebellious stomach,' he observed.

The pudgy woman bustled off to prepare the food while Fidelma and Eadulf remained seated at the table.

'I presume the others – Solin and the young man – are going to the feast?' Cruinn called over her shoulder as she set about her task.

'Young Brother Dianach is in the bath house. But he has said that he is going,' Fidelma volunteered. 'We have not seen Brother Solin this evening. I am sure he will be going as well.'

Fidelma rose and went to Cruinn's side, watching the large woman's dexterous hands preparing the meal.

'Have you always lived in Gleann Geis, Cruinn?' she asked abruptly. Then: 'I have heard that there are many newcomers to the valley.'

'I have always lived here,' the woman confirmed. 'Those you speak of are the Christian wives and some husbands from the surrounding areas who have married among the original settlers in this valley.'

'Do you approve of Christians?'

The fleshy woman chuckled.

'You might just as well ask whether I approve of the mountains. They are there. What else to do but live with them?'

'You are wise,' Fidelma smiled. 'Are all the people of the valley as philosophical as you?'

The big woman did not understand the word.

Fidelma sought for another means of explaining her question.

'Do all the others in the valley feel as you do? Or do they feel an insecurity about the Christians?'

'We are very secure in this valley for there are only two ways in and two ways out,' Cruinn said, misinterpreting her.

Fidelma was about to explain that she had not meant physical fear when she realised what Cruinn had said.

'Two ways? I thought that there was only one path through the ravine?'

'Oh, no. There is the river path.'

'But I was told that the river is unnavigable through the rapids.'

'That is so but there is a small footpath that runs beside the river. Difficult and hidden in places because it goes through caves. A sure-footed person can manage it. It emerges into the valley beyond. As children most of us explored it. But no one could . . .'

The woman paused and then her eyes narrowed. It suddenly occurred to her that perhaps she was speaking too freely. Her embarrassment was covered when Brother Dianach emerged and confirmed that he would be going to the feasting. When questioned about Brother Solin's intentions he replied that he had not seen the cleric for a while but would presume that he was going too.

Fidelma announced that she would take a short walk before having her evening bath. Promising to be back soon, she left the hostel leaving Cruinn preparing the evening meal.

It was with some reluctance that Eadulf decided to also use the facilities of the second chamber to have an evening bathe. He decided that a cold bath might relieve him of the sweaty alcohol-induced discomfiture from his body. He felt a shame that he had succumbed to the excess of drink. Even though everyone had told him the wine had been bad, he felt it no excuse. He felt more humiliation since Fidelma had not been as reproving as she might have been.

Fidelma had actually left the ráth. She knew exactly where she was going. It took fifteen minutes or so to walk down to Ronan's hamlet, having first ascertained from the sentinel at the gate that both Ibor of Muirthemne and Murgal had returned to the ráth for the evening's festivities. She spotted her goal when she saw two horses grazing in the field next to Ronan's farmstead.

She made directly into the field by climbing over the low stone wall which surrounded it.

Fidelma was not without knowledge when it came to equestrian matters. She had been raised on a horse almost before she could walk. If the truth were known, her name was still spoken of in awe at the famous Cuirrech where a great annual race gathering had been held since time immemorial. A few years had passed since she had solved the mystery of the slaughter of the king of Laighin's prize race-horse and his jockey. She knew much about horses.

There were two horses in the field. A black stallion and a white mare. The mare was skittish but the stallion stood docilely enough as Fidelma ran her hands over his shoulders and fetlocks. She stroked him gently on the muzzle until he allowed her to open his mouth and examine his teeth. The mare was more difficult to examine but after a while she managed to calm her sufficiently to inspect her also.

'What are you doing?' cried a harsh voice.

Bairsech, the wife of Ronan, stood regarding her with a sour expression from the doorway of the farm building.

'Just examining these horses, Bairsech,' replied Fidelma unruffled. 'Are they the horses that belong to Ibor of Muirthemne?'

The woman recognised Fidelma but scowled even more.

'Yes; they are his.' It was said ungraciously.

Fidelma pursed her lips reflectively as she gazed at the animals. 'Has he no other horses with him?'

'Why do you ask? Do you want to buy them for he is not here but up at the ráth.'

'Indulge me,' replied Fidelma patiently. 'Did he bring any other animals with him?'

'No, just those two beasts.' Bairsech was wary. 'What does that have to do with you?'

'Nothing,' Fidelma replied. 'Nothing at all. I shall doubtless see him at the ráth later.'

She left the field and began to climb back towards Laisre's fortress.

By the time she reached it, Eadulf had finished his bath. Cruinn was placing the food on the table and there was no sign of Brother Dianach. Eadulf told her that Dianach had gone to the feast but Brother Solin had not returned to the guests' hostel. Fidelma debated with herself for a moment as to whether she should have her evening bath and decided not to allow the soup to chill but to eat first and bathe later.

Cruinn, asking if they needed anything else and ascertaining that they did not, bade them have a good evening and left them to the meal.

Fidelma gave herself to the meal in silence while Eadulf ate moderately and stuck to water as Fidelma sipped at a beaker of mead.

'What are you puzzling over, Fidelma?' Eadulf finally broke the quiet that had fallen between them. 'I know when your mind is active for you have that far-away look in your eyes.'

She brought her gaze from the middle distance to focus on Eadulf.

'I have no other thoughts but to conclude the matter with Laisre tomorrow morning, providing we have no more prevarications from Murgal and Solin. After that, as I told you, we must follow up the mystery of the slaughtered young men.'

'Do you really think that you can find some clue that Colla has missed?'

'I will not think anything before I have examined the evidence. There is some ominous, oppressive mystery – something which is staring me in the face and yet I am not recognising it. However, one thing I have just confirmed about that strange young man who claims to be a horse trader.'

Eadulf looked up with interest.

'Apart from the fact that he does not know his law of trading?' he asked brightly.

'Not only does he not know about the law of trading but the so-called thoroughbred horse from Britain he says that he has brought to sell at such a grand price . . . it is no thoroughbred at all.'

'You saw it?'

'I went to Ronan's farm where Ibor is lodging. I saw the two horses he has brought with him. One is a mare and the other a stallion. They are not young horses, either of them, but they are good working horses. Certainly they are trained, too well trained, as war horses. Both of them have scars and it seems they have seen service in battle before now.'

'Are you saying that he is a complete impostor?'

'I am saying that neither horse is what he has claimed it to be. He said that he had brought a thoroughbred from the kingdom of the Britons, from Gwynedd. All such horses are short-legged and broad-chested, they have thick, wiry coats and a dense undercoat that insulates the body against the hard winters. But the horses that he has brought are not pure bred at all. They are long-legged and of the sort imported from Gaul for racing or bred for battle. His horses are too old to be worth anything that would justify him journeying all the way from Ulaidh to this remote part of our kingdom. In other words – Ibor of Muirthemne is a liar!'

Eadulf felt helpless for he could offer her no advice or even begin to think of anything which might be of help in solving the mystery.

They finished their meal in meditative silence. Faintly, they could hear the sounds of merry-making from the feasting hall of Laisre. It was Fidelma's suggestion that, if Eadulf was feeling up to it, they take another turn around the walls of the ráth before turning in. Eadulf would have preferred to retire immediately to bed for he had still not entirely recovered from the swimming feeling in his head. Yet guilt made him accede to Fidelma's suggestion. At least they had a rapport in which they did not have to talk but still retained a closeness of thought as if knowing what was passing through each other's minds as it did so.

They walked from the hostel to the steps leading up to the battlement walkway.

A shadow moved at the top of the stairs. They could hear an embarrassed giggle and the slight, small figure of a young girl disappeared into the darkness. A second shadow emerged and a harsh male voice challenged them. When they identified themselves the figure of Rudgal emerged into the flickering light of a burning brand torch.

'You are not at Laisre's feast, then?' The wagon maker and part-time warrior seemed embarrassed by their appearance.

'One of Laisre's feasts is enough for me,' Eadulf confessed plaintively.

Rudgal's features seemed to be sympathetic.

'Bad wine,' was his verdict. 'It happens sometimes.' Then he turned to Fidelma, changing the subject rapidly. 'I heard from Artgal that there was nothing to be found on the plain where you discovered the bodies; nothing which would explain how that terrible event came to happen.'

Fidelma leant against the battlement and gazed out into the gloom of the evening.

'You are a Christian, Rudgal. What would you make of this slaughter?'

Rudgal coughed nervously, and cast a look about. He lowered his voice conspiratorially.

'As you say, Sister, I am of the Faith. Life has been difficult for those of us who follow such a path in Gleann Geis. Then it became obvious that we are becoming a substantial portion of the population in this valley and we began to press the chieftain and his assembly to make recognition of our existence. For years now we have been blocked by the chieftain and his council. Then, suddenly, the chieftain seemed to reach enlightenment for he over-ruled his council and sent to Cashel. I never thought I would see the day. However, there are still many here who cling to the old ways. I will say this about this matter . . .' He paused. 'This ritual slaughter, as you claim it to be. There are many people who would like to see those of the Faith demoralised and the old ways triumph again.'

Fidelma turned and tried to read any hidden message in the features of Rudgal's face in the gloom.

'Do you think this act was done as a means of intimidating the Christian community here?'

'Why else would it be done? It serves no other purpose.'

'But who were the victims? Laisre says that no one in Gleann Geis is missing.'

'This is true. We would soon know if any of our people were missing. Perhaps the victims were travellers who were waylaid and slaughtered? Who killed them? I think the answer lies not far from where you hear that laughter emanating.'

A burst of rowdy laughter had just echoed from the feasting hall.

'Who do you accuse? Laisre? Or Murgal?' prompted Eadulf. 'Or is there someone else?'

Rudgal glanced briefly at Eadulf.

'It is not my place to point a finger of accusation. Just ask yourself this – whose interest does this action serve? Laisre was the one who decided to allow the Faith some freedom against the wishes of his council. Examine who opposes Laisre. I can say no more. Goodnight.'

Rudgal made off into the shadowy darkness.

'There is a logic in what he says,' offered Eadulf after a moment or two of silence.

'*Cui bono?* "Who stands to gain?" is an ancient precept of the law. Cicero demanded it of a judge in Rome. It is logical but is it too logical?'

Eadulf shook his head, puzzled.

'That is too clever for me. Logic is surely the art of making truth prevail?'

'Yet logic can often disguise truth from us. Logic can often ruin the spirit, the creative side of our mind, so that we go running along a straight track when our answers lie in the shadows of the forest glades beside those tracks. Logic alone confines us.'

'Do you think there can be some other explanation then?'

'One thing occurs to me – if this slaughter was done merely to frighten and coerce the Christians of Gleann Geis, why not slaughter some of the Christians of this valley? Why enact this ritual in the valley outside and use the bodies of strangers? Why not give more forceful strength to the message of menace? That logical deduction, as you see, has its faults.'

'Well, turning the same facts over and over without anything new to add makes the mind sterile,' Eadulf observed.

Fidelma chuckled.

'At times I need your wisdom, Eadulf,' she said. 'Let us complete our circuit of the walls and return to a restful slumber.'

Eadulf hesitated.

'Perhaps Rudgal was trying to put us off the scent? Who was he conspiring with up here just now?'

'Conspiring is hardly the term,' Fidelma said in amusement. 'Even you must have recognised Orla's daughter.'

They circuited the walls and returned down the steps. They passed across the courtyard, listening to the sounds of merry-making and music echoing from the feasting hall. There came a moment of comparative quiet, a brief lull in the noise, during which the sound of an angry voice and a slamming door could be plainly heard. The sound was unexpected and Fidelma seized Eadulf's sleeve and drew him back into the shadows of the wall.

'What is it?' whispered the Saxon perplexed by her action.

Fidelma shook her head and placed a finger against her lips.

Across the courtyard the door of the building where Murgal's apartment and library were housed was opening and there was no disguising the thick-set figure of Brother Solin as he came out and slammed it shut. He had one hand against the side of his face as if nursing it. He paused for a moment in the light of an oil lamp which hung outside the door, illuminating his angry features. He looked up and down, as if to ensure he had not been observed. The way he carried himself demonstrated his tense attitude and anger. Then he seemed to smooth his clothing and run a hand through his dishevelled hair. He straightened his shoulders and began to walk across the flag stones with a purposeful tread towards the feasting hall.

Fidelma and Eadulf pressed back into the shadows so that Brother Solin did not observe them. They waited in silence until he had vanished through the doors into the chieftain's building.

Eadulf pulled a face in the darkness.

'It was only that pompous idiot,' he remarked. 'No need to hide from him.'

Fidelma sighed softly.

'Sometimes you may learn things if people are unaware of your presence.'

'Learn what?'

'For instance, Brother Solin passed under the light of that lamp there. What did you observe?'

'That he was angry.'

'True. What else?'

Eadulf thought a moment and gave up.
'Little else, I think.'
'Ah, Eadulf! Did you not observe that someone seems to have struck Brother Solin hard across the cheek? Did you see the dark mark of blood on the corner of his cheek?'
Eadulf made an impatient negative gesture.
'And if that is so, what does it tell us?' he demanded.
'Earlier, I saw Brother Solin with a nose bleed. I think someone had struck him on the nose. It tells us that someone does not like Brother Solin of Armagh.'
Eadulf burst into sardonic laughter.
'I could have told you that. I do not like him for one.'
Fidelma regarded Eadulf in amusement.
'True. But you have not gone so far as to assault our pious cleric. Twice blood has been drawn. Wine has been thrown over him. Let us see if we can find the person who is responsible.'
She led the way across the courtyard to the door that Brother Solin had exited from. She was about to open the door when it swung open and the dark-haired figure of Orla came out. She stopped in surprise as if not expecting to find anyone outside.
'What are you doing here?' she demanded ungraciously.
'We seem to have missed our way,' Fidelma returned evenly. 'Where does this door lead?'
The sister of Laisre glowered.
'Not to the hostel, that is for certain,' she replied. 'There is no need for you to have missed the way to it. You can see it from here.'
Fidelma turned and then feigned surprise.
'So you can.' She went on unabashed. 'Tell me, have you seen Brother Solin recently? I wanted to speak with him.'
Orla tossed her head in annoyance.
'I have not seen him. Nor do I wish to. I told you this afternoon that I do not want that pig near me. Now, if you will stand aside . . . ?'
'Are these your chambers, then?' Eadulf stopped her, lamely feeling that he ought to make a contribution.
Orla simply ignored his question.
'I have other matters to attend to, if you do not,' she said as she pushed by them and headed towards the feasting hall.
Fidelma and Eadulf waited until she had gone.
'She must have seen Brother Solin,' Eadulf ventured.
'Perhaps.'
'But they both came through this same door.'

'True, but it leads into a large building with several apartments, including Murgal's. Also, as you can see, there is the apothecary's shop in the building.'

They went through the open door and stood in the dimly lit hallway. An oil lamp hung in the centre giving a dancing shadowy light. There were several doors along one side of it leading, presumably, into the apartments. Fidelma looked across to the stairs which Laisre had conducted her up earlier that day.

She was about to suggest that they withdraw, for there was little to be seen, when the tread of someone descending the stairs caused her to pause. Laisre appeared abruptly around the corner and started in surprise at the sight of them.

'Are you looking for me?' he greeted, having swiftly gathered his composure. 'Or did you come seeking more books?'

Fidelma made a hurried decision.

'I thought that I would show Brother Eadulf where the library is located in case we stood in need of consulting any of its volumes tomorrow.'

'Ah.' Laisre shrugged. 'Time enough for work tomorrow. You should be at the feasting. Yes, I know,' he went on hurriedly, 'you have explained all about your religious *geis*.'

'The feast is where I thought you would have been,' countered Fidelma. 'I hear from the music that it is still continuing.'

Laisre shrugged.

'I had to leave it for a moment. I needed to instruct Murgal on a matter for tomorrow. He left too early for me to mention it. But now I shall go back. Are you sure that you won't join me?'

Fidelma shook her head.

'The *geis* lasts from dusk until dawn,' she replied, wishing Eadulf would not look so bewildered. 'We should have retired some time ago but merely called in to look at the library on our way back to the hostel.'

'Then I shall bid you a good night.'

Laisre left the building with a friendly nod at the two of them.

Fidelma and Eadulf stood at the bottom of the stairs. Laisre had not closed the door and so they could see his shadowy figure crossing the stone-flagged courtyard. Almost immediately that he left the building, a large, portly figure hurried out of the shadows and intercepted him. Fidelma and Eadulf could not mistake the rotund figure of Cruinn, the hostel keeper. She seemed animated and even grabbed the chieftain by the arm. He appeared uncomfortable, glancing round towards the door behind him, but Fidelma and Eadulf were well back in the shadows. Laisre drew the portly hostel-keeper swiftly to one side. They could faintly hear his voice raised slightly as if trying to calm her.

Fidelma placed a finger to her lips and motioned Eadulf to follow her. Her idea was to draw closer to where Laisre and Cruinn were engaged in conversation. However, the sound of another woman's voice within the building raised in vehemence reached their ears. A door opened and shut with an abrupt bang. The sound came from somewhere along the corridor. Fidelma quickly propelled Eadulf out into the night, closing the door behind them.

Laisre and Cruinn had disappeared by now and they were scarcely across the courtyard when the door behind them opened and the figure of Rudgal was hurrying behind them in the darkness. He hesitated and then halted as he saw them.

'Did Murgal pass you a moment ago?' was his breathless greeting.

'No, we have not seen Murgal at all this evening,' Fidelma replied.

Rudgal raised a hand in brief acknowledgment and hurried away.

'Surely this is a place of great restlessness?' muttered Eadulf, stifling a sudden yawn.

Fidelma agreed without amusement. It was time to turn in anyway. Perhaps Brother Solin's nocturnal adventure was not of importance to her after all.

They made their way back to the hostel. The sounds of revelry were still echoing from the feasting hall. Eadulf had no regrets as he made his way directly to his bed chamber, bidding Fidelma good night. Fidelma sat for a while in the main room of the hostel. She sipped at a beaker of mead as she turned matters over in her mind. In the end she had to accept that Eadulf's proposition was right. It was no good turning the same information over and over without adding any new material to point her on to a new pathway. Eventually she made her way to bed, undressed and fell asleep.

Chapter Eleven

Something had awakened her.

She was not sure what it was. It was still dark. She lay on her bed listening carefully. Then she realised the cause. It had been the sound of whispered voices. They were low but intense enough to penetrate into her fitful sleep.

'Very well. It has to be done.'

She sought to identify the voice. It was a moment or two before she realised that it was the young monk, Brother Dianach, who was speaking. Then she located where the voices were coming from, Brother Dianach's sleeping chamber. The rooms were only partitioned by wood and so the sounds were not exactly muffled.

She did not move but lay listening intently for the second voice. She had already guessed who it would be. She was not disappointed.

'Give me the vellum and I will hand it to him.'

It was Brother Solin's voice.

'I have it here.'

Solin gave a hiss. 'Not so loud, boy, otherwise you might wake our fellow guests. We would not want that to happen.'

Brother Dianach gave an uncharacteristic laugh.

'The Saxon will not wake. He quaffed enough mead and wine to sleep a week. Listen, you can hear him snoring like a pig!'

'Quickly, now!' Brother Solin became impatient. 'It is essential I keep the rendezvous.'

'Here is the vellum, Brother.'

There was a silence as if Solin were checking the object that he had been handed.

'Good. Now back to sleep with you. I will report to you in the morning. If all goes well, Cashel will fall to us before the summer is out.'

Fidelma started up with a jerk. It was a reaction which she could not help. It was lucky that her movement had been drowned by the departure of Solin himself. Fidelma sat for a moment, heart pounding. She could hear from the soft footfalls that Solin was tip-toeing past her sleeping chamber. She swung out of bed and dragged on her robe and leather-soled shoes.

Solin had left the hostel by the time she had reached the head of the stairs but she had to refrain from any hurried descent for it would alert Brother Dianach. There was no time to wake Eadulf who slept in the chamber opposite. She went as swiftly as she could down the stairs and out into the cold darkness of the early morning.

The night was so still; so quiet. Yet the moon, although passed its full, shone with a bright white light, bathing the courtyard with its eerie glow. The figure of Brother Solin was hurrying quietly across the courtyard. She could see that he was carrying something, something white and rolled up in one hand. She found she had to wait in the darkened shadows of the hostel door because the moonlight was too intense to venture straight across the courtyard after him.

Brother Solin vanished round the corner of the building complex which she and Eadulf had visited a few hours before. Only after he had turned the corner did she hurry forward. Having reached the corner, she halted and peered carefully around it. Fidelma stood still, frustrated. There was now no sign at all of Brother Solin; no indication of where he could have disappeared to. She peered into the twilight, turning in all directions. Burning torches throughout the ráth enhanced the curious flickering twilight which spread over the buildings. There was no sign of the northern cleric's stocky figure or even inviting shadows which might indicate where he lurked. The main pathway led directly towards the stables of the ráth and she took a few hesitant steps along it, then stopped and shrugged.

There was no point in attempting to find Solin now. He had gone to ground. There was little choice left to her but to return to the hostel and her interrupted sleep. What had Brother Solin meant? Cashel would fall before the summer had ended. That was what he had said. Summer had but one more month to run. What threat was here and how was Solin involved? That the key to the mystery lay with Solin was now abundantly clear in her mind. But what was the mystery? She still could not see any possible explanation.

She had already moved a reluctant pace or two in the direction of the hostel when she heard a scuffling noise. She held her head to one side. It had come from the direction of the stables. She turned back and moved quietly into the shadows, moving slowly down towards the stable entrance. A brand torch was lit above the stable door throwing a pool of flickering light over the entrance.

Had she heard a smothered cry, drawn out as if in agony? She waited some moments trying to detect any further sound.

A figure abruptly emerged at the stable entrance, standing for a moment as if examining whether it was observed.

It was clad from head to foot in a cloak and a hood which was held by one hand across the lower part of the face. Only the eyes and nose were visible. It was a slender figure, Fidelma could tell that in spite of the cloak which almost shrouded it. It was as the figure glanced along the path that the torchlight fell on the visible portion of its features – fell only momentarily and with shadows dancing this way and that, obscuring the exact contours of the face. However, Fidelma felt in no doubt that she had recognised the distinctive dark eyes and the features of Orla.

The slender figure hurried abruptly into the darkness towards the building which housed Murgal's apartment and others.

Fidelma stood in indecision. Should she follow the furtive figure and if so for what reason? She still had to find Brother Solin. Solin would surely be the last person that Orla would wish a tryst with in the middle of the night after her threat to kill him.

Perhaps Brother Solin had gone elsewhere? Why shouldn't the sister of the chieftain and wife of his tanist visit the stables of the ráth at any hour she wanted to do so? It was no business of Fidelma's and yet . . . yet it was clear that Orla had no wish to be seen. Why? By the time Fidelma had considered the problem the figure had vanished into the darkness and Fidelma was alone in the silence of the night.

Fidelma suppressed a sigh and turned away. If the unlikely had happened and Solin had met Orla in the stable then he must have departed by another exit.

The groan was so low that for a moment she thought it was some movement of the night wind. Then it came again. It was a human sound, she realised within a moment, and it came from the stables.

She turned back and hurried to the doorway, peering into the darkness beyond. There was a gasping of agonised breath.

She could see only the shadowy outlines of the horses now moving restlessly in the dark. She moved to the brand torch outside and took it down from its metal holder. Then, carrying it aloft, she moved forward looking carefully to locate the source of the sound.

The figure lay at the far end of the stable, stretched on its back, one hand across its chest, the other stretched out behind its head.

Fidelma had no trouble recognising the thick-set figure of Brother Solin of Armagh.

She moved quickly to his side but one glance at the blood pumping from his lower chest, where his hand was vainly trying to stem the flow, was enough to show that Brother Solin was dying. His eyes were closed, his lips twisted in pain.

'Solin!' she spoke sharply. 'Who did this to you?'

The man rolled his head but did not open his eyes. The lips twisted further in agony.

'Solin, it is Fidelma. Who stabbed you?'

The lips parted and Fidelma had to lean close to hear the painful gasping breath.

'*Suaviter . . . suaviter in modo . . .*'

The head fell back. Brother Solin of Armagh was dead.

Fidelma sighed and finished off the aphorism, '. . . *fortiter in re*.'

She compressed her lips and stared down at the body. And what did that mean? 'Gentle in manner,' Solin had begun. The end of the aphorism was 'resolute in deed'. Well, his killer had been resolute in this deed but certainly it was not done in gentle manner. Orla had said that she would kill Solin if she saw him again and she had, apparently, kept her word.

Realising Solin was beyond mortal help, she made a quick search of his body. The piece of vellum which Brother Dianach had given him, and which she had seen him carrying, was nowhere in the vicinity. She held her torch aloft and peered carefully around. There was no sign of anything remotely resembling the vellum. Had Orla taken it? If so, why? And what had Orla's anger with Solin to do with Solin's threat of Cashel falling before the summer ended?

Fidelma began to rise, torch in hand, and as she did so she felt a sharp sensation in her back. A harsh male voice hissed: 'Make no further move, lady.'

She recognised the voice of Artgal.

She stood still.

'I shall not move,' Fidelma assured him. 'What do you want of me?'

The man gave a sharp bark of laughter.

'You have a droll sense of humour, lady. Stand still.'

To Fidelma's surprise he suddenly raised his voice in a loud cry for the members of the watch.

'What are you doing?' she demanded, less certain of herself.

'You may turn and face me,' Artgal replied. 'But slowly.'

Fidelma did so, facing the grim warrior-blacksmith who stood sword in hand, its point towards her. In the distance she could hear answering shouts.

'What are you doing?' she demanded again.

'Easy to say,' Artgal smiled sourly. 'What does one do when one finds a murderess bending over the body of her victim?'

'But I did not . . .' she began to protest but was unable to finish before Rudgal and another guard hurried into the stable followed a few seconds later by Laisre himself. The chieftain wore a heavy cloak wrapped around his person as if just aroused from his bed. Artgal stiffened respectfully before his chieftain.

'What does this mean, Artgal?' frowned Laisre, peering around the stable.

'I was on night watch, Laisre. I was passing by the stable and saw the torch which usually lit the doorway was gone. There was a light inside the stable. I entered and saw this woman . . .'

He jerked his head towards Fidelma. Laisre frowned at Artgal's discourtesy and interrupted.

'Do you mean Fidelma of Cashel?'

Artgal was not to be put off.

'I saw this woman bending over the body of the Christian priest, Solin. She is the killer.'

'That is not so!' protested Fidelma aghast at such an accusation.

Laisre had now caught sight of the body on the ground. He exclaimed in surprise and bent forward.

'By the long grasp of Lugh,' he whispered, 'it is, indeed, the Christian envoy from Armagh!' He straightened up and stared in bewilderment at Fidelma. 'What does this mean?'

'I did not kill him,' Fidelma asserted.

'No?' Artgal sneered. 'I am a witness to the deed. Lies will not help you.'

'You are the liar,' replied Fidelma, 'for I defy you to say that you saw me plunge a knife into this poor soul.'

Artgal blinked at the vehemence of her denial.

'I came in and saw you bending over him. There was no one else here.'

'What have you to say in reply to this, Fidelma?' asked Laisre, regarding her in some bewilderment.

'I was following Brother Solin,' Fidelma explained. 'I lost him on the path outside. I was turning back to the hostel when I heard a sound from the stable. A figure came out and disappeared into the night. Then I heard a groan. I went inside and found Brother Solin. He was dying. He whispered something to me that does not make sense. A piece of Latin. Then he expired. I was just about to call the watch when Artgal stuck the point of his sword against my back.'

Artgal guffawed in derision.

'There was no one here except you,' he repeated.

'You have the word of a *dálaigh* of the Brehon courts for the truth of what I say as well as the word of an Eóghanacht princess!'

'Perhaps that is not enough,' replied Artgal, refusing to be intimidated by her.

Laisre held up his hand for silence.

'In this case, Fidelma of Cashel, Artgal is right. Your word is not enough. Why were you following Solin in the first place?'

'Because . . .' Fidelma hesitated, not wishing to reveal her suspicions. If there was some plot to overthrow Cashel, she wondered who else would be involved. Artgal misread her hesitation for guilt and turned in triumphant amusement.

'Because she was angry at his presence,' the warrior interposed. 'We all saw her anger in the council meeting yesterday. There is always some conflict among these Christians. I heard her saying that Armagh and Imleach were rivals, both seeking power over our lives. They are squabbling with one another for the right to dictate to us. That's the root of this matter, believe me.'

Everyone knew of the animosity between Solin and Fidelma. Laisre cast a dubious look at her.

'It is a plausible motive.'

'No. My reason to be suspicious of Brother Solin was a simple one.' Fidelma had been thinking furiously. 'He rose in the night and left the hostel. What good intention does someone have for so doing? I was suspicious of that. So I followed him.'

'You claim that you saw a person standing at the stable door?' Laisre reflected. 'I don't suppose that you could identify who it was?'

'Of course she can't!' interrupted Artgal.

'Let her reply,' advised Laisre, gazing intently at Fidelma.

Fidelma felt a conflict, not wishing to reveal Orla's presence until she had investigated herself, but she realised that she must now justify herself to Laisre.

'Yes, I can,' she answered to Laisre's visible surprise. 'But I would prefer not to reveal the name until I have had a chance to investigate.'

'Investigate?' They were startled by the voice of Murgal who had entered the stable unnoticed. 'If there is an investigation, it is not you, lady, who shall conduct it. I am the Brehon here.'

Laisre glanced at his Druid as if he would dispute this but then shrugged.

'Murgal is right, Fidelma of Cashel. You are a suspect in a murder. You can no longer act as a *dálaigh.* So you must cooperate with us. Tell us the name of the person who you saw outside the stable.'

'If you can,' Artgal added with a sneer.

'I saw the lady Orla,' Fidelma said quietly.

Laisre gave a sharp intake of breath. There was an expression of astonishment on his face.

'What perfidy is this?' demanded Artgal angrily. 'She seeks to put the blame of her deed on the sister of our chieftain! The wife of our tanist!'

'I seek only the truth,' replied Fidelma firmly.

Murgal was staring at her with open suspicion.

'Will this bring the truth nearer, by insulting your host, the chieftain of Gleann Geis, by claiming the lady Orla is a murderess?'

'I said that I saw her emerge from the stable . . .'

'The lady Orla, indeed?' snapped Artgal. 'This is an affront to all our people, Laisre!'

Laisre's face had grown taut.

'If you had given any other name but that one, Fidelma, I might have inclined to a lenient approach and might have even believed you.'

Fidelma thrust out her chin defiantly.

'I can only speak the truth. Find Orla and bring her forth to deny my truth.'

Laisre stood undecided for a moment.

'This is a bad business, Fidelma of Cashel. But this business is better discussed in my council chamber. Artgal, go to the chambers of Colla and Orla and request my sister's presence. Do not even hint at what has happened here or why she is summoned.' He turned abruptly to Murgal. 'You are my Brehon. You will come with us and advise on procedure and judgment.'

Murgal inclined his head gravely. He signalled to Rudgal and the other guard to come forward.

'One of you stay here with the body. Ensure that nothing is touched until I say so. The other may accompany us.'

'Wait!' cried Fidelma as Rudgal moved forward and took her by the arm.

Laisre was moving through the door but halted and turned to regard Fidelma questioningly.

'What is it? Do you wish to change your story?' he demanded.

'How can I alter what is the truth?' replied Fidelma in irritation. 'No; if I am supposed to have killed Solin, even as Artgal entered the stable, then I would have used a knife to kill him. Examine the wound in the body, Murgal. You are a Brehon. How did he die?'

Murgal moved over and took the torch from her hand, bending over the body and examining it carefully.

'One wound, a stab straight through the lower rib cage,' he announced.

'It is not disputed that Brother Solin was stabbed to death,' Laisre said, with a quick glance at Artgal, who had also stayed after Fidelma had called out.

'Artgal says that he saw me bending over Brother Solin's dying form; saw me rising from the body, believing that I had just killed the man.'

'That is exactly as I saw it,' Artgal agreed.

'Very well. I demand to be searched now for the knife.'

'What?' frowned Murgal.

'Search me for the weapon with which I killed Brother Solin. I have not moved from this spot since Artgal came upon me. There has been no time for me to have concealed or cast away that weapon.'

Laisre hesitated and exchanged a hesitant glance with Murgal.

The saturnine Druid rose from the body and handed the torch to Rudgal.

'Then with your permission, Fidelma of Cashel . . . ?'

He moved forward and ran his hands impersonally through her clothing. His search was thorough, systematic and dispassionate.

'She has no weapon hidden on her person,' he reported.

'Now look on the floor by the body,' instructed Fidelma. She knew that no weapon would be found there as she had already cast around in a quick examination when she had seen how Brother Solin had come by his mortal wound.

Laisre sighed deeply.

'We will search, Fidelma. Though you must already be sure that we will find nothing.'

'I am only sure that I did not commit this killing.'

Murgal turned to Rudgal's companion, for Rudgal himself had taken up a position just behind Fidelma in the manner of her escort.

'Search, then, and if you find anything at all, bring it to us in the council chamber. Artgal, you have your instructions. Bring Orla to the chamber. Rudgal, you will escort Fidelma of Cashel.'

With Laisre leading the way and Murgal following, they made

their way across the courtyard. Only a few people had been disturbed by the noise of Artgal's alarm and had gathered, whispering among themselves in the courtyard. Fidelma looked anxiously for Eadulf but he was not there. However, she saw the white-faced Brother Dianach at the hostel door.

Rudgal leant close to her and whispered apologetically in her ear.

'I hope that we will be able to solve this mystery quickly, Sister. But there will be much ill feeling at your accusation of Orla. She is well liked in Gleann Geis.'

In the council chamber Laisre clapped his hands and a servant came forward to relight the oil lamps and stir the embers of the grey fire into a dancing display of sparks before adding fuel to rekindle it.

Laisre sat uncomfortably in his chair of office and motioned Murgal to be seated at his side. He indicated Fidelma to be seated before them while Rudgal took up a discreet position just behind her chair.

'This is a very bad business, Fidelma,' muttered Laisre uneasily. 'This morning we were due to conclude an agreement.'

'I am fully aware of that.' There was coldness in Fidelma's voice. 'Perhaps that is no coincidence? We have already been prevented from such a discussion once before.'

She stared directly at Murgal when she spoke. His face showed anger as he realised her implication.

'My chieftain,' he said harshly, 'as your Brehon, I should conduct this matter from now on.'

Laisre gestured that he relinquished the matter to Murgal. The Brehon gave Fidelma a sallow smile.

'At the moment your case is not good, Fidelma. What have you to say to the proposition put forward by Artgal as to your motive?'

'No argument on theology is worth resorting to violence as a resolution,' replied Fidelma.

'Yet it is not unknown that people of your Faith have violent arguments on matters which are pointless to most people. We know, for example, how many clerics here argue against the authority of Rome and now we hear that Imleach does not even agree with the authority of Armagh. Surely you all worship the same God?'

Fidelma smiled thinly.

'That itself is arguable.'

'This Brother Solin was so certain that he represented the true way to your God and that all others dwelt in ignorance. I suppose you also argue that your way is the only way?'

Fidelma shook her head.

'I would not be that impertinent, Murgal. There are many paths to the same objective. We can be absolutely certain only about those things that we do not properly comprehend. To have a path through life made certain is the aspiration of most people in this unclear and uncertain existence. But certainty is often an illusion. We are born to doubt. Those who know nothing, doubt nothing.'

Murgal's expression was one of amazement.

'If I did not see that you carry the symbols of the new Faith, Fidelma of Cashel, I would swear that you were of the old Faith. Perhaps you are wearing the wrong cloak?'

'My Faith is the best armour in which to travel through life but it is the worst cloak.'

There was a silence as they tried to work out her meaning. It was broken by the sounds of voices outside and Artgal threw open the door. Colla, looking as if he had just risen from bed, a cloak wrapped around him, entered. Behind him, came Orla, looking sleepy and tousled-haired. Fidelma was surprised to see Orla's dishevelled appearance as if she, too, had just been awakened from a deep sleep. She also had a cloak wrapped around her nightgown.

'What is it?' demanded Colla. 'What demands our presence in the middle of the night? What has happened? There are people standing around the courtyard in whispering groups.'

Fidelma noticed that Artgal was standing just inside the door with a grin of satisfaction on his features.

'Has Artgal not informed you of what has taken place?' Fidelma asked suspiciously.

Colla shook his head emphatically.

'He simply roused us and told us that Laisre wished to see us in the council chamber at once.'

Murgal intervened in annoyance.

'I am in charge of these proceedings,' he announced. 'I am conducting these proceedings in my office as Brehon.' He turned to Orla. 'Orla, were you at the stables within the last hour?'

Orla's look of bewilderment could surely not be feigned. Fidelma began to have a sinking feeling. Could she have been mistaken? No; she was certain.

'Are you making some jest, Murgal? If so, it is in poor taste.'

'I am not jesting. Where have you been this last hour?'

'In the same place that I have been since returning after last evening's festivities,' Orla replied perplexed. 'In my husband's bed. We have not stirred until Artgal came knocking upon our door.'

The tanist's wife was very convincing.

'And Colla will doubtless confirm this?' smiled Murgal grimly.

'Of course I will,' Colla snapped irritably. 'We have not stirred these last few hours. Now, what does this mean?'

'I can sympathise with your annoyance, Colla,' Murgal replied. 'There is worse to come. The cleric from Armagh, Solin, was stabbed to death in the stable within this last hour.'

Colla let out a low whistle of astonishment and Orla's expression of bewilderment seemed to grow broader.

'But what has this to do with us? Why do you ask if I had been at the stable . . . ? Oh!' Her eyes grew rounded as she stared at Fidelma. 'I had told you that I would kill that pig! You think that . . . but it was just a figure of speech. I did not do so.'

Laisre intervened diplomatically.

'Someone thought that they had seen you there.'

'Well, it was not I,' replied Orla firmly.

'And I can vouch for that,' added Colla.

Murgal glanced at Fidelma.

'I do not think there is anything to be gained in pursuing this matter, Fidelma. Do you?'

However, Fidelma turned to Orla.

'Yet you do remember telling me that if you met Brother Solin again you would kill him? That was yesterday afternoon?'

Orla flushed.

'Yes, but, as I said, I did not mean . . .'

'You said that you would kill him,' repeated Fidelma firmly. 'Why was that?'

Orla bit her lip, glancing at Colla under lowered eyebrows.

'He insulted me.'

'In what way?' Fidelma pressed.

'He . . . he made a lewd suggestion.'

Colla started angrily at his wife's confession.

'What? You did not tell me this.'

Orla was dismissive.

'I was able to deal with the lascivious pig. I slapped him hard. When I said that I would kill him if I saw him again . . .'

'You did not mean it?' intervened Laisre. 'Of course, we understand.' He looked at Fidelma. 'The fact is, my sister's movements are now accounted for whatever opinions she held of Brother Solin.'

Fidelma opened her mouth to protest but then shrugged her shoulders in silent acquiescence.

The testimony of Colla and the apparently genuine look of astonishment on Orla's face told her that no amount of questioning would change their story. Fidelma was a pragmatist. She knew that it was no use pounding away at an immovable object even if she had irresistible force on her side and that she had not. Only she knew what she had seen at the stable door had been a reality.

'I will not pursue the matter for the moment. Let Orla and her husband return to their disturbed slumber.'

Colla hesitated. He looked to Murgal and to Laisre in curiosity. When he spoke, his voice was tinged with a belligerence.

'Just what is going on here? Why does Fidelma of Cashel accuse my wife of this deed apart from those hasty words which she uttered?'

Murgal held up a hand in pacification.

'As to who killed Solin, we have yet to be certain, Colla. And it seems that it was only a mistake of identity by someone passing in the darkness that involved Orla. Best go to bed now and we will discuss this in the morning.'

Reluctantly, Colla escorted his wife from the chamber.

Artgal was still standing, with folded arms, grinning smugly at Fidelma.

'I was right all along, eh?' he sneered at her. 'Your ruse did not work.'

Murgal appeared annoyed at the warrior's attitude.

'I would return to your tasks, Artgal. You may leave Fidelma of Cashel with us and remember this, she is still the sister of the king at Cashel. Respect is her due, whatever she has done.'

Artgal ground his teeth in anger at this rebuke but turned on his heel and left.

Murgal returned a troubled look to Fidelma.

'Artgal is in many ways primitive to the extent that he has little respect for anything which cannot hurt him. Cashel and the reach of its king is too abstract a thought to him. He cannot give you respect unless he experiences the power your brother represents.'

Fidelma shrugged indifferently.

'If you have shame, forebear to pluck the beard of a dead lion.'

'An interesting thought,' Murgal mused. 'Is that your own epigram?'

'Martial. A Latin poet. But I do not want respect for who my ancestors or relatives are. Only for what I am.'

'That is an argument that might not count with Artgal,' interposed Laisre. 'At the moment you are someone accused of murder.'

Fidelma felt that they had fenced enough.

'The one thing that I am sure of is that I saw Orla at the stable.'

'It cannot be so,' Laisre rebuked her. 'Unless you now accuse both Orla and Colla of lying.'

'I can only say what I saw,' Fidelma insisted.

'Orla is my sister.' Laisre was unhappy. 'I can assure you that she is not one to lie. Colla is my tanist, my heir-elect. You accuse him of lying to protect his wife? If that is the sum total of your defence then you would do well to reflect on matters.'

'So you have both decided that I am as guilty as Artgal claims that I am?'

Murgal's expression was dour.

'You are a *dálaigh*, Fidelma. You know the procedure that must now be undertaken. Tell me, what else am I to conclude from what I have heard? We have a witness in Artgal. In counter claim, you have accused the sister of our chieftain. Her husband is a witness to the fact that she was not where you claim she was. And your only argument is to call her and her husband liars.'

Laisre was flushed. It appeared that the offence of Fidelma's charge had finally sunk into him. He was unable to restrain the anger from his voice.

'I have to warn you, Fidelma of Cashel, and with all respect to your rank, when you accuse my sister of murder and then lying, you go too far.'

'I saw what I saw,' replied Fidelma stubbornly.

'Fidelma of Cashel, I am chieftain of my people. We do not share a religion but we share a common law, a law far older than the time when Patrick the Briton was allowed to sit on Laoghaire's council to study and revise it. The law guides me, as chieftain, to the path that I must take. You know that path as well as I. The matter is now entirely in the hands of Murgal, my Brehon.'

Laisre rose abruptly and left the chamber.

Fidelma had also risen from her chair to face Murgal.

'I did not kill Brother Solin,' she insisted.

'Then you must prove that. As the law prescribes, we will meet in this place nine days from now at which time you will have to answer this charge. In the meantime, you will be placed under guard in our Chamber of Isolation.'

'Nine days?' Fidelma gasped in astonishment. 'What can I do while I am incarcerated?'

'It is a matter prescribed by law, as well you know it,' confirmed Murgal. 'For the crime of murder, I can do no less.'

Fidelma felt a sudden cold foreboding.

'How can I prove my innocence if I am not even allowed movement within this ráth?' she demanded.

'Then you must find a Brehon to act for you as anyone else must do in your place. We cannot make special allowances to rank and privilege.'

'A Brehon?' Fidelma was cynical. 'I do not suppose there is an abundance of lawyers in Gleann Geis?'

Murgal chose not to answer her. He signalled to Rudgal who still stood behind her chair.

'Take Fidelma of Cashel to the Chamber of Isolation. Make sure you treat her with respect and obey her wishes as regards comfort and access to anything which may help her defence . . . within reason, that is.'

Rudgal moved forward to touch her elbow. He gazed compassionately at her for a moment before averting his eyes to focus just above her head.

'Come with me, Sister Fidelma,' he said softly, his voice a monotone.

Fidelma glanced again at Murgal but the austere Druid had turned away, hands behind his back, and seemed intent on examining the flames of the iron brazier which heated the chamber. There would be no sympathy forthcoming from any pleading with Murgal, the Brehon of Gleann Geis.

Chapter Twelve

Rudgal led the way from the chamber and Fidelma followed without another word. There was nothing more that could be said. For the first time in her life, in spite of all the occasions when her life was under threat, Fidelma had a feeling which she could only describe as coming close to panic. Nine days incarcerated in a cell with the accusation of murder hanging over her and being unable to question anyone or gather evidence in her own defence was an appalling prospect.

Rudgal conducted her silently across the stone-flagged courtyard. Among the knots of people gathered, the animated conversations were no longer in suppressed whispers. There was an anger among the people. Fidelma looked in vain for a sight of Eadulf. Rudgal took her to a building on the opposite side of the ráth, behind the stables. It was a squat, single-storey building of grey granite. Its sole means of entrance was a great wooden door. Rudgal pushed it open and Fidelma could hear the loud clamour of voices interspersed with coarse laughter coming from the interior. Rudgal seemed to anticipate what was passing through Fidelma's mind.

'This is the quarters of those who volunteer to serve the chieftain as a bodyguard, Sister Fidelma. When we stay at the ráth we use this as our dormitory and it is the only building where we may imprison any who transgress the law. There is a single cell at the far corner of this building. It is called the Chamber of Isolation. Take no notice of the noise. I am afraid that some of the men are still a little drunk after the feasting last night.'

Rudgal was punctilious in his treatment of her. She appreciated that. She was glad that it was Rudgal who had been given the distasteful task of escorting her to the prison and not Artgal.

Fidelma preceded him inside the building. He followed and closed the door before conducting her along a short passage, beyond the room where the guards were still engaged in noisy revelry, and which then turned at a right angle to where there was a door with a heavy iron key in its lock.

'It is poor accommodation, I am afraid, Sister Fidelma,' Rudgal said as he opened it.

'I will try to manage,' Fidelma smiled wanly.

Rudgal looked embarrassed.

'You have but to call on me and I will do what is in my power to aid you providing that you do not ask me to break my oath of loyalty to my chieftain.'

Fidelma regarded him solemnly.

'I promise you that I shall not call on you to break such an oath . . . unless there is a greater oath involved.'

The warrior wagon-maker frowned.

'A greater oath? You mean a duty to the Faith?'

'Not even that. Your chieftain has sworn an oath to Cashel. Cashel is supreme in all things. If your chieftain breaks an oath to Cashel then you are absolved from breaking an oath to him for he will be in rebellion against his lawful king. Do you understand that?'

'I think so. I will do what I can for you, Sister Fidelma.'

'I am appreciative of your service, Rudgal.'

She examined her cell distastefully. It was a cold, damp place with only a straw palliasse on the floor and little else. It smelt foul and had obviously not been used for a while. There was only a tiny slit of a window high up in one wall. Rudgal found an oil lamp and lit it. He gazed around and was also filled with aversion.

'It is the best I can do, Sister,' he apologised yet again.

Fidelma felt almost inclined to smile, so mournful a countenance did he have.

'You are not responsible for my being here, Rudgal. But misfortune has brought me here and now I must apply my mind to extracting myself from this place.'

'Do you need anything, Sister?' he asked again.

Fidelma thought rapidly.

'Yes. I need some personal items from the hostel. My *marsupium*, for example. Would you go there and ask Brother Eadulf, who must still be asleep, to bring them to me at once.'

'Bring the Saxon here . . . ?' Rudgal seemed hesitant.

'Do not worry, Rudgal. Brother Eadulf must act as my *dálaigh* now that I am unable to move freely. It is my right to appoint him to represent me and, as my *dálaigh*, he can visit me without restriction.'

'Very well, Sister. I will fetch the Saxon.'

He hesitated a moment longer before leaving, remembering to bring the great wooden door shut behind him with an ominous clang. Fidelma heard the key turning in the great iron lock on the door and felt an unfamiliar sinking sensation. She had never felt such a feeling of despair in her life.

She tried to be practical and brought her mind back to the matter of her immediate survival, looking around the darkened, damp cell with repugnance. The odour was foul. She shivered and placed her arms folded around her shoulders as if she found comfort there.

Something moved amidst the straw palliasse of the mattress. A dark grey shape of a rat scuttled out and went disappearing into some hole between the granite bricks. She shivered violently and began to pace up and down. She hoped Eadulf would not be long. After she had given him instructions, she would try and find escape in the art of the *dercad*, the act of meditation, by which countless generations of Irish mystics had calmed extraneous thought and mental irritations, seeking the state of *sitcháin* or peace. She was a regular practitioner of the ancient art in times of stress. But never in her life had Fidelma found herself in need of the art of meditation as she did now.

It was only fifteen minutes later, though it seemed like days, when a pale-faced Eadulf entered the cell. He was followed by Rudgal. There was an expression of anxiety on his face which pinched and distorted his features.

'Fidelma, what ill-fortune brings you hither? Oh, I have heard the briefest details from Rudgal here. But tell me how I can secure your release?'

Fidelma was standing in the middle of the room and smiled placatingly in answer to Eadulf's anxiety.

Rudgal spoke before she could respond.

'While you instruct the Saxon, I will see if I can bring you something to make life more bearable in this hovel.' He left them both together, shutting the door behind him.

'What can I do?' demanded Eadulf again in such anxiety that his voice sounded unnatural in the echoing cell. 'God, how I chastise myself. I was so dead to the world, I did not awake until Rudgal came and told me that you were here. Why didn't you wake me when you left the hostel? I might have been able to prevent this from happening. If I had been with you . . .'

'Firstly, you must be calm, Eadulf,' instructed Fidelma sharply. 'You are now my only hope for release.'

Eadulf swallowed hard.

'Tell me what I must do.'

'Alas, I cannot bid you sit down in this place and I do fear that the straw palliasse is filled with vermin which may not provide a comfortable resting place. So we must stand a while and I will explain what happened.'

She was finishing her story when the door of the cell opened again. It was Rudgal who carried a wooden bench with him.

'Forgive me, Sister, for taking such a time but I have foraged for a bed and something to sit on. I will bring the bed in a moment, something to keep you off this wet, chill floor. In the meantime, this bench will serve.'

Fidelma thanked the man warmly.

'Rudgal has offered his help and I think we may trust him,' she added for Eadulf's benefit.

Eadulf nodded impatiently.

Rudgal pushed the bench against one of the drier walls of the cell before he left them again.

Fidelma sat down and brought Eadulf quickly up to date with her ordeal. Eadulf groaned in anguish when she had finished and spread his hands in a hopeless gesture.

'With both Laisre and Murgal against you, I do not know what to do.'

'You must find a way,' Fidelma said firmly. 'After all, that is a task of a *dálaigh*.'

'But I am not a trained advocate of your law,' protested Eadulf.

'But I am. I will give you advice and you must find a way of demonstrating that I have told the truth. It is perplexing. Orla and her husband, Colla, are so persuasive in their argument. But, Eadulf, I swear that I saw her coming out of the stable. She and Colla must be lying. The fact that I identified her seems to have greatly troubled her brother, Laisre. I suppose that I can understand this as an affront to his family honour but I do believe that if the matter was down to a conflict of opinion between Artgal and myself, Laisre might have rejected Artgal's word. The fact that I implicated his sister has caused him to take great anger at me.'

'I do not understand why he should be so angry as to deny you a fair hearing.'

'Ah, family honour is always a hard thing to understand. I cannot say that his behaviour is unfair. Nor Murgal's actions, come to that. Both are behaving within the law.'

'Well, I must get you out of this place. How should I go about it?'

'I have to clear my name and find out who murdered Brother Solin. I cannot do that while I remain in this cell. Murgal says that I must remain here for nine days according to law until my trial.'

Eadulf ran a hand through his hair, frowning.

'But if I remember rightly, in your courts, people of rank and who can pay a fee can be released after swearing an oath that they will reappear before the court when the trial is held.'

Fidelma smiled appreciatively at Eadulf's knowledge.

'You remember correctly. There is such a law. You must see if you are able to operate that law to secure my release. There is a library in this place. Murgal has control of it. Do you recall that I showed you the building where it is housed?'

Eadulf made an affirmative gesture.

'Then you must look up the law on this matter. You must then apply to Murgal, for remember Murgal is the Brehon in this valley. Demand a hearing as to why I may not be released, under the law, to appear in nine days' time. If I am at liberty, we have a chance to prove whose hand was on that knife which ended Brother Solin's life.'

'Would they have such a library of law books here?' demanded Eadulf doubtfully. 'Murgal is a pagan.'

Fidelma chuckled softly in spite of her condition.

'Pagan or Christian, we are a literate people, Eadulf. The Druids kept books long before the coming of Patrick and the adoption of the Latin alphabet. Did we not worship Ogma, the god of learning and literacy after whom our first alphabet was named? And the law was the law eons before the new Faith came to these shores.'

Eadulf pursed his lips disapprovingly.

'Are you suggesting that I ask Murgal if he has such law books?'

Fidelma took him seriously.

'Pagan or Christian, advisor to Laisre or not, Murgal is a Brehon and sworn to uphold the law.'

Eadulf shook his head dubiously.

'And even if he did, what book should I look for?'

'Firstly, you must study the text called *Cóic Conara Fugill* – the five paths to judgment. Also, examine the *Berrad Airechta*. I believe you will find the necessary procedures relating to my condition in those works. Acquaint yourself on procedure and seize the path the law provides to secure my release.'

'I must remind you, Fidelma, that I did not study law in this land,' protested Eadulf. 'I studied the Faith and the practice of medicine only.'

'You have often told me that you were an hereditary magistrate in your own land, Eadulf. Now is the time to use your talent. You have seen my methods and seen me plead in the courts many times. Turn to "the five paths to judgment" and consider the law of security called *árach.* I am placing my trust in you, Eadulf.'

Eadulf rose uncomfortably.

'I will try not to destroy that faith.'

He reached out both hands and held her shoulders, extending his arms for a moment. Their eyes met and then, with a faint colour to his cheeks, Eadulf turned to the cell door. It opened almost at once as if Rudgal had been standing awaiting him. He stood aside as Eadulf brushed by.

A moment later Rudgal carried a wooden cot into the cell. Then he brought in blankets and a pitcher of water. The warrior-cum-wagon-maker looked anxious.

'The Saxon brother looks preoccupied, Sister Fidelma,' he muttered as he manipulated the cot into position. Before she could comment, he added: 'This will make your sojourn more comfortable, I hope.'

'As a favour to me, Rudgal, or as a favour to the Faith, I would like you to keep a watchful eye on Brother Eadulf. He may need help. Help him as you would help me.'

'I shall, Sister Fidelma. Leave matters with me.'

With no further word, Fidelma sat herself down on the bench and began to compose herself for the *dercad.* She did not even notice Rudgal leave the cell or hear the clanging of the door.

It still lacked several hours until dawn and Eadulf realised that he would have to wait until then before approaching Murgal for permission to use his library. Murgal, in fact, would have only just retired after the excitement of the night. Eadulf realised that if he were to help Fidelma he needed to be fully alert. For two nights he had not slept well and so he decided to attempt to sleep for a further hour or two. In spite of his mental state, he had barely laid his head on the bed when he was dead to the world.

He awoke hearing sounds of activity in the main room of the guests' hostel. For a moment Eadulf did not remember the activities of the night before. Then they came to him in a depressing flood. He rose and went down to the bath house.

Cruinn was there staring balefully at him. And the young monk, Brother Dianach, was sitting obviously distressed in a corner. As Eadulf came down the stairs the boy's face creased in anger. It was clear that the death of Brother Solin and the arrest of Fidelma had been the talking point of the ráth that morning.

'Why did she do it?' Brother Dianach's first words in fierce accusation struck Eadulf like a whip. The boy half rose to his feet as though to physically threaten Eadulf. 'Did she hate him so much?'

Eadulf stood at the foot of the stair for a moment regarding Brother Dianach sadly.

'Sister Fidelma did not kill Brother Solin,' he replied calmly.

Cruinn muttered something beneath her breath in suppressed anger. The cheery, portly woman had vanished and in her place a fierce harridan had appeared.

Eadulf looked from one to the other of them and shrugged. He could see that neither of them was in any mood to hear Fidelma's side of the story. He turned into the bath house. By the time that he had finished his toilet there was no sign of Cruinn or Brother Dianach. He made his way up the stairs to his room and dressed. Returning, he found that Cruinn had not left him anything with which to break his fast. It was obviously her protest. Eadulf sighed and went in search of what he could forage.

After a meagre meal of dried bread and some cold meat and mead he sallied forth on the first of his quests. At the building where Fidelma had indicated Murgal's library to be housed, the first person he encountered was the attractive apothecary, Marga. After what Fidelma had told him about her outburst when she had discovered that he had studied herbal medicine, he expected her to brush by him but to his surprise she stopped in front of him.

'I cannot express regret,' she said without preamble. It was clear that she, too, had heard the news. 'Either for the pig Solin or for your Christian friend. They deserve to be with each other in your Otherworld. I can understand any woman who encountered Solin wishing to end his life.'

Eadulf stood his ground.

'You are entitled to your opinions, Marga. But Fidelma did not kill Brother Solin.'

The girl's eyes filled with disbelief.

'So? And you will prove this?'

'I shall prove it,' he corrected. 'I shall discover the truth.'

Marga's lips parted in a sneer.

'Ah, yes. Speaking of truth – I gave you a gift of the foxglove when I thought I was helping someone heal themselves who had no knowledge of medicines. Since you lied to me, there is now a charge. You see, I place a value on truth, Saxon. I think our Brehon would also like to know what value you place on truth.'

Eadulf flushed. He reached into his purse and held out a *screpall*.

'Take it and prosper by it,' he said shortly.

Marga took the coin, examined it, and then deliberately, she let it fall to the ground. There was a smile of contempt on her lips. She seemed to expect Eadulf to scramble on the ground to retrieve the coin. Eadulf simply stared back into her cold eyes for a moment before proceeding into the building.

His task was not going to be easy if the people of the ráth of Laisre had all decided that Fidelma was guilty before her trial.

He made his way up towards the tower where Fidelma had said Murgal's apartment and library were. But there were many corridors and several doors. He stood hesitating, wondering what to do.

'Ha, the Saxon! What are you doing here?'

Eadulf found himself gazing at the flirtatious features of Esnad, the daughter of Orla. She stood in the doorway of an apartment. She was leaning against the door jamb regarding him with a seductive smile.

'I am looking for Murgal's library,' he said.

She pouted.

'Oh. Books! Why don't you come in and join me for a game of Brandub instead? If you don't know how to play it, I will teach you.' She gestured invitingly into the room beyond. 'These are my apartments.'

Eadulf flushed in his confusion at her wanton expression.

'I have much work to do, Esnad,' he said respectfully, remembering that she was, after all, the daughter of the tanist. 'If you could tell me where Murgal's library is . . . ?'

'What do you want with my library, Saxon?' came the deep tones of the Druid. The inquisitorial figure of Murgal stood at the bottom of the stairs.

Esnad let out a hiss of disapproval and flounced into her apartment, slamming the door.

Eadulf was somewhat relieved and turned to the Druid almost in gratitude.

'In truth, I was looking for you to ask your permission to examine your library.'

Murgal's eyebrows rose slightly.

'And what service can it provide you?'

'I am in need of two law texts and it may be that you might have these.'

Murgal was obviously puzzled.

'Why would you need such law texts?'

'You have incarcerated Fidelma of Cashel.'

'I have,' agreed Murgal simply.

'She has appointed me her Brehon.'

Murgal looked surprised.

'You will plead for her? But you are a foreigner and you are not qualified as a *dálaigh.*'

'A person who is not qualified in law has the right to conduct a case before a Brehon if they wish to take the risk,' Eadulf pointed out. 'Even a foreigner. I know enough of your law to argue that.'

Murgal thought for a moment and then agreed.

'Such a person is called a "tongueless person" but if he wastes the court's time he could be fined heavily. Are you prepared to take that risk?'

'I am.'

'Well,' Murgal admitted, 'I cannot say that I am surprised that you will support her. But you will have little enough to do. The case is quite clear. Her guilt is obvious.'

Eadulf was quietly outraged.

'And have you decided what Fidelma's motive was for killing a fellow cleric?' he demanded.

'Oh yes. Christians are always fighting with one another when they cannot find anyone else to fight with. What is it that you supporters of Rome call it? *Odium theologicum?* There is always mutual hatred among you.'

'I see. As a Brehon you have already pronounced judgment,' snapped Eadulf. 'Perhaps I should expand your knowledge of Latin with the phrase *maxim audi alteram partem* – hear the other side.'

Murgal blinked and for a moment Eadulf thought he would explode in rage. Then, to Eadulf's surprise, he started to chuckle.

'Well said, Saxon; well said! You may examine the law books in my library and I wish you well of them.'

'There is a second thing I would ask of you?'

'What further service do you wish of me?'

'Fidelma of Cashel is incarcerated until her trial.'

'Yes. There is a statutory limitation of nine days in a murder trial,' agreed Murgal. 'After that, she has to answer before the law. No one is immune from this process.'

'But Fidelma of Cashel cannot prepare her defence unless she is at liberty.'

'The law is the law, Saxon. Even I cannot change the law to suit an individual.'

Eadulf bowed his head in acknowledgment.

'The law is the law,' he echoed softly. 'But the stricture of the law is often open to interpretation. Surely the word of Fidelma of Cashel, one of rank in this land, is enough to secure her release and to act as *árach* or surety until the trial. Imprisoning her is not justice.'

Murgal regarded him thoughtfully.

'You seem familiar enough with our law to make use of such concepts as *árach*, Saxon.'

Eadulf decided honesty was a better policy.

'I know little enough. That is why I need to consult some law texts. But as I am representing Fidelma of Cashel, I would like to officially request a hearing before you tomorrow so that I might plead Fidelma's case for release before her trial.'

'What law books do you want?' Murgal inquired with interest.

Eadulf named the texts which Fidelma had advised him to look at. Murgal was thoughtful.

'You have made a wise choice, Saxon,' he said begrudgingly.

He gestured to Eadulf to accompany him, leading him up the steps into a tower room. Eadulf was surprised to find it was filled with lines of pegs and book holders. There were even some stands containing wands which he recognised from previous occasions as 'wands of the poets' – texts written in the ancient Irish Ogham script which dated back centuries before the Faith was brought to Ireland. Unhesitating, Murgal went to two satchels and took out the volumes.

'These are the texts you require. Take them to the guests' hostel and study them but they must be returned as soon as possible,' he instructed, handing them to Eadulf.

'I shall look after them carefully, have no fear.'

Murgal ushered him out of the room and locked the door again.

'And the hearing?' pressed Eadulf. 'Will you hear the plea on Fidelma's behalf for her release pending her trial?'

Murgal shook his head negatively.

'It is not a matter I can give an answer to immediately. Some thought must be given to it. To call a hearing necessitates some fresh arguments and might go against the wish of my chieftain, Laisre.'

'Doesn't the law stand above a chieftain's wishes?'

Murgal smiled thinly.

'Is that your only argument?'

'No. There is the undeniable argument that Fidelma of Cashel is not just a religieuse, or just an advocate of the court. She is also sister to the king of Muman and as such she has a rank that must be respected. It is her right to be heard as to why she may not stand liberate on her own recognisances.'

'I will let you know my answer before this night is over. It will also depend on whether you tell me that you have found the right path to judgment in those law books you hold. May justice guide your quest, Saxon.'

Thus dismissed, Eadulf made his way carefully towards the guests' hostel. He was passing along the wall of the building under the walkway against the wall of the ráth when some sixth sense made him swing aside from the path. He did not know what prompted him to do so. Perhaps it was some extra-sensory perception, or some faint sound heard in a fraction of a second, or some other inexplicable sense. A large, heavy stone, dislodged from the battlement, crashed at his feet, so close that he felt the hiss of air and had his foot been so much as an inch or so before him it would have been smashed.

Eadulf sprang back, losing hold of the law books which dropped to the ground.

His heart beating fast he peered up quickly. A shadow darted back before he could identify it.

He stood for a moment or two with the sweat standing out on his forehead. He had passed within a fraction of death.

Then he was aware of a figure hurrying down the steps from the battlement towards him. He stepped back to defend himself.

The figure was Rudgal. There was an odd expression on his features.

'Are you all right, Brother?' he asked anxiously.

Eadulf composed himself as the threat receded.

'I seem to have put my heart in the place where my throat is,' he admitted.

Rudgal was bending down and picking up the fallen law books.

'It was a near thing, Brother. Such accidents can be dangerous.'

Eadulf's eyes narrowed.

'Accident you say?'

Rudgal's expression was bland.

'Wasn't it an accident? Some of these stone blocks on the battlement are ill-placed and loose.'

'There was someone up there on the battlement who gave that particular stone a helping hand.'

Rudgal was shocked.

'Are you so sure, Brother? Did you recognise anyone?'

'I saw no one that I could identify,' confessed Eadulf. 'But you were up on the battlement. You must have seen whoever it was?'

Rudgal shook his head.

'There were a few people about. I was walking along and heard only your cry. When I peered over, I saw you and the stone at your feet. You seemed to be shaken. I saw no . . .'

He paused with a thoughtful frown.

'You saw . . . what?' prompted Eadulf.

'Probably nothing. There was the young brother, what is his name – Dianach? Yes, I saw him walking in the other direction with Esnad and, of course, Artgal was walking nearby with Laisre, who was talking with him. Perhaps they saw something, though I do not think so otherwise they would have come to see what was wrong. No one else had apparently heard your cry of alarm.'

Eadulf shook his head firmly.

'I do not think that will get us very far,' he reflected, taking the books from Rudgal's hands. 'Artgal is the chief witness against Fidelma and young Brother Dianach made his dislike of me very clear this morning. No. We will not say any more about this.'

He left Rudgal and continued back to the hostel. Inside, he put the books carefully on the table and sat before them. He yawned and wished that he had had even more sleep. Then he thought of Fidelma in her cell and felt suddenly penitent for there would certainly be no sleep for her alone in that unfriendly place. But even the hostel was deserted. Neither Cruinn nor Brother Dianach had returned to the hostel. It was plain that they were avoiding him.

Slowly he began to turn the pages of the law texts.

Time passed, the characters on the pages began to take on a life of their own, twisting and swimming before his eyes. He seemed unable to take in the easiest of concepts. His eyelids felt heavier and heavier and his head began to droop.

He must have fallen asleep.

There was a sound at the door.

Eadulf jerked his head up from the manuscript, blinking rapidly and uncertain of where he was for the moment.

It was Rudgal who stood on the threshold.

'What is it?' Eadulf asked, yawning and feeling ashamed that he had dropped asleep. He pushed the law book away from him and turned to Rudgal.

'I come with a message from Murgal, Brother. It is about the hearing which you requested.'

'And?' Eadulf was fully awake now and he rose to his feet. 'Will he grant me a hearing tomorrow?'

'Murgal says that you are within your rights to demand such a hearing before him as Brehon of Gleann Geis. I am to return the books to him – he said you would know which ones he wants. And, further, if you can assure him, through me, that you can cite procedure under law, he will accede to such a hearing. But the hearing must be held in the chieftain's council chamber this afternoon before the evening meal.'

Eadulf was startled.

'What hour is it now?' Eadulf demanded, feeling that Murgal was playing cat and mouse with him.

'Nearly an hour after the noon meal.'

'That means I have only a few hours to prepare.'

Eadulf tried to quell his sudden panic. Rudgal's face was expressionless as he watched him.

'Murgal says that if you are unable to make your plea by this afternoon, then you have not comprehended the necessary law.'

Eadulf ran a hand distractedly through his hair.

'At least Murgal is prepared to hold the hearing,' he admitted. 'You will have to tell him that I shall need another hour or so with these books. I shall return them later.'

He looked down at the open law book on the table in apprehension.

'It seems my only hope is that he will accept the oath of Sister Fidelma, take into account her rank and her position as an Eóghanacht princess to free her until the hearing in nine days' time.'

Rudgal smiled warmly.

'It will be good for the Sister Fidelma to be released from the Chamber of Isolation, Brother. It is not fitting for one such as she to be incarcerated there.'

'I wish I were optimistic about the outcome.'

Rudgal's eyes narrowed.

'You do not think that you are knowledgeable enough to secure freedom for Sister Fidelma?' he demanded. He gestured to the books on the table. 'What do these books tell you to do?'

Eadulf gave a painful laugh.

'They tell me that my knowledge of law is poor and that the little that I do possess is not sufficient to ensure her release.'

'Surely there is something you can do?'

'There is only one thing other than Murgal's acceptance of the oath of Fidelma as sister of the king of Cashel as guarantee for her appearing before him at the time of the trial.'

'What is that?' demanded Rudgal.

'The other thing would be if I could show that Artgal is not a reliable witness.'

Rudgal rubbed his chin thoughtfully.

'He is an ambitious man. A first-class blacksmith and a good warrior, I know that.'

'Perhaps he has some secret. Maybe he betrayed a colleague in battle?'

Rudgal chuckled.

'Look somewhere else, Brother. We fought together, side by side, at Hill of Áine against the Arada Cliach last year. He showed himself courageous in battle.'

Eadulf was staring at the man in surprise.

'You fought there against the Arada Cliach? But that means that you fought against the army of the king of Cashel?'

Rudgal dismissed the matter with a grim smile.

'We answered the call of our chieftain, Laisre, who in turn served Eoganán of the Uí Fidgente. But now Eoganán is dead and there is peace between the Uí Fidgente and Cashel again. So there is peace between Laisre and Cashel, too. But Artgal's ambition lay not in wars. I know this, for he said his ambition was soon to be fulfilled in peace.'

'I swear I do not understand your internal politics,' muttered Eadulf. 'Even if I did it still would not help me. Apart from Artgal's prowess as a blacksmith and a warrior, is there nothing you can tell me about him? What is this you say about Artgal's ambition?'

'Ambition is no crime.'

'But you said that he indicated that his ambition might be fulfilled.'

'In fact, he swore as much this morning.'

'What ambition?' insisted Eadulf.

'To expand his small farmstead and smithy and employ an apprentice, to be able to afford to have a wife. You'll find nothing sinister in that.'

'Indeed. Innocent enough. Why did it become an ambition?'

'He had not been able to save enough to buy milch cows to form the basis of his stock. His smithy is inactive because Goban is the chief smith here. Most people go to him for more crafted work. Artgal's farmstead is poor and he is always looking for work. He mainly ekes out an existence on the largesse he receives from Laisre as his bodyguard. But now he has been able to purchase two milch cows.'

'Well, there is nothing in that which I can use to show that his word is not to be trusted.'

Rudgal agreed.

'True enough. Though I don't think he actually saved to buy the cows. Two days ago he was without money. We were gambling at Ronan's farm and Artgal was losing heavily. At one point, he even offered to put up his farmstead and smithy shop as surety for his bet.'

Eadulf was not particularly interested.

'So he won the cows or the money for them by gambling. That, too, is not to be condemned.'

Rudgal shook his head.

'But he didn't. He won sparingly enough to ensure that he did not lose his farmstead. He did not make any money. He left the game as broke as he had entered it. He took out only what he had put in.'

Eadulf felt a flicker of interest.

'So where did he get the two cows from and how do you know about this?'

'Only a short while ago I heard him talking to Ronan about nearly losing his farmstead in the game that night. He said, and I overheard this clearly, that fortune had smiled on him because he had just been given two milch cows as a reward for telling the truth.'

Eadulf looked up sharply.

'He used those very words?'

'The very words. He also said that in nine days' time he would have a further milch cow to make three. With three milch cows he would be secure.'

Eadulf was staring hard at the fair-haired warrior who did not seem concerned at the effect that his words had.

'Just repeat this – you said that you heard Artgal say that he had been given two cows as a reward for telling the truth and that in nine days' time he would receive a further cow? Are those the exact words?'

Rudgal scratched his head as if this helped him to concentrate.

'Indeed. Those are the words he said.'

'But are you sure that he particularly used the expression "in nine days' time" he would receive another cow? That is what he said?'

'Oh yes. Nine days were mentioned.'

Eadulf sat back and drummed his fingers on the table top.

'Is this helpful?' inquired Rudgal after a moment or two when Eadulf did not make any further comment.

Eadulf brought his gaze back to the man absently.

'What? Helpful? Yes . . . perhaps. I don't know. I must think on this.'

Rudgal coughed nervously.

'Then shall I return to Murgal? If so, what answer shall I give him?'

Eadulf hesitated a moment and then broke out into a broad smile.

'Tell Murgal that I am now prepared. I shall pursue my arguments on procedure and stand by them. Take these books and tell him so.'

'I thought that you wanted them for another hour or two?'

'No longer. I think I now know the path to follow.'

'And you agree that you will be able to present your case to Murgal this afternoon?'

'I do agree,' Eadulf said emphatically.

Rudgal collected the books and Eadulf accompanied him to the door.

'Once I have told Murgal,' Rudgal said, 'I will take this news to Sister Fidelma. I wish you luck, Brother, in your effort to free her.'

Eadulf raised a hand in brief acknowledgment but it was plain that his mind was elsewhere. After a while he turned his gaze to the notes that he had been making from the law texts. Then he sat down again with a frown on his features as he drifted into deep thought.

Chapter Thirteen

Eadulf was plainly nervous as he took his stand before Murgal the Brehon who sat in his traditional place at the left-hand side of Laisre. The chieftain himself looked far from happy as he slumped silently in his chair allowing Murgal to conduct the entire proceedings. Fidelma had been brought from her place of confinement by Rudgal who stood just behind her chair which was placed in front of Laisre and Murgal.

It seemed that the entire inhabitants of the ráth had turned out to witness the event. Eadulf was aware of the presence of the tanist, Colla, and his wife, Orla, on the right-hand side of the chieftain. There was the scowling youthful Brother Dianach. Esnad sat next to him. Artgal stood at the back, his features still fixed in a derisive grin. There was the attractive apothecary, Marga, and the handsome young horse trader, Ibor of Muirthemne, was seated by her side. Even Cruinn lurked in the background with her large girth. The atmosphere was one of tense expectancy.

Murgal had called for silence but there was almost no need. A hush had already descended from the moment Fidelma had been brought in and told to be seated.

The clan of Gleann Geis had never witnessed such an entertainment, as Colla admitted afterwards.

Having established order, Murgal formally opened the proceedings.

'It is my understanding that Fidelma of Cashel wishes to make a plea to be released on her own recognisances and to remain at liberty until such time as she appears before this court after the nine days prescribed by law when she may answer as to her culpability in the murder of Solin of Armagh? Is that so?'

'It is so,' Eadulf responded. 'And I speak for her in this place.'

Laisre was unhappy.

'Does the Saxon have that right, Murgal?' the chieftain demanded.

'He does, lord.' Murgal sounded almost apologetic.

Laisre's mouth was set in a straight, thin line but he indicated that the proceedings should continue.

'Forgive me, Laisre of Gleann Geis,' Eadulf began hesitantly, stepping out of procedure to address the chieftain directly. 'Perhaps I might set your mind at rest as to my position. You rightly call me Saxon; it is true that I am not born in this land. I was a hereditary *gerefa* in my own land which is a magistrate similar to a Brehon, giving judgments under the law of my own people. I was converted to the path of Christ by a man called Fursa; a man of this land, who came to preach the new religion in my own land of the South Folk. He persuaded me to come and seek education in this land and I did so, studying at Durrow and Tuam Brecain, although my knowledge of your tongue and your laws is still imperfect.'

Murgal answered for the scowling chieftain.

'Your speech demonstrates that your judgment of yourself is harsh, Saxon. You are a tribute to Fursa's faith in you. You have but to ask of this court and we will be indulgent in guiding you through our laws. On what grounds do you bring us hither to judge whether Fidelma of Cashel shall be released pending trial?'

Eadulf glanced at Fidelma and smiled swift encouragement for she sat pale and stiff, unused to being in the position of the accused before a Brehon. She remained with an expressionless face gazing into the middle distance. Eadulf continued.

'I am here to offer a plea for the release of Fidelma of Cashel by virtue of her rank.'

Laisre shook his head and leaned towards Murgal.

'Does he plead law?'

Murgal ignored his chieftain's question. He was, after all, a Brehon sitting in judgment.

'This is an unusual step, Saxon. The charge against Fidelma of Cashel is one of murder. Even rank does not automatically grant rights in that respect.'

'I would argue against that. The *Berrad Airechta*, if I have understood the text, says that even with a charge of murder, if the suspect is of princely rank and of good character and the evidence is unclear, then they may be released on the decision of the Brehon until nine days expire when the trial must be held.'

Fidelma had turned to study Eadulf, her expression one of approval at his acquired knowledge. He had spent his time among Murgal's books well. She vaguely recalled this law but she doubted that it would work to gain her freedom for the next nine days in these hostile circumstances.

'You have studied well.' Murgal echoed her thoughts and even he spoke approvingly. 'That is, indeed, the law. Let me hear how you think it should apply in these circumstances.'

Eadulf gave a nervous jerk of his head.

'You will correct me if I am in error?' he asked.

'Be assured of that,' Murgal affirmed with grim humour.

'The legal commentaries, as I understand them, say that the status and character of a suspect must be taken into account in this decision. Will anyone in this court deny that Sister Fidelma is of noble status and degree not only in her birthright but in her legal qualification as a *dálaigh*?'

There was a stirring among the people in the chamber.

'We have never denied this,' Murgal replied with a tired voice.

'Is there anyone in this court that challenges the fact that Sister Fidelma is of unblemished character and her name is spoken of with affection not only in Cashel but in Tara's halls?'

Again his voice rang through the chamber in challenge and there was silence.

'No one denies this,' affirmed Murgal.

'Then you must accept that, according to law, if Sister Fidelma takes oath, the *fír testa*, as you call it, then you must accept her word until proof is sworn against her. Sister Fidelma can leave this court on her own recognisances.'

Laisre looked at Murgal sharply, an eyebrow raised in question, but Murgal shook his head and spoke directly to Eadulf.

'That is the law. As you say, we can accept her oath until proof is sworn against her. But we have a witness whose testimony cancels out her oath.'

Fidelma had seen this coming. She had seen enough cases being tried before competent Brehons to know that Murgal would know that a witness to the murder, making a statement to that effect, would cancel out the oath Eadulf had alluded to. The fact that the witness was only relating what he or she thought they saw did not invalidate the statement until disproved at the trial.

Eadulf's eyes had sought out Artgal who stood grinning at the back of the chamber.

'Bring forward your witness,' Eadulf instructed coldly. 'Let him testify.'

'He will testify at the trial in nine days' time,' Murgal replied sharply. 'This is not the time for his testimony.'

'He must testify now!' insisted Eadulf raising his voice above the murmur from the people. 'It is today that we are dealing with the competence of Fidelma's oath and if his testimony cancels out that oath then he must testify now.'

Murgal swallowed hard. He stared at the Saxon with a mixture of surprise and growing admiration. He had brought forth a legal stratagem to examine Artgal's testimony without waiting for the trial.

Artgal came swaggering forward even before Murgal had instructed him to do so.

'I am here, Saxon,' he announced boastfully, 'and I am not changing my testimony in spite of your strutting and pretence at being a *dálaigh*.'

Murgal stirred uncomfortably at the hostility of the witness.

'Artgal,' he warned sharply, 'the Saxon is a stranger in our land. Let us show him that we respect our laws of hospitality by giving him respect.'

Artgal drew himself up but the sneer did not leave his face. He remained silent.

Eadulf glanced towards the Brehon and imperceptibly grimaced his thanks before he turned to the warrior.

'I have no wish to make you change your testimony, Artgal,' he began quietly. 'I accept that you have related what you thought you saw.'

There was an intake of breath from several people and even Fidelma turned with a puzzled stare wondering where Eadulf was heading with his strategy.

'Then why do you wish to question him?' demanded Murgal, somewhat perplexed, putting the question that had sprung into her mind.

'Forgive me, Murgal,' Eadulf almost looked as if he were pleading, 'I merely need advice on the law at this point.'

Fidelma was not the only one who wondered if Eadulf had realised the advantage that he was throwing away by not pursuing Artgal's evidence and seeking to destroy it. For Fidelma it seemed the only logical route that he could take.

Murgal cleared his throat noisily.

'Well, my advice is that if you have no wish to interrogate Artgal to make him change his testimony against Fidelma, then he need not be summoned and his testimony against Fidelma stands. That being so, your argument for her release falls.'

Artgal gave a bark of sardonic laughter and started to move back to his former position.

'Stay where you are!'

The sharpness in Eadulf's voice was so unexpected that it rooted Artgal to the spot in astonishment. Eyes turned to Eadulf as if they could not believe that the mild supplicant of a second ago had spoken so harshly. Even Fidelma was momentarily shaken by the stern manner of his command.

Eadulf had turned back to Murgal and resumed in a quieter tone.

'I have yet to put my question,' he protested mildly, though it seemed that there was a tone of rebuke in his voice.

Murgal blinked a little in wonder.

'Then proceed,' he invited after a moment or two.

'I know little of the procedure of the court but I have consulted the text called "the five paths to judgment". Artgal is called as a witness which you call *fiadú* – one who sees.'

'That is correct,' affirmed Murgal.

'The text says that such a one, in giving testimony, must be sensible, honest, conscientious and of good memory.'

'I am all that, Saxon,' intervened Artgal, relaxing with a smile again. 'So what?'

'Tell me, learned judge,' went on Eadulf, ignoring him, 'what does the legal maxim given in the text mean when it says – *foben inracus accobar*?'

The question was asked innocently enough but there was a sudden silence in the chamber, an instant tension.

'It means that "greed detracts from honesty",' Murgal interpreted, though everyone felt that Eadulf already knew the meaning well enough.

'It means that a man cannot give evidence if it brings advantage to himself, doesn't it? His evidence is thus excluded from the hearing and justified by that legal maxim.'

If a grain of sand had fallen in that chamber, the silence had grown such that Fidelma felt it might well have been heard striking the floor. She wondered to what position Eadulf was proceeding with his arguments.

He had turned to face Artgal whose expression was no longer contemptuous. His features had grown grave, the face slightly ashen.

'Artgal, do you stand to profit by your evidence against Fidelma of Cashel?'

Artgal made no reply. He seemed to have difficulty speaking.

After several long moments, Murgal spoke slowly and clearly: 'Witness, you must answer – and, remember, you stand on your oath not only as a clansman but as a privileged warrior-bodyguard of our chieftain.'

Artgal realised the bad impression he was making by his hesitation and tried to recover his poise.

'Why would I profit?'

'A question is no answer to the question that I asked you,' snapped Eadulf. 'Do you stand to profit from your evidence?'

'No.'

'No? You have sworn an oath.'

'No.'

'No, again? Do I need to remind you of a certain sum of two *séds* that has already exchanged hands and a further *séd* which will pass into your possession when Fidelma's trial is over? Each *séd* representing one milch cow?'

There was a gasp through the chamber.

'You will need to prove this accusation, Saxon,' Murgal called sharply.

'Oh, I shall prove it, never fear,' Eadulf smiled grimly. 'Do you wish me to name the person from whom this largesse came, Artgal?'

The warrior seemed to deflate before Eadulf's confident stand. He shook his head.

'Then tell us why you were to receive this money?'

'It was no bribe,' Artgal began to protest.

'No bribe?' It was Eadulf's turn to sneer. 'Then why should you be paid for your testimony if it was not a bribe?'

'I did see Fidelma in the stable. I did see her bending over the man, Solin. She *must* have killed him.'

'*Must?* This is a change from saying you actually witnessed her do so,' interposed Murgal gravely.

'One thing must follow from another,' protested the warrior-blacksmith.

'Much play on this word "must",' Eadulf observed. 'Must is merely saying "should" or "ought" but not that something actually was.'

'This court is well aware of the meaning of the word,' interposed Murgal testily. 'And we take notice of Artgal's change of testimony. But, Artgal, do you admit that you were paid to tell that story?'

'Not to tell it,' protested Artgal. 'To ensure I did not change the story.'

Eadulf let out a low breath and only now did he give a triumphal glance towards Fidelma. She was staring at the floor, her shoulders bent in tension.

'I am at a loss to understand this,' Murgal was saying. 'Why would you be likely to change your story?'

'I would not. It is the truth. However, I was approached a few hours after Fidelma had been incarcerated, by a man who offered me two *séds*, for sticking to my story. He would pay me immediately and promised a further *séd* once Fidelma of Cashel's trial was over. Money has little value in Gleann Geis and so I agreed that this was the value of three milch cows. I accepted such a payment. With such a sum I could be assured of security for the rest of my life.'

'Who was this man who gave you this money?' Laisre asked heavily, intervening now for the first time since the revelation was made.

'I know not, my lord. It was dark and I did not see him. I heard only his voice.'

'How did he sound?' demanded Murgal.

Artgal raised a hand helplessly.

Something prompted Eadulf to gamble.

'You heard his voice clearly enough, Artgal,' he pressed. 'Did he have a northern accent?'

Artgal's expression was pitiful now. The bombast had disappeared entirely.

'Did he speak with the accent of a man of Ulaidh?' insisted Eadulf.

Artgal nodded miserably.

All eyes turned to the seated figure of Ibor of Muirthemne whose face had coloured but he kept staring stonily in front of him.

'What did this voice tell you?' Murgal asked grimly.

'The man told me that if I went forth this morning I would find the two milch cows tethered near my farmstead. In nine days' time I would find a third, that was if I did not change my testimony against Fidelma. I swear I had no choice but to accept. He stood in the darkness by my bed. He could as easily have pressed a dagger's point into my throat as offer me money.'

'And did you go forth in the morning, this very morning, and find the milch cows?' asked Murgal.

'I did.'

'And so, in short, your testimony was bought,' Eadulf summed up triumphantly.

'I made clear my testimony before I received the cows,' protested Artgal.

Laisre spoke to Murgal almost with an eager tone.

'He has a point there. Surely this cannot be considered a bribe to give evidence?'

Eadulf was about to protest but Murgal rubbed his chin thoughtfully before replying to the chieftain.

'It means that, according to the law, we cannot use Artgal's evidence against Fidelma. He has rendered himself without honour and cannot be believed. There is no evidence other than his against Fidelma of Cashel.'

Laisre turned to Artgal with scarcely suppressed fury.

'This man who offered you the cows spoke with the accent of the northern kingdom, you say?'

'He did, my lord.'

'Are you sure he spoke with a northern accent? Could it not be a Saxon accent for example?'

There was a loud gasp as all those gathered were amazed at the chieftain's overt accusation.

'My lord,' Murgal urged anxiously, 'it cannot be suggested that the Saxon trapped Artgal to discredit him in order to bring this decision about.'

Laisre glowered at Eadulf.

'Why not? One explanation is as good as another.'

'My lord, reconsider your hasty words. The evidence is clear. Artgal would know a northern accent from a Saxon one and would have said so. For you to argue this would be to bring your office into disrepute.'

Laisre looked as if he wanted to prolong the argument but with Murgal's discouragement he could not.

'Very well. We must question all those with northern accents, I suppose.'

Brother Dianach stood up and protested. Even Eadulf was surprised at his sudden leap out of character for he had always been shy and nervous. But anger and presumably fear provoked his outburst.

'You all know that apart from Brother Solin, only myself and the horse merchant there are from the northern lands. I deny any accusation against me!'

His voice had become almost a falsetto. His face crimson.

'It wasn't the boy,' agreed Artgal hastily. 'It was a deeper man's voice.'

Only Fidelma noted that Laisre's anxiety was now replaced by a look of momentary satisfaction.

Eyes turned to where Ibor of Muirthemne had been sitting. He was no longer in his place.

'Learned judge,' interposed Eadulf hurriedly, 'before we lose sight of the main business of these proceedings, this witness has said enough to prove my argument that his acceptance of this money invalidates his evidence.'

Murgal agreed sombrely.

'It is true. Artgal, you may leave this chamber but confine yourself to the ráth. I will have to consider what shall be done with you. You have disgraced your chieftain and your clan.'

Artgal had barely left his place when Eadulf spoke again.

'I suggest that as Artgal's evidence falls, Sister Fidelma be released *fír testa* immediately.'

Murgal was about to agree when Laisre, surprisingly, held up his hand and bent forward from his chair towards Eadulf.

'One charge prevents that, Saxon.' His voice was harsh. 'When she was charged with this crime, Fidelma of Cashel demeaned herself by seeking to lay the blame on another – namely my sister, Orla. She swore that she had seen Orla coming out of the stable door. But Orla was, by the testimony of her husband, Colla, able to prove she was not at the stable. Now to swear false oath is enough, as I understand the law, to keep Fidelma of Cashel under lock and key until we consider her guilt or otherwise. I say this notwithstanding the dishonesty of Artgal.'

Most people were taken aback by the tough and unsympathetic attitude of the chieftain. Eadulf let the murmur of the court fade away before he spoke again.

'Chieftain, believe me when I tell you that I know just how insulted you must feel by a claim which you believe falsely impeaches your family. Yet I would argue that it is no grounds on which to ignore what has happened here this day.'

He now addressed himself to Murgal for his was the final judgment and he would obviously guide Laisre as to the law.

'In Druidic teachings,' Eadulf continued softly, 'so I am told, there is always a Middle Way to approach things. A third way. Maybe Sister Fidelma made a mistake about identifying Orla. It is easily done in the darkness. Just as Artgal, before he fell a victim to avarice, made a mistake in thinking that because Fidelma was bending over the body of Solin of Armagh she therefore must have killed him. Fidelma and Artgal leapt to conclusions. The third way was not considered.'

Murgal was clearly impressed with Eadulf's argument.

'Is there any other reason why we should accept your argument?' inquired Murgal.

'There is the practical evidence, of course.'

'Oh?'

'The fact that, as Fidelma had rightly suggested, she was searched and not found in possession of the murder weapon. Nor when the stable was searched was such a weapon found. The conclusion is that the murderer took that weapon with him or her. It may be that it would have identified him or her. Laisre will confirm that his warriors searched diligently. There was no place that the weapon could have been hidden between the time when Artgal entered and when he claimed he saw Fidelma rising from the body. In other words, the facts exactly fit Sister Fidelma's account . . . but with one exception – she thought she saw Orla. I ask you to believe that she saw someone.'

Murgal turned and leaned close to Laisre and held a whispered conversation. His voice was urgent. Laisre seemed to protest but Murgal was insistent and reluctantly the chieftain finally gestured his indifference. Murgal sat back.

'You have argued well, Saxon. So well, in fact, that in arguing that Fidelma of Cashel be released until her trial you have dispensed with all the evidence against her. It seems to me that if we find the man who bribed Artgal we might also find the weapon which slew Solin. It has not escaped our notice that Artgal said the man spoke with the accent of Ulaidh or that the horse dealer, Ibor of Muirthemne, has now left this assembly. The fact that Solin was also a man of Ulaidh might suggest that this tragedy was the result of some private quarrel. There is no reason to hold Fidelma in custody any more.'

A burst of noisy voices thundered around the chamber.

Eadulf turned with a smile which was a mixture of relief and triumph to Fidelma. Fidelma was rising for the first time, her face still serious.

'Murgal,' her voice was strong and steady, 'I thank you, as I also thank Laisre, for the justice you have dispensed this day. But there is still the killer of Brother Solin to be caught. I would like your permission to investigate this killing. If Ibor of Muirthemne is responsible, let me bring him to justice. It is my contention that there is a link with Brother Solin's death and the curious ritual of the thirty-three dead young men.'

Laisre interrupted before Murgal could reply.

'I would prefer that we finish the negotiations which you are here to conduct and that you then depart in haste back to Cashel. You may be assured that we will do our best to find this man, Ibor of Muirthemne, who has bribed one of my best warriors and destroyed his honour.'

'Is that your command?' insisted Fidelma, to Eadulf's surprise, for, had it been his decision to make, he would have left Gleann Geis with the utmost rapidity.

'Call it my preference, Fidelma of Cashel. The most important business we have between us is to finish our negotiations. There will be no joy between us in any further relationship. The sooner that you are gone from our valley, the better, for I cannot forget the insult to my family – even if I accept the Saxon's explanation that you were mistaken in your identification. Let us rest this night and commence our deliberations in the morning. Now . . . I think we have finished our business for the day.'

Laisre rose abruptly and left the chamber. There was no happiness on his face. Orla and Colla followed him swiftly. It fell to Murgal to dismiss the court. Across the chamber, Eadulf saw Brother Dianach hurrying away. His face was flushed with anxiety. Of Artgal, there was no sign at all. Eadulf was about to move to Fidelma when he noticed the young girl, Esnad, smiling at him. Orla's daughter had a warm, alluring smile on her features and when he met her eyes, she did not drop them in maidenly fashion but met his gaze in an open, provocative manner. Embarrassed, it was Eadulf who dropped his gaze first.

The fourteen-year-old daughter of Orla and Colla was being deliberately flirtatious.

Chapter Fourteen

Once Fidelma and Eadulf were alone in the hostel, Fidelma whirled round to the Saxon monk with a warm smile and seized his hands with both of her own.

'You were brilliant!' she pronounced enthusiastically.

Eadulf blushed furiously.

'I had a good teacher,' he mumbled with some embarrassment.

'But you found the right laws to argue. And the way you led Artgal into that trap! I have never seen an advocate manipulate a witness better. It was brilliant to use the law to develop your argument. You should claim a degree as a *dálaigh*.'

'I had some help from Rudgal,' admitted Eadulf. 'Without his information, I could not have shown Artgal to be an unworthy witness.'

Fidelma became serious.

'Are you saying that it was Rudgal who gave you the information about the payment Artgal was to receive?'

'It was. Luck was with us because he mentioned Artgal had received the cows and I was able to piece the rest together.'

Fidelma moved in search of a pitcher of mead and beakers for she needed strength after her ordeal.

'Then we should thank Rudgal. But you used his information well. It was the way that you forced Artgal to confess the bribe without having to present the evidence yourself. That I admire.'

Eadulf laughed skeptically.

'If it had come down to having to give proof of my allegation then I fear we would have been worsted. Thank God that Artgal thought I knew more than I did.'

Fidelma paused in the act of drinking.

'You did have the evidence of the bribe, didn't you?' she asked hesitantly. 'I mean, evidence to support your allegation?'

Eadulf forced a smile and admitted the truth.

'It was a bluff.'

Fidelma stared at him in consternation. Slowly she sank to a chair.

'Only a bluff? You'd better explain.'

'Easy enough. Rudgal had heard Artgal boasting of his new possession of two milch cows. Artgal was boastful but he was not that loose tongued. He did mention, however, that he would have a third milch cow in nine days' time. I saw the connection at once. Rudgal had mentioned this to me not realising its significance.'

Fidelma felt suddenly weak as she considered what might have happened.

'And *that* was all you knew when you challenged him before the court?' she pressed faintly.

Eadulf spread his hands expressively.

'It seemed a reasonable assumption that Artgal's new-found wealth was something to do with his testimony against you. I simply took a gamble.'

Fidelma was staring at him in dismay.

'But no Brehon would have dared to make such a gamble, to claim something before the court without certain knowledge or proof. Have you not heard the saying *sapiens nihil affirmat quod non probat*? A wise man states as true nothing he cannot prove. What if Artgal had not confessed? What if you had been challenged to prove your accusation?'

Eadulf grimaced ruefully.

'Then, as I say, it would have gone badly with us. Artgal could have simply called me a liar and walked away. But his guilty conscience made him confess and I was counting on that.'

Fidelma was shaking her head dumbfounded.

'I have not known the like of this in my years as an advocate,' she finally said.

'Then let me give you Latin aphorism for Latin aphorism. *Si finis bonus est, totum bonum erit*,' smiled Eadulf complacently.

Fidelma was forced to duplicate his smile as she repeated: 'If the end is good, everything will be good. I cannot argue that all's well that ends well but do not repeat this story to anyone else, especially not to Murgal or Laisre. Confession extracted by deception is not a principle of the laws of the five kingdoms.'

Eadulf held up his hand, palm outwards.

'I swear! The secret will remain between us. But that doesn't make it the less true. Artgal was, indeed, bribed.'

Fidelma regarded her empty beaker as if searching for the answer in it.

'This is what I do not understand. He did not have to be bribed. I think he might have genuinely believed what he thought he saw. He would not have changed his testimony anyway. Why would Ibor of

Muirthemne risk all by offering to pay him such an extraordinary sum of money?'

'We must seek out Ibor of Muirthemne,' Eadulf announced. 'He will provide many answers.'

Fidelma glanced at him with resignation.

'You heard what Laisre said? I am forbidden to inquire further.'

'When has that stopped you before?' countered Eadulf in humour.

'Well, tomorrow we conclude our negotiation here and then we may turn our minds to the matter. Certainly I would agree that there is some mystery here which emanates in part or in whole from Ulaidh, from the north. I cannot yet fathom it. Do you recall my finding the warrior's torc of northern workmanship near the bodies?'

'I have not forgotten,' Eadulf replied. 'But we do not have to wait until tomorrow. It is only early evening, and there are two milch cows at Artgal's farmstead. Even dumb animals may talk.'

Fidelma was confused.

'Animals do not appear out of thin air,' Eadulf elucidated. 'They must have come from somewhere. Perhaps they have brands. We might learn where they came from. If so we might be able to track Ibor himself and find out who he represents and what his purpose here has been.'

Fidelma regarded him with satisfied approval.

'Sometimes one is so concerned with examining the tree that one loses sight of the wood. A splendid idea, Eadulf. More and more you are proving that you are equal to a *dálaigh*. But we must proceed carefully. Laisre will not approve of our investigation.'

'Laisre will not know. He and his friends will be starting their feasting soon,' Eadulf pointed out. 'Rudgal told me that this evening feast is a regular affair. I think,' he added with a grim humour, 'it will be a long time before I will go willingly to such a feast again.'

Fidelma now became aware that it was approaching meal time and they were the only people in the hostel.

'Where is Cruinn? She should surely be here to prepare our food?' she asked.

'I am afraid that Cruinn has been disapproving of us. She seems to have taken a personal dislike to us and withdrawn her services. We have to fend for ourselves. Brother Dianach is nowhere to be seen. I suspect he, too, has not accepted the finding of the court.'

Fidelma was puzzled.

'I can understand Brother Dianach being upset. But I cannot

understand such animosity from Cruinn. Even if I had been proved guilty, what was Brother Solin to her?'

'Her anger comes from your accusation against Orla. Orla is well liked here in Gleann Geis.'

'Ah well, her absence might be good. It gives us a free hand. We can move without the constraint she would place on us . . .'

She had not finished the sentence when the door opened and Rudgal came in. He looked rather sheepish.

'I came to tell you that Cruinn, the hostel keeper, refuses to come here to cook for you. She is rather old-fashioned . . .'

'We have just been discussing that,' Fidelma informed him.

'But Fidelma was exonerated by Murgal,' protested Eadulf indignantly. 'How dare she refuse to fulfil her duties?'

Rudgal shrugged.

'She is one who takes the view that there is no smoke without fire. She refuses to set foot in this hostel until you have both departed. Even the chiding of Murgal, who admittedly has not been too forceful, has failed to move her. Therefore, I have come here to offer to tend to your needs, though I am no great cook.'

'I thank you, Rudgal,' Fidelma smiled appreciatively. 'We can manage well enough if we have a supply of food and drink. We shall, after all, not be here more than another day. And I am sure Brother Dianach will be able to look after himself. Where is he, by the way?'

'I have not seen him.'

Fidelma was disappointed. She remembered the whispered conversation between Solin and Dianach before he went to his death in the stable. 'If all goes well,' Solin had told the young cleric, 'Cashel will fall to us before the summer is out.' To *us*? Who was the *us*? It was clear that Dianach was party to whatever mischievous plot was being hatched. She wanted to question the gauche young scribe as soon as possible, especially now that he had not the protection of Solin to fall back on. But, if he couldn't be found, there were other things that could be done and Eadulf had made a good suggestion.

'There is another favour we would ask of you, Rudgal,' Fidelma went on, having considered the way forward. 'We would like to go to Artgal's farmstead and examine these two milch cows with which he was bribed.'

Rudgal looked uneasy.

'Is that wise, Sister? Laisre forbade further investigation.'

'Wise or not, we would like you to take us to his farmstead where we may examine the cows. Even a king cannot forbid a *dálaigh* to investigate a crime. A king is a servant of the law, not its master.'

'I am not questioning the wisdom of you wishing to investigate but I think you should know that in spite of Laisre's command that Artgal should not leave the ráth, he has done so. He is nowhere to be found. Artgal might contemplate harm against you for the ruin which you have brought on him.'

Fidelma rose to her feet resolutely.

'Do you think that he is gone to his farmstead perhaps to destroy the evidence of his wrong doing? In that case, we must certainly go in search of him, for he is our only link to Ibor of Muirthemne and those cattle are confirmation of the deed.'

'But he could have gone anywhere,' Eadulf pointed out. 'Anywhere to escape Laisre's justice.'

'I do not think so,' interposed Rudgal. 'His cabin lies not far away on the hillside overlooking Ronan's hamlet. Ronan was sent to his farmstead in pursuit of Ibor of Muirthemne. Ibor has fled the valley. But Ronan told me on his return that he had caught sight of Artgal on the hill path going to his farmstead. He did not think it his duty to stop him as he had only been told to bring Ibor back to the ráth. Besides, Artgal was a friend and cousin to Ronan. Ronan will say nothing to Laisre unless directly asked.'

'So Ibor has fled the valley?' Fidelma repeated quietly. 'Well, that was to be expected.'

'Ibor of Muirthemne and his horses must have left the ráth even before Murgal finished the hearing,' Rudgal agreed. 'However, as for Artgal, I cannot see him willingly parting with the cattle now he has them. If he intends to leave the valley to escape Laisre's wrath, he will collect his possessions first.'

'Then let us find out if he is still at his farmstead,' Fidelma insisted, moving towards the door.

They left the ráth of Laisre without being challenged. As Eadulf had pointed out, although there were several hours of daylight left in the warm summer evening, everyone appeared to have taken themselves to Laisre's feasting hall. Laughter and the noise of feasting echoed over the empty courtyard. There was no one about or at the gates of the fortress. It was Rudgal who suggested that they did not encumber themselves with horses as they might be spotted more easily on horseback if Artgal was trying to avoid them.

In any case, it was scarcely a mile to the farmstead which Rudgal indicated on the side of the hill, just above the hamlet dominated by Ronan's farm. Rudgal led the way at an easy pace with the two religious following close behind.

It was still warm, for the summer's day had been hot beyond the shelter of the ráth. Although it would not grow dark for two hours at least, a few dark storm clouds were hanging over the mountains and there was a threat of rain beyond their peaks. They could hear a distant rumble of thunder from the other side of the surrounding pinnacles. At least the clouds were hanging around the summits of the hills, as if anchored to them, and not moving across the bright blue sky above the valley.

Rudgal caught Eadulf's anxious gaze and chuckled softly.

'With God's help, the weather will pass us by on the other side of the mountains.'

They continued on their way skirting Ronan's farmstead and Nemon's dwelling, before climbing the hill towards the small cabin perched above, which Rudgal had indicated belonged to Artgal. The fair-haired warrior wagon-maker led the way up a steep path whose ascent had been made easier by the placing of large stones every so often. This gave the path the appearance of a stairway. Fidelma followed next and then Eadulf. There was little conversation between them except when Rudgal pointed out areas along the path to be avoided, springy patches of boggy turf or the occasional pit hidden by gorse.

They came to a narrow shelving area of stone-hedged small fields among which stood the grey stone cabin. It was a simple beehive-shaped cabin with a straw-thatched roof and a fence around it. Adjacent to the cabin was a smithy's shop but with the fire dead. It looked as if it had not been used in some considerable time. Even some of the tools were rusting.

Fidelma could see no sign of any cattle in the vicinity.

They paused at the entrance of the cabin to recover their breath. Then Fidelma called sharply: 'Artgal!'

There was no answer. A curious silence permeated the place.

'Artgal!' echoed Rudgal more loudly. Then in an aside he added apologetically: 'I was sure that he would come here. Perhaps he has already been here, taken the cows and fled. But he could not have gone far in the valley herding cows. We would surely have seen him.'

When there was no reply from the second call, Rudgal pushed open the door of the cabin and went inside. The others followed. The cabin seemed deserted but its few meagre possessions were placed in orderly fashion. There was no indication that the owner had made a hurried departure. The only object out of order was a cloth lying on the floor as if dropped unobserved by its owner. Fidelma went over to it and picked it up. She suddenly realised that it was an apron. She placed it on a nearby hook, thinking it was a curious item for a man like Artgal to have. But then it did seem to fit in with the tidy personality of the cabin. It was probably normal for Artgal to wear such an outsized garment to protect him if he were so fastidious.

'Perhaps I was wrong,' muttered Rudgal. 'Perhaps he has gone elsewhere but where I would not know.'

'I saw no sign of the cows around here,' Eadulf remarked.

'And if he took them we would surely have spotted him,' Rudgal repeated. 'A lone herdsman and two cows in this countryside are easy to observe.'

This was true for there were few trees in the valley itself.

'But there seems to be no other explanation,' he added. 'Artgal must have gone and taken the cows with him. I will see if there are any tracks which we may follow.'

He left the cabin. Fidelma was still standing in the middle of the single room, her sharp eyes moving cautiously around it, examining every nook and cranny keenly. She suddenly realised that there were two pottery beakers standing on the table. It seemed that Artgal had had a visitor recently; recently enough for him not to clear away the remains of a shared drink and to have failed to observe the discarded apron on the floor.

She bent to examine the beakers, sniffing cautiously at the aroma left by their contents. She had scented the distinctive pungent fragrance before but, for the moment, she could not place it.

'This Artgal is a very tidy man for a blacksmith and warrior,' she reflected softly.

Eadulf grinned.

'Are blacksmiths and warriors invariably untidy, then?'

'You have seen Artgal. I would have expected Artgal not to be so fastidious. One may tell much from a person's attention to their clothing. Yet the cabin here is scrupulously clean.'

'I have known of such people who are slovenly in their appearance but fastidious in their homes and vice versa,' Eadulf observed.

There came a sudden cry of alarm outside the cabin.

'Sister! Brother!'

It was Rudgal's voice raised in horror.

Eadulf and Fidelma exchanged a glance and hurried outside. Rudgal was at the back of the cabin. He was standing staring down at something on the ground. It was sprawled half in and half out of a small shed. Eadulf recognised it by the clothing.

It was the body of Brother Dianach.

'I was walking round the cabin to look for tracks when I stumbled across the body,' Rudgal explained unnecessarily.

Eadulf genuflected while Fidelma went down on one knee beside the body.

The young religieux lay on his side, his feet and lower body were in the small shed, the torso was sprawled outside, face down, one arm flung in front of him. There was fresh blood staining the ground. Cautiously, Fidelma pushed the body over on its back. Blood was everywhere. It was clear that Dianach had had his throat cut; one long stabbing cut had cleaved through the neck almost to the back.

Fidelma suddenly looked at the lips and gums of the dead religieux. They had a faint blue tinge about them which she could not explain. Clearly the knife cut had caused his death and the wound was still bleeding. Distastefully, she reached out a hand to touch the skin. It was still warm. Brother Dianach had only recently died, probably even as they had entered the cabin.

She sprang to her feet and looked around. Her eyes scanned the landscape.

'Did you see anyone near here, Rudgal?'

The wagon maker dragged his fascinated gaze away from the corpse and regarded her in bewilderment.

Fidelma was impatient.

'The boy has only just been killed. Perhaps while we were in the cabin. Look, the shed is small, you have to bend down to peer inside. Perhaps Dianach was hiding from us when we approached the cabin. His killer must have come upon him in this fashion and slit his throat. It happened only moments ago.'

Rudgal whistled softly.

'I walked around the cabin but there was no one in sight, it was only when I was looking for the tracks of the cattle that I suddenly saw the body.'

Eadulf had moved swiftly to a stone wall and clambered up. He swept the surrounding countryside with his keen gaze.

'Can you see anything?' demanded Fidelma.

Eadulf shook his head in disappointment.

'No,' he replied in disgust. 'There are so many gullies and walls around here that anyone, knowing the area, could hide themselves easily from our sight.'

'Any sign of the cattle?'

'None at all. But while a man might hide among these gullies, I would say that it would be difficult to hide cattle.'

Fidelma turned back to the body in frustration.

'Why kill him, I wonder?' Rudgal said. 'And what was the lad doing up here anyway?'

'When Artgal said that he had been offered the bribe by someone with a northern accent, Dianach grew upset,' she reflected. 'He jumped up to deny that it was him.'

'But Artgal corroborated that by saying it was a deeper voice whereupon Ibor of Muirthemne disappeared from the ráth not attempting to deny the logical conclusion that it was he who had bribed Artgal,' Eadulf called from the wall, still scrutinising the surrounding countryside. 'And now Ibor has fled the valley.'

'If it was not Ibor of Muirthemne who tried to bribe Artgal, why did he disappear?' added Rudgal.

There was no escaping the logic.

Eadulf had jumped down from the wall and joined them again.

'Moreover, why would Artgal disappear?' he asked. 'Surely Laisre's wrath is not so terrible. Artgal would have to pay a fine under your law to reinstate his honour but better to do that than flee to a life of wandering exile outside his clan?'

Fidelma rubbed her chin thoughtfully.

'It is a good point, Eadulf. I wonder if we might be overlooking a more pertinent question. Did the cattle really exist in the first place?'

'That is a question beyond my understanding,' muttered Rudgal. 'Artgal would not have made up such a story.'

'Think about it,' invited Fidelma. 'We are told that Artgal was given two milch cows by . . . shall we just call him a man with a northern accent? Did this man buy them from a farmer within this valley? It is small and the news of such a purchase ought to spread instantly for gossip does not need the flight of birds to cover the ground swiftly.'

'Perhaps they were brought from without the valley,' suggested Eadulf.

'The same would apply. A man herding two or three milch cows into this valley would easily be observed and identified.'

Eadulf had begun to examine the ground at the back of the cabin carefully.

Fidelma glanced towards Rudgal. The warrior stood waiting patiently for instructions.

'I think that you should go back to the ráth and tell Murgal what we have found here.'

'Won't Laisre be angry with you for disobeying his decree not to pursue this matter?' asked the wagon maker.

'That is my problem to deal with,' Fidelma assured him. 'And, more importantly, this death of a cleric outside of Laisre's ráth is mine to deal with. Go quickly now.'

Rudgal set off back down the hill in the direction of the ráth at an ambling trot.

Fidelma turned back to Eadulf who was now sitting on the stone wall with a frown on his face. His eyes were still fixed on an examination of the ground at the back of the cabin which constituted the farmyard.

'You seem interested in something,' Fidelma prompted.

Eadulf looked up reluctantly in her direction and then pointed to the ground.

'What you have said troubles me. If Artgal had not been given the cows why would he make up the story about them? Yet the evidence points to the fact that what you have said needs some consideration. You see, if Artgal had been given two cows, he certainly did not keep them there.'

'How do you know?'

'Have you ever seen a patch of land where cows have been kept?'

'I do not see what you are driving at.'

'Examine this land, Fidelma. Where are the marks of cattle hooves – moreover, where are the pats of cattle excretions which one can never hide? No, even if the cows were given to Artgal this morning and were here during the course of the day, there would be such signs of their passing. If Artgal had such cattle, they were kept somewhere else.'

Chapter Fifteen

A conflict of expressions flitted across Fidelma's features as she considered what he had said.

'What is it?' Eadulf demanded.

'You have just observed the obvious, Eadulf. I think I may know where we might find these missing cows.'

Eadulf was startled.

'Come with me,' Fidelma said, turning and leading the way from Artgal's farmstead. In bemusement, Eadulf followed her as she confidently swung her way down the hill, following the path directly towards the group of buildings dominated by Ronan's farm. They walked in silence for the most part as Fidelma appeared plunged into deep thought. Eadulf knew better than to attempt to interrupt her when she was in such a meditative mood.

He was astonished when, reaching the bottom of the hill, she turned aside from the main track and approached the small house of Nemon the prostitute. She rapped confidently on the door.

Nemon came out immediately and regarded them in surprise. Then she forced a twisted smile which was not entirely one of welcome.

'You two again? I thought they said that you had killed the man about whom you were asking – what was his name, Solin?'

'They thought wrongly,' Fidelma assured her firmly.

'Well, I can tell you no more about this Solin other than what I have told you already,' sniffed the woman, attempting to close the door.

'It was not Solin that I came to speak to you about. May we come in?' Fidelma had noticed that the burly wife of Ronan, Bairsech, had come out of her house and had taken up her apparently favourite position, standing with folded arms watching them with undisguised hostile curiosity.

Nemon was indifferent. She merely stood aside and allowed Fidelma to push by with Eadulf following.

'Time is money,' the fleshy woman remarked, looking pointedly at Eadulf.

'As you told us last time,' agreed Fidelma affably. 'But this time I am acting as a *dálaigh* investigating a murder. What was the price you asked for your three milch cows?'

Eadulf was more surprised than Nemon, for the woman did not even react.

'I asked the going price. One *séd* per cow. A *cumal* for the three of them. I shall not give it back and nor am I going to milk them any longer. Artgal should have collected them or, at least, the two he promised to collect this morning. That was the arrangement.'

Fidelma turned to look out of the window at the cattle munching in the field outside.

'What made you accept money? I thought barter was the usual form of exchange here?'

'I am not going to live all my life in this place. Money can buy freedom outside Gleann Geis.'

'True enough. What arrangement did you make? That you would look after the cows until Artgal came to collect them and take them to his farmstead?'

Nemon inclined her head in agreement.

'He should have collected them today after milking. Well, two of them at least. I was to keep the third one for a further week and then let him have that one as well.'

'And you were paid in advance?'

'Of course. I am not stupid.'

'No one said you were, Nemon. Did Ibor of Muirthemne give you any other instructions?'

For the first time Nemon looked bewildered.

'Ibor of Muirthemne? What has he to do with it?'

'Wasn't he the one who bought your cows?' Fidelma asked hesitantly.

'That one? Ha! He would not even come to visit me. He stayed over there with Ronan and his wife. I met him on the path but he was not interested in my services. It is the first time I have met a merchant who was far from home who refused to avail himself of the services of a woman. Why would he buy the cows from me?'

Fidelma waited patiently until the end of her observation.

'If it was not Ibor of Muirthemne who bought the cows from you, who was it?'

'The boy, of course.'

'The boy?'

'The boy, what is his name? He is one of you – he has his head shaved like this foreign man. I have seen him with Solin.'

'Brother Dianach?' interposed Eadulf slowly.

'Dianach, that is his name,' confirmed Nemon.

Fidelma was standing staring at her with an expression of perplexity.

'When did Brother Dianach come here and buy the cows?'

Nemon thought about it.

'In the middle of the night, it was. Well, not long after dawn. I was fast asleep when he came knocking. I thought that he wanted my services but he nearly jumped a mile into the air when I suggested it. What is wrong with those who follow your God? Why are they such cavilling prudes? Are there no men among them?' She paused and reflected with a derisory smile. 'Well, the thick-set one . . . Solin could not be called a prude. I have no complaints of him on that account.'

'You were telling us about Brother Dianach,' interrupted Eadulf hurriedly.

'The young boy? He awoke me early in the morning and said he wanted to buy my three milch cows. He explained the conditions. A *cumal* is hard to come by and I could do much with it. Besides, I never really wanted the responsibility of milking cows in the first place.'

'So Brother Dianach bought your cows. How did he explain the arrangement? Did he offer any reason why he should suddenly buy the cows and give them to Artgal? I presume he told you that these were for Artgal at the time?'

'Yes. Artgal is Ronan's cousin. I only see him when he has won at some game of chance. When the boy told me that the cows were for Artgal, I presumed that the boy was in debt to Artgal over some wager or other. I don't care anyway. The boy simply told me that Artgal would collect two of the cows later today. The third cow would be collected in a week or so. Artgal then came to see me soon afterwards to ensure that I had the cows. He confided in me that he thought the boy had been joking with him. He was surprised that I actually had the cows to give him. He said that he would collect them later today but I have seen nothing of him since.'

Eadulf compressed his lips in annoyance.

'So Artgal knew the real identity of his mysterious benefactor all along. He lied to the court when he said it was not Brother Dianach.'

'That much is obvious.' Fidelma was phlegmatic. 'More importantly, Brother Dianach lied. Why would he want to ensure I was incarcerated or found guilty?' She turned back to Nemon. 'Have you seen Brother Dianach since this dawn transaction?'

Nemon shook her head.

'And when was the last time that you saw Ibor of Muirthemne?'

'That was a few hours ago. I saw him saddling his horse over in Ronan's field,' the woman replied. 'He rode off with both his horses. He went as if the hounds of Goll of the Fomorii were chasing him. Then Ronan came riding down in search of him. What is that about?'

There came the sound of horses outside.

Fidelma turned and glanced through the door.

'It seems Murgal and Rudgal have returned. Eadulf, tell Murgal we are here. I want a word with him before he proceeds to Artgal's farmstead.'

Eadulf hurried outside to stop the horsemen before they passed by.

Nemon was puzzled.

'What is happening? What is all this activity?'

'Are you sure you have not seen Artgal since this morning when he came to see the cows Brother Dianach had given him?'

'I have already told you that. Now tell me what is amiss!'

'Artgal seems to be missing.'

Nemon did not even register surprise.

'So long as he appears to collect his cows.'

'You may have to keep them longer than you have anticipated. Not only has Artgal disappeared but Brother Dianach has been found murdered on his farm.'

Nemon's features remained stony.

'Well, if I keep the cows,' she finally said, having apparently thought the matter over, 'at least I will not have to return the money. Dead men kill their liabilities.'

Even Fidelma was nonplussed at this unscrupulous attitude. She decided there was nothing more to be said and left the cabin. She found Eadulf at the gate talking with Murgal and Rudgal; both men were still mounted.

Murgal greeted her with immediate disapproval.

'You were told not to leave the ráth until your business with Laisre was finished.'

'Have you been told that Brother Dianach is dead?' she replied, ignoring his reproof.

'Rudgal brought me the news.'

'You will find his body on Artgal's farm. Artgal himself is missing. It was, however, Brother Dianach who gave the cows as a bribe to Artgal and not Ibor of Muirthemne. Your foster-daughter . . . Nemon is the witness to the transaction. And there stand the cows, still in her field because Artgal has not collected them.'

Murgal regarded her with narrowed eyes.

'Are you telling me that Artgal has killed the young man Dianach?'

'I am not telling you anything,' replied Fidelma solemnly. 'As you have pointed out, I am not allowed to investigate, according to you and your chieftain. You may conduct what inquiries you wish. Eadulf and I are now returning to the ráth.'

They left Murgal seething with irritation and proceeded to walk back to the ráth.

It was obvious that Rudgal had not told anyone else of the discovery of Brother Dianach's body other than Murgal. There were a few people about but no one seemed interested in them and the sounds of festivity were emanating from the feasting hall.

It was dusk when they entered the hostel. There was no one about. Fidelma lit the lamps and made a search for something to eat. While she prepared a meal, Eadulf sat at the table resting his hands on his chin.

'I don't understand it.' He finally broke the silence. 'Why would Brother Dianach pay such a large sum to Artgal, simply to ensure that he did not change his claim that you killed Brother Solin?'

Fidelma put down some dried bread and cheese on the table, all she could find, and sought out a jug of mead.

'I think we can speculate. Dianach was involved in whatever Solin was involved in. If we knew what that was, we would know why he was prepared to risk much to ensure that I was imprisoned or tried for murder. I think there is some inevitable link in the chain of events from the murder of the young men to Dianach's own slaughter. But I do not know where the chain even starts. Why would Dianach want to do me such harm?'

Eadulf cut himself a slice of cheese.

'Retribution? He believed that you killed Brother Solin. Perhaps he was emotionally tied to Solin to the point where he wanted vengeance?'

She shook her head firmly.

'No. It does not make sense. He would have waited until the outcome of the hearing. Why spend a whole *cumal* in a bribe which he did not have to pay? Artgal was prepared to swear against me anyway.'

Eadulf grimaced negatively.

'I don't know.'

Fidelma's expression was firmly set.

'I have made up my mind what we should do,' she announced. 'This is too important to wait until after the negotiations. Ibor of Muirthemne remains the one link from which we might trace our chain. If we find him, we will start on the path to a solution. The way to Ibor lies in tracing those tracks from the site of the ritual massacre. I am sure of it.'

'So what shall we do?'

'We will leave here before dawn tomorrow, when everyone is asleep, and make our way to the site.'

'Laisre will not be happy,' Eadulf sighed.

'Better for him to be unhappy and get these mysteries solved so that there is no bad blood between Cashel and Gleann Geis,' she replied firmly. 'The more that I have thought about this, the more I believe that the answer to this mystery is of greater importance to Cashel than agreeing with Laisre about the placing of a church and school here.'

Eadulf stirred uncomfortably.

'More important than converting this corner of the kingdom to the Faith?' he queried. 'Surely Ségdae of Imleach will not agree?'

Fidelma shook her head.

'I fear that there is a common answer to what has been happening here. According to Brother Solin, he was involved in something that would bring about the fall of Cashel before the summer ended. My oath to my brother and the laws of this land forbid me to ignore such a threat.'

There was a tap on the door of the hostel and before either could answer it was opened and Orla's young daughter entered. She carried a basket on her arm. A momentary expression of irritation passed over her features when she saw Fidelma but then her eyes brightened as they alighted on Eadulf.

'I knew Cruinn was not here,' she said in a husky voice. 'I have come to make some supper for you.' She glanced quickly at Fidelma and added: 'For you both.'

Eadulf rose and glanced down at the dried bread and cheese that he had been contemplating eating. He grimaced wryly then smiled.

'It will be very welcome, Esnad.'

The girl placed her basket on the table and began to unpack fresh bread, cold meats, boiled eggs and some vegetables. She had even brought an amphora of wine.

'Do your mother and father know that you are here?' inquired Fidelma.

Esnad raised her chin defiantly.

'I am of the age of choice,' she replied in an annoyed tone. 'I was fourteen last birthday.'

'Yet your parents might be angry that you are consorting with us after what has happened.'

'Let them be,' the girl said dismissively. 'I do not care. I am old enough to make my own decisions.'

'There is no denying that,' observed Fidelma gravely.

The girl finished unpacking. There was, at least, enough food for a passable supper.

It was clear that the girl felt uncomfortable in Fidelma's presence and it appeared that she wanted to speak with Eadulf on her own. That intrigued Fidelma. She was also amused that Eadulf seemed embarrassed at the young girl's attentions. Nevertheless, she hoped that Eadulf would have the sense to see that the girl wanted to speak with him.

She rose with a smile.

'I promised to discuss something with Murgal,' she said with a meaningful glance at Eadulf, hoping that he would understand her motive.

The Saxon looked thoroughly alarmed but he apparently understood that she wanted him to stay and discover what it was that Esnad wanted of him.

Esnad was looking pleased.

'I hope that I am not interfering with your plans,' she observed coyly.

'Not at all,' replied Fidelma. 'I will be back shortly, so save me some of that excellent supper.'

She left the hostel and found herself in the gloom of the courtyard.

For a few moments she walked without purpose, wondering if Esnad had some information which could add anything towards a solution of the mystery of Gleann Geis. Then she found herself retracing the route that she had taken on the previous night when she had followed Brother Solin. She had not gone far when she saw a portly figure of a woman leave the building which contained Murgal's apartment and begin to hurry across the courtyard. The figure was easy to recognise. Fidelma quickened her step.

'Cruinn!'

The rotund hostel-keeper paused and peered round. She recognised Fidelma within an inward hiss of her breath. She would have moved on had not Fidelma quickly moved to block her path.

'Cruinn, why have you not come to the hostel?' Fidelma asked reproachfully. 'Why are you so angry with me?'

The woman turned and scowled at her.

'You should know the laws of hospitality, you being a *dálaigh*. You insulted your host by insulting his sister.'

'That is unjust,' Fidelma pointed out. 'I know that Orla is well respected but I can only tell the truth. I, myself, was wrongly accused.'

'You only escaped justice on a technical point of law,' Cruinn returned sharply, much to Fidelma's astonishment.

'You seem to suddenly know much about the law, Cruinn,' she replied. 'Where did you learn so much?'

Even in the gloom, Fidelma saw that Cruinn looked uncomfortable for a moment.

'I only repeat what everyone is saying. Had Artgal not been so foolish as to accept the cows then his evidence would have been proven.'

'I did not kill Brother Solin.'

Cruinn turned away quickly.

'I have things to do,' she muttered. 'But do not look for me in the hostel. There are few people here who welcome your presence now, Fidelma of Cashel. The sooner you leave Gleann Geis the better.'

The portly figure hurried away into the darkness. Fidelma watched her go with some regret. It was discouraging how people changed their attitudes because of false information and prejudice.

A door opened and a light fell across the courtyard. Fidelma saw the light came from the apothecary of Marga. Two figures were framed in the door. One was Marga and the other was Laisre. Fidelma stood bathed in the light from the doorway. Laisre's figure stiffened as he turned in her direction. Then he bowed his head to Marga.

'Thank you, Marga. How many times must I take the infusion?' His voice came clearly.

'Only once in the evening, Laisre.'

The attractive apothecary turned and closed the door, cutting off the light from the courtyard.

Laisre stepped away in the gloom which had descended towards Fidelma.

'Well, Fidelma of Cashel,' he greeted her heavily, 'I have just been told by Murgal that you disobeyed my orders and left the ráth earlier.'

'It was not an order as I recall. You stated that it was only your preference,' Fidelma replied solemnly.

Laisre snorted angrily.

'Do not play with words. I did not sanction you leaving the ráth.'

'If I had not left the ráth do you think that Brother Dianach would have been any the less dead?'

'You bring death in your wake. The ravens of death are forever fluttering over your head,' grunted Laisre sourly.

'Do you really think that I am responsible for the deaths that have occurred?'

Laisre made an impatient gesture.

'All I know is that such deaths have never occurred in our community before you came. The sooner that you are gone from here the better.'

He left her abruptly and hurried away towards the council chamber.

Fidelma sighed and decided to return to the hostel. She reasoned that she had allowed enough time for Esnad to unburden herself to Eadulf and say whatever it was she had wanted to say.

She was about to open the door when it was flung open and Esnad nearly collided with her. Fidelma almost lost her footing as the young woman pushed into her and, without faltering herself, hurried off into the night.

A moment later another figure came out of the hostel.

'Esnad! Wait!'

The figure of Rudgal hurried by without even seeing Fidelma in the shadows.

Fidelma stared after his vanishing figure with an expression of perplexity. She entered the hostel and closed the door behind her. Eadulf was seated where she had left him. The food was barely touched.

He looked up with some relief.

'What's happened?' Fidelma demanded. 'Esnad came hurrying out and nearly knocked me over. Then Rudgal came out apparently chasing after her.'

'I've no idea,' confessed Eadulf. 'I begin to think there is a madness in this place.'

'Why was Esnad so keen on speaking to you alone? I thought she had something of importance to tell you which might have helped us solve this puzzle.'

Eadulf shook his head.

'She was more anxious to ask me questions about who I was,

where I came from and what life was like in the land of the South Folk.'

Fidelma was disappointed.

'Is that all?'

Eadulf became embarrassed.

'Actually, no. She wanted to know why I was travelling with you and what our relationship was.'

Fidelma gave a mischievous grin.

'Our relationship?'

Eadulf gestured half-heartedly.

'You know,' he said lamely.

Fidelma decided not to tease him further.

'Why do you think she was asking such questions? Was there a purpose in it?'

Eadulf was perplexed.

'None that I could see. If she was older . . .'

Fidelma examined him closely. There was still some humour in her eyes.

'*If* she was older?' she prompted. 'Remember she is already beyond the age of choice now.'

Eadulf, red with embarrassment, protested.

'She is only a child.'

'Fourteen is the age of maturity for a girl in this land, Eadulf. A girl can be married at that age and make her own decisions.'

'But . . .'

'You felt that she was being more than simply friendly towards you?'

'Yes, I did. To be truthful, I have noticed her wanton attitude before. Well, it is probably only infatuation,' he ended lamely.

Fidelma could not help smiling at his discomfiture.

'So, she could add no more pieces to our puzzle? Very well. But what was Rudgal doing here and what was the meaning of that scene just now?'

'He came in presumably because he had promised to prepare a meal for us, knowing that Cruinn was refusing to come to the hostel.'

'Why was he so put out with Esnad?'

'Maybe because Esnad brought us a supper before he did. He came in and when he saw her he seemed very ill-tempered.'

'And how did she react?'

'I do not think that she was pleased to see him. She left immediately.'

'And he followed,' mused Fidelma. 'Interesting.'

Eadulf stood up.

'It is beyond my understanding, however, it is time we had our supper. The hour grows late and if you still have a mind to depart in search of Ibor of Muirthemne . . . ?'

Fidelma asserted that she did.

'In that case, let us eat and go to bed early. Who knows what tomorrow may bring.'

Chapter Sixteen

It was still dark when Fidelma awakened Eadulf and told him to get ready. She was already dressed and, while he hurriedly copied her, she went down to fill their saddle bags with the remaining food that had been left from their evening meal. When Eadulf was ready, they crept out of the hostel and across the courtyard, keeping close to the shadows away from the flickering torchlight in case a wandering guard observed them. Fidelma wanted to avoid any vigilant eye as much as possible. There was one sentinel on the walls but he seemed to be dozing.

They saddled their horses as quietly as they could and led them cautiously out of the stables.

Eadulf groaned for the clatter of their shod hooves on the flagstones was surely enough to wake the dead. It certainly woke the sentinel who had been napping on the walls. He came down the steps to stand by the open gates. Fidelma realised the hopelessness of attempting to leave without anyone realising it. The only way was to bluff it out.

'Who is it?' demanded the gruff, though still sleepy, voice of the guard.

'It is Fidelma of Cashel,' she replied, summoning a haughty tone.

'Ha! It is not yet dawn,' replied the sentinel, stating the obvious. 'Why are you leaving the ráth at such an hour?'

The man spoke uncertainly, knowing who she was and wondering whether he should speak deferentially or with hostility.

'Brother Eadulf and I are leaving the ráth for a short while.'

'Does Laisre know of this, lady?' came the warrior's still uncertain tone.

'Isn't Laisre chief of Gleann Geis and surely he knows everything which stirs within his own ráth?' she countered, trying hard to steer a cautious path between not telling an outright lie and making an implication which would satisfy the man.

The sentinel's voice was aggrieved.

'Do not blame me, lady, for my ignorance. No one has informed me of your leaving.'

'I am now informing you.' Fidelma tried to sound irritable. 'Stand aside and let us pass. Should any inquire, we shall soon be back.'

Hesitantly the sentinel stood aside and Fidelma and Eadulf trotted through the open gates through into the darkness.

It was not until they were some way from the ráth and moving swiftly along the valley road towards the ravine which provided the exit from Gleann Geis that Eadulf allowed himself to exhale noisily in relief.

'Was that wise, Fidelma? To imply that you had Laisre's permission will only deepen the chieftain's anger when we return.'

'Wisdom rises upon the ruins of folly,' grinned Fidelma in the darkness. 'I told the man no lie. And we shall be back as soon as possible.'

There were grey streaks in the sky by the time that they reached the grim granite statue of the god Lugh of the Long Hand which marked the entrance to the valley. It looked strange and frightening in the grey half-light as they rode past. Eadulf crossed himself nervously at its towering image but Fidelma laughed gaily.

'Didn't I tell you that the ancients saw Lugh as a god of light, a solar deity. You should not fear him for he was a good god.'

'How can you be so calm about such frightening wraiths?' protested Eadulf. 'Antler-headed gods with serpents in their hands!' He shivered violently.

'Didn't your people worship such gods before they converted to Christianity?' asked Fidelma.

'None with antlers from their heads,' vowed Eadulf.

They reached the entrance of the gorge and started through its narrow rocky passage.

'Who passes?' cried a voice from high above them.

Fidelma groaned inwardly. She had forgotten the sentinels who guarded the gorge. However, what had worked once would doubtless work again.

'Fidelma of Cashel,' she called back. Then, as an afterthought, 'Were you on guard here yesterday afternoon?'

A shadow moved above them and emerged indistinctly in the rising light of the dawn.

'Not I. Why do you ask?'

'I wondered if the horse dealer, Ibor of Muirthemne, was seen passing this way or Artgal?'

'Everyone who passed through this gorge came under our scrutiny. The horse dealer certainly passed along here in the afternoon for my brother was on duty here. But as for Artgal . . . no, it would have been mentioned if he had passed this way. The news of Artgal's loss of honour has certainly been spoken.'

Fidelma accepted the information with resignation. She had not really expected to learn much.

'Very well. Can we proceed?'

'Go in peace,' invited the sentinel.

By the time they had negotiated the gorge, dawn had broken across the mountains in streaks of orange, gold and yellow and the countryside was coming to life with a noisy chorus of birds arising from all around them. Fidelma made her unerring way towards the spot where they had encountered the slaughtered bodies of the young men. It was well and truly light by the time they reached the place. The view was clear in every direction. However, in two days the ravens had done their work well. The white bones of the skeletons lay scattered with hardly any flesh left upon them. Eadulf shuddered as he gazed about the bright sepulchre of bones, reflecting in the translucent light.

Fidelma did not give them a second glance but rode directly to where she recalled that the tracks had been. She could not find them. It was Eadulf who attempted an explanation.

'While it didn't rain in Gleann Geis yesterday, there was some rain beyond the mountains. It might be that the tracks have been washed away.'

Fidelma moved forward to view the ground more carefully.

'But not entirely,' she called triumphantly. 'I can still see faint traces of the ruts.'

Eadulf followed her, his eyes sweeping the countryside around them in case of danger for he still questioned the wisdom of what they were attempting. Those who would not hesitate to kill thirty-three young men in a ritual slaughter would not falter in killing any religious if they became a threat.

'Come on,' Fidelma called, 'the tracks lead northwards.'

She began to walk her horse carefully across the floor of the valley.

'How far do you intend to go?' grumbled the Saxon. 'Colla says the tracks soon disappeared.'

Fidelma pointed before her towards the northern hills on the rim of the valley.

'I will go as far as the edge of the glen, just there, where the hills begin to rise. If we see no further signs by then, we will follow the edge of the valley back to the entrance to Gleann Geis and conclude our business there.'

'Do you mistrust Colla so much? Do you really think that he has tried to mislead us?'

'I prefer the evidence of my own eyes,' replied Fidelma easily. 'And don't forget, I did see Orla outside the stable. I know I did. Therefore, the logical conclusion is that Colla lied to protect his wife. By doing so, he placed me in jeopardy. What he did once, he can do a second time.'

In silence they walked their horses on, sitting at ease in their saddles, but now and then Fidelma stopped in an attempt to pick up the signs of the passing of the wagons. The tracks soon disappeared. They had not been visible for long before the stony ground had, indeed, disguised all signs of the passing of the carts. She was forced to admit that Colla had told the truth. They were still a mile or so off from the foot of the hills when all trace completely vanished.

'Perhaps you have done Colla an injustice?' ventured Eadulf wryly.

Fidelma did not grace his comment with an answer.

'If we go back empty handed, what excuse will you give to Laisre?' Eadulf pressed.

Fidelma thrust out her lower lip in annoyance.

'I am not in the habit of giving excuses,' she replied crossly. 'He has no right to question my actions as a *dálaigh*.'

She drew her horse to a halt and raised a hand to shade her eyes. Then she exhaled in irritation.

'I would be happier if I even had an idea of what we were looking for,' protested Eadulf. 'I don't think we are going to find further tracks in this terrain. What else is there?'

For a time Fidelma did not bother to reply. They continued in silence for a while until the stony valley floor began to rise into the surrounding hills. But there was no sign of any tracks at all. After a fruitless hour or so Fidelma called a halt and extended her hand southwards.

'There are some grassy areas if we swing south of here. Perhaps we might find some tracks there,' she volunteered. 'This northern path looks as if it is going to reveal nothing.'

Eadulf suppressed a sigh but still followed her. He already had a feeling that a search of the area would reveal nothing. Not a sign of wagon tracks but Fidelma pressed on. Eadulf was about to make a stronger protest to the effect that they were simply wasting time and ought to return to Gleann Geis when Fidelma halted.

'Tracks of several horses,' she cried triumphantly pointing downwards to the disturbed grassy area.

Eadulf confirmed the statement with a sour glare.

'It means little without wagon tracks. There are plenty of people on horseback who could pass this spot.'

It happened so suddenly that Fidelma and Eadulf had no time at all to react.

Out of nowhere half-a-dozen warriors appeared on horseback with swords ready and surrounded them.

'Hold still, if you value your lives!' cried their leader, a large man with a bushy red beard and a burnished bronze helmet studded with red enamel pieces.

Fidelma had a sinking sensation as she realised that the man spoke in a northern accent.

A second man rode alongside them and, before they could protest, their wrists were expertly bound behind them. Blindfolds were produced and tied over their eyes. Their reins were taken from them and they found themselves being led at a swift canter. They needed their breath to maintain their balance on the fast-moving horses and could not protest or demand an explanation. Neither Fidelma nor Eadulf could estimate the amount of time it took as they were escorted to their captors' destination.

The end of the ride came as abruptly as it had begun.

The horses suddenly halted, there were shouted commands, and strong arms lifted them both down. Their blindfolds were removed and they stood blinking in the centre of a group of warriors. Fidelma noticed that they were in a gorge, no more than a rocky fissure, hardly big enough for four men to stand abreast. Around them the rocky walls rose almost blotting out the sky. It was a dark, narrow passageway.

The leader of the warriors, the red-haired man with a fierce, almost angry expression, stood in front of them and his shrewd scrutiny missed nothing.

'You have come from Gleann Geis.' It was a statement rather than a question.

'We do not deny it,' affirmed Fidelma coldly. 'Where have you come from?'

The man's face conveyed no reaction. His sharp blue eyes examined them both carefully, taking in Fidelma's cross of the Golden Chain and Eadulf's foreign appearance. Then he turned and signalled to one of his men. Silently the man handed him their saddle bags which he had obviously removed from their horses. The red-haired leader peered firstly into Eadulf's saddle bags and then took hold of Fidelma's bags.

'Are you common thieves and robbers, then?' she sneered. 'If you are looking for riches, you will not find any for . . .'

The man ignored her and continued to rummage through the saddle bag. His hand came out holding the gold torc. His eyes glinted.

'Who are you?' he demanded.

'I am Fidelma of Cashel.'

'A woman of Muman who carries the gold collar of Ailech?' scoffed the man. He thrust it back into the saddle bag and then slung both over his shoulder.

Fidelma started at the mention of the name of Ailech.

Ailech was the capital of the northern Uí Néill kings who were in enmity with the southern Uí Néill kings who ruled at Tara.

The red-bearded man had turned and was striding towards what appeared to be the sheer cliff face. His men had closed in around Fidelma and Eadulf. Before they could protest or make further demands of their captors they were forced to move at a rapid trot towards one of the towering walls of the fissure. So fast did they move, even with their hands still tied behind their backs, that Eadulf found himself closing his eyes believing, for a moment, that their captors were intent on killing them by smashing them against the granite wall. Then he felt cold and darkness encompassed him. He ventured to open his eyes and found he was in a cave which was dimly lit by a single torch. Somehow he and Fidelma had been manoeuvred into a hidden cave entrance.

The leader continued to head the way along the dark tunnel. Neither Fidelma nor Eadulf made any protest for there was little point in protesting. The warriors moved them swiftly and professionally. They were propelled through a series of caves and narrow passageways. Then they came to a sudden halt.

'Blindfold them again,' ordered the leader.

Once again they were in complete darkness.

There was a moment's pause and they were propelled onwards once more. It was not long before they came to a halt again. The atmosphere was suddenly warm. Fidelma could feel the presence of a fire from the warmth on her cheek.

'We have caught a couple of spies from Gleann Geis, my lord,' came the voice of the leader of their escort.

'Spies, eh?' The voice was familiar. 'Untie their blindfolds and let them see.'

The blindfolds were taken off again with rough hands.

'Gently!' rebuked the familiar voice sharply. 'Do not harm our honoured guests.'

Fidelma stood blinking in the smoky atmosphere of a large cave which was lit by spluttering torches. She noticed it contained sleeping rugs, a fire in one corner, strategically placed under what appeared to be a natural chimney with a cauldron hanging over its flames, steaming away. At her side, Eadulf was still blinking and not yet taking in his surroundings. Apart from the men who had escorted them into the cave, there were half-a-dozen other warriors squatting on the rugs with one of them standing over the cauldron. At one end, perched on a wooden camp chair, was a familiar figure.

Fidelma smiled grimly as she recognised the young horse trader.

'I thought our paths would meet again, Ibor of Muirthemne.'

The young man laughed good naturedly.

'Untie their hands and let them be seated,' he instructed.

'But, my lord . . .' protested the red-haired man who had captured them. 'Look!' He took out the gold torc and thrust it at Ibor. 'The woman carries this as proof of her guilt.'

Ibor took the torc and examined it. Then he raised his eyes to the man.

'Untie them at once!' he said firmly.

Reluctantly, the red-haired man drew out his knife and severed Fidelma's bonds and then the rope which tied Eadulf's wrists. They stood for a moment rubbing their chaffed wrists and examining Ibor in curiosity. Now he was clothed as a warrior, a costume that seemed to fit him better than his previous form of dress. Fidelma smiled grimly as the former assessment that Ibor looked more a warrior than a horse trader now appeared to be correct. The erstwhile trader from Muirthemne was obviously a fighting man.

'Be seated and accept my hospitality,' invited Ibor as politely as if he had simply invited them as guests to his ráth. 'It is rather poor hospitality since we are camped out here . . .'

'Hiding from lawful authority,' interjected Eadulf sourly.

Ibor shook his head and his smile broadened.

'Not hiding but merely not wishing to announce our presence. Come, be seated. You shall not be harmed while you are my guests.'

Reluctantly, but with no other option, Fidelma and Eadulf sat on the rugs which had been indicated.

'Why did you allow the people in Gleann Geis to believe that it was you who bribed Artgal?' Fidelma opened without preamble.

'I thought that they had already decided that without my help,' replied Ibor humorously.

'By running away you simply confirmed it.'

'A strategic withdrawal to join my men.'

'And to do what exactly?'

Ibor shrugged, still smiling.

'Who knows? Maybe to destroy that nest of vermin.'

'Brother Dianach is dead. I know that he was the person who bought the cows to bribe Artgal with and not you.'

The young man did not look surprised.

'And Artgal? What does he say now?'

'Artgal is missing.'

There was a silence but Ibor's composure did not alter.

'As soon as Artgal started to lie about Brother Dianach, I knew that suspicion would fall on me. I knew that I would be apprehended for something I did not do . . . even as you were, Fidelma.'

'You knew that I was innocent?' Fidelma could not hide her surprise.

'I knew that you had little reason to kill Brother Solin,' he confirmed. 'I was hoping to be able to find out who did before it became necessary for me to withdraw from Laisre's ráth.'

'It is hard to believe that you claim innocence,' Fidelma observed skeptically. 'Who are you and what are you doing here?'

'You know already that I am Ibor; Ibor, lord of Muirthemne.'

'That is a proud title. It is not the title of a trader in horseflesh.'

'I am proud to bear it. It is an ancient lineage. Was not my ancestor named Setanta of Muirthemne who men called Cúchulainn, the hound of Culainn?'

Fidelma looked into Ibor's eyes and saw a pride in his ancestry.

'You have not explained why the lord of Muirthemne in Ulaidh was skulking in Gleann Geis in the guise of a merchant. This is a curiously isolated part of the world for a band of warriors from the north to stumble on without some evil intent?'

'In truth, we did not stumble on it and we did come here with a specific purpose.'

'At least you are honest with me. Why?'

Ibor smiled disarmingly.

'I would ask you to promise that you will be circumspect as to what I tell you.'

Fidelma held her head slightly to one side. Her expression one of curiosity.

'Circumspect? You do not ask me for secrecy?'

Ibor shook his head.

'I trust your discretion and honesty as I hope you will trust mine once you hear my story. I know of your reputation. I told you so before. And I also see that you wear the cross of the order of the Golden Chain. This is why I shall put my trust in you.'

Fidelma continued to gaze at him thoughtfully.

'I would answer that I apply discretion in all things but as to accepting your honesty, that remains to be seen.'

'I would expect no more in the circumstances.' The young lord of Muirthemne glanced quickly at Eadulf. 'Your voice also speaks for the Saxon brother?'

'You may be assured of Brother Eadulf's discretion as you are of mine.'

'Discretion is all I ask.'

'You can expect little more, especially when you hold that gold torc which I found at the site of the slaughter of thirty-three young men,' Fidelma added quietly.

Ibor glanced down at the torc in his hand and nodded absently.

'It is a torc fashioned for the warriors of Ailech,' he commented absently. 'You will hear the explanation for this shortly. To begin, my men and I have been following Brother Solin of Armagh this past week.'

'On whose authority?' Fidelma asked at once.

'On the authority of Sechnassuch, High King at Tara.'

'With what purpose?'

'With the purpose of discovering his reason for coming to this land.'

'You say that as if you suspected him of some transgression against the law?' intervened Eadulf.

The lord of Muirthemne chuckled grimly.

'I would venture that my view has long passed the point of mere suspicion. And as for transgressing the law, he has transgressed every moral code that I know of.'

'I do not understand,' Fidelma said. 'You are a man of the north and yet you appear to be claiming that you are an enemy of Brother Solin? Why is this? Is Brother Solin not only a man of the north but also of the cloth? He maintained that he was on a mission for the Faith.'

'A mission for the Devil!' snapped Ibor. Then he leaned forward, his voice grave. 'Surely you know something about the dissensions among the kings of the north? You have been to Tara and you have also been to Armagh.'

'Is it a coincidence that Brother Solin once asked me this very same question? I have been to Tara and I have been to Armagh but I was not privy to any internal disputes there.'

Ibor sat back.

'I will explain the divisions as simply as I can. First you must know that I am an emissary of the High King, Sechnassuch. As you know, he is of the southern Uí Néill, of the seed of Aedo Sláine. Here is his royal seal as proof of my word.' He reached beneath his shirt and brought out a gold seal on a golden chain and held it out for her inspection. 'You have been to Tara and know it well.'

Fidelma glanced at the gold medallion. On it was stamped a regal upright hand symbolising the duty of the king to reach out his hand to protect his people, for in ancient times it was said that both words *rí* for king and *reach* were the same. Fidelma recognised the seal of the Uí Néill immediately.

'Go on,' she invited. 'Tell us your story.'

'Brother Solin was secretary to Ultan of Armagh.'

'That I know,' Fidelma said, a trifle impatiently.

'Ultan has secretly sworn to support the claims of the dynasty of the northern Uí Néill, the kings who sit at Ailech.'

Fidelma had never had dealings with the northern Uí Néill kingdom. She only knew that Ailech was a fortress city in the extreme north-west of the country where the king was currently Mael Dúin, who also claimed descent from the great High King, Niall of the Nine Hostages.

'Your man said that the torc was made in Ailech,' she observed quietly.

Ibor nodded.

'There is little love lost between the two dynasties of the Uí Néill, northern and southern,' he explained. 'Mael Dúin is not the first king of the northern Uí Néill line to argue that his dynasty are the true heirs of the kingship of all the north, and not only the kingship of Ulaidh but he claims the right to the High Kingship at Tara. He further claims that the High Kingship should not be a matter of conferred honour among the provincial kings but a reality and that the High King should have a real power over all the five kingdoms of Éireann.'

Fidelma examined him suspiciously.

'And what does Sechnassuch say to this?'

'You have met Sechnassuch,' Ibor replied. 'His principle is the law. He is king of the southern Uí Néill of Tara and acknowledges the courtesy accorded by the laws of the *Míadslechta* of being High King. But as the *Míadslechta* says – why are the provincial kings greater than the High King?'

'Because they appoint and ordain the High King,' interrupted Fidelma quoting the text, 'the High King does not ordain the provincial kings.'

Ibor nodded appreciatively at her knowledge.

'You are correct, *dálaigh* of Cashel. Sechnassuch would give his entire honour price of fourteen *cumals* in forfeit if he ever broke this law.'

'Is there any likelihood of him doing so?'

'Not while he is alive. But this cannot be said of the northern Uí Néill; nor of Mael Dúin of Ailech. He has ambition. And that ambition has grown since he went on a pilgrimage to Rome before he took the crown of Ailech.'

'How so? What has a pilgrimage to Rome to do with this matter?'

'He saw the greatness of Rome and became enamoured of the Roman path of the Faith. He went to a Roman-trained confessor and priest who taught him about the great temporal empires and the peoples who fell under the suzerainty of the emperors of Rome.'

'There are several in the five kingdoms who have already accepted allegiance to Rome,' observed Fidelma. 'Allegiance to Rome is surely a matter of individual conscience? My companion, Eadulf, bears allegiance to the Roman ways, unlike myself being committed to the Church of Colmcille. We do not fight but we discuss in fruitful amity.'

'Fair enough, Fidelma of Cashel. Each to his own path. But when one is forced along a path one does not wish to take, then there is dissension in the land.'

'This Mael Dúin believes, then, in forcing his beliefs on others?'

'That he does. And he does so in two ways. Firstly with his religion and secondly he has been fired to create in this island the feudal empire of the type which he has learned about in Rome, a central kingdom ruled by one emperor. And he wants that emperor to be himself.'

Fidelma let out a soft breath.

'I begin to see where you are leading us. Mael Dúin of Ailech wishes to firstly subsume the southern Uí Néill to his kingdom of Ailech. Then he wishes to claim the High Kingship and turn it from an honour alternated between the provincial kings into a single dynasty which will maintain a supreme authority over all of the five kingdoms in the manner of the Roman emperors?'

'That is exactly what he proposes,' confirmed Ibor.

'Then the kings of the provinces must be warned against Mael Dúin's ambitions. They would never stand for such a usurpation of law and morality.'

'But there is something further.'

'What more can there be?' Fidelma's expression was grim.

'Mael Dúin has, as I say, won the support of Ultan of Armagh.'

'I knew that Ultan has long been in favour of adopting the rules of Rome in our Church and prefers to use the title of *archiepiskopos* instead of Comarb. Indeed, many have, out of courtesy referred to him as such. Even I myself. I know he would wish to reorganise our Church on the model Rome has provided but not even Ultan can believe that he can change our law of kingship.'

'Why not? If Mael Dúin of Ailech thinks he can, so can Ultan. If Mael Dúin can create a powerful High Kingship at Tara which favours Roman rite and organisation, then Armagh will also prosper being within the *puruchia* of the High King. Ultan plans to become the head of the Faith in Ireland just as Mael Dúin plans to become a High King with real central power.'

Fidelma was troubled as she contemplated the enormity of Ibor's revelation.

'This explains much of what Brother Solin was boasting about. So then Ultan will use the powerful centralised authority of Mael Dúin to exert the authority of Armagh over all other Churches of the five kingdoms?'

'Just so.'

Eadulf intervened for the first time.

'One thing you forget,' he said quietly. 'Even if this king of Ailech overcomes the southern Uí Néill, he could not be in power in Tara for long. Cashel, supported by Imleach, would be among the first to challenge such preposterous claims.'

Ibor glanced at him almost sadly.

'So therefore Imleach and Cashel would have to be made weak,' he pointed out.

Fidelma jerked her head up quickly; her flashing eyes sought those of Ibor.

'You have news of such a plot?'

'The plot has already begun here in Gleann Geis,' he replied. 'It is Mael Dúin and Ultan who are behind it. If the northern Uí Néill move in force then the southern Uí Néill might not long delay them. There are too many ties of kinship and blood for a serious contention between Mael Dúin and Sechnassuch. Once that happens . . .' Ibor threw out his arms in a gesture of resignation.

'But Cashel would not allow it to happen,' Fidelma vowed. 'Wishing Cashel to be weak does not make it so.'

'True. It has to be made so. Cashel represents the biggest barrier to the northern Uí Néill's ambition to take over the High Kingship. Mael Dúin has been probing for Cashel's weakness for a while now. And where is Cashel's greatest weakness?'

Fidelma paused for a moment's reflection.

'Why, among the Uí Fidgente in north-west Muman,' she said thoughtfully. 'And among the clans west of the Shannon. They have been the most restless clans of Muman. The Uí Fidgente have tried many times to overthrow the kings of Cashel and split the kingdom.'

'There is the weakness of Muman – the Uí Fidgente,' Ibor declared like a schoolmaster summing up his lesson.

'So Brother Solin was sent here to create new dissensions between the Uí Fidgente and the Eóghanacht of Cashel? Is that what you are saying?' Eadulf asked.

'He was sent as Ultan's agent and through Ultan as an emissary of Mael Dúin.'

'And why were you sent here? To kill Brother Solin?'

'No. I told you that I had no hand in his death. I did not kill him. But I was sent to discover the details of Mael Dúin's plot.'

Fidelma was finding difficulty encompassing the fiendishness of what the lord of Muirthemne was revealing. She looked at Ibor directly.

'What of the slaughter of the young men? The ritual killing?'

'You have a reputation for working out puzzles. You came as an emissary from Cashel and Imleach and stumbled across what you thought to be a ritual killing. Who would stand to gain had you reacted as you were supposed to react?'

She stared at him in incomprehension for a moment.

'How was I supposed to react?' she asked uncertainly.

'Those responsible for the slaughter simply knew that a religieuse was due to arrive at Gleann Geis. The ritual slaughter was arranged by them in the belief that such a religieuse would understand the pagan symbolism in it and then see nothing further.'

Fidelma began to understand.

'They thought that the religieuse would panic and go riding back to Cashel and call for a religious war to exterminate the barbarians of Gleann Geis for having perpetrated such a crime?'

'Exactly so,' Ibor agreed. 'Cashel would come down with all its might and fury on Gleann Geis to seek retribution. Gleann Geis would be protesting its innocence and indeed some evidence would be placed in the hands of the friends of Gleann Geis to indicate that it was Cashel's own hand in the slaughter. The surrounding clans would be told that Cashel was the evil doer and had used the slaughter as a justification to annihilate Gleann Geis. Indignant, the clans would also rise up in support of Gleann Geis. The Uí Fidgente would be persuaded, and not with difficulty, to also rise once more against Cashel. Civil war would split the land.'

'But most clans in this kingdom would support Cashel,' Eadulf pointed out.

'Possibly. But the northern Uí Néill, expressing themselves appalled by such acts,' went on Ibor, 'would then encourage and supply its allies to march on Cashel. Once Cashel had been destroyed, Mael Dúin would begin the process of obtaining the High Kingship and exert its will over all the kingdoms. With the Eóghanacht of Cashel destroyed, there would be no one to challenge the Uí Néill.'

Fidelma was incredulous. But she realised the grim logic of what Ibor was saying.

'And all this might well have happened,' she murmured.

She did not have to glance at Eadulf to make the Saxon feel uncomfortable. The Saxon lowered his head when he remembered his advice to her on the finding of the bodies and the realisation of what they symbolised. He had a feeling of growing horror.

'Do I understand you correctly?' he asked Ibor. 'The slaughter of those thirty-three young men was carried out for no more reason than for our benefit? That it was a grotesque charade the purpose of which was to make us return in panic to Cashel and call for a holy war against the pagans of Gleann Geis?'

Ibor regarded the Saxon with some solemn amusement.

'That is precisely what I have explained.'

'And these sons of Satan were watching us all the time,' Eadulf muttered reflectively. 'Do you remember,' he turned to Fidelma, 'that we saw the sun flash on metal as we climbed to that valley? We were being watched. They must have watched our approach and knowing the path by which we were entering Gleann Geis they then arranged their terrible show along the course which we were taking, assured that we would see the bodies.'

Ibor of Muirthemne smiled grimly at Fidelma.

'A war such as they planned might have happened had you reacted in the manner that was expected of you. But, God be praised, you did not. You kept your head and went on into Gleann Geis in search of the truth.'

There was a silence as they reflected on the quirk of fate which had prevented this carefully laid plot from coming to its hoped for fruition.

'Sechnassuch once told me that you were an individualist, Fidelma,' Ibor continued appreciatively. 'Sechnassuch claimed that you were a rebel against the conservative ways of doing things.'

'It was a plot that was well thought out,' she admitted. 'But, Ibor, you have not told us who was responsible for that slaughter?'

Ibor replied without hesitation.

'Warriors from Ailech itself. Chosen men from Mael Dúin's own bodyguard, with sworn allegiance to him and no one else.'

'Did you witness this slaughter?' demanded Eadulf.

'No; we did not witness it otherwise we would have done our best to prevent it,' Ibor replied quietly.

'How then do you know that it was men of Ailech who did the deed?' pressed Eadulf.

'Easy enough. Our small band, there are twenty warriors and myself, were following Brother Solin and Brother Dianach. We knew that they would lead us to the substance of Mael Dúin's plot. We followed them from Armagh on their journey south for many days. Then Brother Solin met up with a strange cavalcade. There was a band of warriors from Ailech. They were escorting the column of prisoners. Each man of them was . . .'

'Shackled in leg-irons?' interrupted Fidelma.

'How did you know?' Ibor asked. 'I saw the bodies after the slaughter and the men of Ailech had removed all signs of identification; leg-irons, clothes, anything which might have identified the perpetrators of the deed.'

'I saw the chaffing and scars left by the irons on the ankles of the slaughtered. I also saw the soles of their feet. They were covered with blisters and abrasions. That told me that the men had been forced to walk a long distance.'

The lord of Muirthemne did not seem astonished by her deductions.

'They had, indeed, marched all the way from Ailech. May the place now be cursed. They must have been special hostages rounded up by the tyrant, Mael Dúin, and marched south specifically for the purpose of this appalling crime. With the warriors were men on foot controlling several large hounds, presumably as a precaution against escape. An interesting thing, which puzzled me at the time, was that this strange procession was followed by two empty carts, large farm carts used for transporting hay.'

'Ah yes.' Fidelma nodded. 'The carts. I would have expected them to be there. What exactly happened at this rendezvous which you witnessed?'

'Brother Solin and the commander of warriors from Ailech greeted each other in friendly fashion and they camped together for a day before Solin continued on with Brother Dianach . . .'

'Did you identify the commander of these warriors?' interrupted Eadulf.

'Not by name, although I do not doubt that we will find him in Mael Dúin's shadow. One person with these warriors I can tell you more about . . .'

He paused, obviously to make a better impact but when he saw Fidelma's irritation he hurried on.

'There was a woman who rode into their camp. She was obviously expected and greeted with courtesy. I have seen such a woman in Gleann Geis. A slender woman of commanding appearance.'

Fidelma raised her head with a satisfied smile.

'Was it Orla, sister of Laisre?'

'I can think of no other woman in Gleann Geis who bears resemblance to the person I saw meeting with the men of Ailech and with Brother Solin,' replied Ibor gravely.

Chapter Seventeen

'Orla!' breathed Fidelma in satisfaction. 'I was sure that it was her who I saw outside the stable.'

'Let me be absolutely correct,' Ibor hastened to add. 'I could not swear to the fact that it was Orla meeting with Solin and the men of Ailech. We were spying on this scene from a distance, don't forget. I did not know Orla at that time. But I saw no one else at Gleann Geis who had the same style of dress and authority of command as the woman I saw. One interesting fact I should point out. There was a disturbance during this meeting. It seemed that one of the hostages had managed to escape. The men with the dogs made ready to hunt him down and the woman spoke with their leader. It appeared that she requested to lead the hunt herself, for the next moment she set off on horseback with three huntsmen and their hounds.'

'Did you try to rescue the escaped prisoner?' Eadulf asked.

Ibor shrugged resignedly.

'It was impossible without betraying our presence. It was only a matter of an hour before he was caught and brought back again. It was then that we noticed that he was a priest because he wore a tonsure. The possible fate of the shackled men did not cross my mind at that time otherwise we would have attempted to rescue them all. I was more concerned with following Solin and, to my shame, I left them to their fate not realising what horror would later be perpetrated against them.'

'Indeed, no one would have guessed the terrible slaughter that was about to take place,' Fidelma reassured him. 'There is no blame on you. What did you do then?'

'It had hardly taken her any time to track the poor hostage down. After the woman returned to the encampment, she spoke a while and then left with Brother Solin and Brother Dianach and two warriors of Ailech. They rode for Gleann Geis.

'Brother Solin and Brother Dianach went directly through the gorge but the woman did not do so. With the two warriors from Ailech she went across the valley to the point where the bodies were later placed. It could be that the woman showed the warriors the place. These warriors rejoined the rest of their company while the woman vanished into the hills.'

'That is a pity,' Fidelma sighed.

'What?'

'That is a pity,' repeated Fidelma. 'A pity the woman did not enter Gleann Geis with Solin and Dianach.'

'Why so?'

'Because we could have easily confirmed that this was Orla by finding out, from the sentinels, who it was that escorted Solin and Dianach into the glen.'

'I was wondering why Brother Solin had gone on into Gleann Geis,' went on Ibor, 'not yet having worked out all the permutations of the plot. Pondering this, my men and I found this hiding place and decided to make it our base until we could discover more details. Then two things happened.'

'What?'

'Firstly, while we were hiding in the hills, my scouts reported that the warriors of Ailech had slaughtered the hostages. The slaughter had been done in the shallows of a stream back in the hills, presumably to hide the deed for the water would have dispersed the blood. By the time my scouts alerted me, the bodies had been stripped, placed on carts and taken across the glen – as I say, to the spot where the woman had previously accompanied the two others. We were about to follow them when we observed the empty carts returning with the warriors of Ailech. There were no bodies. We saw that one cart was piled with the bloodied clothes of the victims. Then both carts proceeded northward with their escort.'

He passed his hand over his mouth distastefully as he remembered the scene.

'Go on,' urged Eadulf, intrigued by the horror.

'Then my scouts reported your arrival on the plain and that you had halted where the bodies had, as my scouts reported, been dumped. After a while, from our vantage point in the hills, we saw you and Brother Eadulf crossing the plain and then being greeted by a band of warriors with a woman at their head. By her appearance, it was the same woman who had met Mael Dúin's warriors earlier.'

When he paused again it was Fidelma who urged: 'Then what happened?'

'I was considering what plan I should adopt when my men saw the warrior I now know to be Artgal ride to the spot where the bodies were and examine them. You two and the woman had disappeared into the gorge. I was not sure, at that time, who you were or what

Artgal was looking for. I did not know even then what exactly had happened. Only after Artgal and his men had left did we venture to the spot.'

He shuddered involuntarily.

'I have seen many vicious acts in war, all made while the battle fever gripped men's minds, but there are none that I recall which approached this horror. I went with my scouts and saw that the hostages had been mutilated – the old Threefold Death of which storytellers used to frighten us as children. Only when I saw how the bodies had been arranged did I realise the significance.'

'Why didn't you tell me what you knew when you came to Gleann Geis instead of pretending you were a dealer in horses?' demanded Fidelma. 'That was a poor disguise, easily seen through.'

Ibor grinned lopsidedly.

'It was the only disguise I could think of at the time which gave me a chance of entering the glen. But as for telling you – I did not know who you were. When Laisre introduced us, I knew you only by reputation. But I was told that you were in the company of a Roman monk.' He glanced at Eadulf. 'He might have been one of Mael Dúin's men or one of Ultan's followers. I could not trust you. I could not know whether you were part of the plot or not.

'I suspected, however, that Orla was involved because she was the one who met with Brother Solin and the butchers of Ailech. The more I thought about it, it was obvious that Mael Dúin could not conceive or work this plot on his own or just with Solin's backing. To work accurately, such a plan would have to have at least one supporter in Gleann Geis.'

Eadulf nodded slowly.

'What happened when Colla came later to investigate? Did you observe what he did?' he queried.

'We hid from Colla and his men. I had sent two of my men to track the warriors of Ailech. They did so as far as the borders of the Uí Fidgente and then returned to report that those scions of evil were well on their way back to their master at Ailech. We watched Colla search the valley for a while. He rode as far as the foothills in which we were hiding. Then he returned to Gleann Geis.'

Fidelma sat back.

'And it was then that you decided to come into Gleann Geis posing as a horse trader to see what was going on there?'

Ibor made an affirmative gesture.

'Then it all fell into place, or so I thought. Some great charade had been enacted to prompt a terrible war. Only your refusal to panic and cry "wolf!" at the first opportunity stopped the immediate outbreak of hostilities. The problem was, Brother Solin recognised me as a warrior of Ulaidh in the service of Sechnassuch.'

'I overheard your conversation at the stable. Why didn't he betray you?'

'He might well have had not I called his bluff and said I would also denounce him. It appears that there are many in Gleann Geis who are not in this plot. I was trying to find out who was on which side when Solin was murdered and you were placed on trial.'

'And you fled!' sneered Eadulf. 'Thus bringing suspicion down on yourself.'

'What else could I do in the circumstances?' demanded Ibor. 'Someone had to be free to inform Sechnassuch.'

'And Brother Solin's death was not at your hands?'

'That much is obvious.'

Fidelma was frowning as she thought over the details of Ibor's story.

'There are many questions to be resolved,' she brooded.

'Such as how Mael Dúin in his northern kingdom at Ailech knew that Laisre was going to send to Cashel for a religious to negotiate on matters of Faith? How could he know that this religious was to arrive on a particular day so that his men knew where and when to place the bodies?' Eadulf interposed.

'Mael Dúin must have been closely informed as to what was going on,' agreed Ibor. 'Orla showed his men to the place where the bodies were found by you. Was she acting on her own? It seems unlikely. But who was in the plot with her?'

Fidelma nodded.

'She is certainly part of this conspiracy. But . . . and this is the question we really need to answer . . . if Orla was thus an ally of Brother Solin, why did she kill him?'

Ibor started forward in surprise.

'That had not occurred to me. Are you sure that you saw her at the stable? If so that also implicates Colla as her accomplice?'

Fidelma was quiet for a moment.

'Yes. But we are still left with a mystery – why, if this matter emanates from such a terrible plot to create civil war here, does one ally turn on another? Why kill Brother Solin and then kill Dianach? It simply does not make sense.'

Ibor spread his arms helplessly.

'I was hoping that you would be able to unravel this knot.'

'Even I cannot perform miracles, Ibor,' replied Fidelma grimly. 'I have never known of such an instance where all paths lead into nowhere; where there is much suspicion but no tangible line of facts. I am afraid that the answers still lie in the ráth of Gleann Geis.'

Eadulf shuddered slightly.

'Better to ride for Cashel and report what we know already to your brother.'

Ibor was immediately in agreement.

Fidelma shook her head firmly.

'I presume that we are now free to travel where we wish?' she asked Ibor with a touch of irony.

The lord of Muirthemne was contrite.

'Of course. My men detained you only because I told them to be suspicious of everyone coming from Gleann Geis. I was going to try to contact you and offer to work with you to solve this matter.'

'In that case Brother Eadulf will remain with you but I shall return to Laisre's ráth,' Fidelma announced. 'It is only there that the final threads of the mystery will link together. However, if you can spare one of your most trusted men to ride to my brother at Cashel . . . ? We need to inform him of Mael Dúin of Ailech's plans and Ultan's involvement.'

'Your brother will be suspicious of a warrior from Ulaidh arriving with this wild tale,' protested Ibor.

'Have no fear. Can one of your men cut me some wands of hazel?'

Ibor frowned in bewilderment but relayed the order to one of his warriors. The man hurried off.

'What do you mean to do?' he asked. 'There might be great danger in Gleann Geis now. If Orla and Colla suspect that you know anything about their plot, about what is really going on, then they will not hesitate to kill you. A person who can willingly accept the murder of thirty-three young hostages merely in order to create disunity and strife will not think twice about further deaths to hide their criminality.'

'This I know,' Fidelma accepted. 'How many men did you say you have with you?'

'Twenty warriors of the Craobh Rígh, the royal branch of Ulaidh,' Ibor replied proudly. The Craobh Rígh were the élite bodyguard of the kings of Ulaidh. Then he hesitated. 'Why do you ask?'

'I think that I am beginning to see a pattern in this muddy picture,' she mused. 'Let me think things through for a moment or so.'

After some moments the warrior returned with a bunch of half-a-dozen pliant hazel rods. Fidelma took them and asked Ibor for his sharp knife. They watched in bemusement as Fidelma deftly began to cut a series of notches along the rods. Then she bound them together with a thong of leather taken from her *marsupium* and handed them to Ibor.

'All your man has to do is to hand these to my brother at Cashel. They are to be placed into his hand and no other. Is that understood?'

Ibor turned to the warrior who had brought the rods to him.

'Do you understand what you must do, Mer?'

The warrior nodded and took the bundle of rods.

'It shall be done as you say, Sister,' the man said.

Fidelma looked up at him.

'I have recorded a message to my brother in Ogham, the old script of our tongue. He will understand.'

'It is vital that this message get through,' added Ibor quietly. 'The safety of the five kingdoms is at stake.'

The warrior named Mer raised his hand in a formal salute and hurried away.

'It will be a few days before my brother receives that message,' reflected Fidelma.

'Have you asked him to march here with an army?' asked Eadulf eagerly.

'And do the very thing that Mael Dúin and his allies want him to do?' Fidelma mocked. 'No. I have merely informed him of the situation and told him to beware of Ailech and Ultan of Armagh.'

'Then what do you propose to do?' Eadulf asked, perplexed.

'As I have said, I shall go back to Gleann Geis and investigate further. But I believe that I will not have far to search now. Ibor is right. We might yet find friends in Gleann Geis who will be as horrified as we are about this plot to destroy Muman. Once I know for sure who is responsible then I can place the facts before them and seek their aid.'

'But is it wise to go back?' protested Ibor. 'You will be in constant danger.'

Fidelma smiled briefly.

'Wisdom is being wise at the time wisdom is needed. I need to provoke some answers. I think I will need but another day to solve this mystery.'

Eadulf regarded her in astonishment but Fidelma spoke with quiet confidence.

'It will be early evening when I get back to Gleann Geis. So I should be ready to act by tomorrow morning. At dawn tomorrow I want you, Ibor, and your men to be in control of Laisre's fortress. Take command of all the key points by dawn.'

Ibor was so amazed at her request that he was unable to speak.

But his face did not hold the total astonishment which Eadulf's expression held.

'It will be no hardship,' Fidelma assured him earnestly. 'I have barely seen more than half a dozen of Laisre's warriors guarding it at any one time and the gates are left wide open all night.'

Ibor still looked doubtful.

'It is not so easy. Even in darkness it would be difficult to reach Laisre's ráth without being spotted. The reason why the gates are never closed is obvious. There is only one narrow ravine entering the valley through which only two might ride abreast and that is always guarded, so no need to close the gates of the fortress. The alarm would be given at the ravine if armed strangers entered.'

Eadulf was in total agreement.

'Even when we rode out at dawn, we were challenged, Fidelma,' he reminded her. 'Ibor is right. His men will not be able to enter the valley at all.'

'But there is another route.' Fidelma ignored their objections. 'There is the river.'

Ibor laughed dismissively.

'A river of rapids and waterfalls which is not even navigable by boat? Only a spawning salmon could hope to get up it into the valley. I have heard about that so-called route from Murgal when he was boasting of the impregnability of the valley.'

'According to Cruinn, there is a tiny rocky path beside the river, room for one man at a time, sometimes passing through caves but eventually emerging into the valley beyond.'

'Is she to be trusted?' The lord of Muirthemne was doubtful.

'She let it slip in an unthinking moment and seemed to regret that she had done so. I think we can trust her on that. It means coming into the valley on foot. Will you find the path and under cover of darkness reach the fortress without being seen? After all, you will face only a few unprofessional warriors while you command a troop of the Craobh Rígh.'

Ibor flushed at the implication that the Royal Branch warriors of Ulaidh were afraid of conflict with a handful of non-professional warriors.

This time Ibor gave no hesitation.

'If there is a way, Sister, my men and I will find it. If we can enter the valley unseen then we will be in control of Laisre's ráth before dawn as you demand.'

'Good. Once you have control then I think I will be in a position to draw the veil from these plots and murders without fear for myself.'

'But we have twelve hours to survive before that,' Eadulf pointed out.

'*We?*' queried Fidelma with a smile. 'I suggested that you remain with Ibor.'

'You do not think that I am letting you return alone, do you?' Eadulf asked in annoyance.

'I do not ask this of you, Eadulf. It is not your fight.'

'Neither was the fight between Cashel and the Uí Fidgente but I became involved and made it my fight,' he said firmly. 'What threatens Cashel is still my fight.'

He placed a certain emphasis on the last sentence.

Fidelma pretended not to understand but she did not argue further with him.

'Then, Ibor, we will see you at dawn tomorrow. We will be banking on you.'

Ibor escorted them to the small ravine where his red-haired lieutenant, more deferential now towards them, had their horses waiting. They bade a brief farewell and the red-haired warrior guided them out of the foothills to the edge of the valley. Fidelma refused to allow Ibor's man to ride further with them in case they encountered anyone from Gleann Geis on the way back. Fidelma and Eadulf continued to ride south keeping to the border of the foothills and not heading back across the valley.

'Do you really think that you can prove Orla was responsible for the death of Solin?' Eadulf broke the silence after they had been riding for a while.

'I need to answer one question and then I might safely put forward a hypothesis,' she replied quietly.

Eadulf's mouth drooped pessimistically.

'A hypothesis is no argument before a judge,' he replied.

'True, but it is going to be the best I can offer,' she agreed. 'I think it will be enough to bring forth those who will support us against Mael Dúin of Ailech.'

'What is it?'

'That I cannot say until I have secured the final link because at the moment it is that one link which worries me. Without it being put in place, the entire argument is destroyed.'

They had made a detour around a small foothill when suddenly a band of warriors came charging at them from two different directions, yelling and waving their swords threateningly. Fidelma pulled her horse around in a tight circle but they were surrounded and without weapons to defend themselves. Eadulf's horse was rearing and flaying out with its front hooves. He had difficulty maintaining his seat but succeeded in doing so and bringing the animal under control.

Eadulf found himself cursing under his breath quite forgetting his religious calling. For the second time that day they had been taken prisoner.

The warriors came to a halt, ringing them in, swords resting easily across their saddle bows, ready to use at a moment's notice. Fidelma felt cold. These were not Ibor's men.

'Hold hard!' cried a woman's familiar voice.

The ring of mounted warriors opened to allow a rider through. The slender figure was undoubtedly their leader. She removed her war helmet and surveyed them dourly.

'We thought that you had forsaken our hospitality, Fidelma of Cashel.'

It was Orla, a satisfied look on her dark features.

'As you see,' replied Fidelma, as evenly as if there had been no threatening behaviour on the part of the warriors. 'As you see, we were making our way back to Gleann Geis. We had not forsaken you.'

The truth of the statement was obvious enough for they were scarcely a half mile from the entrance of the gorge and had clearly been riding in that direction. A slight expression of bewilderment crossed Orla's face as she realised the point. Then she scowled.

'Nor will I forsake you, Fidelma, until I have made you retract your accusation against me.' Her voice was cold and brittle with anger. 'Why did you leave?'

'I would have thought that Murgal might have been able to explain the reason for that,' Fidelma commented with apparent unconcern.

'Murgal? What has he to do with this?' demanded the wife of the tanist of Gleann Geis.

'Murgal is a Brehon. He would know what motivated me to force myself to leave your brother's hospitality.'

'Well, as Murgal isn't here to speak perhaps you will? Better still, perhaps your Saxon friend can explain it for me? Then I can be sure that I am hearing the truth.'

Fidelma glanced to Eadulf anxiously, hoping that he would understand what she had meant or, at least make no reference to Ibor or his men.

'Easy enough to explain,' the Saxon said calmly. 'We came to look at the remains of the slaughtered men and follow the tracks to see if we could discover anything which Colla might have missed.'

Orla regarded him with suspicion.

'I knew that you did not believe my husband's report after he came to examine the bodies.'

'It is not a question of belief or disbelief. Your husband, Colla, is not a trained *dálaigh* of the courts, lady,' pointed out Eadulf. 'He might not know what to look for. There is no substitute for one's own trained observation.'

Orla almost ground her teeth in suppressed fury.

'That is not the reason. I know that you both want to destroy my husband and I. For what reason I do not know.'

Fidelma regarded her sadly.

'If you have done nothing wrong, then you need fear nothing. But it is as Eadulf has said. There is no better way to examine the scene of a crime than at first hand.'

Orla was still disbelieving.

'And why would Murgal know where you were? You did not tell him. He was as puzzled as we were by your absconding from the ráth.'

'Not if he had really thought about it.' Eadulf leaned forward in his saddle in a confidential mood. 'You see, as a Brehon, he would know that a *dálaigh* could not accept the prohibition issued by Laisre. Any *dálaigh* would have to see the evidence for themselves.'

Orla appeared confused for a moment.

'So you followed the tracks?' She gazed questioningly at Fidelma. Was there fear in her eyes? 'What did you discover that Colla could not?'

Fidelma felt it time to deflect the conversation.

'It was exactly as your husband told us,' she replied blandly. 'The tracks vanished and we found nothing else.'

Orla gave her a searching look and then sighed and resumed her scornful countenance.

'So it was a waste of time, your coming here?'

'A waste of time,' intoned Fidelma as if in agreement.

'Then you will not mind if my warriors and I escort you back to the ráth of Gleann Geis?'

Fidelma shrugged.

'It makes little difference whether you escort us or not for that is where we are going.'

Orla signalled to the band of warriors who sheathed their swords and turned their horses to allow Fidelma and Eadulf a passage through their circle. Orla drew her horse close by Fidelma's and they led the way forward with Eadulf behind and the column of mounted warriors bringing up the rear.

'We have told you the results of our inquiries,' observed Fidelma. 'In return you may tell us the news of Murgal's investigation of the murder of Brother Dianach. Has Artgal been found?'

Orla glared at her. For a moment or two it seemed as if she was going to refuse to answer. Then she shrugged nonchalantly.

'Murgal has already resolved the mystery. At least that is one killing that you cannot claim you saw me walk away from.'

Fidelma decided to ignore the thrust. She was, however, interested to hear that Murgal had solved the mystery.

'Who was the guilty party?' she pressed.

'Why, Artgal of course?'

'Then Artgal has been discovered and confessed?'

'No,' returned Orla. 'But his disappearance is his admission of guilt.'

Fidelma lowered her head thoughtfully. She remained silent for a short while before speaking.

'It is true that Artgal's disappearance looks bad. However, it can only be argued that it does not do his case good. To move on and say that it is an admission of guilt is taking the interpretation too far.'

'It seems logical to me,' snapped Orla. 'The Christian monk bribed Artgal. When the bribe was discovered, Artgal killed the monk to prevent him saying what he knew.'

'There is a flaw in that logic, as he had already demonstrated his guilt,' Fidelma observed.

'Besides,' Eadulf added with confidence, 'Nemon could easily testify that Brother Dianach had bought the cows from her to give to Artgal. Artgal had already confessed that he had received them.'

Orla was almost pitying.

'You should inform your assistant more carefully on the laws of the Brehons.'

Eadulf glanced questioningly at Fidelma.

'A prostitute cannot testify,' Fidelma explained quietly. 'According to the *Berrad Airechta* a prostitute cannot give evidence against anyone. So any evidence Nemon offers is not acceptable under the law.'

'But Murgal is her foster-father and Murgal is a Brehon. That is nonsense. Surely, with such a powerful foster-father, Nemon has some rights in this matter?'

'It is our law, Saxon,' snapped Orla.

'Because it is the law does not make the truth any less of the truth,' replied Eadulf stoutly.

'*Dura lex sed lex*,' sighed Fidelma, echoing in Latin almost the same phrase as Murgal had once used to him. 'The law is hard but it is the law . . . for the time being. I hear that Abbot Laisran of Durrow is going to propose an amendment to that law at the next Great Council meeting . . .'

'He hasn't a chance of proceeding with an amendment to allow prostitutes the right of giving evidence,' Orla sniffed disapprovingly.

'That is up to the Great Council which sits at Uisneach next year.'

Orla was silent for a while considering the matter.

'Well,' she said at last, 'whatever the future, the Brehon Murgal is satisfied that since Artgal has disappeared, there is an end to the matter. We can accept that Artgal killed Dianach and fled the valley.'

'Rather conveniently,' muttered Fidelma.

'There is nothing more to be said.'

'Perhaps. Perhaps not.'

Orla stared angrily at Fidelma for a few moments and made to speak, changed her mind and shrugged to indicate her indifference. In such silence they came to the ráth of Laisre of Gleann Geis.

Chapter Eighteen

They rode into the ráth of Laisre. The same two stable boys who had greeted them when they had first arrived were in attendance and took their mounts. It was only then that Orla addressed them again. There was a curtness in her voice.

'Laisre and Murgal will want to speak with you immediately. They will be in the council chamber.'

Neither Fidelma nor Eadulf said anything as they followed her into the council chamber.

Laisre was seated on his official chair speaking earnestly with Murgal and Colla. They broke off their conversation to stare in surprise as Orla ushered Fidelma and Eadulf forward. Laisre did not conceal his expression of dislike as his gaze met Fidelma's. Colla looked slightly bewildered at her appearance while Murgal's countenance bore a look of cynical amusement.

'So,' Laisre said in quiet satisfaction, 'you have caught our fugitives, Orla?'

Fidelma raised an eyebrow disdainfully.

'Caught? Have you given orders for my capture then, Laisre? If so – why? And what is this talk of our being fugitive?'

'I found her and the foreigner riding back here,' Orla interposed hastily. 'She said that had Murgal thought more deeply about matters then he would know why she had left the ráth when she did.'

Laisre glanced at his Druid.

'Did you know that Fidelma was leaving?'

Murgal shook his head indignantly.

'Not I,' he protested. Then his eyes suddenly narrowed. 'Ah, I think I do know . . . now. You went to investigate the ritual slaughter? You did not trust Colla's information?'

'You did not trust me? Why?' demanded Colla, apparently affronted.

'Because she is a *dálaigh*.'

'What has that to do with it?'

'Because it is the duty of a *dálaigh* to judge evidence for themselves. What is the triad? Three duties of a good advocate: apprise yourself of the evidence not trusting to the opinion of others when you are able to form your own; a fair judgment and a strong advocacy. A good *dálaigh* would not trust another's judgment if they could view the evidence themselves. Yes, I should have known, Laisre, that your refusal to allow Fidelma to investigate would have been ignored.'

Neither Colla nor Laisre appeared happy with the explanation.

'I told you that I wished you to have no more to do with the affairs of Gleann Geis than can be helped,' Laisre intoned in annoyance. 'We could have conducted our business this morning and you could have been on your way.'

'We will conduct our business after the matter of the murders is resolved,' Fidelma replied firmly. Laisre seemed outraged at her contradiction of his wishes. He was about to speak when Murgal interrupted.

'Are you saying that you can resolve the mystery?' The Druid's keen gaze had swept the features of Fidelma with a strange, unfathomable expression. Fidelma kept her features implacable.

'I should be able to answer that question tomorrow morning. Tomorrow I shall name the killer of Solin and the cause of the other deaths in this place. Now, it has been a long day, we have ridden far, so we will return to the guests' hostel. Does Cruinn still refuse to serve us? If so, perhaps you would ensure that our wants are seen to. Baths and food are the duty of a hostel under law.'

Her bright gaze swept the astonished company and then she turned from the chamber, motioning Eadulf to follow her.

Eadulf hurried to keep in step with her as she made her way across the courtyard.

'Did you see the way Colla was looking at you?' he asked breathlessly. 'By saying that you will resolve the problem tomorrow, you are inviting Colla and Orla to act against you tonight.'

Fidelma smiled grimly.

'I am hoping that they might. It would be a short cut to resolving the matter.'

Eadulf was unhappy.

'It will be a long night before Ibor gets here.' Then he paused and his face paled. 'I hope you are not telling me that you have no other plan to resolve this matter than to frighten Orla and Colla into an attempt on your life in order to prove their guilt?'

'Ecclesiastics in the book of the Apocrypha,' she replied enigmatically.

'Meaning?' frowned Eadulf.

'Do not reveal your thoughts to anyone lest you drive away your good luck.'

Eadulf snorted derisively but, wisely, said nothing further.

They made their way to the guests' hostel. It was deserted. Eadulf took their saddle bags back to their rooms while Fidelma set to banking the fire in the kitchen to prepare hot water for the baths. She was struggling with the logs when Rudgal appeared bearing a basket with him.

'Let me do that, Sister,' he insisted at once, putting the basket down on the table.

Fidelma, who had been on her knees struggling with the fire, rose with a smile of gratitude.

'I shall not be reluctant to hand over the task to you, Rudgal. I presume Cruinn is still displeased with us?'

Rudgal bent to the task of stoking the fire.

'Cruinn is devoted to the chieftain and his family. I presume she is still angry at your accusation concerning the lady, Orla, and her husband.'

'She is very opinionated for a hostel keeper,' observed Eadulf coming down the stairs. 'She should keep to her place and not pass opinions on those she is supposed to serve.'

Rudgal glanced up at him almost with a scowl.

'Everyone should keep to their place, indeed,' he muttered turning back to the fire.

Eadulf had almost forgotten Rudgal's peculiar manner when he found the girl Esnad with him on the previous evening.

'Have you brought us some food then, Rudgal?' Fidelma asked brightly, turning to the basket, apparently not noticing Rudgal's scowl.

'Yes, Sister,' Rudgal replied shortly. He had enticed the fire into a strong blaze. He stood up and moved to the basket. 'The hot water should be ready soon. Do you want to eat before or after the bath?'

'We will have our baths before eating.'

'I will prepare them then,' Rudgal offered. 'Perhaps you will keep a watch on this kitchen fire for me while I do so?'

After he had disappeared into the bathing chambers, Eadulf grimaced towards Fidelma and whispered.

'The man seems to bear a grudge about something and that something appears to concern the girl, Esnad. You don't think that he is jealous or something? No, that would be nonsense.'

'Perhaps you should discover what ails Rudgal,' Fidelma reflected. 'After we have eaten, I think you should seek out this Esnad and find out what it is all about.'

Eadulf looked uneasy.

'I do not want to leave you alone until Ibor gets here. If you are going to put yourself in the position of lure to snare Orla and Colla, then you stand in great danger.'

Fidelma shook her head.

'After we have bathed and eaten, I intend to go to Laisre's feasting hall and make Orla and Colla feel uncomfortable. They can scarcely do anything to me in front of the assembly. It is my belief that if they intend to attempt anything they will do it in the night when all is quiet.' She gave him a mischievous grin. 'Maybe you will be in more danger from Esnad than I will be from Orla and Colla?'

Eadulf blushed furiously.

'She is only a young girl,' he muttered. 'But you are right. There is something that needs to be explained about Rudgal's behaviour.'

It was an hour or so later when Eadulf left Fidelma at the door of the feasting hall and went off in search of Esnad's apartments. He knew where they were for he recalled that they were in the building where Murgal's library was. The same building was shared by the apothecary, Marga, and by Orla and Colla themselves. Walking across the courtyard he saw the portly figure of Cruinn emerging from Marga's apothecary and he greeted her brightly. The pudgy woman whirled round in the dusk, glared at him, said nothing but hurried away. It was clear that the hostel keeper was firm in her new-found dislike of him.

Eadulf turned into the building. He was surprised to find Laisre standing in the entrance hall. The chieftain also appeared taken unawares to see him and demanded, in a gruff voice, to know what he was doing there. Eadulf felt that he should not mention Esnad and made an excuse that he was going to Murgal's library. Laisre merely gave a grunt and moved off without another word. He seemed as anxious to leave Eadulf's company as Eadulf was for him to do so.

Eadulf climbed the stairs to where he had seen the entrance to Esnad's apartments. He hesitated a moment to summon courage and then knocked on the door. The girl's voice called for him to enter and he braced his shoulders and did so.

Esnad looked up from a chair in momentary surprise. Then she smiled, almost a proprietorial smile. Before her was a wooden table laid out with the Brandub board and pieces set ready. She was seated at the board and had obviously been examining it for a strategy of play. Eadulf cast a look round. The girl was alone. A fire burnt in the hearth for it was chilly in spite of the summer. A cool evening gloom hung outside. The girl already had a lamp lit and suspended from the ceiling over the table.

'Ha, Saxon! I heard that you had returned. Have you come to play Brandub with me?' she greeted.

'Er, not exactly,' he muttered, wondering how to question her.

'Do not worry, I will show you how to play it.'

Eadulf was about to refuse on an impulse when he realised that he would learn nothing from the daughter of Orla if he let his emotions get the better of him.

'Come in and close the door,' she instructed with all the authority of someone of mature years.

He entered and closed the door.

She looked at him with a speculative expression.

'Have you never played Brandub before?'

Eadulf was about to admit that he had played hardly anything else with his fellow students at Tuam Brecain. However, he caught himself in time and shook his head.

'I will follow your instructions,' he announced gravely, as he took the seat opposite her. It was a good opportunity. As the game proceeded he would be able to put his questions to her.

She did not drop her eyes to the gaming table.

'You know what Brandub means?'

'That's easy. Black Raven.'

'But do you know why we call the game so?'

He had heard the explanation several times but feigned ignorance.

'The raven is the symbol of the goddess of death and battles. It is the symbol of danger. The purpose of this game is to survive an attack from the hostile forces of the other player – one player attacks and the other defends. Therefore we call the game after the symbol of danger.'

Eadulf tried to appear engrossed by the information, as if he had not heard it before.

'There,' the girl gestured with her hand to the board on the table, 'you see a board which is divided into forty-nine squares, seven squares by seven squares. In the centre square you have one large king piece, you see it?'

He nodded automatically.

'That symbolises the High King at Tara. Around the High King are four other pieces. Each one represents a provincial king. There are the kings of Cashel in Muman, Cruachan in Connacht, Ailenn in Leinster and Ailech in Ulaidh.'

'I understand,' he said gravely.

'On each side of the board there are two attacking pieces, eight in all. The attacker moves them across the board unless checked by a combination of the provincial king pieces. The purpose is to drive the High King piece into a corner from which he cannot escape. When that happens, the game is won. You follow? But if the attacker cannot overcome the defenders then he loses the game.'

'I understand.'

'Then I shall attack first,' the girl smiled with forced sweetness. 'I like to attack more than I do to defend. You will defend. Are you ready?'

Eadulf nodded compliantly.

The girl began her moves with Eadulf countering in the required form. He had to admit that the girl attacked with determination and while she lacked a carefully thought out strategy she took chances which sometimes paid off. Force before strategy seemed her technique.

The girl was soon frowning in concentration as he played automatically, having quite forgotten that he was supposed to be a novice at the game, once he had been absorbed in it.

'You catch on fast, Saxon,' she finally said begrudgingly as Eadulf continually parried her moves.

'Merely luck, Esnad,' he replied, suddenly realising that he'd better allow himself some mistakes in case of angering the girl before he could extract any information from her. He was gratified when she responded to his poor play with a happy smile as she rushed her pieces to capitalise on his 'errors'.

He gave her a crooked grin.

'What did I say?' he said, after he conceded a defeat. 'The earlier play was mere luck. Let me take my revenge with a second game. I do not mind defending again.'

'Very well.' The girl was smiling at him now with a coquettish expression. 'But let us play for something to make the game interesting.'

Eadulf frowned.

'A wager? What shall we wager on?'

Esnad placed the tip of her finger between her teeth, chewing gently. Her smile widened.

'If I win, you must do what I tell you to do.'

Eadulf was hesitant.

'That might not be a good wager. Without knowing what you have in mind.'

'Oh, I shall not order you to do anything that will harm you or other people,' she replied winsomely.

Eadulf shrugged.

'Then if it is not harmful, I accept. But if I win, what then?'

'You have but to name your wager,' the girl replied, still wearing her flirtatious smile.

'Lay out the pieces,' Eadulf said gruffly. 'And I shall think about it.'

The game started again.

'Why are you so friendly with me when your mother is set against Sister Fidelma and myself?' Eadulf suddenly asked in the middle of a move.

Esnad did not look up. She appeared totally disinterested.

'My mother's quarrels are not mine. Anyway, she is more angered by your companion, Fidelma, than with you. I would not worry about my mother's attitudes. I don't.'

'Your father is tanist and your mother is his wife. Their wishes surely count for something?'

'Why should I be concerned?'

'Are you not interested in their affairs?'

'Not at all. I am more interested in enjoying life than the affairs of Gleann Geis.'

Eadulf paused to consider a particularly dangerous move. It was plain that Esnad did not like his response and she pouted in disapproval as she found that he had countered her attack.

'Perhaps one day you might marry a chieftain, then you might have to be interested in such matters,' Eadulf suggested as he moved his king piece into a new position.

The girl laughed dismissively.

'Perhaps,' she conceded. 'But if I married a chieftain, then I would ensure that I did not have to take an interest because the affairs of the clan would be his, not mine. I would have other interests.'

'Does your mother or father care that you are not interested in the affairs of Gleann Geis?'

'I never speak about such matters to them.'

Eadulf glanced sharply at her and decided it was time to press home the pertinent question.

'Why does Rudgal follow you about so jealously?'

Esnad raised her eyes. Her gaze was one of amusement. She pouted at him.

'You are asking a lot of questions, Saxon. Why don't you concentrate on this game? There is much to play for.'

'It is just that Rudgal seems to have taken a dislike to me after you came to the hostel the other day. I wondered why?'

'Oh, ignore him,' sighed the girl. 'He thinks he is in love with me.'

Eadulf was surprised at the flippancy with which she dealt with the matter.

'I thought that much was plain,' Eadulf conceded solemnly. 'And, of course, you do not love him?'

'No. He is too old and without means to make my life secure. Anyway, his so-called love is the love of a dog for the sheep not the salmon for the river. If I ever marry someone it will be for other reasons. In the meantime, I want to indulge myself before I grow old and settled.'

'But Rudgal is not much older than me,' Eadulf pointed out.

Esnad laughed.

'But you are much more interesting than Rudgal, Saxon. Now, let's get on with this game.'

Eadulf kept quiet. The girl was certainly hedonistic. Life seemed to mean no more to her than pleasure seeking. There did not seem to be any mystery here. He would have to finish the game and extricate himself from the embarrassing position as best he could.

In the feasting hall, the musicians were still playing lively tunes, the instruments making a noisy counterpoint to the laughter and conversation of the guests.

Fidelma had sought out Murgal and seated herself beside him. She could see Orla and Colla on the far side of the hall and among the others she noticed were Rudgal and Ronan. There was no sign of Laisre or anyone else she recognised. Murgal glanced uneasily up at her as she joined him.

'I did not expect you to join these festivities this evening, Fidelma of Cashel,' he observed.

'It may well be my last night in Gleann Geis,' she replied gravely.

'Do you really believe that you can clear up everything tomorrow morning?' Murgal asked dubiously.

Fidelma refused the offer of mead but did not reply to his question. He was about to say something else when the musicians ceased to play and a quiet descended in the hall. Ronan stood forward and began to sing with a surprisingly good tenor voice for the rough calloused farmer who preferred to spend his time serving Laisre's bodyguard. He sang a song of warriors and warfare.

'My straight spear is of red yew –
vanquisher of polished spears –
it is mine by right and no warrior dare
affront it.

'My sharp sword is of white polished iron –
cleaver of the opposing armour –
it is silent in its sheath of bronze for fear of
shedding blood.

'My hardened shield is of golden bronze –
it has never been reproached –
for it protects me from all aggressors and their
weapons.'

He sat down to a resounding applause and Murgal glanced at Fidelma with amusement.

'You sang a good song the other night. Will you sing something else to entertain us?'

Fidelma declined gravely.

'A song must swell out of the soul for the moment and not be summoned from a tired mind merely for entertainment's sake, to while away the passing of the hour. Perhaps you have another song about Cashel to set the diversion?'

Murgal chuckled disarmingly at her gentle taunt.

'Not this time,' he admitted. He hesitated and then he asked: 'Do you feel the apprehension in this hall tonight?'

'Apprehension?' she asked.

'The news that you will name the killer of Solin and the others tomorrow morning has spread through the ráth. Many people wonder who you will name. There is much tension here.'

'Only the guilty need feel anxiety,' replied Fidelma.

'There are many who feel that you will name the innocent merely to escape the guilt yourself. They remember that you only cleared your name on a technicality of law and not by revealing who actually murdered Solin. Many think you still killed Solin because you were rivals in your Faith. Many have not forgiven you for trying to put the blame on Orla, for she is popular among our people.'

'I suppose that I also killed Brother Dianach and made Artgal disappear? Or, indeed, perhaps I slaughtered those thirty-three young men myself?'

Murgal was not perturbed.

'Anything is considered possible about a person in minds that are antagonistic to that person.'

'To your mind?'

'Fidelma, I am a Druid and a Brehon. At first I was prepared to dismiss you as I have most of your Faith. Small, bigoted people, intolerant of the beliefs of others. They will not bear anyone who does not think as they do. I found you unlike those others of your Faith that I have encountered. I trust you. I believe that you are free from any guilt. Perhaps you will trust me to help you?'

For a wild moment Fidelma found herself about to tell him all she knew. She had even opened her mouth to respond when she realised the danger. She shut her mouth with a snap. Murgal had suddenly become too friendly. Perhaps there was another motive for his change of attitude?

At that moment she realised that Laisre had entered the chamber. He had a cloak around him for it was a chill evening outside. He had walked across to the fire where his chair had been placed, just before a carved wooden screen. The screen stood at shoulder height, providing a barrier to the draughts. He went behind the screen for there was a small table beyond it where cloaks and weapons were placed during the feasting.

Fidelma let her eyes follow him quizzically across the room and watched his head atop the screen as he discarded his cloak. He turned. Then she realised that Laisre was looking directly at her across the top of the wooden screen. She could not see his lower face. Only his eyes and the top of his head so that she was unsure of the expression on his face. But for a moment their eyes met. She felt the malignancy of his expression. A cold shudder went through her. Then she inhaled softly and calmly. She turned back to Murgal.

'I am sorry,' she said, 'what were you saying?'

'I was saying that you should trust me, Fidelma of Cashel, for I might be able to help you. Tomorrow you must explain your suspicions or finish your business with Laisre and be gone back to Cashel. If you return to Cashel without offering an explanation for what has transpired here then there will be many suspicious minds left behind. You will still be blamed for Solin's death.'

Fidelma studied Murgal thoughtfully for a moment.

'You and the people of Gleann Geis will have the resolution of this matter tomorrow morning. That I swear.'

She caught sight of Eadulf entering the hall and noticed that his face was flushed and he looked anxious. She made her excuses to Murgal, rose and went across to him.

'What's wrong, Eadulf?' she asked curiously. 'You have a melancholy expression.'

'Wrong?' He asked indignantly. He seemed to have difficulty keeping control of his ire. 'That girl Esnad is wrong. Even Nemon, the prostitute, is more honest than she is.'

Fidelma laid a pacifying hand on his arm.

'Walk with me back to the hostel and tell me about it.'

'Do you know that the girl tried to lure me into her bed?'

Fidelma shot him an amused glance.

'She is youthful and attractive,' she pointed out.

Eadulf made an inarticulate sound.

'I presume that you were not attracted by the offer?' Fidelma added with a mischievous grin.

'She had me play a game of Brandub and demanded a wager be set. If she won she was going to demand I go to bed with her. If I won she expected me to make the same demand of her.'

'Did you?'

Eadulf looked aghast.

'Did I go to her bed?' he asked in horror.

'No, did you win the game?'

Eadulf shook his head vehemently.

'I saw where this matter was leading and was able to win but did not fulfil her expectations. Anyway, that did not stop her trying to persuade me. I barely escaped her seduction.'

'More importantly,' Fidelma said, as they entered the guests' hostel, 'did you find out whether she was involved with her parents' politics? What is her connection with Rudgal?'

'All she cares about is carnal pleasure.' Eadulf sniffed in disgust. 'She knows little about anything else. As for Rudgal, I think he is smitten with a passion which comes close to unquestioning adoration of the little wanton. I feel sorry for the man.'

Fidelma lit the lamp.

'Well, an early night is called for. We have done all we can for now. Hopefully, Ibor will be here before dawn.'

Eadulf's expression changed to one of anxiety.

'We play a dangerous game here, Fidelma. It is one thing to secure this ráth but we must be able to solve the mystery.'

Fidelma seemed happy enough.

'I think I can . . . now,' she added with emphasis. 'But the main danger is tonight. If someone is to take action against me, it will be tonight. We have to be vigilant.'

Eadulf was worried.

'I will not sleep tonight,' he vowed. 'Have no fear.'

It was still dark when Eadulf was roused from the slumber into which he had fallen almost as soon as he clambered between the blankets.

He struggled up in bed his heart beating fast, aware of a figure bending over him.

He recognised Fidelma's scent in the shadows. She bent forward and whispered: 'There is someone outside the hostel. I heard them trying the door. They are downstairs. Stand ready. I think they are going to come up here.'

As Fidelma moved silently back to her room, Eadulf swung out of his bed, hurriedly hauling on his robe.

He could hear the footsteps quietly ascending but betrayed by a creaking on the stair.

He moved behind the door and seized one of the heavy iron candlesticks, resolving that as soon as the intruder had passed his door towards Fidelma's chamber he would hurry out and come on them from behind. He had hardly determined this strategy when he heard the steps falter in the passage outside and then – then the latch of his own door was lifting.

He pressed back against the wall with a pounding heart, automatically raising the candlestick defensively.

The door creaked open.

A shadow entered the room. It was burly and that of a man. There was a sword in his hand.

Eadulf waited for no more. He swung the candlestick. It contacted with the figure's head with a sickening thud. There was a soft grunt. The figure collapsed and fell to the floor, the sword clattering out of its hand.

Eadulf stood trembling for a moment.

He heard Fidelma exclaim in alarm and come hurrying from her room.

'Where are you, Eadulf?' she demanded anxiously.

'Here,' mumbled Eadulf, retrieving the candle and stick and reaching for flint and tinder to light it. It was a difficult task in the gloom and took a time. For he had to find the metal box of rotten beech wood, the wood almost powdered by the action of fungus, and then hold his flint over it and strike at it with a sharp piece of metal to cause the spark. Once the spark caused the wood to smoulder, he could light the wick of the candle.

Once it was burning they could examine the figure on the floor.

'Rudgal!' whispered Fidelma.

'I gave him a hefty blow,' confessed Eadulf. 'His skull looks as though it is bleeding profusely. I'd better dress his wound.'

'But not before you bind his hands together,' Fidelma pointed out. 'He did not come here, sword in hand, in the middle of the night out of friendship's sake.'

Eadulf went in search of a stout piece of cord, finding it in the kitchen of the hostel and returned to bind the warrior's hands. As he did so Rudgal began to moan as consciousness started to return. Eadulf heaved him on to the bed and then found water and a bowl and started to bathe the bloody area of his skull.

Rudgal's eyes flickered and opened. They glanced round quickly and he flexed his arms.

'Stay still!' snapped Eadulf. 'Your hands are tied.'

Rudgal immediately relaxed.

Fidelma stood, hands folded before her, examining the warrior carefully.

'You have some explaining to do, Rudgal,' she observed. 'Were you sent here to kill me or was it your own idea?'

Rudgal stared at her in bewilderment.

'Kill you, Sister?' he gasped. 'I do not understand.'

Fidelma was patient.

'I presume that it was not for my health that you came to seek me in the darkness of the night with a naked blade.'

Rudgal blinked and then shook his head slowly.

'You, Sister? It was not you that I sought but . . .' he jerked his head towards Eadulf, 'but that foreigner. Him I meant to kill.'

Eadulf was shocked.

'Why would you want to kill Brother Eadulf?' asked Fidelma.

Rudgal glowered.

'He knows,' he replied tightly.

'I do not,' averred Eadulf. 'What have I done?' Then he groaned. 'Do not tell me that it is to do with that silly little girl?'

'You have tried to take Esnad from me!' cried Rudgal, trying to struggle forward. 'She told me that you were with her last evening. I will kill you.'

Eadulf easily pushed him back on the bed.

'You must be mad,' the Saxon said slowly. 'I am not interested in that child.'

'Rudgal, listen to me,' Fidelma said, interrupting the fair-haired man's sobs of torment. 'Eadulf has no interest in Esnad. Whatever your relationship with her is a matter for you to sort out.'

'But he was with her last night.'

'At my instructions,' replied Fidelma, realising the logic in his madness.

Rudgal flushed.

'Why would you tell him to go to flirt with Esnad?'

'In Christ's Truth!' snapped Eadulf. 'If any flirting was done, it was that young girl who was doing it. You must know, man, what she is like.'

'I love her!'

'But is the girl in love with you?' Eadulf snapped.

It was clear from Rudgal's features that he was not confident to answer this question.

'Rudgal,' Fidelma said, 'there is no need for anyone to shed blood over a capricious girl.'

The warrior was reluctant to be persuaded.

'Esnad told me that he was in her apartment. She made fun of me saying . . .'

Fidelma held up her hand to quiet him.

'*Aegra amans!*' she muttered. Only Eadulf understood. Indeed Virgil had spoken of possessive love as a disease.

Eadulf looked towards her sourly.

'*Amantes sunt amentes*,' he responded, pointing out that lovers were lunatics.

Rudgal was scowling at them both, not understanding.

'There is nothing between Esnad and I,' Eadulf repeated. 'Now why don't you sort out your problems with Esnad?'

Rudgal glowered.

'It is sound advice, Rudgal,' Fidelma added. 'If you feel so much in love with Esnad then you should speak with her. Surely her opinion is more important to you than anyone else's opinion?'

The man was still angry.

'Can it be that you know she does not love you in return and so it is easier for you to blame other people, saying that they are taking her from you?' Fidelma continued. 'Was she ever yours to take?'

Her words struck home. The warrior and wagon-maker flinched as if she had struck him.

'It is not our business what you do, Rudgal,' Fidelma went on, 'but I would be wise and consider matters more calmly. You would do well to see if you actually loved Esnad apart from being in love. These are two different things. And if you loved Esnad you would care for her opinion and her happiness.'

'What do you mean to do with me?' growled Rudgal, ignoring her advice.

'You have broken the law by launching a murderous attack on Eadulf,' Fidelma pointed out. 'What if you had killed him? What do you think we should do with you?'

'I claim justification on my side,' the man said stubbornly.

'There is no justification at all.' Eadulf was outraged by the man's persistent attitude.

Fidelma laid a hand on Eadulf's arm and motioned for him to follow her into the corridor.

'What do you suggest?' he whispered once they were outside.

'We cannot release Rudgal before tomorrow. It might well be that he is just insane with jealousy over Esnad. However, in case there is something more to his love sickness, we should keep him here until morning. We'll leave him in your room and you can change to another. Is he securely bound? Good. We can sort out his real motives in the morning.'

They returned to find Rudgal struggling with the bonds.

'Stay still,' instructed Eadulf in a harsh tone, 'unless you wish for another clout on your skull.'

Rudgal glowered at him.

'If my hands were free, foreigner . . .'

'That is why you will continue to be bound,' interrupted Fidelma. They used more cord and had difficulty in tying Rudgal's feet together for he flayed around with powerful motions. Even when his feet and hands were secured, Rudgal started to cry out and Eadulf seized a towel and wrapped it around the man's mouth, silencing him.

It took a few minutes more for Rudgal to accept that escape from his bondage was impossible and relax on the bed. It was only when he had quietened down that they heard a movement on the lower floor of the guests' hostel.

Fidelma and Eadulf exchanged a look of alarm. Then Eadulf seized Rudgal's discarded sword in one hand and took the oil lamp in the other, moving quietly to the door. Fidelma came behind him, peering over his shoulder. They moved cautiously along the corridor to the landing overlooking the stairs leading to the lower floor of the hostel.

A figure stood there below them in the darkness.

Eadulf raised the lamp.

Colla stood revealed in its rays at the bottom of the stairs.

'What do you want here?' demanded Eadulf, feeling angry that his voice cracked a little with emotion. Here stood the very person whom they had been expecting to attempt to harm them this very night.

Colla stared up at them in surprise. He blinked as he caught sight of the sword in Eadulf's hand.

'Is there anything wrong?' he faltered.

'Wrong? Should there be anything wrong?' inquired Fidelma quietly.

'I was just passing by when I heard a noise like someone calling for help. So I came in.'

Fidelma examined the tanist carefully. It was a plausible story for after all Rudgal had made considerable noise before they had gagged him.

'It was Eadulf,' she lied blandly. 'He cried out in his sleep and I went to see if he were ill. Then we heard a noise below and thought someone had broken in . . .'

Eadulf nodded hurriedly, wondering what penance he would have to pay for the falsehood.

'It is true. A nightmare,' he added quickly.

Colla hesitated, then shrugged.

'The door was wide open,' he said. 'I'll shut it as I leave.'

He stared up at them for a moment and then turned and left the hostel, shutting the door behind him. Outside they heard him greet someone and there was a muttered conversation. Eadulf moved swiftly to the upper window and peered out into the courtyard and listened to the whispered conversation.

'It is Laisre,' he whispered to Fidelma. 'He was apparently passing the hostel, saw Colla coming out and asked what was wrong. He and Colla have both left now.'

Fidelma heaved a deep sigh.

'I do not think anything else will happen before dawn now,' she observed with a tone of satisfaction. 'I think our mystery comes finally near a solution.'

Chapter Nineteen

Fidelma rose from her bed long before the sky began to turn light and was waiting nervously in the main room of the guests' hostel. She had checked Rudgal and found him still bound and actually sleeping, although his repose did not seem comfortable. Eadulf was also asleep, snoring softly. She listened carefully but could hear nothing stirring outside the hostel. She went to the window and peered anxiously up at the sky as it began to turn grey over the eastern peaks. With a sinking feeling she began to wonder if she had been premature in hazarding all for this dawn rendezvous with Ibor of Muirthemne. What if Cruinn had lied and there had really been no other route into Gleann Geis? Perhaps there was only the one ravine? What if Ibor and his men were not able to get into the valley? What if they had not been able to take over the fortress? What if . . . ?

She paused and tried to still her rambling thoughts. What was it that her mentor, the Brehon Morann of Tara, had once said? 'With an "if" you could put the five kingdoms of Éireann into a bottle and carry them with you.'

She forced herself to sip a beaker of mead and tackle some dry bread and cheese to fortify herself against what she knew would now be an ordeal that morning . . . one way or another.

There came a sound nearby and she sprung up nervously. The sound was merely a sleepy yawn and she realised that it was only Eadulf rising. A moment later he came lethargically down the stairs.

'Have you heard anything yet?' he whispered, becoming more alert when he saw that she was up and waiting. Fidelma shook her head. They listened together for a moment to the silence. It was broken only when a dog barked in the distance.

Then, shattering the early morning stillness, a cock began to crow nearby.

It seemed as if it were a signal for at that very moment the door of the hostel swung open. They swung round, filled with misgiving. Ibor of Muirthemne stood framed in the doorway, sword in hand, grinning.

'The ráth is ours, Fidelma. I have rounded up the guards and placed them under the care of some of my warriors in their own dormitory. The gates are now closed and my men are guarding all points, including the council chamber.'

'Was there any bloodshed?' Fidelma demanded anxiously.

A grim smile met her question.

'None that would be noticeable. A bruised skull here and there but nothing worse.'

'Good. We shall proceed to rouse the people of the ráth and make them gather in the council chamber.'

Ibor hesitated.

'There is one thing that you should know, Sister. We found the passageway, exactly as you told us we would. It was a rocky path leading up alongside the turbulent river which exits from this glen. Now and then, the path ran through a complex of caves before emerging into the valley. We were traversing this path, as you instructed. In one of the caves we found Artgal.'

She showed no emotion.

'He was dead, I presume?'

'He was dead,' affirmed Ibor. 'How did you know?'

'In what manner had he met his death?' she asked, ignoring his question.

'That I cannot tell you. He was lying along the path. He carried a bag with him as if he were going on a long journey. There was no mark of any wound on him at all.'

Eadulf looked at Ibor in astonishment.

'No wound?' he demanded. 'No wound and yet he was dead?'

'Who can say how he died?' Ibor shrugged. 'What slays without leaving a wound? When I examined the body I saw a ghastly expression of fear contorting Artgal's features. The lips were blue and twisted, showing teeth and gums. The eyes were bulging as if he had seen a phantom from hell. I have seen a few such deaths in my time and always among pagans. This is a death inflicted by a Druid. God protect us, Sister. I had to put the fear of my sword into some of my men in order to force them to continue into this accursed valley.'

Fidelma lowered her eyes and was reflective for a moment or two. Then she raised her head and her features showed a tranquillity.

'I think that the last piece of the puzzle is now complete,' she said with satisfaction. 'I am ready. Gather the people of the ráth in the council chamber, leave aside the children. I will be along in fifteen minutes.'

Ibor was already moving to the door when she called him back.

'Above the stair here, you will find a warrior of this ráth – Rudgal. He is bound. Get two of your men to escort him to the chamber but do not allow them to unbind his hands.'

Ibor looked momentarily astonished, then shrugged and acknowledged her order by raising his sword in salute.

When Fidelma entered the council chamber followed by Eadulf, there arose murmurs of hostility and anger. The leading inhabitants of the ráth had been gathered there at sword point by Ibor's men. Their own swords had been removed and at each entrance Ibor's warriors stood sentinel while, by the chieftain's chair, Ibor himself and two of his men guarded the chieftain of Gleann Geis. In all, a dozen warriors of the Craobh Rígh were placed around the chamber. Fidelma presumed the others were acting as sentinels at the gates of the ráth or on the walls.

Laisre, his face white with anger, was slumped in his chair of office. Murgal was seated nearby looking equally unhappy. Colla was standing behind his chieftain, flushed and resentful. Orla was by his side. Her face was filled with antagonism as she scowled at Fidelma. There was no amity or affableness on any face in the chamber with the exception of Esnad. Only she appeared unconcerned by the proceedings.

Fidelma glanced around at the others who had been gathered. There was Rudgal looking wrathful. He had his arms still bound. Ronan and Bairsech, his shrewish wife, were there, along with Nemon, the prostitute, and Cruinn, the portly hostel-keeper, and Marga the apothecary. All these were people whom Fidelma had specifically asked Ibor to ensure were brought to the council chamber of the ráth. The entire assembly, apart from Ibor and his men, focussed on Fidelma with intense hatred as she took her position.

Laisre was the first to speak. He rose to his feet, his body quivering with rage.

'Well, Fidelma of Cashel, this barbarity can only be expunged with blood,' he announced. 'You have transgressed all rules of hospitality, you have used foreign warriors to imprison . . .'

'Barbarism is a good word to describe the evil that has permeated this valley,' Fidelma interrupted him coldly. Her voice cut into his tirade and stilled it before he had time to gather further impetus. 'And I have come to reveal the truth about the evil which haunts you.'

'Aided by warriors from the north, Fidelma?' demanded Colla. 'How can the warriors of Ulaidh force any truth from the people of Muman? Is this how your brother treats his people, by the use of outside force? By mercenaries who do his bidding for money?'

'I fear you do Ibor and his men an injustice. They are not Muman's mercenaries. Neither are they here to enforce the truth, merely to protect those innocent among you from any harm and ensure that the truth is finally listened to. And you will listen to me because I speak not only as the voice of my brother the king but as a *dálaigh* of the degree of *anruth* whose voice can be heard by kings and to whom even a High King is subject.'

She spoke with such calm assurance that her tone commanded a silence throughout the council chamber.

Murgal broke it after some moments by saying quietly: 'Tell us your truth, Fidelma of Cashel, and we will answer with ours.'

Fidelma smiled gently at him.

'If you have a truth left to answer with.' She made the riposte softly.

She stood for a moment head bowed in silence and let a tension build up among those gathered.

As Eadulf was wondering whether she should be prompted and if he should undertake the task, Fidelma began to speak, quietly at first.

'I have been presented with many mysteries since I qualified as an advocate in our courts of law. I will not say that these were simple to solve. Brother Eadulf here knows that many were not, for he has been involved in many of these mysteries. What I will say is that the mystery I found here confounded me for a long time. Shall I remind you of that mystery?'

No one responded.

'On arriving here Brother Eadulf and I were confronted with the slaughter of thirty-three young men in what appeared to have been a pagan ritual; the bodies naked and placed in a sunwise circle. Each one had been killed in a manner known to the ancients as The Threefold Death. Then we were confronted with the death of Brother Solin of Armagh.'

'For which you were nearly found guilty,' Orla pointed out sharply. 'For which you tried to accuse me, and for which you were only released on a technicality of the law in that the Saxon showed that Artgal was an untrustworthy witness. You were not found innocent of the charge. You could still be the killer of Solin!'

Murgal looked uncomfortable at what amounted to a criticism of his judgment. He turned and shook his head at Orla.

'Orla, my judgment stands. I can only judge according to our law.'

Orla scowled at him but did not reply.

Fidelma spoke directly to Murgal.

'There is no need to apologise or even justify the judgment you gave, Murgal. But the death of Brother Solin was quickly followed by the death of young Brother Dianach.'

Murgal leant forward.

'And that is easily explained for it was obvious that Artgal killed Dianach out of revenge or for some other reason once it was discovered that Dianach had bribed him to maintain his evidence against you.'

Fidelma ignored the interruption.

'And having done so, Artgal fled the valley demonstrating his guilt in some people's eyes?'

'Exactly,' Murgal said in satisfaction.

'Poisoning himself on the way?'

There was a shocked silence.

'Yes,' continued Fidelma keeping her voice even, 'Artgal was found dead on the tiny river path, having been poisoned.'

'How do you know this?' asked Colla.

Fidelma indicated Ibor.

'Ibor found him. Ibor and his men,' she corrected pedantically. 'Ibor, you said that there were no wounds on Artgal's body when you found it?'

The warrior took a pace forward and inclined his head in confirmation.

'But you said that the lips were drawn back over the gums in an hideous expression.'

'They were.'

'And were the gums coloured a bluish-black?'

'I did not tell you that. But, yes; they were.'

'So now we have a total of thirty-six deaths in Gleann Geis,' Fidelma said softly. 'Truly, a valley that is forbidden. It forbids life!'

'So you are intent to blame the people of Gleann Geis?' Laisre jeered angrily. 'Your plan is to get your brother to bring punishment on my people as you persuaded him to use the full force of the Eóghanacht against the Uí Fidgente earlier this year.'

Fidelma smiled calculatingly at the chieftain.

'That is certainly someone's plan, Laisre,' she said with intent. 'But you do me an injustice by suggesting that it is my plan. I do not mean any harm to the people of Gleann Geis. My only concern is to punish those involved with these killings.'

Murgal spoke again quelling the murmur of voices which greeted her statement.

'Are you implying that the people responsible are here in the council chamber?' he demanded. 'That people responsible for all thirty-six deaths are among us now?'

'I do not *imply* it. I say that it is so.'

The Druid leaned alertly forward.

'Can you identify them?'

'I can,' she replied quietly. 'But before I do so I shall tell you how I came to the conclusion that I have.'

The tension among those gathered increased almost perceptibly.

'My first mistake, for I made a mistake in progressing a line of thought, which kept me from seeing the truth for some time, was to immediately assume that the killing of the thirty-three young men at the entrance to this valley was inseparably linked to the murder of Brother Solin.'

Colla drew a quick breath.

'Do you say that they are not?' he asked in surprise.

'No, they are not,' confirmed Fidelma. 'Although, to be accurate, there is a link, but not the one I had imagined. It follows, by the way, that the murder of Brother Dianach and Artgal, while linked to Brother Solin's death, was also not part of the ritual slaughter.'

'We are waiting for your so-called truth!' sneered Laisre, above the hubbub which she had created in the chamber.

'You shall hear it soon. I will deal with the matter of the ritual slaughter first. This was simply a crude and foul means to provoke a civil war in Muman. I lay the blame for this at the gates of Mael Dúin, king of the northern Uí Néill in Ailech.'

Again the murmur of surprise interrupted her.

'Ailech is far from here,' Colla pointed out in disbelief. 'And what good would it do Mael Dúin if there was dissension in Muman?'

'Apparently Mael Dúin wants to seize the thrones of all the northern kingdoms and then sit on the throne of Tara as High King. He wants to dominate all the five kingdoms. To do so, he knows that there is only one kingdom powerful enough to counter his ambitions.'

'Muman?' It was Murgal who made the logical conclusion.

'Exactly so. The Eóghanacht of Cashel would not allow him to usurp the dignity of the High Kingship which is an honour bestowed not a power to be grabbed.'

'How does it apply to the deaths of the young men? The so-called sacrifices?' Colla now appeared fascinated by her story, following it carefully.

'When Gleann Geis called for a representative of Cashel, of the Church of Imleach, to come here to ostensibly discuss the establishment of a church and school, the enemies of Muman had already planned that a simple cleric coming here would see the ritual slaughter and think it was a pagan ceremony. The pagan community of Gleann Geis would be blamed immediately. No cleric could ignore the affront to the Faith. It was believed that this cleric would race back to Cashel and that the king of Cashel and his bishop at Imleach would pronounce a Holy War of retribution on Gleann Geis. That they would attempt to annihilate the people of Gleann Geis as condign judgment.

'This would provoke Gleann Geis's neighbours to rise up to protect their kin against the aggression of Cashel and the one step would inevitably lead to another.'

'And what prevented this great plan being fulfilled . . . if such a plan ever existed?' Laisre sounded unconvinced.

'I was the cleric but, also being a *dálaigh*, I believed in proof before action. It threw their plan out of synchronisation.'

'A weak plan,' observed Colla, 'with too many ifs and buts.'

'No. For the plan itself had adherents here in Gleann Geis, people who did not care how many of their clan were killed if it produced the right results because it was a step for them on the road to the greater power which Mael Dúin had promised them should he become High King.'

Murgal laughed outright in disbelief.

'Are you claiming that some of us in Gleann Geis have been bribed by offers of power or riches from Mael Dúin of Ailech? Are you saying that we, or some of us, are working hand in glove with Mael Dúin of Ailech to destroy our own people in return for crumbs from his table?'

'Precisely. Mael Dúin's plan could not work without such an ally or allies. The subversion of Muman had to come from within if it stood any chance to work.'

'You'll have to prove that.'

Fidelma smiled at Murgal and she turned around the room, gazing on them each in turn as if attempting to read their thoughts. Finally she said: 'That is what I now propose to do. I am able to do so thanks to something else which happened here which, as I have said, I had actually thought was related but which was not. Yet this unrelated matter led me to the guilty ally of Ailech.'

'Who is it?' demanded Colla, with tension.

'Firstly, let me do some reconstruction of these events. The plan is set in motion. Mael Dúin has sent a band of warriors with sacrificial hostages to enact the ritual which is to set in motion the wrath of Cashel and Imleach. So far so good. The ally in Gleann Geis has everything arranged. An invitation has been sent to Imleach to ensure that a cleric is on their way to Gleann Geis and will stumble across the ritual killings. Sentinels are set to watch for the arrival of the cleric so that Ailech's warriors know where and when to perform their despicable crime.'

She paused for dramatic effect.

'Now Mael Dúin also has a powerful ally in the north. Ultan, the bishop of Armagh, himself. He has promised to give aid to Mael Dúin in his bid for power. How much did Ultan know of the plan? I cannot say. But he sent his secretary and a young scribe to Gleann Geis. It might be that Brother Solin was sent in order to provide a so-called independent witness to Cashel's awaited march on Gleann Geis who could then report the matter to the other provincial kings so that Armagh could call for the rest of the provincial kings to march on Cashel. Brother Solin however, was certainly in the plot even if Ultan was not.'

'How do you know that?' Murgal asked.

'The fact was that Sechnassuch of Tara surmised that Mael Dúin was ambitious for power and suspected he was plotting something. He also discovered that Ultan was in an alliance with Mael Dúin but to what extent he did not know. So Sechnassuch asked some warriors to keep an eye on Ultan and they discovered Brother Solin's involvement. They followed Solin and his young scribe Brother Dianach and saw them meet some of Mael Dúin's warriors. These warriors were marching thirty-three hostages towards Gleann Geis. Thirty-three,' she added carefully for effect. After a pause she continued.

'The warriors of Sechnassuch witnessed a woman meet with the men of Ailech and with Brother Solin and Dianach at that rendezvous. When one of the prisoners escaped, it was this woman who rode out and hunted him down. The woman escorted Solin and his young scribe to the ravine entrance of Gleann Geis.'

'But Solin and Dianach came into Gleann Geis alone,' interrupted Orla, with a flushed face. 'Any of our guards at the ravine will tell you that.'

'I will not argue,' Fidelma replied evenly, 'for you are correct. Brother Solin and young Dianach entered Gleann Geis alone . . . having left the woman. She showed two of Ailech's warriors the path which the Cashel cleric was likely to come by, the spot where the bodies must be laid out. Then she entered the valley by another way she knew, the secret path along the river where Artgal's body was found.'

Orla was about to say something when her husband intervened.

'You say these warriors of Sechnassuch followed these people here? Where are they? What proof do we have of what you say?'

'You ought to have deduced that the warriors who have secured this ráth are the same men. Ibor of Muirthemne is their leader and not a horse dealer. Ibor is commander of the Craobh Rígh of Ulaidh.'

Ibor took a step forward and bowed stiffly towards Laisre.

'At your command, chieftain of Gleann Geis,' he said formally but with humour in his voice.

'Not my command,' replied Laisre with distaste. 'Get on with this tedious tale, Fidelma.'

'Mael Dúin's men and their hostages approached Gleann Geis. The men from Ailech, for I will not grace them with the term "warriors" as they were no more than butchers, were watching for the cleric from Cashel. In other words they were watching for me. As soon as Eadulf and I had been spotted, the ritual slaughter began. The bodies were placed in position for me to find. The rest was going to be up to me.

'I hindered their plan, however, because I did not flee in horror from the spot to raise Cashel's wrath against Gleann Geis and plunge Muman into civil war.'

'Yes, yes, yes! You have made your point, Fidelma of Cashel,' Murgal said hurriedly. 'But the fact is that once you knew of this matter, it provided you with the best motive for killing Solin. Better than anyone here.'

'Anyone except the killer. The fact is, I did not know about this plot at the time of Solin's death nor his involvement in it. The fact of his involvement was only later revealed to me by Ibor of Muirthemne. That was when I realised there were two different affairs taking place. The barbarous, to use Laisre's well-chosen word, plot against Muman and a simple murder . . . though murder is never simple.'

She paused and shrugged.

'Before I go further I should present the evidence of who in Gleann Geis was involved with the terrible plot of the king of Ailech. I would remind you of the woman who met Mael Dúin's men. Ibor and his warriors saw her . . .'

Fidelma turned directly to Orla.

'The person was a woman, a woman of commanding appearance.'

Orla suppressed a cry of rage.

'Do you see what she is doing? This is the second time that she has accused me of murder. Not content with claiming that I killed Solin of Armagh, she would now accuse me of a heinous crime against my people. I shall destroy you for this, Fidelma of Cashel . . .'

She tugged out a knife from her belt and made to spring forward.

Ibor had moved towards her but Colla already stood in her path, placing himself defensively in front of his wife. He reached forward and took the knife gently but firmly from her hand.

'This is no answer, Orla,' he said gruffly. 'No harm will come to you while I defend you.' He rounded on Fidelma, his eyes blazing in anger. 'You will have me to deal with, *dálaigh*,' he told her menacingly. 'You will not escape the penalty for your false accusations against my wife.'

Fidelma spread her arms nonchalantly.

'So far, I do not recall having made any accusations, false or otherwise. I am simply stating facts. You will know when I have made accusations.'

Colla grew bewildered, he took a step forward but Ibor touched him lightly on the arm with his sword point and shook his head, reaching out a hand for Orla's dagger. Automatically, Colla handed it to him without thinking or protesting. Ibor then motioned him to resume his place.

'Let us return to what became a weak link in this terrible tragic chain. Brother Solin of Armagh. Brother Solin was a man of ambition. He was ambitious and sly, a worthy plotter in this affair. But he had a weakness. He was, in a word, a lecher. He made a lewd suggestion to you, didn't he, Orla?'

The wife of the tanist's face went crimson.

'I could take care of myself,' she muttered, 'especially with such a man.'

'Indeed, you could. You hit him once.'

'I dealt with him,' replied Orla softly. 'He did not lay a hand on me. He just made a lewd suggestion. A thing he swiftly regretted. He learnt his lesson.'

'No, he didn't,' contradicted Fidelma. 'He was an incurable lecher. He lusted after someone else. Someone else not only slapped him but threw wine over him. You will recall, Orla, that I asked if you had thrown wine over Solin?'

Orla was still suspicious.

'I told you I did not and I did not.'

'True. You see, there is another attractive woman in the ráth, isn't there, Murgal? In fact, a woman who has some resemblance to Orla, tall and with a commanding appearance.'

The Druid frowned, trying to understand her path of thought.

'You found out that she was unappreciative of your own advances, didn't you? At the feast, Marga the apothecary slapped you across the face.'

Murgal blinked with embarrassment.

'Everyone saw it,' he muttered uncomfortably. 'Why should I deny it? But I do not understand where you are leading us.'

Fidelma now faced Marga. The apothecary's face was an interesting study of emotions.

'Brother Solin had not only made a lewd suggestion to you . . . he came to your chambers and tried to force himself on you.'

Marga raised her chin aggressively.

'I threw wine over him to quell his ardour. I slapped him. He did not bother me again. I did not kill the man.'

'But he had made advances to you, Marga,' insisted Fidelma quietly. 'And for that reason Brother Solin was murdered.'

There was a sudden quiet in the chamber broken only by a sob of denial from the apothecary. Everyone was staring at Marga. The pudgy figure of Cruinn moved forward and put an arm around the girl.

'Are you telling us that Marga killed Solin?' gasped Murgal.

'No,' Fidelma replied immediately. 'What I said was that Solin's attack on Marga was the triggering point for his murder.'

'Are you also claiming now that it was not Orla but Marga whom you saw at the stables?' pressed Colla.

Fidelma shook her head negatively.

'It was someone who looked exactly like Orla, and that misled me. They were clad in a cloak and hood so that I saw only the top part of their face as the light fell on them.'

She turned to Laisre.

'It was not until I saw the top part of your face above the wooden screen last night, Laisre, in just such a light, that I realised the mistake I had made. It was you, Laisre of Gleann Geis, who came out of the stable, not your twin sister, Orla.'

Chapter Twenty

Laisre sat back in his chair as if he had been struck a blow. He stared in open-mouthed dismay.

There was no mercy in Fidelma's eyes as she made her accusation.

He swallowed and then, curiously, the chieftain of Gleann Geis seemed to hunch in his chair and throw out his hands in a curious gesture halfway between defence and surrender.

'I will not deny that you saw me,' he quietly confessed to an audible gasp of astonishment from those assembled. 'What I will deny is that I was the one who killed Solin of Armagh.'

They waited for Fidelma to make a further accusation but she merely turned away and said: 'I know that you did not kill him. Even if Brother Solin had raped Marga, whom you profess love for, you would have tried to keep him alive because it was in your best interests to do so, wasn't it?'

Laisre did not reply. He licked his dry lips, staring in fascination at her as a rabbit might look at a fox before the moment of death.

'You went to the stable that night because you had an assignation with Brother Solin of Armagh, didn't you?'

'I went there to meet him,' Laisre agreed quietly.

'But someone else was there before you.'

'I went into the stable from the side door. Solin was already on the floor having been stabbed. I immediately left when I saw that he was dying. I admit that you saw me leave the stable.'

'The mistake I made was thinking that you were your twin sister because you were so well cloaked and disguised that all I saw was the top of your face. No wonder you grew so angry when I accused Orla. Your anger was from fear; you were afraid for yourself. You were afraid that I would eventually realise my mistake. Your fear was what made me suspicious of you for you suddenly switched from friendship to hatred and that was very marked. You were so afraid that, when you heard from Rudgal that I had appointed Eadulf here as my Brehon, you pushed a loose stone from the parapet of the ráth on him as he was walking underneath. God be thanked that you did not kill him.'

Eadulf swallowed hard as he recalled the incident.

'So it was you?' Eadulf focussed on Laisre for a moment before turning quickly to Fidelma. 'But how did you know that it was Laisre, you weren't there?'

'Rudgal told you who was walking along the wall at that time. Once Laisre was connected with other parts of the puzzle his role became obvious. Do you deny it was you, Laisre?'

Laisre remained silent.

'Now, do you want to tell us why you chose to meet Brother Solin that night in the stable?'

The chieftain of Gleann Geis continued to sit as if he had been carved from stone.

'Then I will do so,' continued Fidelma, after he made no reply. 'You and he were fellow plotters, or allies, if you like. You were the one who was in league with Mael Dúin of Ailech. You took and destroyed the incriminating vellum message from Ailech. Is that not so?'

Laisre laughed, perhaps a little too hollowly.

'Are you saying that I would betray my own people? That I would sacrifice them to gain personal power?'

'That is precisely what I am saying. You need not deny it. It occurred to me during that first council meeting, when you were supposed to negotiate with me, that it had been you who had made the decision to send for a religious to come here. I learnt that most of your council had been in opposition to that decision which you had made quite arbitrarily. Now, why would you, who still clung to the old faith, and who, according to Christians like Rudgal there, was so obstinate about recognition of the Church here, suddenly go against the wishes of your council to send such an invitation? The answer becomes obvious. You had to send the invitation to ensure a cleric came here to see the ritual slaughter. No other person at Gleann Geis could have had the authority to make that decision.

'I was confused when I realised that you stood alone against Colla and Murgal and your sister as well as other members of the council in this matter. Why were you putting your chieftainship in jeopardy by refusing to accept their will in council? The reason was because you had your sights on other power. Mael Dúin had obviously promised you better things than the chieftainship of Gleann Geis.'

Colla, Murgal and Orla were staring at Laisre in horror as they began to follow the irrevocable logic of her accusation.

Laisre's features reformed in an expression of defiance; almost contempt.

'You would have destroyed Gleann Geis for ambition?' asked Murgal amazed. 'Deny it and we will believe you. You are our chieftain.'

'You are right. I am your chieftain.' Laisre rose suddenly, his voice stentorian. 'Let us make this day ours. There are only a few of them if we act together. Mael Dúin will still succeed with his plan in spite of this woman. Join me, if you want to be on the winning side. Declare for Ailech against Cashel. Take hold of your destiny.'

Colla stood facing Laisre, his face white and strained with disbelief.

'I will take hold of the only destiny that honour now demands,' he said quietly. 'You are no longer chieftain of Gleann Geis and shame is your portion for that which you have tried to do to them.'

Laisre was momentarily angry.

'Then you will have to live with your shame in denying your lawful chieftain!'

Even before he had finished speaking he had sprung forward, taking a dagger from his belt. Before anyone could move he had dragged young Esnad from her chair, drawing her in front of him as a shield, placing the blade of the dagger across her throat. She screamed but the pressure of the sharp blade caused the cry to be stifled. A thin line of blood showed on the whiteness of her throat. The girl's eyes were wide and staring in fear. Laisre began to back towards the door of the chamber.

'Stay still if you do not wish to see this girl killed,' he called as Ibor and a couple of his warriors began automatically to move towards them.

Orla screamed sharply.

'She is your niece, Laisre. She is my daughter! Your own flesh and blood!'

'Keep back,' warned the chieftain. 'I am going to leave this ráth in safety. Do not think I will hesitate to use this dagger. The bitch from Cashel will tell you that I was prepared to sacrifice the people of this valley to ensure my ambition and I shall not hesitate to sacrifice even this indolent child – flesh of my flesh or not.'

Marga then started forward towards him with a joyful cry.

'I am coming with you, Laisre.'

Laisre gave her a cynical smile.

'I cannot have you as well as my hostage delay me now. I must travel alone. Fend for yourself until I return here with Mael Dúin's victorious army.'

The girl stepped back as if she had been slapped in the face.

'But . . . you promised . . . after all we have been through . . . After what I have done for you.' Her voice became inarticulate as she understood his rejection of her.

'Circumstances alter cases,' the chieftain replied easily, his eyes still warily watching the warriors of Ibor. 'Clear the way. The girl dies if anyone tries to follow.'

Orla was almost in hysterics. Colla tried to comfort her.

Fidelma, scrutinising him, realised that the chieftain of Gleann Geis was totally insane. She also realised that Esnad would be discarded as soon as he secured a fast horse and reached beyond the gates of the ráth. Not even his own niece meant anything more to him other than a means of gaining what he coveted. Power was his god. Power was a desolating pestilence polluting everything it touched.

'He will do it,' she warned Ibor who was still edging slowly forward. 'Do not attempt to detain him.'

Ibor halted, accepting that she was right, and ground his sword, calling on his men to do likewise.

The warriors of Ibor halted and looked helplessly at their leader for guidance. Ibor simply rested his sword point on the ground before him and gave a sigh.

Laisre grinned triumphantly.

'I am glad that you are so sensible, Fidelma of Cashel. Now, Marga, open the door for me. Quickly!'

Marga was still standing in shocked disbelief at Laisre as if she could not believe her abandonment by her erstwhile lover.

'Move!' yelled Laisre in anger. 'Do as I say!'

Orla turned tear-stained eyes to the apothecary.

'For the sake of my daughter, Marga,' she pleaded. 'Open the door for him.'

It was the rotund Cruinn who took a pace forward.

'I'll open the door for him, lady,' she offered.

Laisre glanced towards the portly woman.

'Do so then. Quickly!'

The hostel keeper, her face set sternly, moved to the door. Then she turned swiftly.

Abruptly Laisre stiffened. His face contorted. The dagger blade fell away from Esnad's throat as his grip loosened. Sensing his slackening grasp, the young girl broke away and ran sobbing into the arms of her mother. The chieftain of Gleann Geis stood swaying for a moment. It seemed as though he had suddenly acquired a red necklet. The dagger finally dropped from his nerveless fingers and he fell face forward on to the council chamber floor. Blood began to pump from his severed artery on to its boards.

Marga let out a series of long, shuddering sobs.

'He was going to betray me,' she whispered almost in disbelief.

'I know, I know.' Cruinn gazed at her in sympathy. She was still standing before the door, behind Laisre's body. There was a large knife in her hand, still stained with the chieftain's blood.

Ibor ran forward and bent down, feeling for Laisre's pulse. There was no need. It was obvious that the chieftain was dead. He glanced up at Fidelma and shook his head. Then he slowly stood up and removed the knife from Cruinn's limp hand.

Cruinn turned away and, taking Marga by the arm, led her to a seat.

Colla had his arm around Orla who was clutching at Esnad. The young girl was shivering with shock at what had happened.

Only Murgal seemed in total control and he was regarding Fidelma with restrained emotion.

'Truly, there is much barbarism here. Was he also responsible for Dianach's death . . . ?'

'In a roundabout way,' Fidelma confirmed. 'Brother Dianach knew that Laisre was in the plot with his master, Solin of Armagh. Of course, Dianach was also involved but he thought that Solin's cause was just, not realising just how corrupt and corrupting it was. He was a mere servant of his master. In many ways he was a naive young man. Laisre went to Dianach after I was incarcerated. He knew I was innocent and was afraid that if I was discovered to be so, then suspicion would come his way. Orla could prove her innocence through Colla and eventually I would realise what I had seen. The fact that Orla and Laisre were twins would eventually lead me to him. Laisre felt that he had to ensure I was found guilty. So he instructed Dianach to purchase the cows from Nemon as a bribe for Artgal to maintain his story about me; to make certain that I was blamed.'

'To escape from his guilt? But why did he kill Solin in the first place?' Murgal was puzzled.

Fidelma shook her head quickly.

'It was not Laisre who killed Brother Solin. You forget that Solin was his ally. Without Solin the plot would not work.'

Murgal was totally bewildered.

'But I thought . . . ?'

'I was not lying when I told Laisre that I knew he had not

killed Brother Solin. Laisre only wanted to ensure that I was made the scapegoat because he knew who the real culprit was. The trouble was that Brother Dianach, once I was released, had brought the attention of the real killer on himself. The real killer mistakenly thought that Dianach and Artgal had somehow become a danger to them. The killer was waiting for Dianach and Artgal at Artgal's farmstead after the farce of my trial. The killer had prepared a poisoned drink for both Artgal and Dianach, to stop them speaking further. But it was a slow-acting poison. It gave the killer time to send Artgal out of the valley on some pretext, perhaps to escape punishment. But the main purpose was to have Artgal disappear. The killer told him to leave Gleann Geis by the second route along the river path, through the caves, knowing that the poison would eventually act and that Artgal would never come out of the caves alive.

'The killer was then left alone with Dianach, waiting for the poison to work. It was obvious, by the way, why Dianach had to be killed. But, as I say, the poison was slow working. The killer suddenly saw Rudgal, Eadulf and myself approaching the farmstead which Artgal had recently left. There was only one thing to do. Pretending to take Dianach to a hiding place, pretending that we intended him harm, the killer took the opportunity to cut his throat just as he was bending down to crawl into a shed.'

Murgal was following her argument keenly, nodding as she swiftly made her points.

'I see no fault with this logic. All right. It brings us back to the identity of the killer. From what you have said – it can be only Marga.'

Marga was even beyond reacting. Her head was still bent with the shock of her rejection by Laisre. Fidelma surprised them all with a negative gesture.

'You must have deduced by now that Marga was in the plot with Laisre to support Mael Dúin's bid for power. That we can all agree. She was the emissary whom Laisre sent to meet the men of Ailech. Why was she involved? Because she was in love with Laisre. He had promised her marriage. Promised to share his forthcoming power under Mael Dúin with her. Promised to make her his coequal.'

She paused to let her words sink in before continuing.

'As part of the plan Laisre was to send someone to meet Mael Dúin's men and show them the best place at which they were to enact their terrible charade of the ritual slaughter. He could not go himself for obvious reasons. The person he sent would have to be someone of commanding position to deal with the men of Ailech and not a mere apothecary. So he had Marga dress in Orla's clothes in order to give her an appearance of position and she was told how to act the part. She played that part well, even hunting down an escaped prisoner. Mind you, Marga had no love for Christians and so she was quite happy to do so and was not bothered about the fate of the hostages.

'Now as much as she disliked Brother Solin, the last thing that Marga would do was to kill the ally of Laisre before the plot came to fruition. No, there was too much at stake for her, or, indeed, for Laisre, to kill Solin simply because he had insulted her.'

'Who is this killer then?' demanded Colla, somewhat petulantly. 'For the sake of our shattered nerves, tell us and let us have done with this awful business.'

'Will you tell them why you killed Brother Solin or shall I, Cruinn?' asked Fidelma quietly.

The rotund woman who was sitting comforting Marga did not even stir. Her face was stony.

'Tell them if you must,' she finally said without emotion and then closed her mouth tightly.

Marga had given a sob of heartrending anguish as she clutched at the elder woman.

'You? You killed Solin?'

'How could I not do so, child?' replied Cruinn calmly.

Marga swung round, eyes wide, looking at each of the company in turn before finally letting them alight on Fidelma.

'I did not know,' she whispered.

'No. I did not think you did.' Then she looked at Cruinn. 'You killed Brother Dianach with much the same stroke of your knife as that with which you despatched Laisre. And you also poisoned Artgal.'

'What nonsense is this?' demanded Orla, her old poise somewhat recovered by now but unable to follow these new developments. 'Why would this old woman kill anyone?'

Colla agreed. 'That you must explain, Fidelma. Why would this old hostel-keeper commit these murders? It is madness.'

'If madness it was, it was the madness of a possessive mother.'

Cruinn was implacable.

'How long have you known?' she asked Fidelma.

'A little while now but I could not be sure what Orla's part in it was. I was still convinced until last night that I had seen her leaving the stable. Once I knew that it had not been Orla, everything began to come together rapidly and Ibor, this morning, brought me the last piece of the puzzle when he reported that he had discovered Artgal's body in the caves.'

'Will you tell us why Cruinn did this?' invited Murgal.

'Cruinn is the mother of Marga.'

'Most people in the valley know that,' affirmed Murgal. 'That is no secret.'

'Assumption can create secrets,' replied Fidelma. 'I am a stranger here. I did not know. Had I known, perhaps some deaths might have been prevented. I had to reason this out for myself. I should have listened more carefully when Cruinn said that she went picking healing herbs with her daughter. Then she later mentioned that she picked herbs for the apothecary. It took me some time to make the link. The apothecary was her daughter. Then I remembered that when Murgal made an advance to Marga at the feast Marga had slapped him and walked out. It was Cruinn who went after her to comfort her, casting an angry look at Murgal.'

'Marga is a beautiful woman,' confessed Murgal, embarrassed. 'No harm in paying tribute to beauty.'

'It depends how that tribute is paid. And harm might have been your lot if you had been as blatant as Brother Solin was. You might have ended your life as Solin did if you had pressed your unwanted attentions further. Cruinn wanted to keep her daughter pure for the marriage to her chieftain.

'I should have paid more attention to Cruinn when she was asking about the marriage laws to chieftains. I thought she had some fantasy of her own. In fact, Marga had told her mother that Laisre had offered her marriage. Cruinn was pleased, for she was ambitious for her daughter. But she was slightly concerned and asked me about the law of marriage, especially between chieftains and commoners. Cruinn was protective of her daughter's interests. Hence her anger at you, Murgal, for insulting her daughter in front of Laisre. Then, when she found out that Brother Solin had tried to force himself on her daughter, her fury was absolute. Not realising that Brother Solin was essential to Laisre's plans, she saw Solin creeping from the hostel one night and thought she had found her chance for vengeance. She followed him into the stables and killed him. Just then Laisre entered to keep his assignation which concerned their plot.'

'You are right,' the pudgy-faced woman intervened diffidently. 'Absolutely right. Laisre came in, even as Solin was falling to the ground. I told him that I had done it for Marga and for their future happiness. He was agitated for a moment or so but then told me to leave, taking the knife with me. He ordered me to clean it so that I would not be suspected.'

Fidelma took up the story.

'He left the stable immediately and there I saw him wrapped in his cloak and I mistook him for his sister. Now Laisre could not accuse Marga's mother. He was wondering what to do when I fell by chance into the situation. How perfect it would be if I, of all people, could be successfully accused of Brother Solin's murder. If I were charged with the murder of Ultan of Armagh's secretary, it would cause the same friction which Mael Dúin has sought. My brother might even send warriors to secure my release. It would make up for my not responding to the ritual killing in the way he had initially hoped.'

Cruinn stared at Fidelma dispassionately.

'How did you connect me with the killing of Artgal and Dianach?'

'You left the poison beakers in the cabin. I scented the poison hemlock that had been left in them. You knew enough from your daughter's apothecary about preparing such a poison. Once I saw blue on Dianach's lips I knew that he had been poisoned. But you also left an apron in your haste to get out of the cabin with Dianach once you saw us approaching. Even if Artgal had been the sort of person fastidious enough to use such a garment, the apron was too large. Besides I had seen you wearing a similar garment in the guests' hostel. Then when Ibor told me that Artgal's body had been found in the very passage which you had told me of, I realised that you had poisoned them both.'

Not for the first time there was a total silence in the council chamber as those gathered contemplated her horrendous story.

Murgal spoke quietly to Colla.

'You are now our chief-elect, Colla. The decisions are yours to make.'

Colla stood uncertainly. He exchanged a glance with his wife Orla before he turned with a questioning expression to Fidelma. 'Is it true that I am to make the decisions at Gleann Geis now?' he asked, looking meaningfully towards Ibor and his warriors.

'Now that this mystery has been solved, Ibor of Muirthemne and his men will await your decisions,' confirmed Fidelma. 'You are still chieftain-elect of Gleann Geis.'

Ibor brought his sword smartly up to salute the new chieftain.

'Yours to command, Colla,' he said.

'Then Cruinn and her daughter must be restrained until such time as they can be brought to trial for what they have done; Marga for plotting the betrayal of her people in league with Laisre; and Cruinn for her cold-blooded murders. I would have been inclined to treat Cruinn with leniency due to the passion of her crime had she not gone on to encompass the deaths of the boy Dianach and Artgal.'

Colla took hold of his wife's hand.

'If I am approved by the council to be chieftain of Gleann Geis, I will denounce and repudiate Laisre's pact with Mael Dúin of Ailech and pledge anew this clan's allegiance to Cashel and its lawful kings.'

Ibor of Muirthemne was smiling with satisfaction.

'Excellent. That is the report I shall be pleased to take back to Tara. Sechnassuch will be delighted. But be vigilant for this is nothing but a check to Mael Dúin's ambitions. The northern Uí Néill will not discard their objective. While Muman presents the only obstacle to their dominance over the five kingdoms, Mael Dúin will try to devise new ways of overthrowing Cashel. So be warned.'

He turned to his warriors.

'Release the men of Gleann Geis and tell them that they have a new chief in Colla. We will then begin our journey north back to Tara.'

He glanced across to Fidelma.

'It has been . . . perhaps "pleasure" is the wrong word, but it has been "rewarding" to work with you, Fidelma of Cashel.'

'And for me, with you, Ibor of Muirthemne.'

Ibor saluted the company again by raising his sword with a flourish before he followed his warriors from the council chamber.

Colla suddenly pointed to Rudgal, who still stood in the background, wrists tied behind his back.

'And what of him, Fidelma? What charges do you bring against Rudgal?'

She felt a twinge of guilt for she had almost forgotten the fair-haired lovelorn warrior. She turned to Eadulf.

'That is up to you, Eadulf. It was your life that he threatened.'

Eadulf asked Colla for the loan of his knife. Hesitantly, Colla drew it out and handed it to the Saxon, hilt first. Eadulf then called to Esnad, who seemed to have recovered from her ordeal quite quickly.

'Take this, Esnad,' he instructed her, 'and release Rudgal. Then take him away and speak earnestly with him. Above all, try to explain that you do not care for me any more than I care for you.'

Esnad coloured a little, her eyes meeting those of Eadulf for a moment before falling away a little in shame. She simply inclined her head and took the knife to Rudgal.

Ronan had taken charge of Marga and her mother Cruinn and ushered them away. Nemon had departed in the company of Bairsech who seemed almost friendly towards her neighbour.

Eadulf gave a wry grimace towards Fidelma.

'I was wondering how you would lead us from the maze that I thought I saw before me. I think you dumbfounded me as much as anyone here.'

Fidelma responded with a swift gesture of deprecation.

'You exaggerate, Eadulf. It only seemed complicated because we were dealing with two separate motivations for the wrong doing.'

Orla came forward, her face still strained from the shock of her brother's perfidy. She was doing her best to control it and was also a little embarrassed as she stood before Fidelma.

'I just wanted to ask your forgiveness for my attitude when I thought . . .'

Fidelma held up a hand to silence her.

'You had every reason to think of me as you did for there is always indignation when innocence is accused. I regret that there was no love in your brother's heart for you or yours.'

'Poor Laisre.' The woman forced a reflective smile. 'Yes, I can say *poor* Laisre even now. He was ill. I believe this powerful madness was just that – an insanity like a disease, like a cold that one cannot fight. He was still my brother, and I knew him before the disease warped his mind. I shall remember him from that time and not this time.'

Colla came forward to take his wife's arm and he smiled contritely at the *dálaigh.*

'You have taught us many things, Fidelma of Cashel,' he observed quietly.

'Some that you may profit by, I hope?'

'The meaning of Christian love and forgiveness, perhaps?' Eadulf intervened brightly. 'That would be a good lesson to have learnt.'

Colla roared with mirth so heartily and unexpectedly that Eadulf felt offended.

'No, no, Saxon! That is the last thing that I would have learnt here. Is not Mael Dúin of Ailech a Christian? Were not his warriors who conducted that terrible massacre of the hostages Christian? Were not Brother Solin and the man who sent him, Ultan of Armagh, Christians? Ha! Christian love is the last thing that has been demonstrated here.'

Colla resumed a more serious expression.

'No, what I have learnt here is something about perseverance in the face of adversity.'

Taking his wife by the arm, he made for the door of the council chamber. There he paused and glanced back.

'Tell your brother at Cashel, and tell the bishop of Imleach, that Gleann Geis is not yet ready to accept a closer relationship with the new Faith. We have seen too much of Christian concerns for our welfare.'

He and Orla were gone abruptly through the door.

'Ingratitude!' muttered Eadulf, offended. 'How can you take such insults from these pagans?'

Fidelma was smiling, not in the least perturbed.

'Hardly insults, Eadulf. A man must speak as he finds. He is right. The Christianity of Mael Dúin, Brother Solin and, if he is truly part of this terrible plot, the Christianity of Ultan of Armagh, leaves one yearning for the old morality of the beliefs of our people.'

Eadulf was scandalised. He did not have time to reprimand her before Murgal approached her also with a grave expression on his face.

'We have, indeed, much to thank you for, Fidelma of Cashel. I have seen the true worth of a moral advocate of the laws of the five kingdoms. It is something to aspire to.'

'You do not have to aspire, Murgal, for you have achieved it. You are a brave and honest Brehon. We may be religions apart but morality often transcends differences in Faith.'

'It is heartening that you recognise that.'

Fidelma bowed her head.

'It is something one is taught when one studies the ancient law. Intolerance is made up of the shells of lies. No natural disaster has cost as many human lives as man's intolerance towards the beliefs of his fellow men.'

'Truly said. Will you stay in Gleann Geis a while as our guests, or, like Ibor of Muirthemne, will you leave for Cashel immediately?'

Fidelma glanced through the window at the sky.

'We still have the best part of a day before us. There is no other reason to stay in Gleann Geis. Maybe one day I might be able to return here and discuss how Christianity might truly be brought here. But not now. We will start our journey home immediately. First to Imleach, to consult with Bishop Ségdae, and then on to Cashel. The sooner Muman is fully aware about the plot that was devised here, the sooner we can be on our guard against Ailech and any similar plots against the peace of this kingdom.'

Two men were carrying the body of Laisre out of the council chamber.

Fidelma observed them quietly and then said rhetorically: 'What shall it profit a man, if he shall gain the whole world, and lose his own soul?'

Murgal looked impressed.

'Now that is a wise sentiment. Is it a quotation from one of the teachings of the Brehon Morann of Tara? I do not know it.'

Eadulf sniffed sardonically.

'No: that was from the Gospel of the Blessed Mark. Even we Christians have books of philosophy.'